My White Cocoon

To Tracy and Tara!
It's a pleasure meeting you.
Enjoy the story!
Carol James Drolet

by

Carol James Drolet

PublishAmerica
Baltimore

First printing

ISBN: 1-60563-412-3
PUBLISHED BY PUBLISHAMERICA, LLLP
www.publishamerica.com
Baltimore

Printed in the United States of America

~ Dedication ~

To my loving husband, Michael,
without whom none of this would have been possible.

~ Acknowledgments ~

To all my children and grandchildren because you are my life!
Special recognition goes to my magnificent editor, Karen Vedane.
Her patience and guidance through the years helped me find
"my voice".
James Beardsley, my cherished friend, thanks for listening!

Foreword

Not one of us remembers our humble entry into this vast, ever-changing world. Birth is an alluring mystery, sacred for the human beings whose union of passion and love has created a fragile, joyous life. The bundle enters the world and is instantly swaddled in a warm blanket, wrapped tightly like the protective layers of a cocoon.

Each life intertwines with numerous pathways, while the threads lead to a search for the fabric of its heritage. Frequently, the unraveling strands reveal an empty shell but inevitably, the metamorphosis transforms the familiar security of our cocoon into a wondrous new experience. As we soar, our humble beginnings would be lost without the loved ones who share with us life's gift, our story.

To those precious souls who weave the threads into our lives, we are forever grateful.

Carol James Drolet

Prologue

As we bounced together over the bumpy road, not noticing the musky stench of the Jeep Cherokee, I gazed through the windows of grime, sensitive to my son's excitement on this crisp, January day. At twenty-six, he still gnawed at his nails, biting them to the quick, which was always a sure sign of his nervousness. Predictably dressed in his khakis, freshly ironed Polo shirt, and highly polished Timberlands, Peter was strikingly handsome. Taller than his three siblings, his strong Celtic features were unmistakably a product of the ancestral Feagin Clan. His honey blond hair was closely cropped, and his deep caramel brown eyes and flaxen skin were truly an image of his grandmother, Rachel. A closer scrutiny often revealed a remarkable resemblance to the kindly face of his grandfather, Truman.

I grasped the seat belt, clumsily pushing the clasp downward into the lock. Peter's size ten shoe pushed lower on the gas pedal. The Jeep thrust past the modest clapboards needing a fresh coat of whitewash. I hadn't visited this curvy, kudzu-draped island in years. The long afternoon shadows extended their arms through the windshield, lulling me into a trance. My eyes were open, but I didn't notice that my journey had suddenly come to a silent halt. I sat motionless until I heard my darling chauffeur say, "Mama, are you all right?" Peter searched my eyes as they welled with tears. Speechless, an uncommon trait for me, always known as a perpetual chatterbox, I was unable to utter a sound as I leaned forward overwhelmed. I was truly silenced by what lay before me. "I told you it would be tough but, I promised I'd do it some day, and I did! I've built another plantation house, and this one's yours, Mama!"

These were the words my adorable offspring announced as he hastened around to open my door. As I stepped out into the afternoon breeze, Peter gently placed a parcel wrapped in tattered brown butcher paper in my arms. "I have more excitement in store for you. This will be the first treasure that enters your new home, because you're going to need it."

My eyes burned with salty tears as they overflowed down my round cheeks. I cherished the contents in this carefully done-up bundle. I trembled as I held my life's memories. Peter's smile widened as he watched for my expression. I looked into his eyes and smiled as happiness danced over the lines of my face. The anticipation of another generation vividly dashed through my mind.

The story begins on March 16, 1943 in the port of Charleston where tall steeples adorn church tops with bells ringing joyously together. The smell of horses fills the air as their giant hooves trek over cobblestone streets carrying smiling passengers to stately single houses as the steep chimneys puffed willowy smoke skyward. A heavy fog engulfed the marina boats near Riverside Infirmary on this day. The Infirmary was by far the tallest structure on the peninsula and it towered over the moored vessels that bobbed below.

Truman Jaffe pressed his weary cheeks against the frosty window, peering toward the skiffs as he tried to remember how many days had passed. Had it really been four agonizing days? His thoughts were as heavy as the fog blanketing the harbor.

Rachel Jaffe was exhausted, unable to deliver the child that was desperately yearning to be born. Softly, she heard his voice, that lazy southern drawl, "Rachel, it's time. This is taking way too long! I'm going to help you end this, honey! You're exhausted. We all are."

Dr. Rhett started preparing. "Forceps!" The nurse quickly handed over the sterile instrument. Without warning, blood splattered rich with life. A fragile wail...the oppressive silence at last ended. "It's a girl!" He smiled as he placed the child in her mother's arms. "You have another daughter, Rachel!" His icy blue eyes narrowed as he glanced at the nurse, neither of them daring to divulge a hint of the mishap they'd just witnessed. Exhaustion, excitement, and relief encircled the Jaffes on that wintry March morn. Catherine, as they named her, was the perfect image of a cherub.

I remember Mama saying, "It was eerie when a clipping listed under *White Babies Born, three days prior* to the birth of my baby, appeared in the local newspaper. 'A leap year baby girl born to Mr. and Mrs. Truman Jaffe.' Predestination, she'd say. I'm sure it was." Mama's Presbyterian roots lead her to believe that my birth was predestined. Maybe others knew my destiny, but I, Catherine Drayton Jaffe had been determined to enter this world at my own pace.

Days passed before my family took me home from the sterile hospital. Photographs show my homecoming as an important ceremony. Mama had me dressed in my tiny white day gown, and she and Daddy were beaming as they held me in their arms.

Waiting impatiently at home for everyone's arrival, Beth Rutledge Jaffe, proudly wearing her chalk pink dress, crisp white pinafore, and big satin hair ribbon, peeked from behind the sheer curtains, hoping for a glimpse of her new baby sister. How long should a four-year-old have to wait? Beth had no idea what a new sister would be like, she only knew what Mama and Daddy had told her. Mama had been gone for such a long time and Beth missed her deeply. How dare this sister take her away so long!

Mama often told this story of my homecoming, and she never neglected the part where she exclaimed, "Beth touched your tiny fingers Khaki and I'm sure I saw you girls become dear to one another that very day. I saw it in the eyes, my two daughters, perfect princesses. I know you two girls will be very close sisters forever," she assured us.

Mama always encouraged Beth to participate in my care, even if she didn't want to. Unable to enunciate Catherine clearly, "Ka Ki" eventually settled into "Khaki." In pictures of me as a child, I had hair as blonde as a sunflower, and a contagious smile. Beth often laughs, "You had enough energy to wear Mama and me out, and she continues, you were an imp who often gave this sister a fright."

In 1946, Charleston Naval Shipyard was booming with post-war expansion. The salty waters of the Cooper River were crowded with military ships going in and out of the harbor. The massive tons of gray navigated past historical sites glorified from previous wars, both Revolutionary and Confederate.

Heading out to faraway seas, ships slid past Fort Sumter as it stood proudly guarding Charleston's entrance. As the ships sailed, they left behind visions of the elaborate Battery mansions and carriage houses. These fine homes are filled with beauty, charm, history, and cultural richness. Often adorned with intricate architecture, they have shapely white piazzas and are topped with widow walks that hauntingly whisper. Majestic oaks solemnly stand with moss-laden branches swaying back and forth, but offering no relief from the scorching heat. Lanky palmettos and walled gardens enclose the rooftops and private walkways as they welcome the loneliest sailor to the Lowcountry refuge.

1
Daddy

Truman, a strong name for such a gentleman, was well known for his generosity, kindheartedness, and profound pride. He was the kind of man who would give the shirt right off his back to a needy stranger, saying, "Here. Take it. You need this more than I do," and know that he could round up another one for himself. He was not a man obsessed with class or privilege; he hobnobbed with the poor as well as the rich.

Daddy came to Charleston in 1938. He was a hardworking apprentice who was also a gifted storyteller. Bedtime was a delight because he charmed us with outlandish tales. The evening usually began with the adventurous account about his hometown near the Okefenokee Swamp. "In the dark green, slimy waters of southern Georgia, that's where I was born. Right there in the middle of thousands of acres of 'gators and snakes creep'n in and out of that huge bog. Big and little birds chirpin' their songs, wings flutterin' from tree to tree, hidin' from the eyes of those curious, hungry wild animals lurkin' behind the branches wait'n for supper!" Then, there was another story about a swamper named Obediah. "He was said to be King of the Okefenok. Seems he and his daddy were the first white folk to build a cabin and stay right there in that big, dark swamp." I always suspected Daddy was really Obediah because he was well over six feet tall and more handsome than any photographs of the kings that I'd ever seen.

But, I guessed if he was Obediah that he got restless and moved from the swamp because he'd continue his merriment with the yarn about his best friend Clifford. "Clifford, a colored, would come into the grocery store while I was workin' behind the counter. He'd grab himself a handful of hard candy. Now the owner, Mr. Will, would look up just in time to see Clifford slick the candy! Mr. Will would order me to take Clifford in that back room and whoop him."

"I'd politely reply, 'Yes, sir, Mr. Will.' Then I'd fuss at Clifford, 'You know better than to take Mr. Will's candy! Get yourself on into that back room right now!' Remember now, girls, Clifford was my very best friend. I'd help Clifford stuff filled flour sacks inside his trousers, and then I'd start with the whoop'n. Let him have it real good. I'd take that paddle and whoop his behind. Each time I'd hit those feed sacks, Clifford would grin and wail, 'Ouch, I won't do it again!' After I thought Clifford had done enough wailing, we'd come out of the backroom together, Clifford rubbing his behind. He would put back the candy, except for what he ate while I was whoop'n. He'd walk on home to his house and wait for me to get to there after work. We'd have a good cackle together, just the two of us."

Daddy always talked about his place in his family, "I was the tallest in my family, stuck right in the middle of the rest…born back in 1915, two years after my older brother Albert, and my sis, Margot, and two years before my brothers Mark and Roger. Five young' uns for my Ma to feed. My Pa died when I was just a teen…he was a Railroad Man! Before my day, back in the early 1900s, Waycross was the cat's meow and the railroad's heart in south Georgia. My Pa died during it's heyday, so I had to work even harder to support your Grandma and my brothers and sister. I finished high school, saw your Mama at that big college in Statesboro, got smitten…she's such a beauty, grabbed her up and eloped…right here to Charleston! Been over at that Navy yard ever since!"

Then, he'd turn the stories to his days at the loft. "I was barely able to catch a glimpse of the palmettos from the loft and it was built way up top at the Naval Shipyard. I was really busy drawing sketches so we could build those giant ships. While I was going over my blueprints, I began thinking about my own little family—you girls and your mama. Putting down my slide, I looked out toward Charleston's beauty. Dreams of a rich future for my Jaffe girls kept popping into my head. "

As Beth and I drifted off to sleep, I could still hear his voice softly in the background. The strength of our family sat lightly on the edge of our bed, sharing his memories.

Years passed swiftly as the shipyard prepared for the certainty of war and uncertainty for the future. An eager achiever, Daddy became one of the best workers in shipbuilding, arriving on the job before 7:30 in the morning. The whistle didn't blow until eight o'clock and he always returned home long after the five o'clock whistle in the evening.

By now, I had learned Beth's daily rituals..."Walk to the edge of the road...entertain yourself...wait...you'll see Daddy at the gate in a few minutes...do this faithfully, every afternoon, little sister. This is a very important task you have!"

All the houses around us looked exactly the same, but of course ours was the neatest and best kept. Mama made absolutely sure of that. They were rows of red brick, railings made of iron rods and shared concrete porches and stoops. Each had its own patch of a yard. What could be more perfect? All our friends lived in the red brick. Everyone lived within these bricks except Aunt Barb and Uncle Albert. Well, the Gerard's didn't either, or the Jacobs, but I think everyone else did. Our school was red brick. I thought the world was built of red brick. The red bricks meant love and family.

The houses were just outside the guarded main gate of the navy base that was filled with soldiers. Surely, we were protected from danger. I'd often watch the men dressed in their crisp uniforms, carrying big guns, walking back and forth. They looked like toy soldiers that I'd seen in Edward's 5 & 10. I was so impressed each time a guard lifted his pretty white-gloved hand to salute as Daddy and the other men walked pass carrying their lunch boxes, thermoses and secrets in their heads..."Top secrets"I'd hear Daddy say to Mama.

Daddy said all the people in the red brick houses had become my very best friends. Mama sent out invitations to my friends for my birthday party. I took a daily walk through the neighborhood offering the news of the day. I shared everything I could think of to entertain the folks. They encouraged me as they chuckled and smiled and said, "You are so little and very precocious." I didn't know what precocious meant, but they always smiled as they said it, so it had to be good. I invited every single person, old and young, to my upcoming party.

March 16, 1947, was certainly a glorious event, the most wonderful day of my life because all my guests came. Mama baked a beautiful pound cake in her special pan with a hole in the middle, and topped it with that soft, white coconut icing piled as high as the clouds! Daddy wore his strong arm out churning my favorite vanilla ice cream made with evaporated milk. As the boys and girls Mama invited came, everyone was smiling, especially me. As the guests I invited started to arrive, Mama and Daddy's smile froze into place. They started putting a plan together. They must be gracious…Daddy would drive to the store and purchase a ready-made cake and a store bought gallon of ice cream. Well, Daddy made that trip to the store three times before those brick house people stopped coming. Daddy said, "They crawled right out of the woodwork!"

Following the grandest party I have ever thrown, Daddy got really sick and started throwing up, doubling over with pain! I never got to thank him for my wonderful party. Weeks after he had his appendix out, he came home from the hospital. A few days later, we had a talk. He made me promise never to invite anyone to our house again without checking with him first.

Beth grew busier in her world of basketball, friends, and school. Her time away left me alone with Mama, waiting and watching the clock'til time for Daddy. Beth taught me to sit at the edge of the ditch, dip my toes in the water and watch the shadowy bugs floating and spinning, entertaining myself. Sometimes on the edge of the ditch, I'd spy a cocoon tucked away on a leaf. I'd watch the roly-polys taking turns in the mud. Suddenly out of nowhere, a gentle hand would hold mine, and Daddy would swing me high across the ditch. Together we'd walk home. Sometimes I'd hitch a ride on the tops of his feet to 161-D, the most wonderful of all the homes.

Mama was home cooking supper, sipping sugary coffee, her Lucky Strike burning in the ash tray as its smoke curled up to the ceiling. Daddy quietly eased through the screen door as I mimicked his large steps. I hoped to see it, but there wasn't a hug or kiss, not a single pucker. "What's for supper?" This was the usual beginning for Daddy's conversation with his bride. Mama snapped open the oven door, coughing uncontrollably, and showed Daddy the golden-brown meatloaf. The kitchen smelled so good that my mouth filled with so much water I thought a faucet had turned on inside of me. Naturally, Mama kept lifting lids, one cast iron pot filled with her famous mashed potatoes, another with fried green beans, and in one more there was the okra gumbo. I knew the lumpy potatoes were chock-full of butter and evaporated milk because Mama told me to get a can out of the pantry for her. I couldn't read the word on the label so she insisted I read it and repeat *e-vap-o-rate-d*. I didn't know exactly what evaporated meant but I sure did know it was the right thing for Mama's potatoes. "Man, Rachel! You sure can whip up a meal in a blink of the eye!" Daddy said as he winked at me. "Where's Beth?" he asked.

"Off with her friends. She'll be home in a few minutes. How was your day, Truman? How are things going at the shipyard?"

"Oh, the same as usual, seems there're people who can't be trusted...the guards caught a few tools in lunch boxes yesterday! I do my job; don't ask questions. What'd you girls do all day?"

"Khaki and I stayed here, didn't do much...cleaned, washed, cooked...she played dolls and you should have seen the outlandish outfits she concocted when she played dress up. Talked to Barb about the new house, said to tell you that the supplies you ordered are in. When will you start building the house for them?"

"In a few weeks, got to finish clearing first."

"She said to tell you that Al got drunk and loud down at the tavern again last night...didn't come home. The boys went out looking and found him this morning. She's afraid he's going to lose his job if this behavior keeps up."

"That drunken brother of mine is going to kill himself with that whiskey. I'll try talking to him one more time. Go wash up, Khaki, and help your Mama set the table!" I sniffled in the corner where I was playing with my dolls and quickly headed for Mama's special drawer. They lay in the box shinning brightly. The sterling engraved with the perfect *D* on the handles...Mama's treasured sterling silver was as shiny as ever. Mama's family had lots of money, and the silver had belonged to them.

Gingerly opening the second drawer, I saw the familiar freshly starched, linen napkins, their color as white as my porcelain doll. They, too, were embroidered with Mama's family initial, for her *Drayton* family.

Mama always insisted on the best-laid table. After all, she was a Drayton and a college graduate. Her daddy was somebody important in the state of Georgia. After her Mother had died, she got a stepmother. Mama didn't think too much of that stepmother, so I never was told much about her. As I laid the napkins down on top of the fancy tablecloth, I touched each perfectly stitched *D,* admiring the beauty of the handwork. I saw Beth's shadow as she reached for the fine china plates in the cupboard. She'd rushed home from cheerleading practice, and wanted a bath but knew chores must be done first. "Daddy home yet, Khaki?"

"Uh huh…brought him up the path a few minutes ago."

"Good girl. How low is the water down at the ditch?" 'Bout the same as last week, you can really see the little wings on those wigglers."

"Let's eat," Mama said. And so we sat together at our table unfolding, blessing, and passing the bowls of Mama's piping hot delicious creations. She always urged us to eat just a little more. I always said, "More, please!" because it tasted so delicious and I couldn't handle the guilt if I didn't. Beth and I were stuffed and wanted to be excused, but just then Mama pulled out her famous Georgia peach cobbler. "Got these peaches from a truck coming straight from Savannah." Daddy started humming as he grabbed the ice cream scoop. "I'll need this to dip that vanilla ice cream frozen in this churn," he hummed as he pulled the churn out of the pantry. I was sure I hadn't heard that churn, but like magic it appeared…creamy vanilla full of evaporated milk…ready to go on the very top of Mama's warm cobbler. I could barely lift the fancy *D* spoon to my lips but I managed a smile rattling off, "Delicious, yummy, especially the crust, Mama."

Beth initiated clearing the table. As usual, I carried the sterling back and put the napkins in the proper laundry pile. Daddy's big hands began assembling the pots and Mama marched off puffing on a Lucky Strike and fixing herself a cup of coffee…adding two spoons of sugar and a touch of that evaporated milk. She used it in everything. Beth always got to wash the dishes and insisted it was my great privilege to dry. I tried to explain to her that if she left the dishes alone and came back later they'd be dry. As I whined, "Just let the air do it!" she shoved the towel in my hand. Following supper, Mama and Daddy went out to sit on the stoop of the brick front porch, and Beth and I went out to find our friends. Beth was off to find Linda, Cheryl, Ronnie, and the gang to play Red Rover.

She said, "You'll have to ride your tricycle and stay near the house. I'll try to bring the gang back here so you can watch us play."

Waiting for the gang to arrive, I sat down real close beside Mama. "Go play somewhere else, Khaki!" Feeling rejected, I walked beside the wisteria twig that I had recently planted. To my amazement, that vine was really growing high and low; it was everywhere. Beneath its tangled vines I saw my little rubber ball. I picked it up and went to the sidewalk just in front of Mama and Daddy. I bounced my ball high, and Mama said, "Move back!" I bounced it again, and she said, "Move farther back away from us!" This time I bounced my ball as high as I could, all the way up to the big, blue August sky. I looked up, losing the site of my ball in the afternoon sun. As I watched the mysterious shape of the clouds drifting above...wouldn't you know it...that ball came right down near Mama. In fact, it plopped right there in her coffee cup. I was so proud of that ball; I grinned like a Cheshire cat until I saw the look in her eyes! I could see she wasn't very proud of that ball or me. "Go inside for your bath, young lady!" She began yelling, "Beth!" who I knew would come right away because Mama was shrieking.

As Beth breathlessly climbed the stairs, she knelt down beside the tub with the washcloth in her hand. Her eyes looked like dark brown stones and all she said with her teeth clinched was, "You had to do it again, didn't you?"

As we grew older, Saturdays were always a day to get up early in our house because Mama liked it that way. Coffee and toast—that's what she ate for breakfast and so did the rest of us. By nine o'clock, I had taken off my long, white cotton nightgown and neatly hung it on the hanger. Putting on my shorts and halter-top, I hurried downstairs to get the dusting rag. It was my chore to keep the dust away and polish Mama's silver. Beth looked angry, busily beating the beautiful rugs that had come from a country far, far away. Daddy guaranteed that once chores were completed, he would take all of his girls to the beach. He was hustling back and forth, busily packing the gigantic cooler with Cokes and drinks. I knew he'd stop by the old icehouse to pile frozen crystal shavings on top of the drinks before we made our way down to the beach. This was our routine, and after the beach we'd get freshened up, drinks still in the cooler and Daddy'd take us to the drive-in movie where I'd climb on the merry-go-round and we'd eat hotdogs smothered in chili. A great day was in store for the Jaffe's this Saturday. As Daddy's huge hands continued to carefully separate the fishing lines, sticks, sinkers, rods, hooks, I watched him thoughtfully pick up a knife. Wondering what it would be used for, I saw him grab a pound of bait shrimp and wrap their prickly tails in special brown paper. It sure looked like Daddy was planning for a big catch out of the Atlantic Ocean. Mama tirelessly worked in the kitchen, her cigarette burning in the ashtray. Her manicured nails were busy fixing pimento cheese sandwiches, fried chicken, potato salad just the way Daddy liked it, macaroni and cheese, and that delicious pound cake she knew everybody always raved over. Once she finished wrapping and boxing, Daddy started stuffing the Studebaker. As he quickly slammed the trunk, he said, "Get in. Let's go before something falls out!" We were off. I knew it would be a long ride, at least twenty miles. That's why my whole family made sure that I went to the bathroom repeatedly before we left. Uncle Al, Aunt Barb, the Gerard's, the Shafer's, and the Copelands were all meeting us at the point on Seabrook Island. The hot wind kept blowing through the front window into the back seat. I could barely breathe, and ashes from Mama's cigarette flew into my hair, almost catching it on fire. Beth kept flicking at the ashes whispering in my ear, "Be a good girl and don't complain, Khaki, please!"

"Trade places with me," I whispered back. "No!"

"What are you girls whispering about?"

"Nothing, Mama!" Beth chimed as she flicked another ash from my eyebrow.

Daddy rolled the inner tubes over the hot sand to us as soon as we climbed out of the car. "Wait for your Mama or me before you go traipsing off into the water, girls." Off we raced, squealing for the other children to join us.

Seabrook Island was legendary for its spindly palmettos that lined the beach back in those days. In stark contrast, great oaks spread their arms decorated with the ghostly moss creeping to the ground. I remember shadows lurking beyond the background, and making me nervous. It was such a big piece of land but I knew Daddy was a personal friend of the prominent landholder.

I can still feel the white grains of sand blistering my feet as I dashed toward the ocean for relief. The greenish-blue water waved for Beth and me to dive in. Beth, much taller than I, climbed quickly onto her tube and headed out to the inviting sea, not waiting for Daddy, Mama, or me. My burning feet, soothed by the water, barely kept the waves from knocking me over. It was then that Mr. Shafer came to my rescue. "Thanks for putting me in my tube", I said. "Where's my Daddy?" He asked me if I could get you girls going. He's headed farther down the beach, going fishing for a big one. Says he's gonna fish like Jonah today. Look over there where your Mama's chatting with the women folk, she'll be watching out for you!" Off he trotted to join Daddy, leaving his funny footprints in the sand. As I watched the tide wash away his tracks toe by toe, I saw Mama waving her arm several times, pointing, and letting me know to move down closer toward her. The undertow was pulling me away.

People were always talking about somebody drowning in the undertow. Splashing in the waves trying to catch up with Beth, who moved faster and farther away, I focused on the undertow. Visions surrounded me, like the salt water, of this ugly giant toe that was attached to a huge foot. As I paddled, this toe was thumping along after me, clumsily, pulling me under the water. Once it wrestled me into the sand, it whispered that I was a captive never to leave again. It held me down with the rest of its big scary foot. Beth's giggling with her friends brought my attention back to the lapping waves where I saw her long legs gliding across the water. Her motions were as graceful as the swans I fed at Hampton Park. I wondered if the big bully undertow lurked to faraway waters where swans gathered.

Suddenly, Mama and the other gossiping women folk started scurrying up the beach toward Mr. Shafer and Daddy, arms waving high into the air. I could barely hear their voices but I knew the words must be "get out of that water!" Paddling toward the edge of the water, leaving the creatures behind, I arrived in the shallow wash, exhausted. Listening, I figured out that old Mr. Shafer had landed a baby shark on his fishing hook. The hook wouldn't budge, so Daddy came to his rescue. That shark must have been a little older than they thought because it had a full set of teeth that clamped together tightly on Daddy's huge hand, ripping it wide open. The gash was so big that blood gushed everywhere and left a big bloody stain in the sand. Daddy's face looked whiter than a ghost. My legs felt like water balloons as I tried to get out of my inner tube. Just as I trudged through the sand to the horrible chaos, Mama gathered Daddy and rushed to the Studebaker. Daddy's hand was wrapped in beach towels and the two of them were heading for Charleston and the hospital's emergency room. Off they sped...Daddy slumped in Mama's seat and Mama peeping over the steering wheel, clinging to it tightly, coughing, her left hand hanging out the window, the Lucky Strike burning close to her lovely fingernails. The same manicured fingers that had made the pimento cheese sandwiches, potato salad, fried chicken, macaroni and cheese and that pound cake. Hopefully, they had already moved the picnic basket onto the beach. "Poor hurt Daddy, I hope he'll be okay," I thought as my sister and I headed off to find the picnic basket.

Mr. and Mrs. Shafer didn't have children and were happy for the opportunity to watch over Beth and me. They drove us home later in the day after sharing their food with us...a feast, as they called it, a peanut butter sandwich, apple and milk. Neither Beth nor I had the heart to tell them we didn't like white milk, and anyway that wouldn't be polite. Instead, when they weren't looking, we made tiny holes in the sand and poured drops of the milk into the sand, pretending we were feeding the milkweed. The Shafer's stayed with us until after dark when Mama finally pulled up in the Studebaker. Daddy staggered into the living room, his huge hand bigger than ever wrapped about fifty times with a soft white cloth looking like the biggest cocoon imaginable. Daddy acted a little strange, mumbling funny words about his dental work creating thirty-five stitches and all he received was one filleted shark and a whopping bill.

Right before Labor Day that year, Daddy mentioned to me that I'd be going to first grade. "Now, I know you didn't like kindergarten very much, Khaki. Your teacher wasn't very pretty, but all women don't wear lipstick and nail polish. First grade is very important and Mama's going to take you and Beth shopping tomorrow for new clothes. You'll be a big six year old and go to school."

I knew there'd be no more discussion about going to first grade because Daddy had given his word that I was going. Mama coughed more and more during these days, and I was really worried about leaving her at home alone. One sticky night just before school began I silently tiptoed into Mama and Daddy's bedroom, careful not to squeak the door. Daddy was snoring so loud it sounded like he was sawing logs. I knew he was really sleeping. Mama wasn't making a peep, nothing at all. I stood very still. My eyes ached I was starring so hard at the sheets on top of her. I couldn't see if they were moving. I crept closer, stopping right beside her and gently putting my ear to her chest, listening carefully for the sound of her heart. As I heard the boom, boom, I said right out loud, "Yep, she's alive!" Without warning, Daddy flipped over in the bed, scaring the dickens out of me. I was so startled that I got down on my hands and knees and quietly crawled toward my room. My favorite white cotton nightgown got tangled and wrapped tightly around my legs. I tugged as it caught under me and ripped it. Now, I'd have some explaining to do. My mission completed, I climbed into the bed that I shared with Beth, a bed that had an imaginary line drawn right down the middle by Beth. "Don't cross over this line, little sister, and you'll be just fine," she'd tell me every night. I couldn't understand her problem. How much space could she need? It really gave me comfort to put my cold feet on her warm ones, and draping my arm over her waist made me feel safe. I knew tonight that I'd better not try to go over that line. The next morning when I woke up, my white cotton gown was wrapped around my legs like a wet blanket. I had wet the bed again, now my gown was soaked and ripped! As I slowly went down the stairs, I pretended to trip and fall just a little. "Oh, Mama, I'm so sorry I've torn my beautiful gown!" I cried. "I'm wet again, too". Mama assured me that mending the gown was not a problem as she told Beth to get me into the bathtub. The metal window fan, its sharp blades moving the humid hot air around our room, was a sure sign that this was August.

Daddy had spoken, so Mama prepared us for our shopping day in Charleston. "Girls, we'll get you new finery and, of course, shoes." Shoes were always her favorite. Her size five feet could always find the most stylish selections at Rob Ellison. Mama made sure we wore brand names, only the best quality. Some stores Mama never shopped in, but I never knew why…just that they weren't important.

Choosing the prettiest dresses with sashes, ruffles and lace was so much fun for me, a girl shopper full of magical ideas. The fabrics were gorgeous, with their colors of purple, red and bright pink. My heart pounded excitedly at the thought of wearing them, just like Cinderella going to the ball. Beth and Mama covered their mouths with their palms as they snickered at my choices. Mama came prancing into the dressing room, where I had already stripped waiting for my delivery, carrying hangers of outfits. I quickly separated the hangers looking for the ones I'd picked, but there hung only dresses I'd never seen. There was no lace, no ruffles, just plain and simple "earth tones" as Mama called them. Mama patted me on the back and said, "You're a little too short and pudgy for those others. These are better suited for your size, Khaki." My heart broken, I started to tear up just as Beth appeared in time to remind me to be grateful. I modeled Mama's selections with an unmoving smile, praising Mama for knowing what was best for me.

Nauseated was a word I heard her use often after she violently coughed and coughed. So, I thought that shopping on King Street in August was quite nauseating for me. The heat hit me in the face, turning it red. The warmth from the sidewalk was making me feel funny. My body was sweating, even though Mama didn't like that word. The stinky odors of the tall people passing by and squishing me reminded me of those smelly sardines that Daddy liked to eat from that flat can. A few of these people made funny noises from their behinds and often smelled stinky. Some made really loud noises; others little soft squeaks or a puffing sound, but I never saw any of these people move their lips with all these noises.

We shopped King Street the entire day in the awful heat, only stopping for a quick sandwich for lunch from Woolworth's soda counter, and Mama promised to return for ice cream later. After lunch, we were off to more fancy shoe shops. In the late afternoon, we were just outside the door to Woolworth's again, with its ceiling fans inviting us inside. "Let's get some iced tea, too!" Mama said, as she glided through the open door. Beth sat primly on her stool while I tried to hoist myself up onto the red, rotating seat, slipping several times. Sipping her Coke Cola slowly, Beth watched me strangely. My face was bright red, from the heat and my throat felt like sandpaper. As I gulped my tea right down, Mama said, "Khaki, you drink like a sailor. Stop that!"

"Okay, ladies, now that you're refreshed, let's get to those shoes!" The rotating ceiling fans had magically cooled her off, and she was ready to hit the road. The ice-cold tea had just reached my stomach, where it was slowly churning with the chocolate ice cream that I just finished. My hands were now as cold and clammy as the ice that had chilled the tea.

As I placed the bottom of my white sandal out into the heat of the sidewalk, waves of nausea shot through my stomach. I briefly caught the horror on Beth's face as she hastily jumped back toward Mama. I could hear Mama's harsh coughing as I wretched and jerked, trying to hold onto something as I upchucked right there on the cracks in the streets of historical Charleston. I don't know how Daddy heard the news about my throwing up but when we got home I could see the disappointment in his eyes. I knew I'd ruined the day for my Mama and Sister.

I rested quietly on the sofa while the three of them ate supper. Beth scooted me upstairs for my bath, tucking me in on my half of the mattress, reminding me about that line. Later Daddy came up to tell me a story, in fact he told me several new tales, on this evening, before I dozed off. I stayed on my side of the bed for almost three days. I made a pact with God and myself that at no time in the future would I throw up in front of Woolworth's or any other place that was historical.

Daddy came home from work early the Friday before I was to start first grade. I knew it was early 'cause I hadn't heard the first whistle blow for the men with the black lunch boxes. I was busy playing with my doll in the closet. Mama wouldn't let me sit on the bed once it had been properly made. She'd say, "You mustn't mess the covers!" Well, my doll didn't care where she got to sit, so we stayed in the living room closet with a curtain for our door. Daddy was talking softly with Mama. "How long has this been happening? Did you call your doctor." Then, I heard him dialing numbers; I tried to figure them out each time his large finger turned the dial. Daddy's voice was gentle on the phone. I heard him say, "Yes, sir, right away." Daddy drove away in the Studebaker, returning with Beth from practice. She began packing my clothes and some of hers. We climbed in the Studebaker with Mama, not saying a word. Daddy was heading the car toward Aunt Barb's house. Aunt Barb quickly came to the car and gathered my bag and me. Daddy and Beth sped away in the Studebaker with Mama now lying in the back seat on her way to the hospital.

Aunt Barb said, "Your Mama's got a little problem. She's spitting up blood and the doctors are a little worried about her. They're going to keep her in the hospital for a few days, and you're going to stay right here with me. Your Daddy will come back to get you soon." I was so worried about my poor Mama. I tried and tried to remember what I could have done this time to upset her. I knew Daddy must be worried sick about her, too.

2
Mama

I'm told that my Mama, Rachel Elizabeth Drayton Jaffe was quite a high-spirited swinger in her day. Born in Columbus, Georgia, near the Chattahoochee River, her wealthy family moved to Americus and Valdosta because her daddy was a big man with the phone company. She was the youngest of the Drayton family's two daughters and the only one who was extremely prideful. "The Drayton family has always been known for its heritage." I can still hear Mama saying. Her older sister, Cornelia, was very unlike Mama. The five years separating them must have had a huge log fall right between those two sisters. It didn't help matters that their mother had died young from "female problems." Mama said, "I was ten years old when my mother passed away. So, I only knew about the 'female problems' and very little about her life."

Mama really didn't remember many stories about her mother, but boy, could she tell some stories about Cornelia. Those sisters must have been at each other all the time.

I'm told that many times their daddy, Zachary Drayton would take my Mama to work with him and sit her on a big phone stool. The phone operators were told to keep an eye on her. Well, Mama learned the tricks of the trade at the phone company by the ripe age of eleven. She could imitate the operator's high-pitched voices and mimic their movements at the switchboard like any twenty year old. She even learned to puff on cigarettes just like the rest of them. Mama said that her daddy was so busy with his work and being a "lady's man," he decided to put his girls in the finest boarding school in Georgia. Cornelia, who was seventeen at the time, decided boarding school wasn't for her, and she ran off and married her long-time boyfriend, Daniel. Mama, who was twelve at the time, decided boarding school would be a new adventure. Making friends became her new hobby, and Mary Emiline was her nearest and dearest friend of the time. They bonded like two sisters eating boiled peanuts in the summer.

As the story goes, afternoons were spent down by the Flint River. Mama and Mary Emiline sat barefoot, sharing stories they'd studied in history class. On this particular spring day in 1927, the story was about the Yankee, Mr. Nelson Flint, coming down south from Connecticut when he was a young man. Albany in 1836 was not more than a few log cabins built. One a store and a few other buildings and that was it. Mr. Tift, the founder of Albany, had given a speech not far from where the girls spread their quilt and stretched out. They lay there with their skirts hiked up to reveal slender ankles. Mary Emiline stood up pretending to be Mr. Tift. "My good people of the south, I find this southern country mild and pleasant, therefore I shall settle here and never be a Yankee again. I shall name this new town Albany because it reminds me extremely of another town that I have walked, Albany, New York." Mary Emiline looked up to see an assembly of passersby's, listening to her every word. Mortified, her face flushed and her brilliant green eyes began swelling with tears. Mama ran over grabbed her arm and they scrambled into the trees that were blocking the river.

Mama said she told Mary Emiline, "You were great, they really liked what you were saying and it was all mostly true…some of it anyway. Come on let's tiptoe through the river on our way back to Roosevelt Hall. We have to be ready for Miss Hadley's afternoon tea and cucumber sandwiches by three o'clock."

During the '20s, Albany bloomed and Mama's friendships did, too. She and her friends enjoyed many special outings, eating pecans and candy from the Famous Candy Company. They watched the town folk flock daily to the natural spring called "Skywater." Their history teacher had told them all about the Creek Indians and how they'd named that spring. It bubbled with elements of radium and was the largest natural spring in all of Georgia. Mama and Mary Emiline were curious as folks filled jars and containers of all sizes with the potion from the artesian wells, hoping to cure their coughs and brittle bones.

Roosevelt Hall played a big roll in Mama's life. The Cotton Mill had brought a slew of new faces to town. Miss Holly Winthrop was one of those new faces. Miss Winthrop, as the girls from Roosevelt Hall called her, was established as the finest teacher in the fine state of Georgia. She was really beautiful with long blonde braids. Mama always said, "I vividly remember Miss Holly Winthrop because her nails were covered with the finest French colors. Miss Winthrop said that her chic shoes were imported from Paris. She made sure that you could see the tiny bits of lace or a piece of exquisite linen peeking from her clothes. Her soft voice captivated us as she prepared us for college."

I can still hear Mama coughing and telling me stories about Miss Winthrop.

"Often, she and Miss Putney would take us girls to the municipal auditorium to hear the tunes of the great bands. Miss Winthrop led us girls like a principal of a school—marching all the way back to Roosevelt Hall. During her first term at Roosevelt Hall, I learned to "Do the Chal'ston" like a professional dancer." Then she'd cross her feet, wiggle her knees and raise her arms to the tune of the music. She laughed as she remembered how she wished that she could really jiggle her hips in the sandy Charleston beaches. I could almost see her visions of the breezy beaches and of course those darlin' boys she'd talked about at Porter School.

I almost held my breath listening to Mama cough as she continued her story with her deep, soft voice. "In spring 1932, Miss Winthrop happily escorted her girls, 'the cream of the crop,' through graduation ceremony. Looking almost as beautiful as Miss Holly in our long white gowns, we carried clusters of deep red roses, breathlessly waiting to hear our names. Sitting in my assigned seat, I glanced over to see who was sitting in the rows reserved for my family.

"I recognized three rows of well-to-do great aunts and a few aunts, my mother's sisters and aunts, dressed in their finery and sitting by some dapper uncles, truly southern looking gentlemen. I panicked when I couldn't find Cornelia or Daddy. I thought, 'Cornelia probably stayed home with her two boys and Daniel. Where's Daddy?' Frantically searching the faces, I saw him smiling proudly, his crystal blue eyes dancing with joy. He blew me a kiss and then I noticed the worst thing of all...beside him was Taffy, his new bride. I could have spit right there during my special ceremony, but I saw Miss Winthrop glancing my way. Spitting would not have been a good thing for Miss Winthrop to see. Miss Winthrop always said to me, 'Good girls do not complain or make others unhappy!' You should always remember what she said too, Khaki."

After graduation, Mama was ready for the world. Georgia Southern was her choice to further her education. She wanted to become a professor, another Miss Holly Winthrop. Since Georgia's first governor, Archibald Bulloch, had come from this part of Georgia, she felt she surely could become a teacher here. Her daddy had arrived to escort her to Statesboro.

As they drove through the beautiful state, they talked about its uniqueness. "The Georgia clay was almost the color inside of those peaches over there. The clay's holding back those groves, Rachel. I've spent many a day digging in that clay. It has no mercy for the weary. I do believe that the roadside stands are spaced just far enough apart to invite every passerby to stop and taste the peaches, watermelons, and boiled peanuts. We're going to have to stop soon because I can taste those peaches." The giant oaks hung over the roadway as my Mama and her Daddy sped along in the fabulous new Cadillac. Granddaddy Zachary had just bought "my new machine" as he called it. The smell, the new leather seats, and the richness of the interior reminded Mama of her childhood just before her mother passed away. She focused on the hood ornament as the mild winds blew gently through the windows thinking about her mother. "Too bad, Daddy had married Taffy, but thank goodness he didn't have her join us today. At least I have him for a few hours all to myself", Mama thought. "Daddy, you sure did buy yourself a fine automobile."

"Thanks, honey...I wanted you to go to school in a new car, only the best for my baby girl. We're almost to Statesboro. Wanna stop for a Coke

Cola and stretch our legs, maybe get some peaches?"

"Sure daddy." We freshened up and bought a basket of peaches, then climbed back into the comfort of the Cadillac, driving past Akins Farm on Old Register Road to Savannah Avenue and straight into town. We crossed the railroad tracks on Vine Street and turned on to Cherry Street. I could see the old Courthouse. Turning right on South Main Street, we headed for Georgia Southern."

"Khaki, I tell you, the years I spent at Georgia Southern were filled with money and lots of courting. There were glorious parties, plenty of friends, and gentlemen callers from all parts of Georgia. As a debutante, I was well known in those parts. My friends Sarah Donehoo, Emma Thomas, Grady Caldwell, and your daddy, whiled away many evenings together down at the Jackson Hotel listening to 'Blind Willie' playing the Blues on his wonderful twelve-string guitar.

"Then, we'd be flapping to the tunes, tassels swaying, pearls rocking back and forth to the great bands, and, of course, dancing the Chal'ston! One evening, it was late August, your Daddy, handsome as ever, swept me right off my feet! I had barely completed my term at Georgia Southern when he asked me to elope to Charleston. My Daddy was as furious as a wild boar with Truman and he begged me to come back home."

"At nineteen," Mama said, "Charleston and your daddy were the two loves in my life. Besides, Daddy had his Taffy, back in Valdosta and Lowndes County." I finally had someone to love me who was all mine.

Later as both of my parents continued to share their adventures, Mama and Daddy said they began building their new life together in 1938. Mama was working for Southern Bell Phone and Telegraph Company and Daddy was an apprentice at the Charleston Naval Shipyard, struggling much harder than expected. Other than the lack of money, life in Charleston was just what Mama had hoped for. Happily married...with plenty of time to swing to the music that played throughout the city.

Wartime was approaching. Talk was everywhere about compromise, but there was no compromise that would end this conflict. Would Daddy have to go, or would he be needed to build the huge gray ships? As President Roosevelt made speeches about total victory, Mama said things were scary and peaceful at the same time. The talk of war brought the country closer together, and I guess my parents too because Beth was born in the fall of 1940.

Mama often said Beth was a hand full, a difficult baby, crying all the time, colicky, needing to be rocked or walked constantly. Fortunately, Daddy didn't go to war...I don't remember why except that he said he was there to take care of his country and us...building ships, bigger than ever and keeping those secrets.

As I grew older, I learned more about World War II. "People made many sacrifices on the home front, and many lives were lost, but your Daddy and I were so lucky because we got two bundles of joy during this time, Khaki, your sister and you," my Mama often told me. We moved from our Trapp Street home to Tom Macmillan Homes near the Naval Base so Daddy could reach his job quicker during the difficult times.

"I didn't go back to the Southern Bell Phone and Telegraph Company any more because I wanted to stay home and raise Beth and you, Khaki," Mama said as she started to cough. I guess Mama must have been smoking since the days on her phone stool, but it seemed to really latch on to her these days. She coughed constantly.

When I was about eight years old Granddaddy Zachary arrived in Charleston with his oxygen tank in tow and a cough that sounded just like Mama's. I still remember that day...Mama hooked up his breathing machine and the long tubes stretched like a vine throughout the house. As Mama puffed her Lucky's, sparks flew like the fireworks on the fourth of July. I ran into the other room and hid in the closet as the two of them yelled for Beth and gasped and coughed. By the time all the gauges were refitted on the tank, Mama and Granddaddy were breathing like twin dragons. They had no eyebrows, eyelashes, or hair left on their arms, and the room was filled with a strange smell that I later learned was burning hair. Pondering over this sight, I resolved right then and there that oxygen was the most confusing stuff I'd seen yet.

By the time I was almost ten, Mama had been in the hospital so many times that I was sure Daddy owned part of the building. Each time she visited Roper, I visited my large, jolly Aunt Barb. Her long, long hair framed her beautiful face. It was always twisted into huge rings and wrapped neatly around her head. Her enormous fingers played her grand piano with the great harmony. She always let me try to play with my right hand. I could play my favorite chopsticks like a pro. Each time Aunt Barb would wander over to sit on the narrow rectangular bench beside me, I would leap to my feet in fear: I didn't want to be flattened before my performance. We were quite a duet, Aunt Barb and me. She'd leave me banging away while she went off to round up the yummiest refreshments imaginable. There was poor Mama laid up in the hospital, Beth taking care of her after school, and me stuck at Aunt Barbs and barely able to visit her.

I remember Daddy calling one afternoon to say he would pick me up after work, take me to our house while he changed his clothes, and we'd pick up Beth at the hospital, have dinner and then visit Mama. I was so excited…pleased as punch.

While Daddy changed, I decided that Mama needed to know that I had grown up during her absence. I changed my clothes wanting to make a good impression on her. I borrowed a pair of her red shoes. They were tiny but beautiful with special little heels called pumps. Mamas size five feet were just a tad smaller than my size five and a half but those pumps should do the trick—they'd be perfect. Knowing that I had never worn pumps before, Mama would be proud of my choice for this special evening. She wouldn't mind that I had borrowed from her collection. Stuffing my chubby toes all the way down into the end was harder than I thought, but I was sure they'd stretch. Leather always did, I was told. I glanced in the mirror feeling as proud as Sambo with his purple slippers, in my favorite book *Little Black Sambo.*

Daddy drove the Studebaker to the hospital, gathered Beth, and headed for Robertson's Cafeteria. Daddy, six feet, three inches, and Beth edging right up there with him, had no mercy for my very petite legs, wearing Mama's rigid red leather pumps. Their wide gaits moved them down the sidewalks quickly, and they had no sympathy as I whined, "Wait for me!"

Dinner became much more than splendid, as I chose dishes from each selection on the display: the salads, soup, two entrees, fried chicken and shrimp. I had trouble with the vegetables so I took fried okra, green beans, mashed potatoes and rice and gravy. Of course, there was a problem when I got to the cornbread and the biscuits and the lady kept saying move along...I just took both. Daddy repeatedly said, "Take what you want, Khaki, but you'll eat what you take!" Well, I really thought most people got two trays until Beth gave me the evil eye at the table moving away to the side nearest Daddy. Looking at his watch, Daddy said that if I didn't hurry and finish my food visiting hours would soon be over. I slowly finished my pie and struggled with the rest of my bread pudding before waddling to the car. Laden with food, exhausted from my day, and definitely feeling pressure from the red pumps, I climbed into the back seat of the Studebaker.

As Daddy drove to the hospital, I sat in the dark trying to wiggle the straps loose on my feet. Those red stranglers on my feet only got tighter. I began to feel so confined that I was sure it felt just like choking. My toes were numb; I couldn't move them at all. They were swelling as big as the great undertoe in the ocean, totally out of control. My heart was now in my feet, beating thump, thump, thump! As my luck would have it, the parking area was loaded with cars, so Daddy decided to park around the corner. He said it was only a few blocks farther to walk. By the time the doors opened on that giant, funny-smelling elevator, my feet were redder than the lipstick I'd seen on Marilyn Monroe in a magazine. I bit my lip with the pain because I knew that good girls shouldn't complain. Beth kept looking at me strangely, asking me if I needed to use the bathroom. I guess it was because I kept moving from one inflated foot to the other. As she pressed the elevator button to take us up to Mama, I lost my balance and staggered to the floor. Shrieking, Beth pointed to my feet in the miniature red shoes. Daddy asked where I'd gotten the shoes. As I confessed, I started to feel embarrassed right there in that elevator! Arm in arm, those two laughed so hard that they had to support one another all the way down the hall. Surely, they could see that I needed bracing. But no, they only roared by themselves to Mama's room. I slowly hobbled behind the laughing pair, wondering how much farther I had to go. Finally reaching the room, its door shut, I couldn't go inside. Slumping down with my back against the wall, tears began to swell. I watched as they fell from my cheeks onto my bulging stomach, traveling southward along my body. They dripped onto my legs and stopped just before reaching my toes. There were my toes throbbing out of control, attached to my legs, straight out in the hall for everyone to see except my Mama, her red shoes hidden behind my back. Not wanting to face the jokes, I knew the teasing wasn't over. It would go on for the rest of my life because through the thick, cold wall I could hear Mama laughing, amid coughs, as my Daddy and my sister told their version of the story.

At last, red faced, I gathered my courage, pushed the door open enough for my blurry eyes to glimpse inside. There hooked to a number of unfamiliar, scary machines was Mama.

She stayed in that hospital for six months. Daddy said she couldn't come home because the doctors had taken out one of her lungs and I needed to stay with Aunt Barb and Uncle Al, but Daddy promised to come by and visit with me. Poor Mama, I hoped my wearing those red shoes didn't make her worse.

Staying with Aunt Barb wasn't a bad thing. She and Uncle Al lived in a house Daddy had helped build for them. It was really close to the Navy Yard and across Spruill Avenue, not far away from where we lived. Uncle Al was never home because he was a railroad man and at night he liked to go to taverns. In fact, I only remember seeing him once or twice.

There was the day I sneaked out to cross the railroad tracks. I had planned to sit at the ditch and wait for Daddy to grab my hand, knowing that he would walk me back across the highway to Aunt Barb's. I never got there. The rocks on my bare feet were like hot coals in a fire and burned my feet. I kept stepping onto the metal of the first rail, feeling for any vibrations on the tracks. As I listened carefully for the sound of the big engine, I hopped to the next rail. The July heat on the rails was scorching, but I continued to hop the rails one at a time, always straining my ears for the sound of the Atlantic Coast Line trains. All of a sudden, I heard an awful moaning noise. It was so pitiful and so close to me that I knew I had to find out what it was. Turning toward the bushes to my right, I scrambled straight for the low growling moans. They were getting louder. Then, I saw him laying there, his huge eyes watching my every move. I took a few steps closer, "Are you alright...what's the matter?" He tried to pull himself up and drag toward me. My eyes filled with tears and terror and then I scrambled away from that horrible place as fast as I could. Screaming my loudest, I bumped into Uncle Al coming onto the tracks.

"Khaki, Khaki," I heard Uncle Al repeating my name and then he was shaking me with his skinny hands. "What's wrong with you?"

At last I was able to utter a few words, "He's over there! My dog, Sam! He has no legs! He's still on the tracks."

Sam's big brown eyes were pleading, "Help me."

Uncle Al raced past me back to the house, yelling for me to do the same. Just as I arrived, he darted out again, carrying a huge shovel. As Uncle Al trotted back to the horrible place, Aunt Barb took me inside for a glass of iced tea. Still crying, I tried to smile as she wiped away my tears. Uncle Al came back a while later and wrapped Sam, who was no longer breathing, in an old spread. He dug a great big hole, and the three of us had a funeral for my dog. Uncle Al made a cross from some twigs, Aunt Barb said a few words, and then we went inside where she played *Jesus Loves Me* on the piano and we sang the words to make me feel better.

I didn't know at the age of ten that funerals would become something I had to do. A few weeks after Sam's death, I learned that Uncle Al had beaten Sam to death with the shovel. "It was to put him out of his misery, Khaki. I'm sorry that I had to do it." I excused myself and quickly ran into the bedroom, burying my face in my pillow. I was careful that Uncle Al didn't hear me cry as my heart hurt for poor Sam.

I thought Mama would never get out of the hospital. The time seemed to be dragging along so slowly. Then, early one morning, I heard Aunt Barb whispering on the phone. I knew I shouldn't listen, but I tiptoed to the door and pressed my ear to it as tightly as I could. I heard Aunt Barb say, "Oh Truman, I'm so very sorry! I'll get her ready and tell her you're on the way to pick her up." Hurrying back to the bed and putting the sheet over my legs, I pretended to still be asleep. I yawned as Aunt Barb opened the door. "Good morning, Khaki!" she chirped as her arm jiggled when she lifted my covers. "Would you like a nice stack of pancakes? How about some warm syrup to go with them?"

As I answered, "Yes, ma'am," I wondered why she was babying me so much. Slipping into my shorts and halter-top, I met Aunt Barb in the kitchen. Not only was the table filled with pancakes, warm butter, and fresh maple syrup, I saw a huge pile of crisp bacon and sausage. My chocolate milk had been poured, and I could smell the fresh coffee brewing—just like the trouble I was sure I was about to hear.

"Honey, your daddy's coming over in a few minutes to get you. I have something just awful to share with you. Listen carefully because it's really important." I stopped chewing the mouthful of pancakes and took a big gulp of milk to wash it down. I started to cry before she even finished telling me the news. "Your Granddaddy Zachary has passed away. He went up with the angels just a little while ago. Your Daddy's coming to get you and to go tell your Mama the news. Then, you are going to Valdosta, Georgia, with your Daddy to the funeral. You be a good girl, and take care of your Daddy, okay?" Now, I was really sad…another funeral, my only Granddaddy, gone! My poor Mama!

Daddy arrived just in time to devour a couple of eggs, fried hard, five strips of crisp bacon, two biscuits covered with apple butter, and juice and coffee. He and Aunt Barb chatted about the funeral and all the arrangements. I listened as Aunt Barb politely offered to order flowers and phone friends.

Once we reached the hospital, I felt nauseous, my hands were clammy, and my hair soaked with sweat. Mama always said perspiration and would be disappointed to know that I even thought the word sweat. Just outside her room, I stopped to bite my lip and work up a big smile for her. Beth was waiting for Daddy's arrival. As we watched, nurses ready with their equipment, Daddy gave Mama the painful news. Sheets started flying, people were rushing in and out of the room while I hid in a corner. Mama was crying and screaming, "I want out of here. I've got to go to my Daddy's funeral. Damn you, Truman! Get me my clothes!"

"Now, Rachel, you know that you're still too sick to travel and the trip will be extremely difficult for you. I'm taking Khaki with me and Beth is going to stay right here in the hospital with you. They're bringing in a cot in a few minutes. It's settled, and that's that!" Immediately, the nurse was there to give Mama a shot. Mama's eyes instantly started to close. I was so afraid that she had died, too. Beth took me into the hall as I sobbed loudly, unable to control myself. She told me that Mama was only resting and that she would take good care of her.

Once we reached the South Carolina-Georgia state line near Savannah, Daddy stopped so I could go to the bathroom. I had been sleeping on the seat of the Studebaker. The humidity was so high that I was drenched with perspiration. I had red marks etched into my face and drool was running down my chin. I felt like a ton of bricks was sitting on my chest. Daddy got some Cokes and Nabs for us and off we went, heading toward the dreaded alligator waters and a dead person. The dead person was someone I hadn't seen as much as I wanted, but I loved him with all of my heart.

We arrived in Valdosta around nine o'clock that night. Daddy headed straight for Miller's Funeral Home. There wasn't a car in sight. "Good," I thought. "We won't have to go in tonight." I was really wrong. Not only did Mr. Miller open up, but he also kept the lights down very low. Daddy pointed through the heavy double doors to a lengthy wooden box and said, "There's your Granddaddy." Slowly, Daddy walked me down the long corridor to the front of the chapel where Granddaddy Zachary was just as still as could be. I was holding my breath and praying that he wouldn't jump up in front of me. The stories I'd heard about the dead were scary, but I'd never actually seen a dead person before in my whole life. Looking at him with his makeup on made me feel funny; I was sure that he'd be very unhappy about what they'd done to him. His suit was perfect though. Just as I started to turn around and walk quickly away, I heard my Daddy say to me, "Give him a kiss, Khaki. Tell him 'bye." You could have put me right in that coffin with my Granddaddy, 'cause I thought my heart stopped. I couldn't feel my fingers either.

For the first time in my life, I heard myself say, "No, Daddy!"

Daddy leaned down closer and said, "I told you to kiss your Granddaddy 'bye. Do it for your poor sick Mama. Remember she can't be here."

I tiptoed up to the side of the coffin and my clammy hand touched my Granddaddy's hands folded politely over his heart. Leaning over him, I puckered my lips and placed a kiss on his forehead, muttering good-bye or something like that. Then I ran for the door, out of Miller's Funeral Home.

The next morning, Daddy and I ate breakfast at the motel then drove to Aunt Cornelia's motel down the road. When we got there, the room looked like it was chock-full of crows. There were women everywhere in black dresses with hankies to their noses. They were all going through clothes Aunt Cornelia had brought to sell 'cause she owned a dress shop in Columbus. As Daddy and I came in, they started squeezing me and saying I looked just like my Mama and how sorry they were that she wasn't well. These old crows were Mama's aunts, and they made sure I knew they were my great aunts. But I didn't think they were so great. Daddy left me with them while he went to get a few things. As soon as he was gone, they started arguing over the clothes again and gossiping about the guests who were coming to the funeral. The stepmother, Taffy, was in the group. She was one of the worst gossips.

The next day was Granddaddy's funeral. Daddy and I had trouble fixing my hair. My cowlicks stuck out everywhere on this sad day when I wanted to look perfect for Mama. We got to Miller's Funeral Home early. Daddy took me up to the front row where Aunt Cornelia and Uncle Daniel were going to sit next to the stepmother. He said, "You sit here in your Mama's seat, Khaki."

"Okay, Daddy," I said, thinking he was going to sit with me and hold my hand. Then, he started talking with his old friends. The music started and everybody began taking seats. Daddy sat down nine rows behind me—I knew because I had counted every row.

Just as things seemed to be going just fine, one of the old crows, dressed in black with a thin mask over her face, crouched down beside me and said, "Move somewhere else, Catherine. You don't belong with the adults. Scoot along now." I was so embarrassed! Everybody was looking at me. I tried to quietly climb over all the adults who filled their seats, but I must have looked really out of sorts because a nice lady four rows back put her hand in mine.

"Come, sit here next to me, honey." She moved over and sat me beside her. My poor ailing Mama would have been so shamed if she heard that I couldn't keep her seat of honor at her Daddy's funeral.

As we headed back to Charleston, I finally found the words to apologize to my Daddy for the funeral mishap. He patted me on the shoulder. "Don't you worry about it, Khaki we all make mistakes, and I promise not to breathe a word to your Mama or Beth."

Mama came home from the hospital eight months after her Daddy's funeral. She was much weaker than I remembered her being before she went to the hospital. She still coughed, especially after she smoked her Lucky Strikes, but now Mama seemed really different to me.

3
Beth

Her given name is Elizabeth Anne Jaffe, but we've always called her Beth. Much taller than I, she is the spitting image of Daddy with her dark hair and no cowlicks. It even curled a little, just like Daddy's. "Khaki, your stick straight hair and all those cowlicks must have come from the trolls," Beth often told me when she tried to brush my hair. "Let's put some water on it, maybe that'll help. Now be still or I'll spit on it."

One morning, Beth told me this story: "You were about six years old. Mama had put you outside for the day to play. It was a perfectly usual day, breakfast with Mama, toast and coffee, getting dressed, going outside until lunch. You weren't allowed to come in until Mama called for resting time and then you'd go back outside until time for Daddy to come home. On this particular day, you hadn't been outside thirty minutes when I heard you beating on the locked screen door. 'Mama, let me in, I need to use the bathroom!' 'You can't come in. The floors are wet. Go over to a neighbor's house or find a tree!' 'Mama, I'm going to wet my pants!'

'Sorry!' Beth continued. "It wasn't long before I came outside and found you hiding beside the porch. Oh, Khaki. You're soaked again! Stay here, I'll be right back.' She said she brought me fresh clothes and sent me off to play again.

"It was only a little while before you returned so excited and trembling with excitement. Mama and I both came running out to see what was going on."

"It was the kittens. I remember it vividly," I said.

"You had promised not to bother Mama again for the rest of the day but when you trotted off to entertain yourself you found a surprise. As you turned the corner of the brick buildings, you heard a faint meow."

"I remember that now, Beth. As I looked down, I saw the most beautiful thing I'd ever seen. Cuddled together were five new kittens. Their paws were making dough on their Mama. I was so excited that I ran home to share my treasure with you and Mama. Y'all followed me to the secret hiding place but warned me not to touch them. You told me that the mama cat would pack up and move away. I promised not to touch them if Mama would talk to Daddy about letting me keep one. After much begging, Daddy finally decided that I could keep one boy kitten. I named him John."

"Being your big sister does have its problems. You keep me busy and on my toes!" I was never quite sure what Beth meant by this statement. She was the person who gave me my information. She was the one who always took care of me—except when Aunt Barb was in charge. Beth and Aunt Barb were the ones I looked up to, especially Beth.

It was a rainy summer afternoon, and she was teaching me how to play Pick Up Sticks. "Try using your left hand, Khaki. You know you can bend those fingers. Have you been using the weights Daddy made for you?"

"I can't, Beth. You know this stupid hand won't work. Why doesn't my hand look like yours?"

"Cause there wasn't an accident when you were born. No one found out about yours until you were two. It was when my friend Linda fell from the iron porch rail and knocked you from your tricycle. Remember you broke your left arm? You were so happy when the doctor took off the itchy cast! We were all surprised when you couldn't keep your arm straight. Mama and Daddy took you for lots of visits to the best doctors in town.

"That's when they discovered what happened in the delivery when you were born. Dr. Rhett used long pinchers to help pull you from Mama's tummy. You must have been trying to watch like you always do because those pinchers caught you between the eyes and you started to bleed from your head. That's why your hand jerks and bends funny. It's called a birth defect, Cerebral Palsy. Yours isn't bad, it's mild. You'll understand better one day. Now, take your turn and pick up the sticks."

"Oh, so that's why I got all those new dresses every time I visited with the doctors from New York and California and that's why Daddy tied my right arm behind my back and made me eat with my left hand."

"Yeah, Khaki, and that's why Mama says I have to watch out for you all the time!"

Beth was my really good protector for a while. Each of the three times I fell and broke my right arm, she was right there to make me feel better. She added lots of names and pictures on the casts. If I needed her to stick a long comb down inside and scratch my skin, she'd try her hardest to figure a way to do it.

As I grew older though, Beth quietly disappeared. She was gone all the time. I was never really sure where she was and I missed her so much. I knew she must be busy with something very important or she wouldn't leave me. Every now and then when we were doing the dishes, I would try to get Beth to talk about her friends. "Do you have a boyfriend?"

"Nope!"

"Who's Jeff?"

"A friend!"

"A boyfriend?"

"Nope!"

"Well, he's a boy and he's a friend so he's your BOYFRIEND!"

"Stop it, Khaki, and dry the dishes." Mum was the word. She remained as fuzzy as the test pattern I watched on channel five every afternoon waiting for Flash Gordon.

One day while I was in the kitchen, Beth came home from Lou's Grocery. She'd gotten everything on Mama's list. As I watched them put everything away, I saw a box with the word Kotex on it. I didn't know what this word was, so I asked Mama. "What does Kotex mean?" She laughed as she told me, "It's candy!"

"Can I have some Kotex candy?" Well, Mama started laughing and Beth joined in hysterically. I didn't understand their joke so I went outside by myself to play. A few days later, I saw Beth with the same box of Kotex candy. I expected her to start laughing at me again as she saw me watching her, but this time she told me Kotex was a box of napkins. "Oh," I said, as I went off to play with my dolls.

Several months passed and Mama told me to ride my bike to Lou's Grocery. This was a new privilege I'd earned only because Beth wasn't around. Mama gave me her list and went over my instructions: "Charge it on my account, be careful crossing the highway, don't fall off and break your arm, and be back here within an hour." I couldn't find my Mickey Mouse watch, but I knew an hour was a long time. So, as soon as I left Mama, I stopped by my friend Lorraine's house.

Lorraine was two years older than I was but we got along pretty well. Her Mama, Sally, could make the best salmon patties, fried nice and crisp and full of onions. I was hoping she'd have a batch made today. "Hi, where's your Mama?"

"Gone to a meeting." Sally wasn't home, so Lorraine was ready to ride her bike to Lou's with me.

Off we went, my legs peddling as fast as they could possibly go. Once we arrived at Lou's, we split the list. Lorraine gathered her part of the groceries and put them on the small counter.

"This is more fun than a scavenger hunt." I had all my items but one. Mama wanted white paper napkins. "Lou, where are the white napkins?" Lou pointed in the direction of the paper products. As I went down the aisle, I found them sitting there all by themselves, Kotex. Beth was right; it did say sanitary napkins right on the box. I proudly took them up to the counter. Lou said, "Khaki, are you sure these are what your Mama wanted you to get?" I quickly showed him my list. As he scrutinized each item, he picked up the box of Kotex and carried it back on the shelf. He came with a clear wrapped package of Marcel Dinner Napkins. There was a funny grin on his face and he didn't look at me as he said, "I think these will do better for your Mama."

A few months after my shopping adventure I began to feel really uncomfortable in my own skin. I couldn't quite figure out what was happening to me. It was a scorching hot day; I just needed to do something different. "Should I wear my halter-top or go without it? I'm only a little girl, or am I? Boys don't wear shirts…I'm only ten…no shirt for me today!" I marched proudly outside without my shirt. Mama gave me a strange look but never said a word. I slowly walked across the sidewalk and up to the Turner's porch. I felt like ants were marching over my burning skin. I thought, "Perhaps I'm turning into the son Daddy always talked about. Can girls change into boys?" I asked myself. Who can help me with this question? I knew Mama and Beth would laugh. Aunt Barb's house was too far away for me to walk today. Lorraine's, that's where I'll go!"

Walking down the sidewalk toward Lorraine's house, I felt a sudden drip in my undies. "Oh, drat! I've wet myself again. I'll go home and get dry undies and not tell anybody this time," I thought as I plopped down on the toilet. I started screaming!

"Mama, help me! I'm dying! Come quick! I have a real problem this time! I need to go to the hospital." Mama could barely breathe when she reached the top of the steps. Walking into the bathroom, taking one look at my stained undies she said, "You're too young for this. Beth, come up here and take care of her!"

Pulling a cigarette from the pack and striking a match, Mama walked away. Beth clambered around in our room for a few minutes before coming into the bathroom. "Here. Put this on." She handed me this gigantic funny looking piece of elastic. Then, to my surprise, she opened a box of KOTEX and connected one of those napkins to each side of the strange elastic. "Wear this until it needs changing." she said. "In a few days you can stop wearing it. Every month you'll have to do this." Beth went back downstairs, and I sat on that toilet in total amazement. "How can my body disgrace me like this?" I thought. Eventually, I stood up with the bulky wad between my legs. "What do I do now?"

Walking into my bedroom, I quickly pulled a big shirt from my dresser drawer. Out of the corner of my eye I saw my white cotton nightgown. I wished I could be wrapped in it and climb into my half of that bed. Mama would be furious if I did. Instead, I snuggled John, my adorable cat. Sitting there on the floor with him resting in my lap, I began petting his shinny fur. Soothed by his purring, I thought about my situation. I noticed John had gained a few pounds. "Maybe I should stop giving you a bowl of Mama's evaporated milk every night, boy," I whispered.

It was about ten days after my bleeding ordeal, and I was still feeling very confused and alone. I was sound asleep when I heard Beth screaming wildly, "Get up now, Khaki! Hurry!" Groggy, I scrambled to feet, my nightgown turning in the breeze with me. I was tugging and grabbing it trying to get to my feet. "What's the matter?" A low growling and moaning came from right there on the pillow next to me. It was my handsome John. I was sure he was missing his evaporated milk that I'd stopped giving him. "Poor kitty, I'll get you some milk!"

"No, you won't! He needs much more than milk, little sister!" John picked your pillow as the spot to give birth to HER kittens! "Kittens! How? He's a boy! Oh my goodness…he's a boy and a girl?" Beth and Mama were busy fixing a box for John while I stared unbelievably at him—her. John's stomach went back and forth and rolled all around before the three very tiny wiggly bundles came out. I thought about my new problem and wondered what I should call my cat.

As I grew older, I watched as Beth really grew up. She started inviting boys over to our house. I overheard plans of an upcoming wiener roast but didn't understand what I heard. "The boys are coming to roast their wieners!" The girls all laughed hysterically. "You're not invited, Khaki."

"I really don't care," I said. I thought to myself, "Besides the wiener roast is going to be in Aunt Barb and Uncle Al's back yard and I know about everything in their yard."

"I'll bring you a hotdog just the way you like to eat it," Daddy said, as he walked up busily straightening and untwisting coat hangers. "What are those for, Daddy?"

"Great cookers for the franks and marshmallows, Khaki."

Most Saturday afternoons, Beth and her friends walked to the Dixie Theater. There must have been at least ten in their group. Daddy finally agreed I was old enough to tag along, but Beth had another version of this plan. "You, little sister, will walk five feet in front of us. Do not turn around and when we get there, don't sit near us! Oh! And don't forget, not a word of this to Mama and Daddy!"

"Okay, Beth but what about when it's time to leave?"

"You stand in front of the theater and you'll see me come out, then start walking."

The Dixie Theater was a great for Saturday afternoons and it became my very special outing.

These days it seemed everything that happened in our household was predestined. Mama had grown up Presbyterian and was back into her old beliefs that everything happens for a reason. She always reminded me, "Khaki, God is watching you. He knows what you're doing and going to do. He knows everything. It's all been planned out before you got here. We may not go to church now, but back when I was young we didn't miss a day." I imagined that we didn't go to church because of Mama's coughing and poor health, but I wasn't sure. One of Beth's favorite friends, a dark haired boy named Jeff, came around often; Beth had a huge crush on him. Every Sunday morning she would make me get dressed in my best Sunday clothes and walk all the way to Cooper Heights Baptist Church with her.

On Wednesdays, Beth would start early with her prompting. "Eat your supper in a hurry. I want to finish the dishes early so we can get ready!" She insisted that I go to training union on Wednesday nights to learn more about the Baptist religion. All the teenagers there acted like they were so goodie-goodie. They were always talking about the movies they had been to see, or who was going to drive through Piggy Park drive-in restaurant. They also whispered about dancing at Folly Beach, but they didn't want any adults to hear because good Baptists didn't dance. I even saw some of them sneak outside and smoke cigarettes. I didn't like training union and wasn't sure why everyone was training.

I remember one bright Sunday morning that spring. The whole congregation had joined the choir in singing *Just as I Am* and the preacher was praying and shouting and yelling, "Come on down." I was so moved by the voices that I gingerly stood up. Beth grabbed me by my sleeve, but politely I turned and smiled her way as I marched right down that center aisle to the front of the vestibule. I knew that Jesus had called me to come on down. We were very late getting home from church that Sunday because I had to fill out forms for my Baptism. Beth had to help because I didn't know the answers and I had no parents with me. I could tell that my big sister was angry.

Once she got me outside, she really let me have it. "Mama's going to be furious with you and she'll punish me! You were baptized in the Presbyterian Church when you were a baby, Khaki. "Didn't you know the only reason I kept taking you to church was so I could see Jeff? His daddy's the Preacher!"

Well, Mama and Daddy didn't seem too angry about my new religion. They came to my ceremony after they made sure all the papers were correct. Mama bought me a new white dress and fixed my hair. Everyone watched as Jeff's daddy threw me back into the water and prayed loudly. I thought he was going to drown me when the water started coming out of my nose. "You are baptized, Catherine Drayton Jaffe, in the name of the Father, the Son, and the Holy Spirit." Then, the choir loudly sang *How Great Thou Art.* The only real thing I have kept from my days as a Baptist is singing those beautiful hymns and my name Catherine.

After my baptism, Beth went to that church less and less. It seems that Jeff had a new motorcycle and a girlfriend named Faith. Beth was not allowed to ride a motorcycle and was totally in love with a new boy named Tim. Tim had an after school job working in a funeral parlor. He seemed nice enough and always said to me, "Hey, Khaki, come over and have a cool one at the parlor."

"Catherine, help me get this fastened, please," Beth pleaded. "Tim's going to be here any minute." Mama was buzzing around the room getting Beth's hoop skirt ready. After the clasp on her pearls was fastened, Beth put on her hoop skirt and gently raised her arms. I could see her bobby socks carefully tucked inside her strapless bra. Mama slid the beautiful periwinkle taffeta gown over Beth's hair, careful not to mess a strand. "You look gorgeous," we gushed together. Tim knocked on the door just as Mama finished taking a half roll of film. He really looked gorgeous, too, and the flashing started again. As Beth walked down the front stairs, I noticed that her dress looked pretty wide. When she stood beside Tim's Volkswagen, I knew trouble was in the making.

Tim was politely holding the door open as Beth tried to sit down in the seat. Mama and Daddy helped Tim stuffed and folded her hoop-dress into the car. I watched with my mouth wide open as he walked around to his side of the car to get in. He opened the driver's door, but all I could see was Beth's gown, no steering wheel, and no windshield! I guess Daddy had been trying to figure this out too because he handed Beth a hankie and offered a solution. "Tim, you drive your car to the prom, and I'll drive behind you. Put Beth into the backseat of mine. Once the dance is over, Beth, you can take off your hoop skirt and put it in Tim's backseat."

"Thank you, Mr. Jaffe. You're a life saver!"

"Here, Beth. Dry your eyes before you mess up your make-up." I heard her sob, "Thanks, Daddy, for everything."

Beth was going to college soon, and Daddy decided it was time for us to move. He talked about a repossession and an upcoming bank auction and the deal he was about to make. He came in one day so excited and fidgety.

"Catherine, I've got a surprise for you!"

"What is it, Daddy? You know I love surprises!"

"Get into the Studebaker; I'm going to drive you over to see our new home."

"Where is it? When did you buy it? Do Mama and Beth know about it? How big is it? When are we moving?"

"You'll see in a few minutes." He was so nervous that he twitched in his seat and had a ticklish cough in his throat. I sat there in the Studebaker with visions of one of those stately, beautiful homes on the Battery drifting through my head. When Daddy pulled in front of his property, I almost hid beneath the seat. "There must be a mistake," I thought to myself. "It can be beautiful, just use your imagination!" A few weekends of work, and it'll be as good as new. A fixer-upper, that's what I bought. Beth can lend me a hand before she goes to college, and you can help too, Catherine." Lying was something I was taught not to do, but I couldn't tell him the truth. This place was a real slum. It was just horrible and not anything like I wanted to have my friends visit. Instead I said, "You're exactly right, Daddy. We can make it beautiful!" Shortly after that day, Daddy began the work. It did turn out to be livable and comfortable, but beautiful never.

Beth graduated head of her class and was off to Wilcox College, an all-girls school in Columbia, South Carolina. Mama said she should get proper schooling since she was so bright and such a lady.

I entered high school at the same time. Everyone expected me to follow in Beth's footsteps, and I certainly tried to be polite when I rebelled.

"Catherine Jaffe? Beth Jaffe's little sister? I'll expect A's from you, young lady, and the best behavior!" This scenario was played over and over again throughout my high school years. Beth Jaffe I was not!

"I'm Catherine, not Beth!" I often shouted to my parents. "So what if I got a B! I don't like sports because I don't like running or sweating! "Perspiring or Glistening, Catherine, ladies don't sweat," Mama would immediately correct me. "My hair is mousy, I want to be blond."

"You'd better not color your hair, young lady or I'll keep you grounded in this house forever." Daddy reminded me. Well, little by little, I colored my hair, until Daddy thought the sun had delicately lightened my locks. He never found out about the day I stayed in the bathroom for five hours because I had turned my hair bright orange. Mama's friend Megan kindly brought me more color and helped me fix my hair.

I joined many clubs and kept so busy that sports, except for basketball where I always sat on the bench, were no longer an issue. This was the beginning of the new me—pleasing others and trying to please myself.

Since Beth had gone to college, Mama had gone back to teaching. She said I was old enough for her to start working again, and she'd be home in the afternoons for me. She was coughing terribly with the remaining lung, and I was sure she shouldn't teach. She insisted it would be good for all of us. Mama wrote letters to Beth every day, telling her about the events in our lives.

Dearest Beth,

Let me say first of all, how much I miss you. Life is not the same. Daddy works at the shipyard or tinkers around the house. Catherine is busy being Catherine and you know what that means. The school where I teach is near an orphanage and most of my students live there. My children, as I call them, need me! They're all I have now that you're gone. Daddy and I take some of my favorite students like Bill out to supper to teach him proper table manners. We go to the baseball games and cheer them on with our love and encouragement. Catherine is doing okay in school…not like you, just okay. She is still hanging out with Polly. They drive everywhere in

Polly's old Henry J. I swear we're going to lose your sister one day when she gets hurled out that door. Do remind me to have your Daddy check the passenger door on Polly's' Henry J. Daddy called me in a roar this morning as soon as he got to the shipyard. He was riding to the 'yard with a group of his fellow workers who you know. They stopped at a red light, and right there beside him was Catherine in a red thunderbird with Gloria and your sister was smoking like a stack! Daddy was furious! I guess I'll have to deal with her when she gets home. Stay as sweet as ever and remember...

I love you!

Mama

Shortly after Mama sealed her letter, I walked into the house. She broke the news about the smoking discovery and made me promise never to let Daddy catch me again. "I promise!" Mama and I sat there grading her papers. Lighting her Lucky Strike for her, I puffed seriously on my Winston.

By now Beth was in her second term at Wilcox College and I was becoming a real girl of the sixties. But I was being a good girl. Daddy made sure of it. When a boy brought me home at night, not one minute past eleven, Daddy was there to open the door. If I sat in the car one minute past eleven, Daddy was at the car window inviting me to join him inside the house. Beth's birthday was approaching, and Mama said it would be perfect if we made the trip to see her for her birthday. "There's this football game, it's homecoming at St. Paul's. Can we go on Saturday morning so I can go to the game? Please, Mama? I've got a date with a real cute boy named Johnny from Yonges Island. He's a good friend of Grady's." Mama said she'd check with Daddy and let me know. The deliberations over, I heard Mama on the phone with Beth, telling her that we'd be in Columbia on Saturday morning, a little before noon, and of course she would bring her famous pound cake for Beth's birthday.

Thursday morning as I was dressing for school, Mama stuck her head in and told me to get home early from school. "We're going shopping for new shoes and a suit!"

"What for?" I asked in surprise. "Your homecoming game on Friday night."

"Sorry, Mama, I can't...got cheerleading practice right after school. Anyway, I don't need a suit!"

A nightmare kept me tossing and turning that night: I wore a suit to the game and it got ruined and my shoes were ripped to pieces. I woke up in a clammy sweat. As I brushed my hair, I began to brush the nightmare away. After all, I didn't own a suit.

Polly stopped by to pick me up in the Henry J, and off we went to school. As the last bell rang, my thoughts turned to Beth, and I remembered that I hadn't gotten her a gift. "I do hope Mama has picked up a little something for me to give Beth," I thought as I glanced down the hall looking for Polly. Shorter than myself, Polly was really hard for me to spot. But there she was with her flashing smile and good nature for the world to see, heading right toward me. "Hey, Catherine, ready to go?"

Once we climbed inside the Henry J, I knew my job was to hang on dearly with my right hand and not go flying out of the open door when she turned the corners. Her daddy had tried to fix the latch, but it was hopeless. "I do think you have fun tossing me around in this thing, Polly!"

"Keeps you alert, Catherine!"

"Tell me about this boy, Johnny, you're dating tonight."

"I just met him a few weeks ago, seems harmless. He's an old friend of Sarah's."

"What ya wearing?"

"A skirt and blouse. Can you believe Mama wanted me to get a suit? She said it's only proper to wear suits to homecoming games!" Laughing hysterically, Polly turned a little too hard on the curve near the end of the road. Before I knew it, I had only one toe still inside the Henry J. Gripping as hard as I could, trying to haul myself back inside the car, she jerked the car to a screeching halt and I landed face first in the grass, right next to a ditch. Polly looked at me like she was seeing a ghost. "Catherine, are you okay?" she said as she wiped the mud from my face. "Here's a belt. I'll tie you in for the rest of the trip." We stopped by her house for munchies and I washed up a little. The more we rehashed our ordeal, the harder we laughed. Polly drove me home and blew me a kiss saying "Love ya, girl! Be sweet" as I trotted up my walk.

Mama was already home when I got there. I couldn't tell here about the Henry J. ride because she'd never let me ride in that adorable car again. Sitting there grading her papers, she looked up smiling. "What time's your date tonight?"

"We have to go early because it's so far away; he'll be here probably around six o'clock." Mama was saying something else but I didn't hear her. Walking into my bedroom, I gasped! I saw it lying there on my bed, tags hanging from it. A brown tweed suit! There was also a lovely linen blouse and deep brown penny loafers, Bass, of course. I was flabbergasted! Mama came through the door just in time to say, "Shut your mouth, Catherine, or you're going to catch some flies!"

"Mama, you shouldn't have…when did you find time to do this?"

"Don't you love them, Catherine?"

My honest words would have been, "I love the shirt; I hate the suit," but I couldn't aggravate Mama. So, instead I said, "They're divine! You shouldn't have…they're gorgeous…I'll save them for something really special!" Mama's eyes lit up brighter than the tip of her Lucky Strike, and I saw a defiant side of her that I knew I didn't want to see very often. "Now, you listen to me, young lady. These clothes will be on your back this evening. You will look proper and refined, or you won't step foot out of this house!"

Bathing early allowed plenty of time for hair fixing as I sat in front of the mirror rehashing my nightmare. As I reflected, I caught a glimpse of the homely tweed suit lying there on my bed, the jacket stretched with its arms waiting for an occupant. I scowled as I started taking the giant rollers from my hair.

Joanne, our obese mutt, stood there wagging her tail as I fed her another "cookie" while she waited for her supper. She barked happily and danced all over as Daddy came through door. "Ooh, la la!" Daddy said as he walked through the door. "Must be a really hot date tonight."

"Catherine, do change your shoes," I heard Mama saying as Daddy piped, "I hate those things you've got on as well." I had already put on the suit but it had begun a misty rain and I actually liked the loafers and didn't want to get them dirty. I heard a masculine knock at the door as I marched off to change shoes. It was Johnny, right on time. Mama and Daddy forgot about my shoes, and I scooted out the door without changing, promising to be home before eleven.

Once inside Johnny's car, I gave him careful directions to my friend Gwen's house. She had a date with Johnny's best friend, Richard, this evening. Neatly packed inside the Chevy the four of us headed for the homecoming game. We were giggling and talking up a blue streak. We had only gone a few miles when I noticed a difference in Johnny. As the car climbed the ramp to cross over the new Ashley River Bridge, I realized that Johnny was acting really strange. He kept driving faster and faster. "Are you okay? What's going on?" He and Richard cackled like hyenas. "Oh, we boys have been drinking a little 'Purple Jesus.' I promise we'll have more when we get to the game. You girls will get something real goo…d to drink," Johnny slurred. Crossing over the bridge to West Ashley, I looked out on the murky waters of the river below. My spirits were like the waters, churning rapidly. I wished I'd stayed home and gone on to see Beth. Johnny raced down the bridge heading toward the first crossroad. Nothing but woods surrounded this area. In the darkness, I started to panic. Our two lanes of road were crowded with the weekend traffic, and Johnny's head was clouded with Purple Jesus. The taillights in front got closer, closer, getting extremely bright. I finally shouted, "Watch out!" Johnny swerved to the left, going around the car. The car in front of that one turned left. As we hit the station wagon, I saw a woman and her child directly on my side of the car.

The crash was horrendous. I heard screeching tires and the crumbling twisting steel. The nauseating taste, a combination of blood and metal, and the smell of the rain and my mud-soaked clothes overcame me as I lay unmoving on the floor of the mangled car. Wailing sirens broke the deafening silence. People gathered out of the darkness; Johnny and Richard leaped from the car. I could faintly hear their voices outside as they rehearsed their story. Lights shone down through the windows as the police diligently pried open the passenger's side of the car. I was stuffed under the dash, and my body ached. I couldn't close my mouth without pain shooting through my jaw. "I'm going to lay you in the rear seat of my cruiser, young lady. Stay still and don't move until the ambulance arrives." Gently, the officer put me in his arms and carried me away.

"Would you try to find my missing shoe?" I begged. "My Daddy will kill me if I lose my shoe."

A hysterical Gwen kept crying, "Please, don't die, Catherine!" One of the kindest strangers in the crowd took Gwen away and came back to my side.

"Would you like for me to call someone for you?" a soft voice asked.

"Please call my Daddy, Truman Jaffe. The number is 555-3284. If my Mama answers, don't tell her please…she's very sick…this might kill her."

Sirens came and went as the mother and child were taken to the hospital. I faded in and out of consciousness until the wailing sirens stopped, ultimately arriving for me. Carefully strapping me to a gurney, the paramedics hoisted me inside the narrow passage. Gwen was already seated for our jaunt to the hospital. "Dear God, please don't let Catherine die," she prayed. "Please, God, save her!" I heard over and over. As I regained consciousness, I thought I saw angels in white. Was I dead?

When we arrived at the emergency room, I could sense the hustling and bustling around me. The hospital staff was dashing in and out but I didn't know where they were going in such a hurry. The door flew open and in walked Mama, tightly controlling her emotions. She looked so pale and weak, I was afraid she was a goner. Right behind her, grabbing her tightly, was Daddy. "Catherine, you're going to be just fine, honey. It may take a while, but you'll be fine. We'll get the best doctors and dentists in town."

"Are the others okay, Daddy?"

"Don't you worry, baby. They're all okay."

"The mother and child?"

"Who?" I heard Daddy say. "Oh yeah, a few breaks but they're okay. In fact, my old friend Andy Sylvester just called the hospital to say he wants to represent your case. Heard all about your friend, Johnny, and what a good boy he is."

I watched as the nurse got a needle ready. I woke up several days later to see Beth standing over me smiling. "You sure know how to get out of taking trips. You missed the birthday cake! I saved you a piece, though."

"Oh Beth, I'm so sorry I ruined your birthday! How long have you been home? How do I look?"

"I've been here a few days. Daddy got Greg to pick me up and bring me. You sure scared everybody out of their wits. I hear you've been calling my name, so here I am, little sis. You look a bit ridiculous without your teeth, kind of like an old lady. The doctor said your jaw, arms, left leg and ribs will heal in time. As far as your concussion, it can't be too bad...I know how hard your head is!"

"Thanks! Give me a hug. Ouch, that hurt!"

I missed several months of school during my recovery, but Mama was a teacher so the school allowed me to continue my work at home. Studying had become the most exciting part of my day. I'd get all my work done before Mama got home from school, knowing full well she'd want to check it. If it wasn't completed, she'd make my friends wait to come over.

Bessie Lou, our maid for a long time, wasn't much older than I was. She wasn't much of a conversationalist, either. But, she sure took good care of us. She arrived on the scene permanently, about the time Beth left for college. She was always around polishing, cleaning, ironing, and cooking. During my convalescence, she couldn't cook for me because my jaw was wired shut. Milk shakes became my regular diet. She made milk shakes day in and day out. They became pretty boring, and I longed for the cabbage and cornbread I smelled her cooking. I wondered how a cabbage milk shake might taste. Bessie laughed as she whipped up supper for Mama and Daddy. "Bessie Lou, you finished; ready to go home?"

"Yes sir Mr. Jaffe, I'm finished for today." Daddy hummed as he went to grab his keys.

The months passed slowly, and finally it was winter. It was time for basketball season to come to an end. The final game, my last sitting on the bench night and I desperately wanted to be there.

"Daddy, please let me go to the game! Please!" I begged. "Okay, but your Mama and I are going to go with you. We'll take you out for supper first. No running around and no jumping. You can wear your uniform but no playing. Promise?"

"I promise!"

I was so excited about getting out and especially seeing all of my friends. I knew they'd ooh and ah over my freshly healed wounds and make me feel important. Now that my jaw was unwired, I could chat with the girls and get the latest gossip. Boy, would they be jealous that my uniform was two sizes too big. I'd lost so much weight drinking those milk shakes and not eating real food. I grabbed my coat, wrapping it around me and got Daddy's keys for him. "Let's go get some supper!" Joanne started wagging her tail when she heard supper, so Mama told her that she could go, too. I climbed in beside Joanne, and my stomach felt a little queasy thinking about my last ride. I hadn't been in a car since my accident. When I had appointments with the doctors and hospitals, I was always sedated. "Eve's Diner isn't far away, we'll be safe, and Daddy's a great driver," I told myself.

When we got to Eve's, Mama told Joanne to wait in the car like a good girl. She politely moved over to sit in the driver's seat and proudly took control, her hot breath fogging the windows. Inside Eve's, the smells were awesome. I caught a whiff of the chicken and dumplings as soon as the door cracked. "Where's Beth this week?" the waitress asked.

"Back in college. It's not the same without her being with us!" Mama chimed. Mama ordered first, her favorite calves' liver with onions and gravy. Daddy picked his favorite meatloaf and mashed potatoes. Everybody got the delicious collard greens and the fried okra. As the waitress delivered our food, Daddy asked, "You got some of that special hot vinegar for my greens, honey?" We ate every morsel except for the small amount that we all saved for our four-legged child waiting in the car. I always knew it was time to go when Daddy placed his customary tip on the table. It was like a ritual: thank the waitress, get the money out of his wallet for the tip and fold it, then place it on the table. The finale to his ritual was to carefully place the salt shaker on top of the bills so they wouldn't blow away.

Delighted with her treats Joanne's tail wagged profusely as she climbed back into the rear seat with me. The windows were so fogged from her breath that it took five minutes for all three of us to wipe them clean using the napkins from the doggie bag and our coat sleeves. "Okay, Falcons! Here we come!" Daddy joked as he cranked the car.

Chugging slowly down Dorchester Road, Daddy was humming with the big band tune on the radio. We hadn't gone very far, maybe a mile and a half, when I heard Mama say, "What's that?" I saw her head shoot forward, and I leaned toward the back of the front seat to get a peek at what she'd seen. Daddy almost came to a complete stop, and then I heard a thunderous bang. I only saw the bright headlights as they rammed head-on into our car.

Mama, blood gushing from her head, wasn't moving. Daddy was hobbling toward the other car, and Joanne was moaning. As I realized what had happened, I began screaming hysterically, "Somebody help me!" The wailing ambulance arrived shortly and the paramedics gently placed Mama on the stretcher, mindful of her breathing condition. Thanks to Daddy, they gave me a little something to calm me down.

"It will help you not be so anxious. Can you climb in by yourself? Here, let me help you," one of the technicians said as he handed me Joanne's leash. I heard the wails of the sirens as I rode with my mother and dog for yet another venture to the emergency room. My thoughts were of Daddy and his hobbling. I prayed that he would be okay.

Fannie, a close neighbor, appeared at the hospital emergency room. "Let me take Joanne home, Catherine. I'll call and check on y'all in a little while."

Mama and I were admitted to the hospital for a stay. Daddy showed up hours later, his knees severally banged and bruised. "The doctor said I'm going to be okay. Mama's injuries are pretty severe. You're going to be all right, Catherine, after you rest. You've had another concussion and are suffering from stress." I heard Daddy in the hall on the phone calling Beth home to help our injured family.

Mama was released several weeks after the accident, just in time to finish her last days with her students. Her hospital room looked like a florist. We tried to pack the treasures that had been sent. Daddy said, "Thank goodness we gave most of the stuff to the nurses!"

I went back to school my sophomore year knowing that the next year would definitely have to be better. Beth came home for summer vacation and got a job at Edward's 5 & 10. She worked every minute she could, saving to buy her things for school and her upcoming wedding. She got engaged to Greg Pennington at Easter. I knew the wedding would be grand because Mama was in charge, and I'd gotten a glimpse of her plans. She poured over them when she wasn't teaching. She had plenty of time to complete the arrangements and the date was a year away. I was ecstatic that I was going to be the maid of honor.

Since the accidents, Daddy and Mama wouldn't let me go anywhere without calling when I reached my destination to tell them I was safe. I called when Howe, my new date, and I arrived at the movie. Afterward, I didn't call them. Friends climbed into the backseat of the car with us, and we had a grand old time driving through Piggy Park until I noticed that it was 10:45. "I've got to go home NOW!" I cringed. Howe said he'd scoot me to my house and return with the others back at the hang out.

Zipping along, we came upon another car as we approached a curve on Ashley Phosphate Road. It was swerving as it drew nearer. With no other cars on the road, we assumed there was plenty of room for us to pass. Just as that car turned the curve, it crossed the double yellow line, scraping paint and trim from the entire driver's side of Howe's mother's car. Then, it roared on down the road. Howe was so scared that he started crying. We were okay, sitting in stunned silence except for Howe's whimpering. There we sat with no lights, no phones and very few houses that just might have a phone. Trying to determine the damage was by touch only, so we climbed back into the car and ventured on to the closest house with a light on. An elderly gentleman peeked through the window and listened to our story before kindly letting one of us in to call the police. After hearing our version of the story and getting the make and model of the car from one of the boys who had tagged along with us, the police decided that it was time to call our parents. I begged with all my might to "please, let me call mine."

I knew if Mama heard, "This is the police" when she answered the phone that she would surely die. It was after eleven o'clock, and Daddy was going to kill me for being late. As the ringing began, I felt the tears whelping. I heard his "Hello?" and blurted out "Daddy, I'm all right. A car hit Howe's, took the side off pretty good. The police want to talk with you," and then I sobbed uncontrollably. The officer offered to bring me home but Daddy said he'd be there shortly. I'd barely hung up that phone when Daddy was by my side assuring me he'd take care of everything. Beth was waiting at home with Greg and Mama. As I went to my room, Beth came in and looked at me pitifully, shaking her head, saying, "Catherine, you're going to have to do better than this."

Beth had disapproved of just about everything I did during my teen years, but the final straw came in the spring of the next year. I always poked around Beth's room when she was away. Her room was larger than mine, and she still slept in the bed with the imaginary line. I'd sleep in her bed and cross that line every single night. She never knew...not even a clue.

One Friday, my friend Dana was over. Smelling like garlic as usual, Dana loved to brag about being Italian. Her daddy looked like one of those men who play an organ and has a monkey and a hat. Dana was telling me stories about people she knew. Today's gossip was about Dana's Mama and Daddy. They didn't sleep together. "My Mama says it's better to pretend to be sleeping or get a headache and sleep in another room. That way they'll leave you alone...won't paw at you, grope you all night long!"

I looked at her in amazement. "Really?"

"Uh huh," she said. "Dana, who's pawing and groping and anyway, what's groping?"

"My daddy and yours!"

"Mama says all men are alike."

"Well," I retorted, "My daddy snores all night, I'm sure of that...come on, let's get a Coke." After the Cokes and brownies, we returned to our hide-out in Beth's bedroom. Dana started to open Beth's closet.

Now, this was something Beth had forbidden me to do and I wasn't having any part in this escapade. "You'd better not do that. Beth will be furious if she finds out!" I sat as still as a statue upright in the middle of the bed, crossing imaginary lines in all directions. Dana pretended she was highfalutin', a fancy lady with Beth's gloves and purses, opening and snapping closed the latches, deciding which matched her outfits.

Unexpectedly, she started screeching, "Look at this!"

"Get out of Beth's stuff," I responded.

"Look at this," she continued to screech," waving a paper in her hand. I carefully unfolded the official-looking document. "Miss Elizabeth Anne Jaffe and Mr. Gregory Fowler Pennington are MARRIED. This can't be true! They're getting married next year. I'm going to be in the wedding!"

"Your sister's married, and I'm gonna tell," Dana sang as she danced around the bedroom acting like a bride. "Give me that piece of paper and go home. Don't you tell a soul, or I'm going to tell your daddy what your Mama said about him and all men!"

"See ya!" Dana chided as she slammed the door. I had just straightened up Beth's room and fixed the covers when I heard Mama's footsteps.

"Where's Bessie Lou?"

"I took her home early for you; Daddy left his car here today. He rode with Parker."

"What have you been up to?"

"Nothing much. Dana was over." Now, my hand was burning from the hot news it had just held. Mama and I sat down to smoke as usual before Daddy came home. He hadn't caught me again just like I had promised. Mama kept looking at me like something was up. She could read me like a book. "Okay, what have you done...tell me before Daddy gets here!"

"I DIDN'T DO ANYTHING!" I told her Dana had made a discovery but that she, Mama, wasn't to tell a single soul. As soon as I received the "I promise," I ran into Beth's room, dug out the marriage paper and thrust it into Mama's outstretched hand. I was so excited for Beth; all married and grown up, until I saw Mama's face as she reread each word five times. Mama shuffled off, mumbling obscenities and going to find her phone directory and another pack of cigarettes. I knew Beth would never speak to me again.

In the beginning, Mama kept her promise. But the hostilities continued, and the story came out. As the weeks of tears and frustration continued, Beth became more and more distant. She graduated from college and moved to the Clemson College campus, where Greg was a senior. "The fairy tale wedding was cancelled because of your silly snooping and meddling." I can still hear Beth's bitter words today.

4
Carter

I had many beaus during my senior year in high school but none seriously. High school was finally behind me, and I was trying to decide what to do with my life. Following a graduation that occurred without notable honors, I was bound for none other than the infamous Wilcox College, South Carolina's all-girl's school. I pleaded with Daddy "Please let me go to Carolina. I promise I'll study and be a good girl!"

"You are going to the same fine school your sister attended, and that's that, Catherine!"

"But, I was accepted at both places. I'll make better grades, I promise!"

"No is no!"

Packing for my departure for the "breathtaking hallowed halls," as Beth put it, was like revisiting the dentists I had recurrently seen—sheer pain and misery.

"Once we leave you'll be fine, busy making new friends like you always do!" Daddy was saying. "Your roommate seems like a dear girl, and her family was as nice as can be. Now, I've put money in an account for you. It's time for you to learn to manage your finances, and here's a little something extra." I looked down at the crisp hundred-dollar bill with Ben Franklin's face on the front, wondering what Granddaddy would have put in Daddy's hand when he was about to be deserted.

As my parents drove away, tears streamed down my cheeks and soaked the front of my dress. I realized I was left on my own, and I'd better get my act together and make the most of it. Branson dorm was well worn from the years of late-night parties and all night study sessions. Inside my room, I searched the orientation package for the time of the freshman meeting. I had ten minutes to get there, but I didn't know where there was. Then I heard a voice in the hall, "I'm your House Counselor, and I'll lead you to the orientation meeting. Let's go!" Dabbing water on my puffy eyes, I looked swollen and red as I began my days at an all-girl's school. I had faith that God and Daddy wouldn't let me down.

Wilcox was perfect for Beth, but not for me. I suffered through the first semester, wishing I could transfer. But there was no way to convince Daddy to let me do it.

Then, one day at the end of the second semester, the house counselor asked me to join her and several other advisors in her room. I couldn't imagine what was going on so I went right away. They had questions about my roommate and the girl in the room next door, asking if I knew about their affair. I told them that I had no idea what you're talking about. "Catherine, you do know what a lesbian is, don't you?"

"Well, I'm afraid I don't," I answered. They proceeded to tell me the ghastly details of sex between two females as I turned fifty shades of red. "My roommate's engaged to be married," I insisted. "The girls are good friends. They dance together slowly. I've seen them do that. But surely, they're practicing for a dance. Yes, they sleep together, and I have been awakened with pillows over my head, but maybe they're afraid of the dark and turned on the light."

"Listen, Catherine, complaints have been filed about their behavior, and they're going to have to explain before the Judicial Board."

"Oh, my goodness, what should I do?" We recommend that you move across the hall immediately because they'll think you issued the complaints. Dumbfounded, I strolled down the empty hall to the nearest phone booth. "Hello?"

"Hello, Mama...Where's Daddy?"

"I'll get him."

"No, don't let him pick up the other phone, please!" I told Mama about what had happened and then I heard Daddy from the extension phone saying, "I'll be there in the morning!"

I moved across the hall for the rest of the year, saddened for my roommate and her dear close friend. Never really happy at an all-girl's school, I simply couldn't face returning in 1963, especially after the tragic assassination of President Kennedy. Wilcox closed its doors like the other colleges due to the uncertainty of the situation. I went home. I picked up all of my things a few weeks later and then, I was home again this time for good.

I happily enrolled at the College of Charleston, and a multitude of handsome young men gladly helped carry my books. During the summer of my senior year, I was working at the Employment Company. The elderly director was an old friend of Mama's. I went to see him to apply for part-time work anywhere in the city. When I completed the forms, he asked when I was available. I was surprised to learn that I had been selected as the receptionist for his entire operation at the Employment Company. My job was fun and developing nicely, but I vividly remember a particular afternoon several months later.

It was very late in the day, and I was busy finishing my paperwork and answering the phones. I looked up as a short young man with a dark complexion and blond highlights in his hair walked through the door. He was as handsome as could be. Truly, he resembled Richard Chamberlain. His soft voice asked, "How do I apply for a summer job?" I handed him the appropriate form and told him to have a seat and fill it out. He returned with the completed form, and I noticed his name right away, Carter Rutledge Duvall. "Are you related to William Duvall?" I asked.

"He's my younger brother. Do you know him?"

"Oh, yeah I've gone out with him several times. He's really got a gift for gab. Sure likes himself and his bodybuilding a lot. I haven't seen him in months. What's he up to?"

"That's William for sure. We're not at all alike! What's your name?"

"Catherine Jaffe."

"Well, Catherine Jaffe, would it be okay if I called you some time?"

"I guess so but I'm dating someone else right now."

"Is it serious?"

"I don't think so. Here's my number." As he left the Employment Company that day, I noticed that his torso was fairly long but his legs were equal to mine.

Carter did call, and we went out once but the date was miserable. He was so quiet and he was nothing like his brother. I learned that he was entering his senior year at Clemson and knew Beth and Greg. About three weeks after our date, he came into the office again. To my surprise, he asked me out again. The sailor I had been dating had gone out to sea for three months on the USS Pulitzer, so I said, "Sure." I had no idea that a deep affection between the two of us was just beginning.

Carter arrived at my front door in stark white pants and a navy blue shirt, his blue eyes blazing with anticipation. He drove me out to Folly Beach for dinner at the Atlantic House. As we ate, we reminisced about the days when we were teenagers, wondering how we'd never seen one another as we danced to Maurice Williams and the Zodiacs. "I'm not much of a dancer," Carter said.

"Oh, I love to dance…learned from both of my parents. They're like Fred Astair and Ginger Rogers! 'You can really cut a rug,' my Daddy always tells me. I learned to Shag right here under the boardwalk on Folly." Swaying to the music, I began telling Carter about my earlier days dancing in the breeze, sometimes influenced by the "Purple Jesus" that the boys from the Military College supplied my friends and me.

Dinner was a tedious task, as I carefully watched his face and tried to select the appropriately priced entrée. "I wonder how much money he has?" My thoughts were of Carter's financial situation. The waiter was standing there smiling at me.

"I'll have a cup of the She Crab soup, sautéed shrimp, fries, and a salad with vinaigrette."

"I'll have the exact same thing but I want blue cheese dressing on the salad, please."

"Shall we walk on the beach later, Catherine? The tide's going out."

"If you want?"

"What are your plans after you finish college in December?"

"I'm going into the Army as an officer, ROTC, you know."

"Do you think you'll go to Vietnam?"

"I'm not sure what's happening over there...all the protest and everything."

"This soup is really delicious. Would you like a little more sherry in yours?" As delicately as I could, I poured a minute amount into his bowl. I couldn't stop staring at his beautiful blue eyes. "The sherry really adds to the flavor!"

"I've never tasted She Crab soup before."

"Where are you originally from?"

"I'm an Army brat. My dad has moved us all over the world. I was born in Hattiesburg, Mississippi, lived in Germany, New York, and Virginia. My family's been in Charleston since I was thirteen. My mother's parents live here in Charleston. My father's parents are French Canadians. Speak fluent French, they do. My father does, too. I am the oldest of my four brothers. "How do you survive with four brothers?"

"It's not so bad now that I'm older. I used to take care of all of them. My mother stays in the bed most of the day. She's not well."

"I'm sorry to hear that. I know what it's like with a mother who isn't well. My mother has been ill all of my life."

"My mother is a different kind of sick! I don't want to talk about her though."

"Do you want dessert?"

"No thanks. I'm really full. Dinner was awesome.

Thank you so much!"

On the pier, we chatted, laughed, and wiggled our toes in the sand as we sat on the steps of the boardwalk. We neatly placed our shoes behind the support post. Treading down the well-worn staircase that towered above the dunes, he reached over carefully, placing his warm, gentle hand over mine. My heart fluttered as though I were a seagull racing against the heavy winds. We walked hand in hand without a whisper, feeling passion radiating between us. The unruly breeze whipped against our faces as we stared into the darkness of the night, longing to explore those feelings that were stirring. The heat from our bodies rose as the wind tore at our clothes. We walked to the far end and turned for our journey back to the pier. Facing one another, our eyes searching in the darkness, he slowly settled his warm lips on mine, his tender hands gently caressing my body.

Days turned into weeks, and the August heat led to Carter's departure to Clemson. Our courtship had grown into a whirlwind romance. A daily routine of phone conversations and visits developed. "What time do you want me to pick you up tonight?"

"I'll finish at the Winn Dixie around nine o'clock this evening. Do you mind picking me up that late?"

"I'll be there...do you want me to fix dinner for you?"

"Great! You know that if I eat at home it'll be on paper plates and out of a can. My brothers never leave me a morsel, and my mother won't get out of the bed to fix anything. Will your parents be home?"

"Yeah. They'll stay in the family room and watch TV or go to bed early."

At nine o'clock that evening, I was sitting in the parking area waiting for him. He came out carrying an enormous bunch of the most beautiful fresh cut flowers I'd ever seen. Climbing in the passenger side of the Studebaker, he kissed me as he said, "These are for the most beautiful girl in the world!"

"You're incorrigible! You're supposed to be saving your money."

"The lady in the flower shop likes me...gave me a good deal. Look, I've got something else to show you!" There on his finger was his senior class ring. His grandfather had given him the money to buy it. The shiny gold ring was inscribed with the year 1965 and a C for Clemson. A Palmetto tree was engraved dead center. Clemson University's newly expanded name was wrapped around the surface just beneath the beaded roping. "It's gorgeous!" Smiling, I asked when he was leaving. "I have to be at Clemson on the third of September. Tomorrow's Friday. Let's get a marriage license and get married right after I get back to school."

"You're kidding, right?"

"No!"

"We've barely known each other for two months!"

"I love you and want to marry you, now! We'll get the license and rings and get married on the seventeenth of September. I'll arrange everything."

"I love you, too, but I'm not sure about marriage so soon. I'll have to talk this over with Mama and Daddy."

The next morning, my stomach was filled with flutters and doubt. Was he serious? Would he show up this morning? What was I getting myself into? "Catherine, Carter's in the living room, bright and early he is. He said that y'all have a busy day scheduled today. Aren't you going to work?"

"No Mama, we're going shopping."

"What time will you be home?"

"Not sure but I'll call you after you get home from school." We ate breakfast at a local café before heading to the courthouse to fill out the necessary forms. Leaving the courthouse, Carter drove straight toward Friedman's Jewelers. "Let's do it, Catherine! Let's get the rings now!"

"Carter, I promised my parents that I'd never run off and elope. I can't!"

"Okay, then we won't elope. You can tell them!"

"Are you sure?"

"Yes!"

"These rings are perfect bands of gold, 'his and hers,' the jeweler said. "Everybody's having double ring ceremonies these days," he said.

Later that night, I quietly walked into Mama and Daddy's room where they were reading. "Carter's asked me to marry him!" Mama looked up and said, "Really." Daddy said, "If it were anybody but Carter I'd be upset, but he's a good boy, Catherine."

"When's the big event?"

"In two weeks." Mama about jumped out of the bed. "You're joking?"

"No, Mama! September 17."

"I've got work to do!"

The next morning, I met Carter for brunch. "I told my parents and they're pleased that I'm marrying you."

"Daddy wanted to know if I'd told you about the Cerebral Palsy. Mama wanted to know about the size of the wedding."

"Catherine, I'm sorry. There won't be a size to the wedding. I told my parents, and they're so upset with me that they refused to come. My insane mother chased me around the house screaming, 'You can't get married! You need to support your brothers and help send them to school!' I don't want to go back to my house. They're the reason I wanted to elope."

"I'm sorry, Carter, but if they don't want to come, we'll make it beautiful anyway."

"If my family isn't coming, I don't want yours there either, Catherine! Just let it be us and some of my college friends."

"Carter, I'm not sure I can do this."

"Sure, you can if you really love me."

Leaving Carter that morning wasn't hard for me. I certainly had more than food on my plate. How was I going to handle this? Did I really love him enough?

Daddy came home from work at his usual time. As I shared the uncomfortable wedding news with him, Mama came through the door. She had been ordering a cake and flowers and shopping for a new dress. Tears streamed down my cheeks as I sadly asked my parents not to attend our wedding. Daddy shuffled around in the kitchen making some cheese toast to go with the vegetable soup Mama had made earlier. "You know, Catherine, your Mother and I are extremely disappointed about not seeing your big day, but we'll manage. It is your day, and we'll support you anyway that we can. We'll make sure you have a honeymoon, flowers, car, and the best that we can offer."

Listening to the words of my kind-hearted father made me feel worse. "Maybe I shouldn't get married," I cried. "Only you can decide that, honey. Now, go wash your face, and let's eat this delicious soup your Mama conjured up."

Coming back to the kitchen I heard Mama whispering about the surprises she was planning. Somehow I knew my family would make our wedding day perfect without being there. As we finished our soup and delicious cheese toast, Carter walked in. Hugs and handshakes later, he turned toward me with his charming smile, "Catherine, there's one more thing I forgot to tell you. I am a devout Catholic and really want to share our vows before God in my Catholic faith." Looking at Mama I asked, "Does it matter to you?"

"It's totally up to you, Catherine."

"Daddy, do you mind if I become Catholic?"

"Well, Miss Catherine, your mama and I had you baptized Presbyterian and you had yourself baptized Baptist, so why not be baptized Catholic?"

"What is she required to do for the ceremony, Carter?"

"She'll have to complete some forms, and visit with Father Condon and Father O'Malley. I imagine we can get all of this done before the 17th. You and Mrs. Jaffe will need to meet with the priests also, Mr. Jaffe."

"No problem."

I sat there pondering over my Baptist experience and wondered whether the Catholics were really statue worshipers like that minister had said back in those days. I'd been to Carter's church several times and thought being a Catholic suited me just fine. After all, I did like to dance, smoke and party with the best of them.

Meeting with the priests, I learned that Carter's mother had been ill for quite some time. She was dependent on her prescription medicine, unable to cope with daily life. Mrs. Duvall was confined to her bedroom most days, except on the rare occasion when she attended mass. Mr. Duvall kept busy with his job and caring for his wife. According to Father O'Malley, Carter's brothers were pretty much on their own, surviving the best way that they knew how. "Carter is an admirable boy who wants a family and that's why he wants to marry you so quickly, Catherine. Father Condon and I are going to quickly approve your documents and give you our blessings. Take good care of him and yourself. Let's see now...did you sign the form promising to rear your children in the Catholic faith?"

"It's right here, Father."

On our wedding day, I drove alone in Mama's new Chevy to Clemson. Carter had arranged for me to dress at a friend's house. I only got lost once during the trip, but I still arrived an hour later than anticipated. The look on Carter's face when I arrived that evening was shear relief. "I was afraid that you changed your mind, Catherine!"

"I'm here...where do I change? It's almost six o'clock."

The Catholic chapel was perfect in every way. I don't know how Mama had performed her magic, but my favorite yellow roses were placed throughout the chapel. The most exquisite bouquet imaginable was waiting for me. As I walked down the aisle, I could feel the arms of my parents around me as if they were right beside me. Oh, how I wished to see their faces.

Our hotel room was lavishly filled with the fragrance of yellow tea roses and there was an exquisite champagne chilling in the silver container—compliments of Mama and Daddy. As I picked up the receiver and dialed their number, melancholy replaced my earlier merriment. "Hi...we're married! I really missed y'all. Want to speak to Carter?" I was filled with gratitude for the family I so adored. I could hear them as Carter held the receiver to his ear..."Welcome to the family, son!"

"Thank you very much for all you've done for us. I promise to take good care of her, forever."

Hanging up the phone, Carter poured us a tall glass of champagne. Walking off to shower, I gulped it quickly. As I began dressing for my groom, I knew I'd leave the bathroom sooner or later. At last, I decided I was radiant enough to make my entrance. I knew my eyes were shinning like the heavenly bodies twinkling beyond the tightly drawn curtains. He sat nervously on the edge of the mattress. He stood up as he saw me. Slowly he reached forward, gently bringing my fingers to his sweet lips. As I ached for his kiss, it appeared to be an extraordinarily long, agonizing interval before our lips passionately joined in celebration of sanctifying love.

The morning arrived quickly, and we dressed for the football game. From our seats in the bleachers we watched the Clemson Tigers race down the hill. I should have known that Carter had arranged our wedding the night before a very important game. All football games were very important as far as he was concerned. Here we were, newly married and watching the game before leaving on our honeymoon. Thankfully, the fans around eventually ran out of things to tease us about our wedding game appearance. The final score was Tulane-7, Clemson-23 as we headed for the car and privacy.

The mountains greeted us with their colorful splendor as we traveled through the Blue Ridge Parkway. We dreamed of our future. "I want a new Mustang!"

"Me too! Please Catherine, let's never eat on paper plates. That's all I ever get at my parent's."

"I promise you'll have the finest dinner table, there will always be sterling silver, china and cloth napkins."

"I want four children…three boys and a girl, Carter. When you become a full-fledge Army Officer, let's have a baby right away!"

"I want one boy and one girl!"

"Nope, we're going to have four!"

"Okay, but you're going to stay home and take care of them. I know you'll be a perfect mother…nothing like mine. By the way, the first weekend that I get back to Charleston, I'll arrange for you to meet my family."

"Do you think they'll like me?"

"It doesn't matter now does it…you're my wife, Mrs. Carter Rutledge Duvall…Catherine Jaffe Duvall."

My new name was lovely. I repeated it several times, adjusting to the sound of it. We spent the honeymoon wrapped in each other's loving arms, sheltered in the vast mountain chain. The days passed quickly. As reality set in, I found it hard to fathom leaving my true love at his college dorm while I trekked to Charleston alone. The solemn ride home took hours.

As I pulled in the driveway at my parent's house, I was greeted with a banner that read *Welcome Home, Mrs. Carter Duvall.* Inside, the house was filled with magnificent wedding presents and a gorgeous, three-tier creamy white wedding cake. My dear, sweet Mama had sent out wedding announcements. I shared the celebration with my family and friends, but woefully not with my groom.

The very next weekend, Carter hitchhiked to Charleston. As promised, I was introduced to his family. All the doors and windows were covered with iron bars. Once inside the living room, I felt like a blind bat. Rooms were so dimly lit that I could barely focus my eyes. Finally, the wait seemed like forever, my new in-laws appeared. Carter's mother,

Margaret was cordial, but extremely distant. His father, Bernard, was quite a talker and chatted non-stop the entire hour that we visited. They were hospitable enough, but I sensed an underlying peculiarity about this strange family and truly couldn't wait to leave.

Carter graduated as a second lieutenant in the United States Army on December 18, 1965. His duty with the Infantry wouldn't begin until March 1966, so I assumed that we would save our money and live with my parents. Carter had other plans. On December 20, he drove me to a furnished apartment off of Richardson Avenue. "Catherine, here's our first home together!" As we hesitantly climbed the fire escape to this one bedroom shanty, I looked around the neighborhood, making a mental note to keep the doors locked. Once inside, I tried to imagine how I could spruce this place up. "I thought we were going to live with my parents, Carter."

"I know but I want my wife all to myself! Come here and give me a big kiss." We wound up working our way to the bedroom, leaving a trail of clothes behind us.

My parents explained all the reasons why we should save our money and stay with them, but Carter had proven to me we should live alone. With Christmas five days away, I packed my clothes and moved into my new "shanty castle" with pride and joy. "I'll make a few changes here and there and this place will be beautiful. Help me rearrange this furniture, Carter."

"Have you tried to open the oven door yet?"

"No, why?"

"You'll either have to sit on the counter or open it from the side. There's not enough room to stand in front of it and open the door at the same time."

"We're only going to be here a few months. I promise our next place will be better, and we'll buy our own furniture!"

Christmas Eve is always a very special time for my family and Carter made sure that it continued into our new life together. Around 9:30 on this Christmas Eve, Carter came up behind me. "Catherine, I love you very much…thank you for loving me and being my wife!" He placed a small gift in my hand. "What's this?"

"My gift for you the love of my life." Ripping the exquisite wrapping from the tiny, expensive-looking box, my hands trembled. Shaking, I unlocked the small black velvet box to see sparkling brightly inside was a beautiful diamond set in antique gold. "Carter, we can't afford this! It's absolutely beautiful...when did you get it?"

"Here, let me put it on my bride. I didn't have the time or money to get it before our wedding but my darling wife deserves an engagement ring...will you marry me and wear my ring, please?"

"I'm already married to you, silly, and yes, I'll wear this ring! I love you so much...thank you!" I stared at the rock throughout the entire midnight Mass at Saint Ann's, unable to take my eyes from the tremendous surprise.

The incense-filled church was crowded beyond belief. Every Catholic in the city assembled to celebrate the birth of Jesus. As one parishioner knelt beside me, I smelled the distinct strong odor of Kentucky bourbon. I didn't know it at the time, but that smell would come back to haunt me throughout my life.

The flu season arrived early that January of 1966. I have always been susceptible to the flu, so it was no surprise when I started throwing up one night. Carter was being such a dear trying to make me feel better. "Here, put this washcloth on your head."

"Thanks, honey...I hope you don't catch this." The flu wasn't getting any better. "Carter, will you come home early today from work today and take me to the doctor?" He was working part time for Conglomerate Services. The company did contract work for the Navy. "Sure, I'll call you in a while and let you know what time."

Carter took me to Dr. Bixley's around four o'clock that brisk January afternoon. Dr. Bixley started the examination as soon as he came into the room. "Did the nurse get a urine sample? How long have you had the flu, Catherine?"

"At least two weeks."

"Are you on any birth control?"

"I was, but Carter said he's Catholic and now I am...so he insisted I had to stop the pill."

"Here's a prescription to help make you feel better. Go home and go to bed and call me first thing tomorrow."

"Okay, thanks, Dr. Bixley."

As instructed I went right home and straight to bed. Unfortunately, the nausea got worse, as soon as I got into bed. The yucky, queasy feeling just had to go away and leave me alone. "From now on, I'm going to avoid going out during flu season," I mumbled as I stumbled my way to the bathroom. I woke up long after Carter had gone to work; the nausea was much better. I was sitting there reading the morning news and drinking coffee when the phone rang.

"Hello, Catherine."

"Hello, Mr. Duvall. I'm sorry Carter's at work."

"I knew he would be. I want to come over when he gets home. Would that be okay?"

"Yes sir. I'll tell him you're coming. Will Mrs. Duvall be joining you?"

"No, no, it'll be just me."

"Your dad called this morning and wants to come over this evening." I said as I bit into my tuna salad sandwich. "Want some more potato salad?"

"Thanks, what did you tell him?"

"Okay and that I'd tell you. What time will you be home? Your dad's coming around six o'clock."

"Then, I'll be home at five o'clock. Lunch is really good. Thanks for fixing it for me. Are you feeling better?"

"I'm so glad you came home…just having you here makes me better."

"Did you call Dr. Bixley?"

"No…I'll do it after awhile."

"Give me a kiss. I've got to go."

"I love you…see you later this afternoon," I said as I turned to pick up the phone.

"Hello, Pat. This is Catherine Duvall. Dr. Bixley asked me to call him today."

"Hold on. He does want to talk with you." Sitting there I lit a cigarette. Carter hates me smoking so much; I really need to quit this nasty habit before I end up like Mama," I thought. "Catherine, are you there?"

"I'm here, Dr. Bixley."

"How are you feeling?"

"Better this afternoon."

"When you were here yesterday, I noticed some darkening around your nipples so I tested your urine. You, young lady, are pregnant."

"Are you sure I don't just have the flu?"

"I'm very sure. All of your tests are positive. I want you to come back in but according to the information you gave me yesterday, you'll be having a baby around September 27."

"I'm having a baby? I can't believe it! I couldn't be more pleased!" Walking into the bedroom to look into the mirror to see if I looked pregnant, I put out my cigarette, deciding it had to be my last.

"Hi...you're home early."

"Yeah, I decided if my dad is coming I'd better take a shower."

"Where do you think we'll be in September?"

"Well, I could be in Vietnam and you could be with your parents, or we could still be at Fort Martin. Why?"

"Just wondered. Supper's ready whenever you are."

Washing the dishes after dinner, I thought of Beth and her baby girl, Ann, who was now ten months old. I didn't get to see them much since Greg was working at Cape O'Malley. Ann's pictures were adorable, and I wished I could see her more. "What are you thinking about?"

"Beth, Greg, and the baby."

"Did you hear someone knock at the door?"

"I'll check."

"Hey, come on in."

"Catherine, my father's here."

"Hello, Mr. Duvall."

"Hello, Catherine."

"Carter, I'm here because your mother and I are not happy with you. Your marriage has not made us happy at all. Catherine is not the girl we would have chosen for you. I need to get your dependent ID from you, your old insurance card. It's getting near tax time, and I am going to claim you on my income tax. I need some information from you to fill out the forms."

I sat stunned as my dear husband listened to his father. How dare he say I wasn't the girl they would have chosen! I was crushed! I waited for Carter to defend my honor, but there was silence as he handed over the insurance card and ID. "Carter, excuse me, but don't you have something to say to your father?"

"Dad, I love Catherine very much, and we're happy."

"Not that! Didn't we decide that I had paid for your clothes and the last portion of you school and that you're going on my income tax?" Mr. Duvall almost had a stroke right then and there. "You're just trash! And you coerced Carter into marrying you. You should be ashamed of yourself for stealing him from his mother and helping his brothers. I hope I never see you again."

"Mr. Duvall, you are a selfish, egotistical man, and I'm glad I married Carter. And I hope I've ruined your life because right now you're ruining mine, so please get out of my home!' I saw Carter standing there in disbelief. His father almost slipped on the fire escape as I slammed the door behind him. "Catherine, no one has ever talked back to my father in his entire military life."

"I waited for you to speak up for me, but you obviously weren't going to do it, so I decided that I had to defend myself. "By the way," I sobbed, "You really hurt my feelings more than he did!"

"Oh, Catherine, I'm so sorry. I love you and I don't care about him at all. I was just hoping he'd take his stupid cards and leave. Please forgive me. The next time I'll do better."

"There won't be a next time because I never want him near me or my baby again."

"What did you say?"

"That's right…I didn't just have the flu. I'm…we're going to have a baby in September. Dr. Bixley confirmed it this morning. I was going to tell you just as he knocked on the door."

"Are you sure?"

"Yes, you are going to be a father on September 27."

"I can't tell you how proud I am. I love you so much," Carter said as he gave me a great bear hug. "Don't worry about my father. He'll come around, I hope."

I couldn't wait to talk to Mama. I was bursting with news. As soon as Carter went in to shave, I gave her a call. "Mama, he was so rude. I couldn't believe the horrible things he said."

"How long was he there, Catherine?"

"Not long, but long enough to tear me apart."

"Poor Carter, no wonder he wanted to run off and get married." Holding the receiver tighter and beaming with a smile I confessed, "I just found out today that you're going to be a grandmother in September!"

"Oh Catherine, I wished you would have waited. Everybody is going to think you HAD to get married. You and Carter need more time together," she coughed. I couldn't believe my ears. How could she not be happy for us? I was so hurt that I slammed the phone down and ran to the bed, sobbing hysterically. In between sobs, I said, "Now my own mother is critical of our baby."

"I hate all parents everywhere!"

Carter answered the phone when it rang a few minutes later. This time it was Daddy. "I'm happy about the baby, Carter. Put Catherine on the phone. Young lady, you need to understand your Mama's position on this. She'll be there every minute for you, but you shouldn't have upset her. You know that will make her sick. I want you to apologize to her."

"But..."

"No buts about it, Catherine. Apologize."

"Let me talk to her."

"Mama, I'm sorry if I upset you. We are having the baby September 27...add it up, Mama, that's almost thirteen months after we got married. I don't think you'll be disgraced."

"Catherine, thank you for your apology I'll talk to you tomorrow."

I showered and found my favorite Christian Dior nightgown. The down comforter was calling my name. The minute I put my head on the pillow, nausea sent me running back to the bathroom. As I hugged the toilet this time, I smiled at the thought of the baby growing within my body.

Just as he predicted on our honeymoon, Carter bought a 1965 metallic blue Mustang. Now, we were bound for Columbus, Georgia, and Fort

Martin. Officers' basic training would last only six weeks then Carter would get his new assignment.

Columbus was definitely not like Charleston, and Benson Army Hospital wasn't anything like Roper. My first appointment with the OBGYN doctors was a fiasco. I waited for hours for my name to be called. Women in the waiting room filled me in on how to navigate the system. "Make sure you stay away from Dr. Goldfinch," one very pregnant brunette told me. "He's heartless," chimed another newly delivered mom. "How do I avoid him?"

"Make your appointments on his day off!"

"Mrs. Catherine Duvall!"

"Come this way, please." My appointment was uneventful, and I made sure to arrange my next visit on Dr. Goldfinch's day off.

It was a gorgeous April Saturday and the smell of fresh spring flowers filled the air when Carter took me out for a surprise drive. He looked so handsome in his uniform. I was as proud as a posy when the guard saluted my lieutenant. Heading to the commissary, I noticed he kept looking at me. Finally, he spoke. "I know you've been very lonely here, Catherine, so I believe it's time to tell you that I have my new assignment. It's right here at Fort Martin. I'll be the chief of the Visitors Bureau; actually I'll be the only person in the Visitors Bureau."

"What will you do as chief?"

"Coordinate trips for VIPs...senators and visitors who want to visit the Infantry School and Center. I'll be in charge of the Hail and Farewell parties for the school. We'll be staying in Columbus until after the baby comes so we need to find a larger place to live." That was an understatement! Our apartment was okay for two people, but there wasn't an inch to spare. "Oh Carter, I'm so excited. Since we're staying here, can I get a pet? I want a toy poodle...they're so cute. Let's go to a kennel now!"

Cars flew past us, blowing my hair to pieces as we stood in the phone booth going through the yellow pages to find kennels. "Did you understand all of the directions? The lady said they're closing at four o'clock this afternoon."

"Yeah, I got 'em right here in my pocket." The Mustang zoomed down the highway as we drove toward the Alabama state line and Ashcroft Kennel. I heard yelping the second the tires hit the dirt road. Climbing out of the car, Mrs. Ashcroft greeted us with several toy poodles in her arms. "This is Blondie and her brother Dagwood. They're twins."

"Hi, I'm Catherine Duvall. I called about thirty minutes ago. This is my husband, Carter."

"Hello, how do you do, Catherine is looking for a companion until our baby arrives in September."

"Well, my dogs must have good homes or I won't sell them, and they can't be companions until babies arrive and then be cast away."

"Oh, you misunderstood. I want to have it as a companion until the baby arrives but then it will be another part of our family. I love animals! Do you have any black toys?"

"There are a few in the next kennel. There's one really small one, but her teeth aren't perfect. You might have a hard time showing her." There sat the tiniest ball of black curls I think I'd ever seen. I put her in the palm of my right hand and held her up to Carter's cheek. Her perky pink tongue licked his face and ears, and we purchased our first love for the whopping price of two hundred dollars. Mrs. Ashcroft assured us that we had the deal of the day.

Ebony, as we named her, was a doll. She filled our days with laughter and love as we awaited the arrival of our child. Life couldn't have been happier as we settled in. Carter and I found a furnished house and planned to move in the summer.

Mama promised she'd come help me decorate the house and baby's room when school was out. She was driving alone because Daddy wanted to save his vacation for when the baby came. About the second week in June, Mama called to say that she'd be arriving the next day. Busily I cleaned everything and prepared for her visit. That night Carter, Ebony and I all cuddled together in our bed. This had become our nightly gathering, although we had to be very careful not to roll on our tiny pup. My excitement over Mama's arrival made it hard for me to sleep. I tossed and turned all night.

It was a scorching late June morning; Carter didn't have to be at the Visitors Bureau until the afternoon and he let me sleep as he prepared breakfast. "Good morning, Sunshine!"

"What time is it?"

"Eight o'clock."

"Mama's not coming!"

"What are you talking about? She'll be here in a few hours."

"I tell you, she's not coming," and I started shaking with fear. "Catherine, what's going on?"

"Remember that dream I told you about when I was a teenager? The one about wearing the suit and it came true."

"Yeah, but that was a long time ago."

"Well, I dreamed Mama was standing in the middle of a road screaming for help! I don't know why she's screaming for help, but I know she's not coming."

"Come on, eat your breakfast, and we'll take Ebony for a walk."

The sense of foreboding did not disappear as I dressed and Carter put Ebony's leash on her. After a long walk in the park, we sat on a bench and thought of baby names as we watched two cardinals taking turns drinking from the fountain. She watched his back, and then he'd watch hers, always mindful of danger.

Walking home, I realized the fear from my dream had almost gone away. As we approached our front door, we heard the phone ringing. Carter hurried with the lock but wasn't fast enough. Nobody was on the other end. "I'll bet it's your Mama. She should be about an hour away. She'll call back." As I started thinking about what to have for lunch, the phone rang again. "I'll get it," Carter said, dashing to the phone. "Hey, Where are you? Do I need to meet you somewhere?" Then I heard his voice change to a low husky gasp. "Really…are they going to be okay? Are you alright? I'm so sorry. No, I'll tell her. When will you be coming?" His ashen face looked straight at me as though I was a monster. "Catherine, your mother is coming in two days. She's sorry for the delay. It seems that there was a little problem. As she was getting ready to leave early this morning, her friend Fannie stopped by to send some baby gifts for us. Your Mama walked Fannie out to her car. Fannie was waving good-bye to your Mama, and just as she drove away, the little girl next door ran out into the street. Fannie ran over her! Your mother said she was hysterical but there was nothing she could do. Before they called the ambulance, she said she was standing in the middle of the road and screamed for help! The child's not going to die, but she'll be in the hospital for a while. Your Mama's going to stay with Fannie; she's worried about Fannie's bad heart."

"Do you think I'm possessed, Carter?"

"No! I do believe that you have some kind of sixth or exceptional sense. I wouldn't have believed this if you hadn't told me before it happened."

"Should I see someone about this? I feel really uncomfortable with it. Do dreams really come true?"

"Talk to your Mama when she gets here." I knew that I wouldn't talk to Mama because she would laugh it off as more of my theatrics.

By August we had moved into our new rental. It was a furnished house with three bedrooms. I had the nursery painted a pale pink. I just knew our first child would be a girl, even though I desperately wanted a boy. I thought reverse psychology on the walls might help, and baby boys look beautiful in pink. I spent my days folding and unfolding baby clothes, trying to imagine the size of our baby. My feet were so swollen I couldn't get them in any of my shoes. I finally found a pair of sandals that tied on to my feet, but my stomach was so big I couldn't lean over to tie them. Carter always put my string sandals on me when I was going out, and today was one of those days. The heat was unbearable, but I had a few errands to do. I saw people cautiously eyeing me as I slowly shuffled through the shops. I knew they thought I was going to have my baby right there on the spot.

When I got home, the window air conditioning units were dripping with condensation because they were working so hard to cool the house. Shopping had completely exhausted me. I flopped down on the sofa and wiped away the perspiration. I looked down the hallway and started to laugh uncontrollably. "Ebony, you silly girl, you know better than this. I'm going to tell your daddy on you!" She jumped and barked waiting for me to pick her up. I trudged over to pick her up and carried her in my arms as I rewound an entire roll of toilet tissue from the living and dining rooms. Then, I noticed that she had knocked over a candy dish and the whole package of M&M's had disappeared. "Oh, Ebony! You're going to be so sick. I should probably call the vet." Carter walked through the door just in time to view the remains of the mess. "Did you call the vet?"

"You think I should?"

"Hello, Dr. Armstrong's office."

"This is Catherine Duvall, Ebony, my toy poodle has eaten an entire bag of M&M's. "Hold on, please."

"Mrs. Duvall, Dr. Armstrong said for you to keep an eye on her tonight. She'll probably throw up and have diarrhea. Just don't let her get dehydrated. Call us back if she's not better by this time tomorrow."

"Thank you so much." Ebony didn't throw up one single time nor have diarrhea. Carter and I decided that she was little, but she sure was mighty.

I thought September was the longest month of my life, but October came and we still had no baby. So far, I had avoided Dr. Goldfinch like the plague. My appointments were so often that I was sure to see him soon. I must have seen fifteen different doctors, and each one would start all over with the questions. All fifteen were told about my Cerebral Palsy and that my Mama was afraid that I couldn't give birth naturally. Thankfully, all fifteen disagreed with her.

Diane, my next door neighbor, looked in on me each day. Mama was calling every half-hour to see if I was in labor. I decided that we weren't really having a baby.

Diane and her husband Bob insisted that we go to the fair with them on this cool autumn evening. It was in the low eighties and Carter was hesitant, but I begged to get out of the house. Walking though the fair grounds, I could barely put one foot in front of the other. My feet looked like large muffins as they rose through the tops of my shoes. Exhausted, I begged to go home. Carter left early the next morning and I fixed myself breakfast and looked again at all the adorable baby clothes. Mama had called twice by the time *Days of Our Lives* came on. Fixing myself a pickle and sandwich, I noticed a pain in my back. As I sat down to eat, there was a stronger pain. I finished my lunch and lay there on the sofa thinking about all the walking that I had done the night before, sure that I had strained my back.

As I got up to answer the phone, I had a few more back pains and a really funny feeling in my stomach. "Hello."

"Hi, honey. How are you feeling?"

"I think I might be in labor, but I'm not sure. Can you come home now?"

"I'm on the way." Sitting on the couch, we timed contractions. Carter and I waited several hours before calling the hospital. "Bring her on in, sir. We'll be waiting for you."

We arrived at Benson Army Hospital at four o'clock in the afternoon. Carter was given my string shoes, my clothes, and my purse in a bundle and told to go sit and wait. After we kissed good-bye, I was put in a labor room with four other soon-to-be mothers. Each one of these traitors delivered right away. Four more were brought into my space…four more deliveries. I desperately wanted to see Carter, but the nurse in charge assured me that it was not an option. The shift changed at the hospital and finally someone told me it was 9:30 pm. There were three of us left.

I had requested the bedpan several times, but the head nurse assured me I was imagining that I needed to use it. I was mortified when I had a bowel movement on the gurney. Just then, the door flung open and I heard a loud, "I smell feces!" Meekly, I whispered, "It's me."

"Clean up the mess, nurse, so I can examine her right away."

"Yes, sir, Dr. Goldfinch!" My heart stopped…Dr. Goldfinch! He was right there in the room with me. The nurse quickly removed the soiled sheets. "Hello, Mrs. Duvall. I hear you've been here for a long time. In fact, you're the last patient left. I don't believe I've seen you before. I'm Dr. Goldfinch."

"No sir, I haven't seen you ever."

"I had the nurse put a fetal monitor on you and your baby. It seems the baby is having a little trouble. I spoke with your husband, and I'm going to take you into surgery in a just few minutes for a caesarian section. Is there anything you'd like to ask me before we begin?"

"Will the baby be okay?"

"I'm sure everything's going to be fine. I'll see you in the operating room." A new doctor entered the room and explained that I needed a spinal to completely numb my body for surgery. As he inserted the needle into my spine, the pain totally subsided as I groggily said, "I love you," to him. Just then, Dr. Goldfinch walked in wearing his scrubs. His face was the last thing I saw.

When I opened my eyes the next morning, Carter smiled broadly at me as he held up a picture, saying, "Our son, Jaffe Rutledge Duvall, was born at 10:54. October 14 will never be the same for us. He weighs six pounds and fourteen ounces and is nineteen and a half inches long and he looks a lot like me! You and I have a perfect little boy, Catherine."

"Will you ask the nurse to bring him in, please? I'm dying to hold him!"

"You have to be very careful with your stitches. Don't sit up without help."

"Get the baby, please, Carter. I'll be all right!" As the nurse handed me the tiny bundle wrapped like a papoose, I immediately began my new motherly responsibility of unwrapping the soft thickness of the white layers that surrounded our precious blue-eyed son.

5

Jaffe

Mama and Daddy stayed for two weeks caring for Jaffe, Carter and me. After they left for Charleston, Carter and I developed our own exhausting and exciting routine. Jaffe was a perfect baby crying rarely, and as happy as a cherub. I swore I heard him giggle at four weeks, but the pediatrician said that wasn't possible. I still believe to this day that he giggled out loud.

Jaffe looked adorable lying there under his first Christmas tree that year in Columbus, Georgia. After taking rolls of pictures, we packed him and all of his baby paraphernalia into the Mustang for the long drive to Charleston. Christmas with the family was glorious for us. Carter and I attended midnight mass at Saint Ann's while Mama and Daddy kept Jaffe. On the cold winter's night of December 27, Carter drove me out to Folly Beach. My teeth were chattering as we stepped out into the blustery night. "Hold me tight, I'm freezing!"

"I wanted to bring you here once more before we have to separate."

"What do you mean, separate?"

"I received my new orders. I'll be leaving in March for Vietnam."

My heart sank. "No not Vietnam!"

"That's what the destination number indicates...Vietnam."

"What am I going to do?"

"I want you to move back to Charleston."

"Get a place of my own or live with my parents?"

"You'll be safer with your parents."

"No Carter, not that!"

"We'll talk with them tomorrow."

"I don't want you to go! Jaffe will miss you so much...you won't know him when you come back."

"I know, I don't want to go either, but I have an obligation. I'll come home, I promise."

The next weeks were agonizing. Carter came home early one February afternoon, as I was feeding Jaffe and getting him ready to go for a walk. "Here let me put his sweater on him, I'll walk with y'all."

"Why are you home early?"

"I have something to show you. Look at this."

"I don't understand what this means," I said as I scanned the piece of paper. "It means that there was a mix up in the numbers. I'm not going to Vietnam...I'm headed for Korea "

"Is that good or bad?"

"It's good, real good...I'm going to be an Army liaison officer assigned to an Air Force base in South Korea. I'll be at J nsu."

"Can we go?"

"I'll have to check on that, but if you go as a dependant, I'll have to stay two years."

"Well, get all the details, please!"

Carter could sign up for an extra year, which would allow me to go overseas with him as his dependant. If I went, I would have to live in Seoul and not see him very often. This didn't seem like the best option for the family so Carter left alone in March for J nsu.

Jaffe, Ebony, and I went to Charleston to stay with my parents. Things were going pretty well except that Bessie Lou was glued to Jaffe all day and Mama and Daddy played with him all evening. If I went to a movie at night, Daddy still insisted that I be in the house by eleven o'clock. Writing Carter every day and rushing to the mailbox to see if he had written me became my biggest distraction.

Early in April there were three letters in the box. Tearing open each red, white, and blue bordered envelope in order of mailing dates, I finally read in the last letter.

My dearest Catherine and Jaffe,

I miss you both so very much. My life is not the same without you near me. I don't know what to do without your smiling faces and gentle laughter. I have received every letter you have sent, and I know that you're miserable, too.

I found a place for us to live just outside of the gates of J nsu, in a nearby Korean village. There won't be many things for you to do all alone. If you don't come as a dependant, you will need to apply for a tourist visa, passport, and get all the appropriate papers and immunizations. It's possible that you both can be here within several weeks. There's tons of work to be done. I'll call on Sunday to make sure you got his letter and to find out if you want to try and come halfway around the world.

Catherine, sell the Mustang and use the money for your expenses. We'll buy another when we get back to the States. Don't try to bring Ebony; she might become someone's lunch here. Ask your parents to keep her. Check with the pediatrician and Dr. Bixley about heath issues for both of you.

This place is very primitive and dirty. The house is a compound owned by an American who is married to a Korean. There is a concrete wall with jagged glass all around the top. Inside there is a courtyard with three apartments. The owners live in one and we'll share the other kitchen and bathroom with another American couple. There will be one living room and large bathroom just for the three of us.

There are only two women, the Air Force general's wife is one of them. Ya'll will be able to use all services on the military base. It is pretty safe here, but there's always eminent danger. I will meet you in Seoul in my Jeep when you get here; we'll drive south together.

You know your parents are going to have a fit and try to talk you out of this. It's up to you! Jaffe will be safe. I'll hire a house girl for the two of you. It won't be easy, but we'll be together and I can watch our son grow. I want to hold you both in my arms in the very near future.

My undying love,

Carter

I broke the news that I would be leaving to my horrified parents. They went over every reason why I shouldn't leave. Mama even went as far as calling the doctor and begging him to tell me not to go. Dr. Bixley assured her that Jaffe and I would be fine and that he thought it would be a great experience for us. Once my parents accepted the fact that I was bound for Southeast Asia, they helped me with the necessary protocol. Bessie Lou dutifully cared for Jaffe while I filled out forms and made countless phone calls. Daddy made sure that I got a more than fair price for the Mustang. Packing was the hardest thing I had to do. How could I pack for one year? Daddy began shipping boxes to Carter as soon as I filled them. The morning of our departure eventually arrived bright and early. We arrived at the airport at four o'clock in the morning.

Saying "good-bye" and "I love you" over a thousand times, Mama and I cried so hard that I almost didn't get onto the airplane. Daddy came to the rescue, but I noticed his eyes were a little damp, too. "It's time to go, Sis." Daddy said fondly to me. "You take good care of yourself and that adorable boy. Give Carter our love, write often and send tapes of Jaffe talking and walking. Call us from Alaska before you cross the Pacific."

"I love you, Daddy! Jaffe loves you, too!"

"I love you."

Once we changed plans at O'Hare, I began to calm down and settle in for our twenty-four-hour trip, but Jaffe had other plans. The sun continually shone in the windows, and he couldn't sleep. He was tired and frustrated and cried all the way to Alaska. Everyone aboard the plane was helpful: They pulled down all the shades, they walked him, some rocked him, and others bought drinks for everyone. By the time we landed in Tokyo to spend the night, we were all looped but Jaffe was quiet.

The Tokyo experience was amazing. We all piled into a bus that screeched through town to our hotel. I was horrified to realize that I was the foreigner as the people shouted everywhere in Japanese. At the hotel, I was so tired I was afraid to lie down because I thought I might not get up again. Of course, Jaffe was wide-awake. Inevitably I fell asleep about an hour before it was time to dress and scramble back to the airport on our transport bus. I dressed Jaffe and began washing my face to freshen up. All of a sudden, I felt a gushing through my clothes. I looked down in horror. As luck would have it, I had just started my period...I hadn't had a period since Carter left Charleston. Quickly trying to repair myself and drag new clothes from the suitcase, I was of the opinion that things couldn't be worse. Jaffe was so heavy for my petite, tired frame to carry.

His wiggling and smiling at everyone all the way to the airplane didn't help either. The airplane was filled with foreigners. I thought they were all Koreans or Japanese. Suddenly, I realized again...we are the foreigners!

I had to tightly hold Jaffe on this plane. It bounced, dropped and hit air pockets for the entire trip to Korea, and all the people eyed me suspiciously. Arriving in Seoul was the biggest shock of my life. No one had round eyes like me, and no one spoke English. I hauled my chubby, blue-eyed baby through this enormous airport searching for Carter's face.

Just as I was about to burst into tears from exhaustion and fear, I saw an American Army uniform carrying a sign high in the air that read "Mrs. Catherine Duvall." I hauled us, my arms aching toward the sign hurriedly hoping to see Carter behind the sign. It was a strange face. "Are you Mrs. Duvall?"

"Yes."

"Hi, I'm Sergeant Stevens, your driver. Welcome to Korea, Land of the Morning Calm."

"Mrs. Duvall, Lieutenant Duvall will meet you once we get out of the airport. He had an important briefing and was afraid you'd be standing alone too long so he sent me to intervene. Would you like me to carry anything for you, Ma'am?"

"How about him? He's getting really heavy." I handed Jaffe to this complete stranger and began following closely as the sergeant parted the crowd for me to exit. At the Jeep he said, "Do you have your baggage *pyo*?

"My what?"

"Your baggage ticket?"

"Oh, yeah...here it is."

He placed Jaffe in my lap inside the Jeep as he returned through the crowd with the ticket in his hand to gather my remaining baggage. I couldn't believe my initiation to South Korea and wondered what I had been thinking when I decided to leave the comfort of the good old USA. The sergeant darted the Jeep carefully around the tiny cars blowing furious horns, as they raced wildly down the narrow street with the occupants again shouting at one another. Suddenly, a Jeep stopped quickly. It was right in front of us, blocking us from moving. I was very tense as I watched the military vehicle. It was very frightening not knowing what was about to happen. Then my heart started to race. Sitting there in his uniform was Carter. The sergeant and Carter exchanged their dutiful salutes before Carter grabbed me up and swung me around, crushing Jaffe between the two of us. "Catherine, I love you. It's so good to see you...you're beautiful...you're so thin! I can't believe you're here...look at you Jaffe...you're such a big boy and so handsome! Here, Catherine, these are for you!"

"They're perfectly gorgeous. Where did you get such beautiful roses?"

"At the commissary, but they do grow roses in Korea. The national flower is the *Mugunghua*, the Rose of Sharon, Catherine."

"Sorry, I guess I have a lot to learn," I said feeling very unfamiliar with my surroundings. "Our new home awaits, let's get going. It's thirty-four miles to go and will take at least two hours on the MSR."

"What's the MSR?"

"Military supply route."

"Why does it take two hours?"

"You'll see!"

I found out that the MSR was the only road to travel from Seoul to J nsu or anywhere. I was almost speechless the entire trip as the Jeep slowly passed livestock, ox carts laden with old tin or what appeared to be clothes or trash, women walking barefoot with baskets and kimchi pots balanced on their heads. Military transport trucks were roaring by with camouflaged troops draped over the rails. Wet noodles lay on the road for the massive trucks to flatten. There was a slight odor of fermenting vegetables in the large earthenware jars buried in the ground. Tired-looking women were washing their clothes in water that appeared dirtier than the left over gray of our bath water.

The houses had thatched roofs and many were just a lean to. I couldn't believe my eyes at the poverty and was totally afraid to see our new home. I was glad to see Carter but desperately wanted to be back in the United States. As a matter of fact, I wanted to be in Charleston, South Carolina, and the comfort of my parents' arms. "What have I done?"

"Did you say something?"

"What...oh, nothing," I mumbled.

The MSR ride was dubious to say the least. At long last we arrived at our new mansion, a flamingo pink stucco fortress. The surrounding walls were piled high with broken pieces of bottles and jagged pieces of glass. Just as we were about to enter the metal double gates, they swung wide open and a winged Plymouth raced forward. Flabbergasted I asked, "What was that Batman and Robin?" Laughing hysterically, Carter informed me, "That, my dear, is our landlord and his wife." Jaffe, needing a change, was getting pretty fussy by this time so I gathered his diaper bag and jumped out of the Jeep walking toward my new quarters. "Which way is our half?"

"Over there...go on in. I'm right behind you!" I went through the kitchen and found an unfamiliar-looking Korean girl with a pan of water and towels standing at the door. "I guess I'm in the wrong spot."

"a-ni-o English. I no speak English."

"I don't speak Korean."

She reached over and began taking my diaper bag and trying to pry Jaffe from my arms. "What are you doing?" I asked as I held tightly to my baby. "Oh, I see you've met Youngee...she's our new house girl. She'll help you with everything, honey," Carter said from behind me. "An-nyeong-ha-se-yo, hello," she said bowing to me. "Give, Youngee," she said and reached for Jaffe. I was so exhausted that I surrendered him to this girl. She balanced him on her hip, while she prepared to wash my feet and give me socks. I didn't take my eyes off of her as I pulled the socks on my sterile feet.

And so my days in Korea began. Youngee was my closet companion. I taught her broken English, and she taught me enough Korean to shop in the village. At the rural markets with their colorful stalls, I learned to select raw fish—*saeng-son-hoe* and rice—*pab*, and haggle over prices with the country farmers.

Jaffe adored Youngee with her warmth and animated gestures. Youngee often sang *Dori Dori* or *Dukkeoba Dukkeoba* Korean folk songs to Jaffe. She carried him tirelessly on her hip. I was certain that he was going to be bow legged. Every time I checked on Jaffe, he was being washed or fed a delicious mixture that Youngee had created. I encouraged the jars of Gerber, but she insisted that the Korean food was better.

I established the only two mandatory cooking rules: She could not eat or feed dog or cat to him, and fish must be cooked properly. This agreement came about shortly after I found her preparing a huge raw fish and after a young Korean boy grabbed my hand as I walked through the village. He placed a tabby kitten in my arms. "You take my family eat. Please, Mommasaun!"

One of the four numbered Air Forces in Pacific Air Forces, J nsu was deeply rooted in Southeast Asia. The officer's club at J nsu was our Korean Country Club. The facility was furnished lavishly with rich oriental treasures, soft luxurious carpet topped with exquisite rugs hand woven by the locals. The beautiful arched windows were covered with fine fabrics in warm colors. The beautiful kidney shaped swimming pool was nestled right outside the stately French doors. The doors had elegant brass doorknobs that were always brightly polished. The tables were neatly dressed and ready for inspection with stark white linens. After all, top brass that flew throughout Southeast Asia was entertained here. Jaffe and I hobnobbed with the stateliest of dignitaries over lunch, dinner and happy hour. Carter, often busy planning attack positions, giving briefings, or doing something-top secret missed our glamorous lifestyle.

Many days, I would carry Jaffe out to the MSR and walk the three miles to the Base. Often a Volkswagen bus filled with locals would stop on the road, waiting for livestock to pass. The driver would point for me to sit in the seat behind him. I noticed that the other women were standing and the Korean men sitting. Some days, I'd walk down the dirt highway and a deuce and a half-ton truck filled with troops would stop. The soldier in the front passenger seat would call out. "You want a ride, ma'am?" When I nodded yes, the soldier would help Jaffe and me into his seat then, climb into the back of the truck with the other troops. On one occasion when I left Jaffe with Youngee a Jeep stopped. "Are you a missionary, ma'am?"

"No, I'm going to meet my husband for lunch."

"Would you like a ride?"

"Thanks...where are you going?"

"Wherever you are going, ma'am."

"J nsu Officers' Club?"

"Ma'am, do you think your husband would mind if I sat with you for lunch? I have been in Puson for over a year and haven't seen a female with round eyes in such a very long time. I'm from Atlanta, and it's so nice to hear a southern accent." Carter was extremely cordial with whatever I hauled in. Catherine's "Catch of the Day," as he called my diversified modes of transportation. "I'm sure my husband won't mind, lieutenant. Please join us for lunch."

Darling Jaffe was growing far too fast for my taste and was the best baby a mother could hope for. Two children lived in the other half of our duplex, but age differences were too big for a playgroup. The boys' father, Ralph, was a writer and wrote the news for the military publications, their mother, Laney, was busy making news for everyone to gossip about. She was having a steamy affair with her husband's boss at J nsu, and the whole base knew about it. Their house-girl, Consugie, cared for the boys while their mother romped with her lover. Unfortunately for me, she was the only other American wife besides the general's, so I spent most of my time shopping with Jaffe and Youngee or eating out at the Officers' Club.

"Do y'all ever discuss her affair, Catherine?"

"No, Carter. It's none of my business. I don't want to get involved. I'm not like her in the least...once married...always married!"

"Do you think Ralph is aware of what's going on?"

"Honey, if he's not then he's the dumbest soldier alive. It's common knowledge. Every fighter pilot that comes into the Officers' Club asks me about the exotic love triangle at J nsu."

"I'm glad you wouldn't cheat on me, Catherine."

Jaffe's pediatrician at J nsu was Dr. Washington, and Jaffe loved him. He was a true southerner from none other than Goose Creek, South Carolina. Here we are on the other side of the world, and I am lucky enough to find a pediatrician who lived fifteen miles from my hometown. "He's advancing rapidly, Catherine. Korea doesn't seem to have harmed him in any way. Let's see...he's fourteen months now. Are you planning a big Christmas for him?"

"The Club's having a big dinner, and we're going to that. Santa's bringing a few things, but I don't want to have to ship too much back to the states when I leave on the twenty-fifth of January. When do you go home?"

"I'm right behind you in February. I hope you, Carter, and Jaffe will stay in touch with me once we all get back to South Carolina."

"I'm sure we will. You've been such a dear to us the whole time here in this new world. It has really grown on me. When I first got here, I thought about going home and now I'm getting nostalgic about leaving. That reminds me, Jaffe screamed all the way to Korea on the plane. Is there anything I can do to prevent that on the return trip home?"

"Stop by before you leave and I'll write a prescription for a sedative for him. He's older now. I'm sure he'll do much better."

"Thanks so much…see you soon…Merry Christmas!"

Carter and I left Jaffe with Youngee on a bitter cold December morning so we could go to Seoul to Christmas shop. We planned to pick up some great Oriental treasures to send back to the states for ourselves as well. The heater in the Jeep was cranking, but it wasn't putting out any heat.

"I'm freezing!"

"We'll be in Seoul soon. Do you want to have lunch first or start our shopping?"

"It's still early. A hot cup of Jujube Tea with pine nuts floating in it would sooth my coughing and aching muscles. Then we can go to the Itaewon shops and look at the silk dresses and tailored suits. We can have lunch in a restaurant at Itaewon."

"I'd like to get a few leather belts and a down jacket while we're shopping. Let's get Jaffe some Korean toys, too, Catherine, and then let's visit a Shilluk Yongmung Temple. I hear the temples here are the most serene. Let's try to visit Changyyong Palace and that working Korean folk village. I heard it has a blacksmith, carpenters, potters and weavers. If we have time maybe we could go Piwon, the royal secret gardens."

"Do you think we'll have enough time, honey? How many days are we staying?"

"I guess you're right, we'll have to choose. We'll get back after dark but Youngee has Jaffe, and they'll be just fine. I can radio my sergeant and have him check on them."

It was very late when we climbed back into the Jeep heading for J nsu. The road was icy, making our journey even slower. I tried to keep the windshield wiped as Carter focused on the road. There was no where else to go on the road except off into a benjo ditch and they were filled with human feces, urine and animal waste, along with who knows what. I looked up to see a huge ox cart swerve out of control and head straight for us. Carter veered the wheel sharply to the left. We hit a thin patch of ice and the Jeep went sharply left, jerked back toward the right, and slid sideways straight into the nasty benjo ditch. The Jeep flipped on its right side, dumping me face first into the vile decaying feces. All of our new treasures tumbled around my head. Carter jumped from the driver's side to pluck me from the mud and feces. Then, he quickly began grabbing the packages before they sank any further. "Catherine, are you hurt? Does anything feel broken? I'll take you straight to the base hospital as soon as I can get us out of this mess." My eyelids were caked with the despicable waste so I held up my hand gesturing for something to wipe myself. "Here, take this towel! Let me do this for you." Spitting the nasty taste from my mouth, I started crying. "How could you dump me in that putrid mess? I don't know if I'm hurt or not...I can't talk with this yuck on me." Locals were suddenly everywhere, deciding how to right the Jeep and get us back onto the MSR.

We didn't understand a word they were saying, but we knew they were trying to help us. I was shivering with the damp waste all over me, and a kind Korean man offered me a blanket. Trying to get warm, I sat in a Jeep that had just come up with some soldiers in it. I watched as several Koreans tied ropes to our Jeep and then to their oxen, quickly up righting our filthy Jeep. Cheers filled the air. Carter thanked the Koreans and offered to pay them for their help. Refusing, the Koreans scattered as we climbed back into the Jeep and headed for the base hospital. I shivered, shook, and cried the rest of the way home. It was very late, and I was very nervous about leaving Jaffe so long.

The tears started again when we got to the base dispensary. All the doctor could understand was the word "baby...my baby" as I blubbered for Jaffe. The poor guy thought I was pregnant and had lost the baby during the accident. I had to shower before anyone would even touch me because I was so gross. Several hours later the examination was finished: the only thing hurt was my pride. The doctor said I may be sore the next day or two but the decay in the benjo ditch had definitely broken my fall.

When we got home, we found Youngee asleep on the floor next to Jaffe's crib. He was safe and snug without a worry. "Shhh don't wake them," I said as I tiptoed off to bed.

Youngee had invited me several times to join her family for lunch. Knowing that I would be leaving Korea in a few weeks, I accepted her invitation to the Pink Flamingo Club. Her family owned the Pink Flamingo Club, which was always filled with soldiers, dancers, and prostitutes in the evenings. It was next to the hair salon that the prostitutes and I used to spruce ourselves. Most of them could speak English and let me get my hair done before them. The stylist used hot coals to heat her curling iron before working her magic on my hair. Bowing and giving the stylist the customary 25¢, I thanked her in Korean, *kam-sa-ham-ni-da*.

Leaving the hair salon, I walked next door where Youngee and Jaffe were waiting. I reached for a hug from Jaffe and then Youngee whisked him away. She came back with her family and extended family. Greetings are very important in Korea. As they bowed their heads and said "*an-nyeong-ha-se-yo*"I politely bowed and said "hello" to Youngee's grandmother, mother, father, aunts, one uncle, and sisters. I presented my host with an inlaid mother of pearl lacquered vase. Youngee had helped me pick it out. I felt right at home, their social hierarchy and customs were as gracious as my deep-rooted southern heritage.

After a beautiful Korean girl washed my feet and placed me in a pair of traditional silk socks, the entire family went in to sit on the floor for lunch. Mealtime etiquette was of profound importance in Korea, and I was hoping my manners would be up to their standards. When drinking together, Koreans customarily pour for one another using both hands. I was wondering if I should pour for all of them. I was nervous about this pouring thing because I wasn't sure how I could eat…I already had enough trouble with the chopsticks. However, Youngee had made it very clear for me not to leave the chopsticks in the rice because that was a symbol that they were used by the dead. "Put chopsticks on table, Mrs. Duvall," Youngee emphasized. As I watched, the grandmother sat at a special table, while the father, mother, and aunt were seated at a large table with me. When my turn approached to sit, I carefully crossed my legs and gently folded on the floor. The food was brought in immediately. A huge array of bowls and dishes was spread out on the tabletop. These side dishes were filled with savory dips and pungent vegetables, raw fish, baby octopus, oysters, and shrimp. The Ku-jol-pans were filled with an assortment of meats, including Yuk-hoe (a marinated steak tar tar), short ribs and bulgogi (a specially marinated grilled beef). Other dishes were full of buckwheat noodles, tofu, hot chili and bean curd paste, bean sprouts, ginger and gingko nuts, and large servings of kimchi. Individual bowls of rice and soup were presented to all of us, but the main course was for sharing. Some of the selections were familiar, but I knew I had to taste each dish. I carefully washed down several strong tastes with my tiny cup of Ginseng tea.

After an hour and a half of eating, I was exhausted. Just as I thought everyone was finished, fresh fruits were brought in for dessert. Youngee made sure I knew the rules so I was prepared to wait. In her broken English, she made sure that I understood. "No one leave table. Eldest eat all, go first." Youngee's grandmother and her father both loved their fruit.

Forty-five minutes later we unfolded from the floor. As soon as I could, I asked where Jaffe was. No sooner had I said his name than Youngee appeared. She pointed for me to walk with her to a bedroom where the covers pulled down for me. "You nap." I was totally stuffed and desperately wanted to climb into that bed, but I remembered the nightlife at the Pink Flamingo. "Youngee no nap. I must go home. Lieutenant Duvall will be home soon. I do not want to offend your family, but I really must leave."

"You nap, Mrs. Duvall." Desperately she tried to encourage me to stay but I was just as determined to get Jaffe and myself out of the Pink Flamingo. I wasn't sure what the next course might be. Giving my thanks and apologies I said, "I go now."

Carter was already at the compound when I arrived. "Your hair looks nice! What time's dinner?" I looked at him in disgust and walked to the bathroom. Looking at the dismal room, I wondered how anyone could even sit very long on the toilet. There was no insulation, no heater, and the walls were covered in ice. Shivering, I threw up. Carter or Youngee must have fixed dinner because I climbed into bed, sicker than I'd ever been.

The next day was Christmas Eve, but I couldn't move. Every muscle in my body ached. My temperature was 103°—and I couldn't stop throwing up. Carter stayed home with me. I tried desperately to get up on Christmas Eve, but my coughing and sneezing were uncontrollable. That evening after Carter put Jaffe to sleep he crawled into bed with me. The next thing I knew, he was throwing up in the pan on the floor. Here we were in Asia with the Asian flu on Christmas Day, Jaffe filled with glee, and Youngee had the day off. Guilt ridden, I climbed out of bed, changed Jaffe's diaper, gave him one present, and climbed back into bed. Carter eventually got up to feed him breakfast and give him another gift and then he clambered back under the covers. There was no Christmas dinner at the Officers' Club for us. There was no dinner at all.

We muddled through Christmas Day 1967 and prayed for Youngee's return the next day. Fortunately, Carter recovered rapidly. The doctor suggested I stay indoors for several weeks. He seemed to think my ditch visit had something to do with the severity of my flu. Recuperating, I played with Jaffe and watched as he clung to Youngee. I started thinking about getting home to the United States, where he would be all mine again. The generator was running as I tried to watch TV. All I could tune in was *Bonanza.* There was big ole Horse Cartwright speaking in Korean. The dubbing was pretty good and funny. The lights in our duplex weren't as bright as candlelight so reading was pretty tough on the eyes. Jaffe jumped into my lap, and I gave him a big squeeze as Youngee went to fix our lunch.

"I sure can't wait for your Granny and Granddaddy to see you, big boy. I think I hear your daddy's Jeep."

"Da Da," he went running to the door. "Hi, honey, I came by to see how you're feeling this afternoon. Youngee has your lunch ready…please try to eat…you're getting too thin."

"I'll try to eat some soup or toast." Carter came back carrying a hot cup of soup. Youngee says it's, "*Twoen-jang-tchi-gae.*" She said that it is made from soybean paste and is the soul of Korean cuisine. She said this soup is an everyday staple and is essential to your health. Eat up! Here, I'll have a bowl with you." I hadn't touched Korean food since two days before Christmas, but I knew I couldn't get out of it this time. "It's really good! Please ask Youngee if I can have a little more." She came walking right into the room carrying the hot liquid and wearing a huge smile. "You like?"

"Yes, I like."

"You get better, now."

"Thanks to you Youngee."

"Catherine, as soon as you feel up to it, I need to take you to the police station to fill out departure forms and finalize your green card."

"I always love going there: the prostitutes and me checking in with the local authorities. Can we go tomorrow, Carter?"

"That will be fine. I'll let you know what time when I get home tonight."

After Carter left, Youngee came into the kitchen with baskets of plants, onionskin, berries, jasmine, safflower, gromwell and indigo, and jars of lye, alum, lime and gallnut. She was teaching me the traditional dyeing techniques for the knot work crafts we were doing together. As she boiled the water in the massive pots, Jaffe followed closely. I gave him some blueberries and took him away from the hot stove. He went back inside to play with "Oopso," the mutt Carter had inherited from a Korean child on the streets just outside of J nsu.

Oopso looked pretty lethargic today and suddenly started retching as if he had caught the flu. Youngee came running. She took one look at him and started pouring soapy water down his throat and yelling for me to get the landlord with his winged car. I wasn't sure what she was saying, but the way her arms were flinging I knew I'd better hurry. The landlord revved his motor and he, Oopso and I flew past the pedestrians. Oopso survived thanks to Youngee and the vet. People Youngee called "slicky boys" had poisoned him with cyanide. She said they had probably planned to rob us and were trying to get rid of him.

It was very cold that January night, so I kept Oopso inside instead of tying him to Carter's Jeep. We had just gone to bed when I asked Carter, "Do you hear someone hammering in the rice fields?"

"Are you crazy? No one would be out on a night like this. And besides, why would they hammer in the dark in a rice field?"

"Okay," I said as I got up to walk down the long hall to the bathroom, dreading its ice-covered walls. "At least it has walls," I thought as I flushed the primitive pot. Shuffling back into the duplex, I had the distinct feeling someone was watching me. Carter was already snoring when I climbed under the covers. I quickly placed my frozen feet on Carter's nice, warm, hairy legs. Lying there I listened carefully, trying to hear the distant rap, rap, rap in the fields, but all was silent. As I closed my eyes, I wondered what the rapping could have been.

Loud voices woke us at four o'clock the next morning. According to the landlord and his wife, the slicky boys had struck again. They'd built a ladder in the rice fields and climbed onto the roof right over our toilet. The landlord was furious because they'd cut a hole in the ceiling. The thieves had climbed down into the compound and taken down curtains and used them to haul away all of our food. They stole the TV next door but couldn't get into our side. Carter's Jeep had been chained to a concrete pillar, so they didn't get it either. Once all the commotion settled down, I rocked Jaffe back to sleep and said good morning to Oopso, who wagged happily at sleeping inside. As I dosed off again, I realized Oopso'd probably be dead if he'd slept outside and then it dawned on me that those slicky boys had been watching me use the bathroom.

Carter took me to the police station the next day to fill out my departure forms. "Want to have lunch at the club before you go home?"

"Sure...Jaffe is with Youngee but I don't want to be gone long." Just as we were finishing lunch, Carter got a message that he was needed right away. "You go ahead. I've got on my tennis shoes so I'll just walk home."

"Are you sure, Catherine? I saw some clouds out there."

"I'm sure, and if it starts to rain I'll get a cab."

Walking out of the main gate of J nsu was like walking into a different world. As I walked, I pulled my gloves on tighter, noticing that the breeze had picked up quite a bit. My jacket had a hood but it wasn't the warmest garment I owned. As I continued toward the MSR, the weather turned into a blizzard. Snow was falling everywhere. Charleston is not known for its snow, so this was as foreign to me as the Koreans had been in the beginning. My tennis shoes weren't the right shoes for a blizzard but I carefully put one foot in front of the other hoping to see a taxi. Not a single taxi came by…nothing. The snow was getting thicker, and the wind was blowing so hard that I could barely make out anything in front of me. Two Korean men approached in a big, old covered truck. The driver motioned for me to get inside between them. I hesitated for about half a second and then scrambled inside. I didn't know how to tell them where I lived, and I wasn't sure if I was being kidnapped. Once inside the cab, I sat there silently praying Hail Mary's. As the truck chugged along in the direction of our compound, I continued to pray that these strangers wouldn't hold me hostage. The snow was blinding as we lurched along the road. Suddenly, the driver slammed on brakes and the giant transport slid to a screeching halt just beyond the double metal gates of my home. Scampering down from the seat trying to touch my frozen toes on the road, I repeatedly thanked these two men who had saved a damsel in real distress. "*Kam-sa-ham-ni-da,*" I said over and over. Their grins were like Jack o lanterns as they bowed and said, "*Cheon-ma-ne-yo*" I knew enough Korean to know that this meant, "You're welcome." The truck roared away just as I fell flat on my behind in the snow. Youngee came hurrying outside to help me up and fuss at me for riding in the truck with strangers. "Jaffe, no Mama. You no be safe."

"I know, Youngee, but the snow was so cold. Believe me, I was worried, too. But an angel must have been watching over me."

Mama and Daddy had listened to Jaffe talking on all the recordings I had sent them throughout the year. They were as excited as I was about our homecoming. I packed a few things each day and started shipping them home. January twenty-fifth was coming fast. Youngee had asked about returning to the states to live with us, and it was a definite consideration. Jaffe loved her so much. Carter and I needed to decide, but we had more time because Carter was flying us home standby and then he was returning to J nsu. His tour finished the first of March. This would give him time to work out the details and help her with her documents. I dropped a quick note to Mama and Daddy, knowing I would beat the letter home.

Dear Mama and Daddy,

By the time you read this, I should be in the wonderful United States. I can't believe Jaffe and I have been here this long. I wish Carter could leave for good with us, but I know he'll be home soon. I can't wait for you to see Jaffe. He's adorable and so smart. He's into everything...can you believe he's going on fourteen months old? His eyes are the bluest I have ever seen, and his hair is so blond that it shines like the sun. The Koreans are amazed at him, because they've never seen blond hair and blue eyes. His skin is still as porcelain as ever. Youngee makes sure he's protected from the sun.

I'm still not well from my bout with the flu. My cough is worse but I don't know what else to do. I keep losing weight...I guess I just miss your cooking Mama. Hopefully, I'll feel better soon. Daddy, I can't wait for you to see Jaffe throwing a ball. He is already totally full of himself.

I'm going to meet Carter for lunch and say my good-byes to all the friends I've made here in Korea. I'll see you in two days.

We all love you both,

Carter, Jaffe, and Catherine

I folded the note into a stamped envelope, kissed Jaffe as I said to Youngee. "It's eleven o'clock now. I should be back here around two o'clock. Captain Duvall and I are having lunch, and I am coming right home."

On January 23, 1968, I bundled up for my last walk to the Air Force base. I had walked just about a half-mile when an Air Force truck pulled up beside me. "Ma'am, it's cold out here...you want a ride?"

"Are you going to J nsu, captain?"

"Yes, ma'am " The captain held the door open while I climbed inside. "Thanks. Are you stationed at J nsu?"

"No, ma'am, I'm at Teagu just coming to J nsu for a briefing."

"I'll be leaving Korea in two days. My son and I are going home."

"What does your husband do?"

"He's the Army liaison for the Air Force. He coordinates air strikes on the ground for all of the troops and he's excited because he just made captain."

"That's a pretty important job! I remember when I made captain. I was excited, too."

"I guess his job's important but I'm not sure because nothing dangerous ever seems to happen."

"I don't think there's anything to worry about around here."

The captain slowly guided his truck up to the checkpoint at the main gate. The gates were closed, and the guards were standing at full alert, weapons drawn. The sentry had waved me through countless times this past year. He saluted the captain saying, "Sir, you are requested not to leave the base once you enter." Then he came around to my side and said, "Ma'am, please get out of the military vehicle."

"What?"

"Get out, ma'am, and come with me!" The captain looked strangely at me before he drove through the now-open gates. The guard said, "Ma'am, you can't go onto the base."

"Why not?"

"I can't tell you, but you cannot go onto this military facility."

"This is ridiculous! I'm going anyway!"

"Ma'am, I have orders to shoot anyone who tries to enter this base. Go inside the guardhouse and call your husband. He'll tell you what to do."

"Captain Duvall, please."

"Ma'am, I'm not sure if he can speak with you. Wait, here he comes now." Carter was very nervous and evasive. "Catherine, get Jaffe and get back to the base as quickly as possible."

"Carter, what in the hell is going on?"

"Catherine, I can't tell you…get Jaffe…I'll find you later!"

"The guard won't let me on base...how can I get on?"

"I'll take care of that while you get Jaffe. Hurry, Catherine! Hurry...be very careful!" I hung up the phone in total shock and started to walk past the guard at the gate when he came to attention with his arms across his chest and declared, "Ma'am, you can't leave this property! I have orders to shoot anyone departing this United States facility." I was dumbfounded.

All I could think of was Jaffe and my conversation with Carter. I looked that guard straight in the eye as I pushed him aside and said, "Then shoot me! I'm going to get my son!" There was a tense moment of silence and then I heard, "Ma'am, please wait just a minute." I turned as the guard brought out his commander to talk with me. "Hello, Jake, how are you? What's this all about?"

"Hello, Catherine. I'm fine. I can't tell you, but I'll get you a cab so you can go and get Jaffe. Carter just talked with me...I'm sending three guards with you. Please hurry, Catherine. Time is essential." The taxi driver was scared to death when I climbed in and Army guards climbed in on both sides of me and one jumped into the passenger seat. All had their weapons drawn and ready to fire. I have never taken such a wild ride. Each time the driver slowed for any reason, the guards insisted he drive faster.

When we reached the compound, one guard stayed with the driver and two guards came with me as I grabbed the baby and the clothes I'd packed that morning and kissed Youngee. The poor thing stood there crying, trying to figure out what was happening. I didn't have time to cry because the guards were telling me my time was up.

I plopped Jaffe on the floor as the guards ordered, and we sped back to the base. This time, my entourage and I were waved through the gates. The taxi driver dropped Jaffe, our bags, and me at the Officers' Club and drove toward the main gate where he was immediately escorted from the base.

It was 1:30 pm; I was frustrated, scared, and worried. Jaffe was hungry, wet, and excited about being at the club. After changing his diaper in the ladies' room, I ordered lunch. While we were sitting at the table, Jaffe whined for some of my Coke. When I put the glass to his lips, he clamped his teeth onto the glass accidentally biting a big chunk out of it. Trying to pry the glass from his mouth without cutting him, I spilled the Coke all over the table. "I'm so sorry, Dan, this has been a horrible day. Do you know what's going on?"

"I heard a few bits and pieces a few minutes ago. Here, let me clean this up, and I'll take Jaffe for a walk. Go sit at the bar with the fighter pilots, and you'll figure it out."

"Thanks. Jaffe, you be a good boy for Dan."

I listened as the guys talked. I could only make out a few bits of the news. "Ship!"

"It was on an intelligence mission."

"We'll probably go to war."

"Captured!"

"North Korea."

"International waters." Dan came back with Jaffe. "Did you get any details, Catherine?"

"Not much, but what I heard sounds serious."

"Jaffe, you want to watch TV over here with me?" Jaffe toddled off again holding Dan's hand. The hours crawled by as I paced, hoping Carter would call or come by.

Happy hour was a great deal more informative. After one Singapore Sling and a glass of wine, I discovered that the USS Pueblo, a United States Navy vessel, had been sent on an intelligence-gathering mission off the coast of North Korea. North Korean jets and naval vessels attacked it. Several men were wounded, one man was killed, and the remaining eighty-two crewmembers were taken hostage. Fighter pilots were coming in from all over Southeast Asia, but I hadn't seen Carter for one minute. After dinner, Jaffe began yawning and rubbing his eyes. He'd been great all day, but now he was tired and needed a bath and bed. Sitting in the Officers' Club rocking him, I watched Colonel Cannon approach. "Catherine, I hear that you and Jaffe have been in here all day."

"Yes, sir. It's been a very long day. I don't know what else to do."

"Carter will be down in about an hour and a half to see you, but I'm going to have my driver take you and Jaffe up to the bachelors' officers' quarters. We'll move you all into Carter's room."

"Mrs. Duvall, you look exhausted…let me carry that." Ben picked up my bags and placed them in the Jeep and then he threw Jaffe up on his shoulders. "Come on, little guy. You're moving right across the hall from me." When Ben got us to the room, I saw that the colonel had ordered a crib for the room. I was so thankful for his kindness that I started to cry. "Thanks, Ben, for everything. And please call me Catherine."

"Since we're neighbors, I guess I can do that. The shower's down the hall. If you want to take one, I'll station a guard outside the door."

"I'll wait, but I would like to wash off Jaffe."

"I'll get wash cloths and towels for you." Jaffe's eyes were closing by the time I pulled his pajamas onto his chubby little body. I closed the door and walked down to the sitting room where there was a TV. Staring absently at the screen, I tried to figure out what was happening around me. "Catherine! Catherine, honey…are you okay?"

I looked up to see Carter looking down at me, a worried look on his face. He put his arms around me as I cried like a baby. I gave him all the information that I picked up at the club. "Catherine, this is very serious. I can't tell you more, but I need to get you and Jaffe out of here as soon as possible. If there is a war, J nsu will be bombed first and, as you know, I'll be very busy plotting where our troops will bomb North Korea. C141 cargo planes are arriving with troops from all over. This place will look like Tent City within a few hours from now. Everyone is making space for the arrivals. I can't fly standby with you and Jaffe. We'll have to buy you a regular ticket even though we don't have that much money saved. There's another problem. No planes can fly out of Seoul, because it's so near the DMZ." As the plane goes up, it will be heading right toward North Korea. It will be shot down. It crosses the demilitarized zone separating the two countries. "What are we going to do, Carter? I'll try to call Daddy to wire the money, but how are we going to get out if we can't fly near the DMZ?"

"I'm not sure yet, but I'm working on it. Come on, let's go to bed. I have to report back in five hours."

I heard Carter as he dressed and left hoping Jaffe would not wake up. Turning over on the small bed, I heard a familiar sound: the booming engines of a C141 cargo plan coming into J nsu from Charleston. I could feel the closeness to my home. Jaffe and I dressed and read stories before I fixed him cereal for breakfast. "Now, what are we going to do my precious angel?" Ben was knocking on the door. "Catherine there's a phone call for you."

"Thanks…I'm on my way. I'll bet its Carter."

"Hello."

"Hello Mrs. Catherine Duvall?"

"Yes."

"My name is Roger Gatch, and I'm with the Red Cross. There are people in the United States who are concerned for your safety."

"Mr. Gatch, it's so good to here from you. Please tell my parents that Jaffe and I are on base at J nsu and we're trying desperately to get home. I'll try to contact them as soon as I can. Can you help me with that?"

"Mrs. Duvall, I am appalled that you would haul your baby into such a place. I can't believe that you'd move into a BOQ with all those men. What kind of morals does a person like you have? I'll give your parents the message that you're okay for now, but that's all the help I can give you. Good day!" My mouth was still wide open when Ben brought Jaffe down the hall to me. "What's the matter, Catherine?"

"You won't believe what that man just said to me!" I shared the conversation with Ben and watched as his face flushed. "What are you going to do?"

"I have no idea, Ben."

"Jaffe, let's put your coat on and go outside for a short walk."

Jumping and bobbing around, Jaffe finally was still enough for me to zip his snowsuit. "Oh, my goodness, Jaffe! Look at this!" I couldn't believe my eyes. Thousands of soldiers and tents were everywhere. The grounds were covered. Jaffe and I watched as the Land of the Morning Calm turned into a full-fledged war zone. The Pueblo incident was bringing in the entire Seventh Air Force, Fifth Army, and the Marines to our little spot on the map.

Ben drove us to the Officers' Club for lunch. Dan got us a good table even though the place was packed. Top brass was everywhere. I quietly fed Jaffe his grilled cheese sandwich and soup before I picked through my salad. Coughing as I chewed the endive, I almost choked before downing my glass of water. "You okay, Catherine?" Dan asked as he passed by. "I'm fine…can't get rid of this cold."

"You need to see the doc…he's over there."

"No, Dan, don't you bother him…I'm fine!"

"Whatever you say, my dear." Looking up, I watched as Ben walked toward our table.

"Are you two ready to go back to the BOQ?"

"Hey, there! We sure are. Where's Colonel Cannon?"

"I just dropped him off and he told me to take good care of you."

"You're the best, Ben."

Back at the BOQ, Jaffe and I played games and sang songs before I put him in his crib for a nap and returned to the sitting room with a note pad and pen. "What are you doing, Catherine?"

"Making a list of possible ways to get out of Korea, Ben."

"How many ways are on your list?"

"Zero!"

The barracks phone was ringing off the hook and finally an officer answered it. "Yes, sir. I'll get her right away, sir."

"Mrs. Jaffe, it's the deputy commander of the base, Colonel Smith."

"Hello, Colonel Smith, I know you are a busy man."

"Hello, Mrs. Duvall. It has been brought to my attention that you and your infant son, I believe his name is Jaffe, are bunking in our BOQ. Is this correct?"

"Yes sir but only because your guards won't let us leave and I don't know what else to do."

"You are here on a tourist visa. Correct?"

"Yes sir."

"You did not come over as a dependant?"

"That's correct, sir."

"Due to the grave situation I find myself in, I must ask you to vacate the primacies of the BOQ within the next few hours. I need the BOQ for my troops not a woman and baby who will distract them. I expect you to follow my order immediately, good day." Hanging up the phone, I couldn't stop the tears. "Where can I go? What am I going to do? Where is my husband?" I lay on the couch, softly sobbing and trying to figure this mess out. "Catherine, I have to go out for a while, but I'll be back shortly," Ben said after I told him about my devastating conversation with the Colonel Smith. "Here. Wipe your eyes and try to rest," Ben said as he marched out the door.

I must have dozed off because I woke to the phone ringing. "Yes sir. I'll get her for you."

"Mrs. Duvall, the phone's for you." Groggily walking to the phone, I wondered who would be the bearer of bad news this time. "Hello, this is Catherine Duvall."

"Catherine, this is Colonel Cannon. I hear there is a big bad man picking on you."

"Yes, sir, he sure is...Ben must be spreading gossip."

"He is...and I'm sending him down to pack you and Jaffe up and move you into my quarters immediately. I share my place with the chaplain. I promise we'll keep you safe up here. The Air Force may not want you, but the Army sure as hell will protect you."

"Sir, you are too kind. I can't thank you enough. I hope I won't inconvenience you too long. Sir, I need to know one more thing."

"Yes?"

"Is Carter allowed to join me?"

"If he promises not to salute me every minute."

"Thank you, sir. I'll be ready when Ben arrives." I grabbed a pen and scribbled a note to Carter.

Honey,

We've moved in with the Army brass. Call me at Colonel Cannon's number. Love you,

Catherine and Jaffe

I had just finished repacking when Ben arrived. "Should we take the crib?"

"Yes ma'am. The Colonel said to bring everything!" Ben began dismantling the crib as I cleaned up Jaffe. "I'm ready whenever you are."

"I'll pull the Jeep up as close as possible and load it. You wait inside where it's warm."

"Thanks again, Ben."

Driving up the hill to the colonel's quarters, I hoped Carter wouldn't feel too uncomfortable living with his commander. The kept villa and its manicured grounds were quite a contrast to the dismal compound Jaffe, Carter, and I had been living in. Henry, the houseman, spoke fluent English as he answered the door. "Welcome, Mrs. Duvall! And this must be Jaffe. Will the captain be joining us?"

"Shortly, I hope."

"Come this way. Your quarters will be in the east wing." Pinned neatly on the door was a note.

Welcome! The only house rules are cocktails at six o'clock sharp. See you then. *Andy Cannon*

Ben and Henry set up the crib and helped unpack all of our things. Henry left with Jaffe in tow. "Come, young man, you must need a snack."

I couldn't believe the villa or the hospitality. After freshening up, I went to reclaim my son. I looked into the kitchen, but there was no sign of him. Then, I heard giggles. Pushing open the door beyond the kitchen, I found Jaffe seated at a formal dining room table large enough for twenty people. The table was covered with an exquisite crisp white linen cloth. Jaffe was giggling as Henry dipped hot dog pieces and flew them through the ketchup and into his waiting hanger. Ketchup was everywhere…it looked like the war had begun with drips of blood drooling out of Jaffe's "hanger."

"Henry, I'm so sorry about this mess!"

"No problem, ma'am. He's so much fun, quite a boy you have here!"

"Thanks. What time will the colonel arrive?"

"He usually comes in around 5:30…in time to dress for happy hour. I've made some delicious hors d'oeuvres for this evening in your honor."

"You're so kind. I can't wait to try them. "Excuse me for a moment, I must answer the phone."

"Mrs. Duvall, it's your husband."

"Hi, yes it's a long story, and I'll explain it when you get here for cocktails."

"What? I can't live with my commanding officer!"

"Well, if you want to see your son and wife, you will," I said as I hung up the receiver.

When I went to get Jaffe, I noticed the linens had been replaced and Henry was off preparing for the Colonels Cannon and D'Antonio, the chaplain. I dressed Jaffe in a white shirt with a Peter Pan collar and his red corduroy overalls. I freshened my makeup, twisted my hair on top of my head, and put on my short, black silk dress and pumps. As I was trying to fasten the clasp on my pearls, Carter opened the door. "Let me help you with that. You look gorgeous!"

"Well it's about time…you look horrible!"

"I love you, too!"

"What are we doing here?"

As I rehashed the events of my day, Jaffe hugged and climbed all over his father. "I can't believe the Air Force colonel kicked you out."

"Well, believe it because here we are in the Army commander's quarters in South Korea!"

"What should I wear for cocktails?"

"A fresh uniform, and don't salute the colonels."

In the living room, Carter and I met Colonel Cannon and Colonel D'Antonio. They warmly welcomed us and treated Jaffe as if he were their grandson. The pleasant atmosphere was a welcomed relief from the events of the day. Henry's aperitif of Brie, baked en croute, topped with chutney, sparkling champagne was perfect and the fine gentlemen and pleasant conversation was soothing until the conversation turned to my predicament. "How is Catherine going to get out of Korea safely and quickly?" I heard Carter saying. "I had planned to fly stand-by with her but now I can't leave." Several martinis later, Colonel Cannon offered to loan us the funds for a plane ticket home. "Sir, that's very kind of you but I'm sure the wire from my Daddy will be here shortly, " I replied. "Do you think the planes will fly from Seoul any time soon?" Carter asked as Henry filled his crystal highball glass with another shot of bourbon. "It'll be another week or so before planes can fly in or out."

"I hope you don't mind us staying here that long," I chimed in as I went to take a piece of silver from Jaffe. "Come here, Jaffe, and let's go check on dinner," Henry declared, reaching for Jaffe's hand just as I did. Jaffe toddled away with him as Henry broadly grinned at me.

The dinner table was set for royalty: silver, crystal, and china, a Ming vase filled with freshly cut roses. The two colonels and my captain sat me then joined me at the table. Jaffe was in his glory sitting next to his father.

Our first course was cream of asparagus soup and giant croutons made from English toasting bread. A luscious truffle, pear, and leek salad drizzled with balsamic vinaigrette. Then came raw oysters and boiled shrimp, followed by the roasted beef, potatoes with hollandaise sauce, sugar snap peas, pole beans, squash casserole, rice and beef gravy, and sesame seed rolls. Delicious red and white wines complimented each dish.

Colonel Cannon informed us, "This extensive spread is traditional for Chaplain D'Antonio and me each evening. We have drivers and rarely get to walk, which explains our expanding waistlines."

"Everything is wonderful."

"Thank you, Catherine; please convey your pleasure to the chef. He'll come in after dessert." Just as the words came from his mouth, crème brulée was brought to the table. Jaffe loved the spoonful Carter gave him. "Let's go into the drawing room and relax." Just as we were settling down…in walked the chef. "Hello everyone!"

"Catherine, Carter, and Jaffe please say hello to our Chef Amyl."

"Hello, Amyl…dinner was exquisite. Thank you so much," Carter and I said in unison.

Once we sat for after-dinner coffee and spirits, Jaffe began falling asleep. "Please excuse me, gentlemen. This is lovely, but my little bundle is about to nod off. I really need to put him to bed. I can't thank you both enough and I'll see you tomorrow. Please, don't get up. Remember, I now live here, too."

As I tucked my tired boy into his crib, I couldn't help feel an urgency to leave Korea and get him to the safety of the United States. Once Jaffe was asleep, I slipped into my thin soft batiste white gown and curled up snuggly under the fluffy down comforter. I must have been sleeping several hours when I felt Carter's warm hands caressing my nipples, searching down my legs. "What time is it?"

"Eleven. Shh." He placed his warm lips gently on my sleepy mouth and pulled my nightgown down from my shoulders. "You're beautiful, Catherine…I need you."

"I'm sleeping."

"I won't keep you awake long." Slowly his muscular arms wrapped tightly around me as he climbed gently on top of me. The throbbing of his body pressed insistently, prying my thighs. As the exciting rhythm carried us along faster and faster, we reached a pulsing outburst of pleasure. Breathing heavily, Carter whispered, "I don't want you to go away, Catherine, I love you."

"I love you, too." We lay there holding one another tenderly, knowing the separation was coming.

I had been asleep just long enough that now I was wide awake. As Carter rolled over and began snoring, I scooped up my gown and tiptoed to the bathroom for a bath. Preoccupied with the gratification we'd just shared, I thought, "Carter is such a passionate lover and as I was preoccupied with my thoughts rushing warm water overflowed, reaching the iciness of my feet.

By the time I came down for breakfast the next morning, scrambled eggs and grits were everywhere because Henry and Jaffe had been flying planes into the hanger again. I finished feeding of my son before a bath and fresh clothes. "Jaffe, today Mama's going to find away to get us out of Korea. We're going down to the Officers' Club."

Just as Colonel Cannon suggested, I struck up a conversation with several of the C141 pilots. "How's Charleston?"

"It's as beautiful as ever, ma'am."

"I'm from Charleston "

"How long have you been at J nsu?"

"One year…it's time for me to go home but as you know there's a problem here. When are you flying out Major?"

"First thing in the morning."

"Any chance that I could catch a ride to Charleston with you?"

"Ma'am, I don't have a problem with that. Can you be ready?"

"Absolutely, I'll get our things together!"

"Our?"

"I have a fourteen-month old son. He's over there with Dan."

"Ma'am, I'll take a chance on getting you out but I can't risk a baby on the plane...it's just too dangerous, sorry." After four pilots, I lost hope on leaving on a C141.

Colonel Cannon came into the club with several dignitaries. After introducing me he whispered, "Any luck, my dear?"

"I'm afraid not, sir."

"We'll figure something else out, see you tonight." Dan was motioning me to the bar. "There's a phone call for you. Take it over there."

"Hello, this is Catherine Duvall."

"Mrs. Duvall. My name is Senator Strom Thurmond. I want to know how you're getting along over there young lady? I've been talking with your Mama. You know her friend, Fannie, and I are close friends. I hear you're having a difficult time."

"Senator Thurmond, it's so good to hear your voice."

I explained my housing situation with the Air Force and how well the Army was treating me and asked the senator to tell my parents that Colonel Cannon would pay for the ticket on the first plane out of Seoul. "I'll be happy to tell your parents, and I'll see to it that you are on that first plane out of Korea. As a matter of fact, I'm calling for a full congressional investigation into this matter. The treatment that you have received is appalling for any American citizen. I'll have my office contact you as soon as you're back in South Carolina, honey. Now, you take good care of yourself and that fine baby of yours."

"Yes sir and thank you so much."

I shared my phone call with all the men in the villa over cocktails. "Yes, I know about the conversation. The senator called my office, too." announced Colonel Cannon. "A congressional investigation!" chided Carter. "My military career's over."

"I'm delighted that the Army's been on your side, Catherine," praised the chaplain. Colonel Cannon walked over and took my hand. "I have news about your departure, Catherine. It'll be day after tomorrow.

They're enforcing limited departures at this time, but I had your tickets purchased today. I'll have Ben drive you to Seoul in my car. Carter, you can go along for the ride. I'll send several guards, too." I longingly looked at Carter as he returned the look. "You are too kind, Colonel Cannon. Catherine and I can't thank you enough." Crying, I babbled, "I'll certainly miss all of you. Please keep yourselves safe. Come here, can I have hugs, please?" Many hugs later, Colonel Cannon added, "Catherine, it's still very risky for you to fly out of Seoul. The plane goes up very near the DMZ, and there's a possibility that your plane will be shot down."

"I have no other choice, do I, sir?"

"No, you don't."

The next two days were filled with tears of joy and fear. And then at six o'clock on the morning of February 11, Carter, Jaffe, and I climbed inside Colonel Cannon's car with two armed guards and Ben positioned behind the wheel. Our journey to Seoul was extremely somber as we passed the same thatched roof bungalows surrounded by rice fields. The backdrop beside the roadway remained the same, but our southeastern interlude had changed our lives forever. The tension mounted as the sounds of rifle fire near Seoul echoed through the distant hills. Our plane was waiting on the runway. "I'll pray that you both make it over the DMZ," Ben said as he hugged Jaffe and me. Carter put his arms around us, not wanting to let go. "I love you, Catherine…just know this. You'll be safe and I'll get home as soon as I can. Take good care of Jaffe and yourself. I love you son. Let me give you another squeeze." I had a lump as big as a baseball in my throat as I uttered, "We love you, too!" As my tears started falling, I reluctantly let go of Carter's hand and blew him kisses.

Walking up the staircase into the plane, I felt like I was walking into doom. The engine noise increased and the winds started rushing from the jets, but the cabin was filled with a deafening silence. Peeking out the window, I spotted Carter waving in the distance. I blew him another kiss as the engines roared and the tires whirred on the tarmac. The plane soared upward rapidly, and I held Jaffe snuggly in my arms. The soldier next to me reached for my hand just as I reached for his. Squeezing tightly, we bowed our heads in prayer. I was sure I had just stopped breathing when I heard. "Ladies and gentlemen, this is your captain. We are now in safe air space. You can breathe, folks. We're going home!"

"Hurray!"

"Thank God!"

"Praise the Lord!" Outbursts came from every passenger on the plane, and I saw tears of joy and relief streaming down every face.

I had filled the sedative prescription from Dr. Washington but decided that I'd hold off giving it to Jaffe for as long as I could. He was wide awake, but I was physically and mentally drained. After about eight hours on the plane, it was time. "Here, honey, finish your dinner. Mommy's going to change you and get you ready for bed."

"Here, honey, take a spoonful of this yummy syrup, open wide!" Obligingly, he took every drop of the medicine. Within thirty minutes Jaffe was sound asleep, and I curled up to rest as much as I could.

When we reached Alaska, Jaffe stirred long enough for me to give him another dose. Twenty hours after we'd left from Seoul, we landed at O'Hare International. It was early morning as I hauled our belongings and Jaffe to the nearest pay phone. "Hello?"

"Daddy, it's me!" Crying uncontrollably, I couldn't say anything else. "Are you okay? Where are you? Where's Jaffe?"

"I'm okay, just exhausted. I'm in Chicago and Jaffe's with me. We're changing planes and will be in Charleston around five o'clock in the morning. Can you meet me? I'm flying Delta."

"Of course we'll be there. Try to stop crying. You're going to upset the baby."

"That's one of the reasons I'm crying. I have been giving him sedatives the entire trip, and I think I've overdosed him. He's so groggy, I can't get him awake."

"We'll take care of him when you get here. Love you, honey!"

"I love you, too."

Our flight continued, but it was scary with really bad weather and huge air pockets. I began praying, "God, please let me get this baby off of this airplane and to safety, and I'll do whatever you want me to do. I'm yours."

Landing in Charleston was like peeking back in time. Racing to the plane, Mama and Daddy grabbed Jaffe from me, chatting incoherently about how big he was. A quick hug for me, and Daddy was off in search of my luggage. Daddy said, "It's so good to have you home, Catherine. I've missed you greatly."

Once we got to Mama's and Daddy's, Jaffe was wild. He'd been asleep more than sixteen hours and hadn't been so close to a TV set, bright lights and doting grandparents. Ebony climbed in my lap and licked me all over. She didn't move as I talked for hours with Mama and Daddy. I shared every detail of the past year with them. Finally, I begged, "Would you mind watching Jaffe while I lie down for a while?"

"Go ahead, honey. We've fixed the front room for you," Mama said.

Their new home was quite lovely, and the front room was perfect for me. I bathed, found a clean nightgown, and climbed into bed shortly before lunch. I didn't wake up until the next morning when I smelled fresh coffee brewing. Mama said, "We were beginning to think you were in a coma. You have a terrible cough, Catherine. Jaffe has been a good boy, but he's been hell on wheels, touching everything in sight. Daddy took him to the park to burn some energy. He loves Ebony, but I think he thinks she's not real. Didn't you have a dog in Korea?"

"Uh huh, he was big though, and Jaffe didn't see many dogs because they eat them over there."

"Goodness! No wonder he loves Ebony. I made you an appointment with Dr. Bixley for one o'clock this afternoon."

"Thanks, Mama."

Daddy drove me to the doctor. Having not driven for a year, I was nervous as Daddy sped down the highway. It seemed strange to see only cars and regular traffic. The biggest surprise was the blue lights on police cars. They were red when I left the country. "Hello, Catherine. How was it?" Dr. Bixley asked as he came into the room. "Really different from the U.S., but I've gained a lot from my experience in Korea. I believe I've really grown up."

"Great…then it was worth the trip. Now, let's see about you physically. Take a deep breath, again."

On the way home, Daddy stopped at the pharmacy to fill the five prescriptions I had been given. "You sit here while I go get them."

"Thanks, Daddy."

"What did the doctor say?" Mama said as she greeted me at the door. "I have pneumonia and if I don't stay in bed until I'm well he's going to put me in the hospital. I'm so sorry to do this to you, Mama. Who's going to take care of Jaffe?"

"Me, Miss Catherine!" Bessie Lou said smiling from across the room where she had Jaffe wrapped in a fresh towel from his bath. "Oh, Bessie Lou…it's so good to see you!"

"I have Master Jaffe under control, honey, now you go on in there and get yourself in that bed like the doctor said."

Recuperating took longer than expected, but I relished that Jaffe was in good hands. He played in the park everyday and walked the neighborhood with Bessie Lou or Daddy. Mama was busy buying him outfits from Church Street Children, a posh children's shop. She and Daddy often took Jaffe to run on the battery, where he could feel the sea breeze blow against his little cheeks or climb on the old cannons. I spent much of my time resting and writing to Carter. I longed for him to be with us and desperately needed word that he was safe. Just after lunch, Bessie Lou brought me a stack of mail. I saw the red, white, and blue edging on three letters and searched for the posting dates so I could read them in order. Carter filled me in on the latest news.

Dearest Catherine,

I've visited with Youngee. She's well but misses you and Jaffe. She has decided not to come to the United States. The situation here is pretty scary. The eighty-two crewmembers are still being held captive. Some kind of action will be taken against North Korea. I'm swamped with the command but only have a few more weeks before I'll be home with you and our adorable son.

I should leave the first of April but will try to call you before I leave.

All my love,

Carter

"No. I don't know whether he's decided to get out of the Army or not, Daddy. I certainly would like to move back here permanently. We'll just have to wait and see."

"Your Mama and I adore having Jaffe here!"

"And you're spoiling him rotten but he loves every minute of it."

Carter returned to Charleston in April 1968 and was honorably discharged. He heard that Metro Power was moving part of its operation down from the main plant in Schenectady, New York. It was due to open in Summerville. Carter had a degree in electrical engineering so he was thrilled when he landed the position as vice president of equipment Installation.

"Truman, thank you for letting us stay here while our new home is being renovated," I overheard Carter saying to Daddy. "You're welcome to stay as long as need be," was the reply. "Carter, Jaffe has a temperature of 104°. He hasn't eaten a thing. I'm calling Dr. Adams."

"Bring him on in, Mrs. Duvall. We'll be waiting."

"I've ordered several blood tests, Catherine. How long ago were you in Korea?"

"Two months."

"Let's keep a close eye on him. Call me if his temp goes up or anything changes."

We carried our motionless child home and put him in his bed, taking shifts sitting with him. The next day his temperature began to rise. Dr. Adams met us at the hospital. "I'm going to admit Jaffe. I have no clue what's going on, but I'm going to find out." I never left the hospital, but Mama, Daddy, and Carter were in and out. Jaffe wasn't responding to any of the medicines. Four days passed before Dr. Adams had news. "Is Carter here with you Catherine?"

"He'll be here shortly. Why?"

"Jaffe has an infectious disease, and I believe that he may have a form of meningitis or encephalitis. It's serious, but I'm sure we've caught it in time and Jaffe's going to be fine. Some symptoms are fever, headache and in worst cases seizures. Don't be frightened by the worst case scenario. The blood tests are not conclusive yet, so try not to worry. I'm staying here until I get the answers. "How did Jaffe get sick?"

"Both of these viruses come from mosquitoes."

"Is he going to die?"

"Not if I have anything to do with it, now try not to worry. I'll be back in a little while."

Just as Carter walked into the quarantined room, Jaffe arched his spine and jerked uncontrollably. I screamed for help. The nurses held his tongue with depressors until the seizure subsided. "He's resting now, I'll stay in here with him, Mrs. Duvall. You go talk with your husband."

"What in the hell is going on, Catherine? Where's Dr. Adams?"

"He just left but he's some where in the hospital. He thinks Jaffe has meningitis or encephalitis. Dr. Adams wants us both to stay here until he comes back with results from the lab."

"Carter paced back and forth while I tried to read a book. I couldn't concentrate because he was pacing so fast.

Finally, Dr. Adams returned with the diagnostic report. "Some of these viruses have no human vaccines available. I'm trying to determine if this is La Crosse Encephalitis (LAC), Japanese Encephalitis (JE), or a type of meningitis. All are chiefly mosquito borne and occur if there is a change in lifestyle, such as a recent move or exposure to the outdoors. There hasn't been an epidemic around this area in a long time. Fort Jackson is renowned for its meningitis outbreaks. LAC is notorious in the Mid-Atlantic States and strikes mostly children under sixteen. It is in North Carolina and could be in South Carolina. JE is extremely serious and several military personnel traveling or living in Asia have contracted it."

"Do you think this is what Jaffe has, Dr. Adams?"

"I don't know for sure, but we should have the final results soon." I looked at Carter. I'm so frightened." Carter put his arm around me and held me tightly.

Back into Jaffe's room, we couldn't take our eyes off him. We watched the nurse as she checked his breathing then quickly put the oxygen mask over his mouth. Over the intercom, she said, "I need help in here, STAT!" As the nurses ran through the door, I grabbed Carter. "What's wrong? Do something!" I sobbed. Carter ran out into the hall, quickly returning with Dr. Adams and several other doctors. I watched as they listened to Jaffe's breathing and searched for a heart beat. "Get respiratory in here STAT," ordered one of the strangers.

The nurse asked us to step outside, but we refused, moving quickly into a corner out of their way. We stared in horror as the doctors pounded on our son's chest. "We're losing him…step back!" He continued working on our infant son as we watched in fear.

Suddenly, the monitors showed a definite heartbeat, and each doctor congratulated the other. "He's back with us…thanks to Almighty God!" Carter and I held one another as we cried softly and joyfully. "Is he going to be okay?"

"We're moving Jaffe to the pediatric intensive care unit immediately, so someone can monitor him around the clock," Dr. Adams explained as he walked us down the hall. "The lab reports are back. Jaffe has La Crosse Encephalitis. He's going to be sick for a while longer, but we're going to get him better. Drs. Martin and Sullivan are two of the best in the nation on encephalitis, and they were both just in the room with me."

The long stretcher pulled up beside us, and we looked down to see our Jaffe lying still. "Can we go down on the elevator with him?"

"Absolutely, let's ride down together. Catherine, you and Carter will have certain hours that you can visit Jaffe. Please try to get some rest because this recovery could take quite sometime. He'll be in qualified hands, I promise. I'll come out and get you after Jaffe's settled."

Dr. Adams followed the stretcher through the carefully guarded doors. "Try to sit down, honey. There's a phone over there. I'm going to call Mama and Daddy and give them the details. Have you talked to your parents lately? You may want to tell them."

"Catherine, my parents don't care about you, Jaffe, or me. I'll call them in a day or two. I will call my brothers though and I definitely want to call a priest. Do you want me to call Father Kelly or Father Condon?"

"It doesn't matter to me, call one of them." Jaffe was in the PICU for ten days before Dr. Adams came out to say, "His temperature is finally normal, he's breathing on his own, and he's asking for his Mommy and Daddy. I think it's time to move him back on the pediatric floor. He's not totally out of the woods, but he needs to be with you both."

Back in Jaffe's room, we examined him from head to toe. His frail little body had lost too much weight and his arms were purple from all the IVs and shots, but he was still gorgeously perfect. His room was filled with toys, bears, balls, balloons and flowers—all compliments of Mama. "Look at all this stuff Granny and Granddaddy bought for you, Jaffe. Do you want to play ball with Daddy?"

Carter rolled the ball to Jaffe and he picked it up and threw it across the room. It wasn't long before Jaffe yawned, put his head down and fell asleep. "Do you think he's alright?"

"I think he's got a good arm and is going to be a baseball player like my grandfather."

"I didn't know Poppy was a ball player, Carter."

"It was in the early 1900s. He played for a team in Columbus, Georgia. From the stories I've heard from my Grandmother, Poppy was quite good. Mommy and Poppy Chamberlain met in Columbus, married and had my mother then moved to Charleston."

"I find it very coincidental that your mother, my mother and Jaffe were all born in Columbus, Georgia, don't you? Maybe there is something to that Presbyterian predestined stuff."

"It is coincidental, but you know how you are about explaining phenomena."

"Okay, we won't go there!"

"How are you all doing?" Father Condon whispered as he entered the room. "How's Jaffe coming along?"

"He's getting better every day, Father. It's so good to see you. Thanks for all your prayers, everyone has been so kind.

Mrs. Roland called to say that all of St. Mary's was praying for Jaffe. Please thank them. "I'll convey your gratitude, Catherine. Carter, have your parents been over?"

"No, Father. It's okay. It doesn't bother me, but I know it bothers Catherine. Her family is so close."

"Don't let them bother you, Catherine. Not seeing Jaffe is their loss. It's a shame that people can't carry peace in their hearts at all times. Mr. and Mrs. Duvall are both living in a world of denial. Let's pray for them today as we pray for Jaffe's continued recovery."

Father Condon guaranteed us that God would not take Jaffe from us at this point and his promise was good enough for us. Two days after Father Condon's guarantee from God, our prayers were answered. "My little man, I believe you are completely healed. You can go home today. I'll go and fill out your paper work," Dr. Adams announced with a big grin. There were plenty of hugs and kisses from everyone before Carter, Jaffe, and I drove away.

Daddy had been overseeing the renovation of our 1869 house while we were at the hospital. "It looks fantastic, Truman. You certainly kept the contractor on track, thanks for all you've done for us. I can't believe you even had them finish the landscaping."

"You just have to stay after them. They're good fellows, but they do tend to get distracted."

Mama and Daddy left just after I put Jaffe to bed. Walking arm in arm through our newly renovated home, Carter and I smiled gleefully at one another. "It's simply gorgeous, isn't it? Come look out into the gardens, Catherine. It's even more beautiful out here." Sipping glasses of wine, we talked around the house. "Can you imagine the hands of the craftsman who carved this Victorian molding? It wraps all the way around a fourteen-foot high ceiling. Glancing down at the heart pine floors, I said, "I'll bet they are keeping secrets, generations of tip-toeing around." As I looked above the heart pine floors, my eyes were drawn to the window casings. They were delicately finished around hand-blown glass. "Carter, what is this?"

"Those are the ropes and counter weights that open and close the windows. Here, I'll show you how they work." As he opened the window, the strong breeze carried fragrance from the luscious roses growing in the garden below.

"Here I can keep you and Jaffe safe like a real plantation owner. Did you know, Catherine that not so long ago plantation families escaped the heavy summer heat and mosquitoes by moving to Summerville? That's why they started moving north of Charleston back in the early 1700s. The pine-ridged landscape sheltered the first colony. Then, early 1800s, the railroad came through and progress took over."

"Thanks for the history lesson, Carter. I see you've been reading my history books again. Well, I did some reading about Summerville myself, darling."

"I can assure you that life in Summerville promises the totally opposite of what we just put behind us in Korea." Carter's off hand remark brought us immediately back to reality and the stressful ordeals of the past months. "Thank God we are home safely, and Jaffe's well! I hope we never have to go through anything like that again, Carter."

"Me too, Catherine, but I know the rest of our lives together will be perfect. We will have a good life together here in Summerville."

The one thing Carter and I absolutely agreed on in 1968 was that this colonial town still had a simplicity and southern gentile atmosphere—the perfect place to heal our souls and watch our children grow.

6
Peter

Jaffe was thrilled with his room overlooking the gardens. The blossoms and shrubs were his playground, and he loved playing hide and seek there. His playmates were a mixture of girls and boys his own age. He knew no strangers and spoke to everyone; he was confident and happy. Jaffe was even more elated when he heard the news about a new baby joining our family. As the weeks and months passed, he was full of questions. "The baby will come out of my tummy around the beginning of August, Jaffe. The weather will be very, very hot then. You will go and stay with Granny and Granddaddy while Mama is in the hospital. Daddy will bring you to see the baby and then Mama and the new baby will come home to be with you and Daddy."

"Is the baby a brother or sister, Mama?"

"I don't know, honey."

"I do…it's a brother. I want a brother. I'm going to have a brother to play football with me."

"Go get your bathing suit on. It's low tide and we're going down to the beach for a swim today."

As I sat in my chair, the hot June breeze blew my hair into my eyes. I was so thankful we had a house at Folly Beach. Watching the lapping waves of the Atlantic Ocean, I wondered about the child growing inside me. "Maybe this one is a girl…I hope she has Carter's blue eyes like Jaffe. What'll we name her?"

"Come dig with me, Mama!" I waddled toward the surf and carefully lumbered down into the sand. I felt like the Loggerhead turtle I'd seen when I was just a girl. I could still remember it vividly. We were out at Seabrook Island around nine o'clock one evening. Daddy had taken us there to look for the Loggerhead. We were holding flashlights near the base of the dunes. "Keep your eyes wide open girls. I know this is the spot. She'll return here if she's coming, I saw her here two years ago. It's nesting time again. " I turned and looked toward the water. There she was, crawling out of the ocean heading up the beach near the high tide line. You could see her tracks in the sand. She stopped right at the base of the dune and started scraping a hole with her flippers. Her three-hundred-pound body labored over the sand. All of a sudden, she stopped scraping. We watched in amazement as she laid about one hundred fifty golf ball-sized eggs in her nest. Then, she used her flippers to cover her eggs with sand. No sooner had she finished covering them and she was off…lumbering back to the sea. The whole process took her less than an hour. No one would have ever known she had been there, except for her two sets of tracks that told her story.

Building a castle in the edge of the sand is hard work when you feel the size of a Loggerhead, but it's even more difficult with an active two-and-a-half year old. "Not a bad construction job, if I say so myself," Carter said as he joined us on the beach after work. Watching his hands cup the sand and mold it into perfect towers, I knew his castle would really out shine mine—particularly in the eyes of our son. "Let's add a mote and tower over here, son! Do you have some soldiers we can station on the edge?" Carter was enjoying his construction much more than Jaffe. "You're a great builder, Daddy. I want to be just like you." As the medieval structure grew, my weary body grew restless. "I'm going inside and start dinner."

Waddling up the sandy boardwalk, I felt the baby stirring…pushing downward. "You still have a while my little one, it's way too early." I watched as Carter and Jaffe continued to build on the shoreline. The evening sun was a bright orange ball moving toward the west. Just as I started peeling the fresh shrimp that Carter had picked up from Crosby's the phone rang. Quickly grabbing a rag, I picked up the phone. "Hello."

"Hi! How are you feeling?"

"Hi, Beth…I'm okay but this baby's really growing. It's good to hear from you. What's going on?"

"I thought that maybe you and Jaffe could drive to Mount Pleasant for lunch tomorrow with Ann and me. Ann's missing her little cousin. We can go to the village antique shops and Mrs. Cramer's. She just put out some of the most gorgeous plants and flowers. We'll go there after lunch just before you leave. How about lunch at that new Greek deli on the corner? I hear they have great gyros almost as good as the Continental Cupboard in Summerville."

"Yum, a gyro sounds awesome. How does ten o'clock sound?"

"Great, see you, little sis."

"I don't feel so little. 'Bye."

"Y'all were certainly busy on that beach this afternoon, boys. Did you have a good time? "Yes, Mama, Daddy's a good builder!"

"Carter, will you bathe Jaffe while I start frying the shrimp?"

"Sure, honey. Come on, son! Let's get cleaned up."

"Yum your shrimp are the best in town, Catherine! You should open a restaurant."

"Someday, I may do just that! Beth called while you boys were on the beach. She wants Jaffe and me to come to Mount Pleasant tomorrow. We're going shopping and out to lunch. It'll probably be late when we get home."

"That's okay, because I promised Len that I'd go fishing with him after work. Y'all go and have a good time but do be careful!"

After dinner the three of us snuggled as we watched a little TV before putting Jaffe to bed. "Honey, check out this moon?" Putting his arm around me, Carter drew me closer and started rubbing my enormous belly. "The moon is gorgeous, but you are just as gorgeous, and our baby will be, too." We sat in a long silence before I said anything. "When are we going back to Summerville? I could stay here forever."

"I know, Catherine, but I need to finish the wallpaper in the nursery. Why don't we go back next Wednesday and then we'll come here for July fourth."

"Okay. I'll invite Beth and Greg to join us for a cookout; I've already asked Mama and Daddy. Do you want any of your family to come?"

"No! I'm tired…let's go to bed." I lay in bed listening to the ocean. In the stillness, I felt the life stirring in my body just like the waves of the ocean. I could almost hear the baby whispering to me.

The next day my sister greeted me with "You're getting really big! "

"Thanks, Beth! You're so thoughtful. Let's go shopping." After several hours waddling around Mount Pleasant, I needed a break. "I'm exhausted. I just love my tea table even though it's a reproduction. Beth, your corner cabinet is going to fit perfectly in the kitchen. Jaffe, stop taking Ann's doll!"

"Are you ready for your usual gyro, Catherine?"

"Sure. Do you think they'll have something plain enough for the kids?"

"I brought snacks just in case Ann gets too fussy. You know how picky she is about eating."

"This is a really good gyro, but not quite as good as the Continental Cupboard. What do you think? "My goodness, do you think they piled on enough feta today? Look at this salad." Looking at Jaffe, I couldn't help but smile. He had the gyro sauce running down his chin. "Jaffe certainly seems to be enjoying his gyro."

"Save room for the baklava, it's perfectly delicious," Beth advised.

After the absolutely marvelous lunch, we drove to Mrs. Cramer's to fill the car with plants. From there it was on to Pennington Place down in the Old Village of Mount Pleasant. This quaint Victorian neighborhood was almost a duplicate of Summerville only it had a fantastic view of the harbor. Shrimp boats, fishermen and aristocracy dated back at least three hundred years. Yawning, I stood. "It's getting late…I think I'll head back to the beach. We're moving back to Summerville next week, but July fourth is just around the corner so we're having a cookout back at the beach. Can y'all come, Beth? It'll be fun, and the kids can play all day. Please come!"

"I'll check with Greg, but I'm sure we'll be there. What can I bring?"

"How about a salad? Bring Greg's mother, too."

"A salad it is. I'll ask Marla. I'm certain she'll join us, but why don't you give her a call? You know how she is about etiquette."

"I'll give her a call tomorrow. Thanks for such a great day. I had fun and I know Jaffe did, too…give Aunt Beth a kiss good bye, Jaffe."

As we climbed into the well-worn Mercedes, I put Jaffe into his car seat, and knew he'd be asleep in seconds. Driving over the Cooper River Bridge, I thought again of my childhood. I remembered crouching on the floor of Daddy's Studebaker afraid to look out the window. "It's okay, Khaki, one day you'll drive over this bridge yourself." I could hear Daddy's voice as if he were in the seat next to me.

Carter was cleaning fish when we pulled into the sandy driveway. He wiped his hands and came to get Jaffe. "I think the new baby likes to shop. It's been moving all day. Feels like it's doing somersaults. Do you mind unloading the car for me? I'm pooped." After dinner we sat looking out at the ocean and listening to lapping waves. Carter put his hand on my stomach, waiting for movement from the baby but there was nothing. "Do you think the baby is asleep or just doesn't like me?"

"Oh Carter, don't be silly. Of course the baby likes you. I could sit out here all night, couldn't you?"

We moved back to Summerville the next week and started decorating the nursery. Jaffe was thrilled when he saw the crib and tiny day gowns. "They're dresses, Mommy. I don't want a sister. I want a brother."

"No, they are not dresses, they are day gowns. You wore these, too." The baby will be tiny and these gowns will fit perfectly…in fact, they'll be too big."

By the first of July, I was more than miserable. As I slowly packed our things to head back to the beach, I realized I hadn't felt the baby move in quite a while. Trying not to panic, I decided not to mention a word to Carter. "Let's not go to the beach until the fourth, honey."

"Are you okay? I thought you couldn't wait to go back."

"I can't but I'm just tired. We'll stay a few days after the fourth."

July third was scorching in Summerville. In the early evening when Carter put Jaffe in his wagon, the temperature still registered in the high 90°s. "We're going for a walk. Do you feel like walking, honey?"

"Let me try and put on my shoes. My feet are really swollen." Walking through the streets gave me a funny feeling, as I slowly put one foot in front of the other, nodding and smiling at our neighbors, I desperately wanted to lie down. "Look at the moon, Mommy. It's as big as my beach ball."

"You're right, Jaffe. That's a full moon." As I looked at the moon, tears welled in my eyes. "What's the matter, Catherine?" Carter asked. I blurted out, "I'm so worried. I haven't felt the baby move in days. I'm afraid something's gone wrong."

"If you don't feel him move by tomorrow, we'll call the doctor. Now come on, let's get you home." The sun was still shining so late in the evenings that Jaffe didn't fall asleep until almost 9:30. After my shower, I lay on the bed like a huge mountain. The soft fabric of my favorite nightgown wrapped gently over my big stomach. Carter dried himself quickly and climbed into bed. He was snoring within seconds.

I couldn't get comfortable so I tried to lie on my side to peek out at the moon. Its brightness gazed back at me between the blinds. In the stillness, I felt a slight tickling sensation inside my tummy. Softly, gently the sensation interrupted my thoughts, had I imagined it, or was it real? The tickling continued. "There it is again," I breathed. I grabbed Carter's watch from the dresser and stared at the glowing hands. The green arrows ticked by for two hours before I woke Carter.

"Something's going on. Wake up," I whispered. "Oh, Catherine, you've had false labor before...not again! Go to sleep."

"The tickles are regular and ten minutes apart. Carter, I'm positive I'm in labor. Hand me the phone book, please."

"It's almost midnight. Who are you calling?"

"Dr. Pinckney!"

"Go to sleep, Catherine."

"Go to hell, Carter!" I shouted as I threw the phone book across the room and started to cry. Groggy and in shock at my behavior, Carter got up. "I'm sorry, honey. You know I don't wake up easily."

"You'd wake up better if you didn't drink so much Jack Daniels."

"Let me hold the watch." Carter put his hand on my stomach and peered at the green arrows of his watch for over half an hour. "I think we'd better call Dr. Pinckney's service and see who is on call."

My fingers trembled as I dialed the number, I could hardly breathe. "Who's on call, please?"

"Dr. Pinckney." A huge sigh escaped as I responded, "Would you have him call me please. This is Catherine Duvall." Within minutes the phone rang. "Hello?"

"Catherine, what's going on?"

"Hey, Dr. Pinckney." I explained the tickling and then I heard. "You're not due for another month but you're certainly big enough to have twins. It would be just like you to ruin this party I'm having here at the beach. Get yourself on down to Saint Francis and have the nurse check you out, if you're really in labor, she'll give me a call." Totally unprepared for an early delivery, I frantically packed a suitcase for the baby and me and tiptoed into Jaffe's room to gather his things.

As I dialed Mama and Daddy's number, I looked at the clock: two o'clock, "I'm sorry to wake you but we're on our way to the hospital. We'll going to drop Jaffe on the way if that's okay. See you in thirty minutes." Carter came into the room with a worried look on his face. "Catherine, when is the last time you had gas put in the car?"

"I don't remember. Why?"

"Well, the light is on and there are no stations opened anywhere in Summerville."

"I'm sorry. What are we going to do?"

"I think I have a little gas in the can out back in the shed. I'll go look."

I watched Carter finagle the gas into the tank and load the bags in the trunk before tucking our sleeping son on to the back seat. Not another car was on the road; it was as if we were the only people on earth. The drive down Trolley Road was haunting: rows of trees loomed over the road.

The headlights of the Mercedes cut through the darkness. As Carter turned left onto Dorchester Road toward Charleston, there was the enormous full moon shining like a beacon. As the rays guided us south, I knew we'd be staying at the hospital. Dr. Pinckney finally arrived around four o'clock in the morning.

"Do you need anything for pain, Catherine?"

"I feel fine…only the tickling in my stomach."

"Well, you're definitely ready to deliver. I'll do the C-section in a little while. Nurse, bring me a pot of coffee, black, I'll have it in here, please."

"You must have been having a big party, Doc."

"It was…I'll finish it after we get this baby here. Carter, do you want to stay in here with Catherine?"

"I'd love to. When Jaffe was born, husbands couldn't be in the room. I felt so lonely and helpless, I hated leaving her."

Dr. Pinckney sat with us, gulping his two pots of coffee before putting on his scrubs and pushing open the doors to the operating room. The nurses wheeled my stretcher out shortly after Dr. Pinckney left the room. "Kiss me."

"You'll be fine, honey. I love you." After the spinal, numbness began to creep over my body. Dr. Pinckney began to touch his sterile, sharp scalpel down the middle of my abdomen. "Can you feel this?"

"Yes." He repeated the same procedure. "How about now?"

"I still feel it."

"Now?"

"Yes."

"Catherine, the spinal should be in full effect by now. I don't understand why it's taking so long…I want to give you some gas."

"No! I want to be awake when the baby comes."

"I'll only give you a few more minutes then." Minutes passed and Dr. Pinckney picked up his scalpel again. "I can still feel that."

"Put the mask on her, Dr. Pinckney said."

I opened my eyes to find Carter standing beside my bed. "It's a girl; tell me it's a girl!"

"Okay, the baby's a girl, Catherine," Carter told me before the drugs knocked me completely out again.

Many hours later, I woke up to see my mother, Carter and the nurse standing over me. "Hi. How's my baby?"

"Beautiful, honey!"

"It's really a boy isn't it?"

"Yes, Christopher Peter Duvall was born at 7:55 this morning. He weighed six pounds, one ounce and was nineteen inches long." Then, the nurse said, "You need to rest, Mrs. Duvall, the gas made you hallucinate, so we decided not to argue with you. You've been screaming and saying really foolish things."

"Can I see him?"

"He's in an incubator right now because he's having a little trouble breathing. His pediatrician, Dr. Adams, wants him to stay in there a while longer. He's worried about the baby's lungs…it's just precautionary. I'll bring him in as soon as I can, Mrs. Duvall. You rest now."

"Thanks, nurse. What's your name?"

"Andrea."

"Thanks, Andrea."

It seemed like years before Andrea brought Peter into my room. As I unfolded the soft white covers swaddled around my tiny infant, I began the inspection. His thin little arms and legs were perfect, and I started counting each finger and toe. His big eyes were a bluish gray and staring right into mine, as if they knew all my secrets. "He's perfect, Carter as gorgeous as can be, just like you said! I believe he looks like Daddy, or maybe it's Mama?"

"I think he looks like you, Catherine, but I do see a resemblance to Jaffe. Maybe he looks like me, too."

"He's so alert," Mama chimed in. I'll bet he's going to be a politician—born on the fourth of July."

"That's right…it's a holiday. Y'all were coming to the beach so what's happening now?"

"I'm staying with you, honey. Your Daddy's keeping Jaffe, and he'll bring him down to see his brother later. I've called everyone else. Don't worry about anything."

"Oh, is Jaffe excited? He wanted a brother so badly."

"Your father said, 'Jaffe is jumping through hoops!' I'm going home to join them now so give me a kiss. "Love you, Mama."

"Love you, too!"

Peter and I stayed in the hospital for nine days. Thankfully, his breathing improved dramatically. The doctor explained to me that babies get a covering over their lungs and that it's still there when they're born prematurely, but usually disappears in time. He said that's what President Kennedy's son died from. "Let me hold him, Mama!"

"Sit down first and I'll put Peter in your arms, son." Watching my two young sons sitting there together, I felt as if my heart was the size of the enormous July moon. I was about to burst with pride and love for two miracles. As I beamed with joy, tears began to stream down my cheeks. "Catherine, what is the matter with you?" Carter had just come inside to see how we were adjusting. "Nothing! You wouldn't understand. It's just a girl thing."

"Well, quit crying before you scare the boys."

My emotional moment immediately came to an abrupt end because I knew that Carter thought crying was a sign of weakness. He said many times, "My mother cried and yelled all the time—particularly when she wasn't taking her meds. Please don't be like her, Catherine."

Peter was such an adorable baby. Jaffe had been a perfect baby, but Peter's toothless grin enchanted everyone. We saw a different side of him once he began solid foods. "Hurry, get his food warm before he wakes up, Carter. You know how he screams between bites, let's be ready for him." This was the only demanding trait he seemed to have. He would coo, giggle, and nestle closely, offering love and comfort to Jaffe as well as the rest of us. "Mama, Peter is such a good brother."

"I know, Jaffe. He's so happy to be with us."

Life was good and moving ahead happily until that August when I started feeling nauseous, morning, noon, and night. I could hardly hold my head up. "Are you sure you're not pregnant, Catherine?"

"I'm sure Carter. I must have a virus."

"I think you probably need to see a doctor."

"If I don't feel better soon, I'll go to Dr. Pinckney." That night the pain in my chest was so sharp that I imagined it was like a heart attack would feel. I was afraid to fall asleep because I didn't want to die at the age of twenty-five. "Catherine, I'm sending you straight to the hospital. I'm ordering blood test and x-rays. You'll be staying for a few days."

"But Dr. Pinckney, the baby is only six weeks old. I can't leave him, now."

"You can and you will, now call Carter to come and get you."

"Everything is going to be okay, Catherine. Your parents are staying with the boys, and Bessie Lou's there, too. Worry only about you and get well," Carter ordered as he sat down to watch TV.

Just then Dr. Pinckney walked into the room looking very grim. "All of the results aren't in but I can confirm that you have hepatitis. It takes a while to present itself and I'm worried that it will cause liver damage. You could have gotten it while you were in the hospital, perhaps when the nurses couldn't get your IVs going properly. The needles could have gotten contaminated. I'm going to keep you here at least a week, and then you'll have bed rest for several weeks or months."

"I can't do that, Dr. Pinckney; I have to take care of my boys."

"Catherine, if you don't do as I say, your boys may lose their mother. This is very serious. Now, promise me you'll follow my advice."

"I promise. But I want to go home real soon."

The weeks following my hospital stay were horrible because I couldn't even pick up Peter or Jaffe. I could only rest, read, and watch TV needless to say that I was bored out of my mind watching Bessie Lou caring for my boys. Thankfully Dr. Pinckney gave me a clean bill of health by October, but still wanted me to keep things slowly. He said no more birth control pills because of liver damage. "Well, what am I suppose to do now? You know Carter won't use anything, it's against our faith."

"I can put in an IUD, Catherine."

"What's that?"

"An internal uterine device, it blocks the sperm and is 99% effective."

"Okay. Let's do it, but don't tell Carter."

Halloween was perfect with my two spooks tricking and treating as Carter carried Jaffe door to door while I passed out treats at our door, holding Peter in his bumble bee suit. He made quite a buzz at the door and all of the adults made such a fuss over him.

Halloween turned into Thanksgiving, Thanksgiving into Christmas and Christmas into the New Year, 1970. As all young couples do, Carter, the children and I transformed into a perfect little family.

Summerville was flourishing and its lazy southern atmosphere still yawned and stretched, separating the bedroom community from the hustle of industry so near in Charleston. The first annual Flower Festival was scheduled for April that year when the southern gardens are glorious for all to see. The park consisted of acres of magnolias, camellias and bushy azaleas that climbed to the height of small trees. The large bushes billowed with blooms of lavender, salmon, rose, flame, pink, red, and white as the tea olives, gardenias and jasmine scented the air. A perfect garden set right in the middle of Summerville, a garden ready to attract visitors and to collect needed revenues. The event began on a Friday afternoon and continued through Sunday.

Carter and I took the boys for a walk through Flower Park on that Saturday in April. It was a dazzling spring day for a walk in the park. People wandered through the booths examining the merchandise, buying flowers, herbs, and produce. The aroma from the food vendors made us ravenous. Jaffe wanted a hot dog, Carter and I wanted a barbecue sandwich and iced tea. The boys and I found a table for four while Carter bought lunch. Peter who was now eight months old and always starving began to fuss. The diaper bag was filled with jars of carrots and applesauce for him. Opening his food, before he had a chance to get louder, I heard someone slide onto the bench beside me. "Hey there, Catherine, how are you? The boys are really growing and they're so adorable."

"Well, hey there, yourself, Miss Lavenia. How are you doing? Do you have a booth here? How are things going at your shop?"

"I'm fine, a little tired but I came down here to see what all the excitement's about. I have enough trouble keeping up with the shop so there's no way I could manage a booth, too. I've missed seeing you at the shop, where have you been?"

"Home with the boys and helping Carter manage his rental properties."

"I need some help at the shop, doing a little rearranging and fixing up myself. You interested?"

"Well, I'd love to but I don't have anyone to keep the boys right now."

"You can come in the evening when the shop's closed or when Carter's home with them."

"Let me talk with him and I'll let you know."

"Hello, Miss Lavenia! Oozing with charm, Carter gave her a big hug. "How are you getting along? How's Clem?"

"I'm fine but Clem had another bout with his back. He really suffers."

"Tell him I send my regards."

"I will, Carter. Now I'll get out of here and let you young folks get back to your eating. Catherine, kiss those precious boys for me."

"I will, Miss Lavenia, and I'll come see you soon."

"Daddy, where's my ketchup?"

"Right here, Jaffe. Catherine, what's the matter with Peter? He's always so good."

"The carrots aren't hot and you know how he likes his food. Let him try one of Jaffe's fries maybe that will calm him down."

Peter squashed the fry between his fingers and shoved little pieces into his mouth, immediately crying for another. "I do believe this child is a bottomless pit, Carter. What are we going to do when he gets older?"

"I'm sure he'll out grow it. Let's finish eating before he's ready for his nap."

Carter carried the boys' home and left me at the antiques auction over at the Bird's Nest Inn. A newcomer to Summerville had recently purchased the property and its contents and everything inside was up for auction. Daddy and Mama were to meet me there at two o'clock. As I meandered through the rooms, I stopped before an etching of ships sailing in the fog. I shivered as if the ghosts of the past were holding my hand and guiding me to a purchase. The longer I looked at it, the more the ships entranced me as I counted them. The fog was so thick and it seemed as though the ships were moving right toward me. "There you are, Catherine, Mama and I have been looking all over for you."

"Hey, Daddy, where's Mama?"

"I had to sit her down over there in that room, she needed some oxygen. She has her number, so you know we'd better hurry and get there before the bidding starts."

"Okay, but first tell me what you think of this picture?"

"Looks like it's been sitting over a radiator, see all the discoloring on the glass. I can barely see anything in it. Why?"

"You don't like it, do you, Daddy?"

"Well, I think it's pretty interesting."

"I find it very soothing and mysterious."

"There you go with that mystery crap. Come on, let's join your Mama."

Daddy wandered off to inspect the rest of the auction items. Mama got ready for the auction by taking out her oxygen tube and sneaking to the bathroom to smoke a cigarette. "I thought you were going to quit. Does Daddy know?"

"Of course not, Bessie Lou buys them for me, and don't you tell him."

"Mama, they're killing you. Don't you want to live a long time?"

"Those butchers told me I wouldn't live ten years and that was when you were ten, Catherine. You're now twenty-five, and I'm going stronger than ever. If they keep giving me morphine for pain, I'll out last all of you. Now, be a good girl and go get your father, the bidding's about to start."

My parents and I bought our fair share of the beautiful antiques that day before I heard, "It's almost five o'clock, Truman, time for my shot."

"Okay, Rachel. I'll give it to you in the car before we go to Catherine's."

After we settled our account with the cashier, we moseyed to Daddy's new Chevy. I thanked the Lord that he'd finally stopped driving a Studebaker. Daddy gave Mama her morphine, and we drove to my house to give Carter a description of our bargains.

"Hi, honey. Did you get anything?"

"Carter, I hope you won't be angry but I bought a whole lot of things. A dresser for Peter, iron twin beds for the boys, a desk for you, and a picture for all of us."

"Where are they?"

"You'll have to go back this evening or tomorrow with a truck and bring them home. Mama and Daddy bought a rocking horse for Peter and a train for Jaffe. We hurried back here because Mama and Daddy wanted to visit with the boys before they go home to Charleston."

It was time for the boys to eat dinner and Mama wanted to feed Peter. "I'll get everything nice and hot and give it to you Mama; you know how he screams between bites if it's not warm enough."

"Hello, darling boy! You're the sweetest child. Don't you think he looks like my side of the family, Catherine?"

"I do…but I think he has a long trunk like Daddy, and there's something about his mannerisms that are definitely Daddy's."

"Come on, big boy; open your mouth for your Granny. Look at that grin! You look just like a cherub. My goodness, you're hungry. Come here, Jaffe. Do you want to help Granny feed your brother? That's right, now fill the spoon again."

"Glad to see you're using your sterling, Catherine, remember to keep it polished because I always have."

"Yes ma'am."

As my parents left my house that day, I had empathy for my mother and sadness for my father. I watched as they drove out of the drive, choking back tears before I went back to my adorable little family. Carter gave the boys a bath before we read stories and kissed them goodnight. Tiptoeing out of Peter's room, I whispered to him. "If all children could be a sweet as you are, I'd pray for a dozen."

"What were you whispering?"

"Oh nothing, honey, I'm just telling him how much I love him. Is Jaffe asleep?"

"He's waiting on you to kiss him."

"Are you ready to go night, night, big boy?"

"Yes, Mama and I brushed my teeth and said my prayers with Daddy."

"Good night, my sweet child. I love you very much."

"I love you, too. Mama, why does Granny smoke cigarettes?"

"Who told you Granny smokes?"

"She smells like smoke. I asked Granddaddy why and he told me that she smokes in the bathroom but doesn't want anyone else to know. He said she doesn't even know that he knows it. He said I should keep this secret."

"I think I'll have a talk with Granddaddy tomorrow, son, don't you worry about it tonight. Just close your beautiful blue eyes and get some sleep, and tomorrow I'll take you to visit Miss Lavenia's shop and we'll get you a new toy or something for your room."

Carter left for work before seven o'clock on Monday and called at noon to check on all of us. "How are the boys? What time will they be up from their naps?"

"Around three and then I'm going to take them to the Ole' Towne Shop to buy some gifts and see Miss Lavenia. I'll tell her that you agreed to the decorating after hours."

"Catherine, don't forget that I invited the Scotts and the Cuthbertsons for dinner on Friday. We'll just cook burgers on the grill."

"Okay. I've got it on the calendar. What time will you be home?"

"Around seven, see you then, my love." As I hung up the phone, Peter began to squeal for his lunch and Jaffe hurriedly got out the food as I warmed the dishes. Together we fed Peter before I put him down for his nap.

While Peter slept, Jaffe and I had a picnic. Just as I started to pour our drinks I felt so lightheaded that I almost dropped the cup. I sat down thinking that I must be catching a virus. I laid out fresh clothes for the boys and dressed myself before going into Peter's' room. He was cooing and babbling silly sounds so I knew he was awake. "You finally decided to wake up. Come here and let me squeeze you before I change you and then we'll get your big brother and go shopping." Jaffe came running out of his room about fifteen minutes later. "Come on Jaf, let's change your clothes. I want Miss Lavenia to see how handsome you are."

Miss Lavenia's historic home was located just across the railroad tracks. The grounds were accented with arbors covered in trumpet vines and Confederate jasmine and the scent of the jasmine was breathtaking. Her Bashful Betty statue, nestled amid the Johnny Jump Ups, was always a friendly greeting before climbing the steep staircase. The exquisite shop was on the second floor of her home. Patrons of all ages climbed the wooden steps to hear Lavenia's charming greetings and browse her fine selections displayed throughout the rooms. I waited at the bottom of the steps while Jaffe searched out back for Mr. Clem, who wasn't in his garden today. Peter was so heavy by now that my arms ached as I stood waiting for Jaffe. "I can't find him, Mama, can I taste the Johnny Jump Ups today?"

"Okay, Jaffe, but hurry, your brother's getting really heavy. Here's a pretty Johnny for a handsome boy, pick that one over there. Now, scoot up the stairs and wait for me just inside the door. Don't touch a thing, just wait." Jaffe's tiny feet bounded the stairs with ease as I slowly climbed the staircase. Finally, reaching the top, I carefully opened the glass door.

Jaffe was waiting patiently for me. The bell jingled on the door as it closed but I couldn't move. Shortly, I heard Miss Lavenia. "Catherine, are you all right? Here, let me hold that baby. "I'll be fine in a minute. Peter's so heavy, and I just felt dizzy for a minute."

"Do you feel faint?"

"I don't know, I've never fainted in my life that I can remember."

"How are you, Mr. Jaffe? You're such a fine lad." Taking Jaffe's hand, I heard Miss Lavenia say, "Come on with me, I'll bet we can find a surprise. I'll get you something to drink, Catherine."

Minutes passed as I recomposed myself and went to the center of the shop where Lavenia was rocking Peter and feeding Jaffe cookies. "Thank you so much! I don't know what came over me."

"Maybe you're anemic. You really look pale. I think you should give the doctor a ring just to be safe. Remember you just had that hepatitis."

"You're right, Miss Lavenia. I'll give him a call tomorrow. Do you want to show me what you'd like rearranged? Carter said that he didn't mind if I worked a few evenings."

"That's fantastic! I really need your help. Come on in the back and I'll show you before other customers come in. Let me hold that beautiful child again. Come here, Peter, I'll carry you."

"Jaffe, hold my hand and come with Mama."

Carter came home at seven just as Jaffe was saying his prayers. "God bless Daddy and Mama...and God make Mama not get sick at Miss Lavenia's anymore."

As we sat down to eat our dinner, Carter was staring into my eyes. "What are you doing?"

"Wondering when you're going to tell what Jaffe was praying about."

"Oh, that. It's nothing. I just felt strange after I lugged Peter up that entire flight of stairs. I'm fine, I promise. Eat your dinner before it gets cold."

Early the next morning I called Dr. Pinckney's office. His nurse Mary was always so helpful. "Do you want to talk with him yourself, Catherine?"

"No Mary, just tell him what happened and ask if he thinks I might be anemic."

"I'll give you a call back later, Catherine." The phone rang while I was outside with the boys. Scrambling up the back steps with Peter smiling in my arms, I was breathless as I said, "Hello." Catherine, Dr. Pinckney wants you to come in tomorrow morning and have some blood work done. Can you manage that?"

"Sure, Mary, I'll be there."

"Nothing to eat after midnight and we open at nine." I immediately called Bessie Lou to have her watch the boys.

Carter came home early on Friday to help get the charcoal going so he could grill the burgers. The boys were scrubbed and dressed for bed, and I was in the kitchen fixing appetizers for our guests. With only a few minutes remaining before their arrival, the last thing I wanted to do was answer the phone. "Catherine, I can't get that. Will you answer it?"

"Hello!"

"Catherine, I know it's late, but I just read the results of your blood test."

"Oh! Hello, Dr. Pinckney. Am I anemic?"

"No. You should stay out of the bed, my dear, you're pregnant!"

"How can that be? You put in the IUD."

"Sometimes they don't work. I'll need you to come in next week so I can examine you and determine when the baby is due. How old is Peter now?"

"Nine months."

"Catherine, are you okay?"

"I'm in shock! Yes, I'll see you next week, Dr. Pinckney."

I sat beside the phone staring at the receiver for a long time before Carter came in and found me. "The coals are hot, and everyone will be here in a few minutes. Are you ready, honey?"

"I'll be ready in a minute but first we need to talk."

"About what? Who was on the phone?"

"Dr. Pinckney, I had some tests run this week. I didn't want to worry you, so I didn't tell you."

"Are you sick?"

"No. We're going to have a baby."

"What?" The doorbell rang and I left Carter standing there with his mouth wide open as I went to answer the door.

After our guests left, Carter and I stood watching our two sons sleeping. "They looked so innocent and sweet. Do you think this one will be a girl, Catherine?"

"It doesn't matter anymore. Let's just pray for its health and strength."

7
Drayton

Dr. Pinckney estimated the baby was due on Christmas day, but warned us I might miscarry because the IUD was still in place and couldn't be removed and it could even cause a birth defect. As I was leaving his office, I heard him swearing to another patient whose fallopian tubes he'd tied the same day he inserted my IUD. "I don't know how this could have happened. We'll have to x-ray, you must have an extra tube. You already have five children! Oh well, number six will join the family on Christmas day." He turned to his nurse Mary and exclaimed, "Lord, I'm really having a bad day!"

Carter and I began to prepare the boys for a new sibling. They were as pleased as any youngsters could be. Peter was too young to care, and Jaffe was as inquisitive as ever. "Where will the baby sleep, Mama?"

"Well, we'll move Peter into the room with you and put the new baby in the crib in the nursery."

"Peter can sleep with me?"

"That's right, but he'll have his own crib in your room."

"Oh boy, how much longer is it 'til Christmas?"

"Three more months. Say them with me, Jaffe...October, November, December."

By Thanksgiving I felt like I was the size of a cow again. Having two babies in such a short time was definitely taking its toll on my body. "Catherine, I promise you that you still look beautiful."

"You're so sweet; Carter, but I can't even see my toes. I'm huge!"

"It's not much longer. You can lose the weight in the new year." When is Dr. Pinckney going to set the date for the C-section?"

"Next visit, I'm going to take a nap. Will you watch the boys?" I could hear Carter, Jaffe, and Peter softly laughing and giggling as I drifted off under my down comforter. As my eyes began closing, I saw my enormous abdomen reaching toward the ceiling and the baby gave me a tremendous kick. I turned on my side and smiled as I whispered, "I love you, too."

On December 17, Mama and Daddy came to stay with the boys while Carter drove me to the hospital. The C-section was scheduled for early morning on the eighteenth but Dr. Pinckney promised me he'd have me home for Christmas day if I'd agree to the date. He wanted to go hunting and would be gone for several days afterward. "Will you be okay tonight, Catherine? I'm going home with the boys but I'll be here by seven in the morning."

"I'll be fine, Carter, give me a kiss." As Carter put his arms around me, I felt a sudden feeling of sadness. "Don't forget to kiss the boys goodnight for me."

I watched Christmas specials on TV until I finally fell asleep. Abruptly, I woke up just after midnight with an excruciating backache. "Nurse, can you give me something for my backache?"

"Mrs. Duvall, you can't have anything after midnight."

"But, I'm in pain!"

"I'm sorry, doctor's orders."

I climbed out of the bed and began to walk, pacing around my room and up and down the hall. As the sun began to rise, I gazed out of the window. In the parking lot below my window I saw Dr. Pinckney getting out of his car completely camouflaged in his hunting clothes and he was showing Carter his rifles. I turned as the nurse entered and said, "It's time to get you prepped. Dr. Pinckney's on his way up."

"I know. I just saw him."

"Yep, he's in a hurry to go hunting. How's your back feeling?"

"It's still killing me." Carter and Dr. Pinckney arrived at my room together: one as tall and thin as a tree and the other as short as his French ancestors. Carter kissed me, "How are you feeling?"

"My back's killing me!"

"Let me examine you, Catherine. Carter, do you mind waiting outside?"

"Well, Catherine, it's a good thing we chose this date, you're ready to deliver right now. Your baby picked its own birth date; I'd better get you into the operating room right away."

"Please let me stay awake and see my baby this time."

"I'll do my best."

As the doctors put on their masks, they joked with me about Dr. Pinckney. Dr. Richards said, "Catherine, you'd better hope a bird doesn't fly by that window because I'm afraid that he'll follow it and forget where he's cutting." As everyone laughed, I looked at the clock: eight o'clock. Dr. Pinckney began his incision on my stomach as I stared straight up at the ceiling. The overhead mirrors had been turned so I couldn't watch the surgery. The doctors began moving rapidly, and then Dr. Pinckney handed the nurse something to rinse. She handed it back to him and then I saw a baby's head coming up...then I heard a soft cry. "It's a boy, isn't it?" I heard myself say. "You have a beautiful baby boy, Catherine." Then, Dr. Pinckney handed me the object the nurse had given back to him. "Here's your IUD, the baby had it in his hand."

I was briefly allowed to see my gorgeous son before I was given a sedative and I heard voices trailing through the air as I drifted off to sleep.

I woke up hours later with Carter sitting beside my bed. "Hi, did you have a nice rest, Catherine? The baby is so tiny. He only weighs five pounds, twelve ounces. He's so cute and I'm so proud of you," Carter whispered as he kissed my lips. "I want to see him. Can I see him now?"

"Let's ask the nurse," Carter said as he pressed the call button. "May I help you?"

"Mrs. Duvall is awake and would like to see our son."

"She'll have to wait awhile; the doctors are in with him now."

"What's wrong with him, Carter?"

"Nothing honey, don't you worry." I watched drowsily as Carter paced the room with his arms folded across his chest, trying to hide his worry.

After what seemed like forever, Dr. Adams came into my room looking very concerned. He looked at both of us sadly. "Your son is struggling to breathe because his tiny lungs still have a partial covering over them, it's called Hylums membrane. It's the same condition that Peter had but if we can keep him breathing and stable until the membrane disappears, he'll be just fine. Right now it's a little uncertain but I believe I can keep him strong. I've called in several experts on his condition; Dr. Marsh and Dr. McNeil are with him now. Have you named the baby yet?"

"His name is Drayton Carter Duvall," we chimed together. Dr. Adams scribbled down the baby's name and left us clinging together in devastating silence. "A priest, get Father O'Malley." I whispered the words so softly that I wasn't sure I'd actually said anything. "Do you want Drayton baptized?"

"Uh, huh, please, I'll go call now and your Mama and Daddy."

"I think you should call your family, too, Carter."

"You try to get some rest," Carter said as he left the room. The nurse came in just as the door was shutting. "I've got a shot for you, my dear, it'll help you rest." She put the needle right into my thigh, gave me a rub and took off through the door.

Hours later, I woke up in darkness with the sound of whispering voices in my room. "Well, hello, sleepy head. Look who's here."

"Who's here, Carter?"

"Father O'Malley."

"Hello, Catherine. How are you feeling?" Father O'Malley said with his beautiful white teeth showing as he smiled. "I'm better now that you're here. How's the baby, Carter?"

"The doctors are still with him, they haven't left his side, honey. Your Mama and Daddy are down at the nursery, too. The boys are with Bessie."

"Did you call your family, Carter?"

"Father O'Malley and I will talk to you later about them."

"Okay, I guess."

"Father O'Malley, will you baptize Drayton?"

"I'm waiting on the doctors to give me time for the sacrament, they said it wouldn't be much longer. Let's bow our heads in prayer." As we all bowed our heads, I couldn't help but wonder what Carter's family had said.

Just as we had made the sign of the cross and said amen, Dr. Adams entered the room. "Father O'Malley, you can baptize the baby now, come to the nursery with me."

"Is he getting worse?" I asked as tears slowly splattered onto the white sheets. "There's no change, Catherine, keep praying for the best. We're doing everything possible." Dr. Adams put his arms around me. "Try to take care of yourself and get stronger; all of the boys need you."

As Father O'Malley left with Dr. Adams, Mama and Daddy came into my room. Mama was gasping for air and Daddy fidgeted with the change in his pocket. "The baby's so precious but he's very small. He has an olive completion and dark hair and looks so different from his brothers but very beautiful. I do believe he looks like Carter and Daddy, Catherine." Mama gasped as she began fussing with the covers on my bed while Daddy fluffed my pillows. "Everything's going to be fine, honey, don't you worry," Daddy whispered as he put his huge hand on my shoulder. "Father O'Malley will do his job, God will watch over Drayton."

"I'm so glad you're both here...thanks for coming." Tears rolled down my cheeks. "I know Carter's glad you're here, too. Aren't you, honey?"

"I certainly am. You know that I feel as though you are my parents, too."

"We love you as our son, Carter," Mama said as she gave him a kiss.

"Have you seen your parents yet?"

"Yes, while Catherine was sleeping I ran by to tell them about Drayton's fragile condition. Mother had taken her medication and didn't want to see me, and my father proceeded to tell me that they'd raised five boys and really didn't care about my children...especially since I had married Catherine against their wishes. Father said that I didn't need to see him or mother again."

"Oh Carter, I'm so sorry. Why didn't you tell me sooner?"

"No need to cry over them, we've got enough to worry about. I don't want you worrying about me." My parents hugged Carter hard and reassured him of their love, while I grew angrier with my in-laws. Father O'Malley rejoined our group just in time to see our sadness. "My goodness, what's going on in here? I just baptized your son, but you all look as if he has just left this world to be with our Heavenly Father."

"They just found out about my conversation with my father, Father."

"I see, Carter. Now, how are we going to deal with this? You all know that Carter's mother is physically and perhaps mentally ill and his father has his own peculiarities so let's focus our energy on baby Drayton because he should be the only concern right now. We'll deal with the other branch of Duvall's later. I've got to go, but I'll be back to check on Drayton and all of you."

"Thank you, Father. Give me a hug, please?"

"I'd love to, Catherine. Please try to stay positive and keep yourself together." Father O'Malley gave me a tremendous hug and blessed all of us before leaving.

Mama and Daddy went home to the boys. Carter settled down in the chair beside my bed and fell fast asleep. The nurses were in and out of the room all night making sure I was comfortable. I watched as they scurried in and out, but my thoughts were only of my tiny son lying helplessly in the nursery. Sleep was out of the question. I had to stay awake to help pull Drayton through until the morning.

Around seven o'clock the next morning, when I asked the nurse about Drayton I heard, "I'm sorry. I can't give you any information. Your pediatrician will come by to see you in a few minutes and I believe I saw Dr. Pinckney heading down this way a few seconds ago." Carter sat straight up in his chair, yawned, and headed for the bathroom as I started shaking all over. My hands were as cold as if they'd been in a bowl of ice. "Carter, hurry, come out here with me, I'm so afraid."

"I'm right here, honey...we'll get through this together." Carter put his arm tightly around me as I trembled and tears flowed down my cheeks.

The door opened widely and there stood Dr. Adams and Dr. Pinckney. I tried to stop sobbing, but the tears continued to flow and my body tensed all over. Then I noticed the gleam in Dr. Adams' eyes as he held a tiny bundle swaddled so tightly that I couldn't see anything but the blanket. As he came closer, I saw two tiny eyes peeking out meeting mine. "The membrane's gone, he's fine...meet your son, Catherine and Carter."

"Oh, my God, are you sure, Dr. Adams?"

"I'm positive." I started unfolding the layers of the blanket, touching each little finger and toe. "He's beautiful, perfectly gorgeous."

"Everyone in the nursery will agree with you, Catherine," Dr. Pinckney declared with pride. "I hurried back to see how you're holding up."

"I'll be fine now." When did you get back from hunting?"

"Late last night. Now, I want you to hold him for a while and then both you and Carter need to get some rest. Carter probably needs to go home for a while and check on the boys."

"Will you let me go home for Christmas?"

"I'll do my best but it depends on Drayton's progress so I'll see you in the morning."

I was so busy inspecting Drayton that I didn't see Dr. Pinckney leave but Dr. Adams was assuring us that Drayton was going to be fine. The next few days passed slowly as I sat up in the chair, tried walking often, but Christmas Eve arrived and I was still in the hospital. Fortunately, Santa had prepared for his visit to our house earlier in the previous months. "Nurse, have you seen Dr. Pinckney yet?"

"No, Mrs. Duvall, I'm not sure he's coming in today. We have very few patients and everybody has gone home for the holidays."

"Everybody but me that is, I shouted! Is there any way you can call him? I want to go home, too."

"Okay, I'll see what I can do."

Christmas specials on TV were playing every tune from *The Night before Christmas* to *Frosty the Snowman* while I sat in the room staring at the walls, trying not to be anxious. I longed to have my three sons at home and watch their tiny faces glow with the excitement of Christmas. Carter called time after time to find out when I could leave. Just as I began chewing on my fingernails, Dr. Pinckney walked in looking just like Icabod Crane, his long thin legs stretching through the doorway. "Hello, Catherine."

"Hey yourself, can I go home?"

"Well, things have been pretty complicated for you and you've only been here seven days and you still need your staples out."

"Take them out now."

"It's too soon."

"I'll come to your office after Christmas, please!"

"Well, okay if you promise not to pick up anything, including the baby."

"I promise."

"I'll sign the release order but please take care of yourself, my dear."

Carter packed us in the car as if we were made of glass, nestling the baby in my arms before starting the car. "Why are we going this way, Carter?"

"There're fewer bumps in this road. I have been testing different ways of taking you home."

"You're so silly; we're going to be fine, just get us home so I can see Jaffe and Peter. Are they excited over Santa and Drayton?"

"Jaffe is bouncing off the walls, and Peter is into everything as usual. I'm so glad you're coming home but I hope this won't be too much excitement for you."

Bessie was waiting when we reached the house. "Miss Catherine, give me that child," she commanded as she scooped Drayton from my lap. "I have your bed ready." Jaffe and Peter came running to see their new brother, quickly giving me a big hug and kiss. "Let's put him under the Christmas tree and get a picture of all three boys," I said. Carter hurried out to the car to get the camera. They were so darling under that Christmas tree, sparkling like the tinsel that hung above their heads. My emotions took over and the tears began to flow but this time they were tears of joy. Our little family gathered safely near the tree of hope and love. Carter and I didn't speak but our eyes met as we smiled. What could be better? Christmas 1970 was picture perfect indeed.

As the boys grew, Carter and I matured into parents filled with love and affection for our children and were absorbed in all that they did. Our every thought was to ensure their safety and well-being and give them with a perfect life. Neither of us wanted the boys touched by the unpleasant childhood memories that still haunted us.

Carter's mother, Margaret, had neglected him most of his life and because of her irrational outbursts. He would often say, "Catherine, my mother didn't write me once the entire time I was in college and she didn't even come to my graduation. How can a mother do that, Catherine? You're a mother, but I know that you'd never neglect our children." I couldn't give him the answers that he so desperately needed because I didn't understand myself.

Our backgrounds were so different because I led an extremely sheltered and privileged life surrounded by my parents. It wasn't always easy because Mama was sick all the time, and I was taught never to make trouble, smile and pretend everything was delightful—even if it wasn't. Just like the time I had to go to the state mental institution to visit my uncle and I saw grown women with their hair as wild and matted as a rat's nest. Their drab clothes hung from their bony bodies, and they rocked back and forth wailing. Others clung to dolls or stared straight at you with eyes that were empty. I remember walking while clinging to my father because I was terrified. When we finally reached the car that day, Daddy said, "Wasn't it wonderful visiting your uncle today?" I replied my usual, "Yes, Daddy, this really was fun."

Carter and I hid the wounds from our childhood as the boys developed into three wonderful personalities. Jaffe was such a devoted big brother, always available to play and teach his brothers, whether they were learning to play sports or jumping off the roof of the house. He led the way as a charmer who was always busy swinging his arms, a bat, or racing around the yard. He was perpetual motion, only stopping for a night's rest and then Jaffe was in full swing again.

Peter, now our middle child, was filled with love and tenderness, adoring his older and younger brothers. He loved Drayton so much that he'd climb out of his crib at night and sneak into Drayton's room trying to pull him out of his crib. Carter and I were so exasperated about his climbing that I called our pediatrician for advice. "Carter wants to make a lid for Peter's crib but my mother thinks this is cruel. I want both boys safe."

"Catherine, I think a lid is an excellent idea. I know how many times you've found him climbing into drawers and trying to get outside. Just make sure the lid is easy to get off in case of fire."

Drayton, the youngest, was gentle and extremely honest. He adored his older brothers while he struggled to be independent. His dark hair and bronze complexion gave him a magnificence all his own as he was a true combination of Carter and me.

I vividly remember a day when he was about four years old when he picked up the pet carrying cage and said, "Mama, I'm going hunting!"

"Oh you are. Where are you going to go, Drayton, and what are you going to hunt?"

"Down the dirt road over there...I've got some carrots and lettuce and I'll catch a rabbit."

"Well, I'll watch you go but don't go any farther than Mrs. Whaley's house, and don't stay too long. I'll come get you in a few minutes."

"I'm a big boy, Mama," he said as he gave me a big kiss. Our neighbor, a retired Colonel, was outside in his camouflaged fatigues overseeing his lawn when Drayton and I passed. "Hey Catherine, how are you today?' "Fine sir, just taking Drayton to the dirt road, he's going hunting!"

"You be careful down there, soldier."

"Yes, sir, I'm gonna catch me a rabbit." I watched Drayton set his trap, looked at my watch and turned around for home. I had just gone back into the house when I heard a blood-curdling scream.

I reached Drayton just after the Colonel, who had taken charge of the scene. Drayton had decided that he'd had enough hunting as soon as I was out of sight and as he turned to come home he saw a mammoth snake sunning itself across the warm dirt road. Drayton was on the other side of the snake from the Colonel and me. "Don't move, son, just stand still. Your Mama's here with you and I'll be right back. Don't you move either, Catherine." I felt like I was in a war zone as the fatigues rushed past me and I knew I couldn't let Drayton know how much I feared snakes. Just as the Colonel returned with an ax and shovel, I saw Mr. Whaley coming up the dirt road behind Drayton. The Colonel kept creeping closer and closer to the snake as he said, "It's not venomous, Drayton. Do you want me catch it for you?"

"No, sir, I don't want a snake, I want a rabbit."

"What's going on here, young man?"

"I was hunting and this snake wouldn't let me go home, Mr. Whaley."

"I see, well it's a good snake for my garden so the Colonel and I will put it there." As the men shooed the snake toward Mr. Whaley's garden, Drayton ran into my arms sobbing, "I'm never going hunting again, Mama."

This day was a defining moment in my life with my precious young son. A deep and profound calmness came over me that day and I knew Drayton and I would always be close and I also knew that Drayton would hunt again.

As we walked home hand-in-hand again passing the dark gray house on the corner, I wondered about the people who lived in it. I didn't know them but I had seen them strolling along the street. Our local neighborhood gossip, Lydia, told me a grandmother and her grandson lived there and that the boys' mother had given him away because he was mentally delayed. The grandmother had raised him since he was very young but now he was now in his thirties and according to Lydia, quite interested in young children. Lydia warned I should keep a close eye on my boys.

My thoughts were consumed with Lydia's words when I heard Drayton say, "Hello." Standing just a few feet away was the thirty-year-old boy. "Hey, what's your name? "Jack." I turned just in time to see Jack hide something behind a bush. "My name's Drayton. Do you like to go hunting?"

"Come on, Drayton, we need to hurry home."

"'Bye, Jack, it was nice meeting you," I said as I swiftly swept Drayton up and hurried away. "Drayton, you must be careful who you talk to," I chided as walked into the kitchen.

I couldn't wait for Carter to come home from the office because I needed reassurance that everything was beautiful in the world around me. Carter could always calm the emotional roller coaster caused by my extra sensory perception. "Now, Catherine, you know that boy is fine, they've been good neighbors. I haven't seen or heard one thing about Jack."

"Well, you haven't talked with Lydia."

"What has she told you that has proof?"

"She said that he hides knives in bushes but that's all. Nothing else...but!"

"But nothing, don't listen to that bagpipe. She just loves to stir up trouble."

"Okay, but I'm still not convinced."

The days flew by, and the boys grew as fast as weeds. I was busy playing on the tennis team, antique shopping, cooking and working part-time in the evening for Miss Lavenia. Carter stayed busy working, and life was good but still, I had an uneasy sense that something was about to happen.

One day Carter said, "I'll be working late and won't get home until a little before midnight."

"No problem, the boys and I will be fine and I'll wait up for you." Just as Carter left, a tremendous summer storm popped up out of nowhere. "Come on, boys, we're going shopping while it's storming."

"Again Mama? Jaffe questioned."

"Yes. Help me gather up the boys. You know how bored you all get when we stay home so let's get going." The phone started ringing just as I was packing snacks for the boys. "Jaffe, will you answer that?"

"Yes ma'am!"

"Mama, it's for you!"

"Hello, this is Catherine."

"*I am going to kill you,*" I heard the deep voice on the other end say. "*I have a gun and I'm going to kill you.*" I was so startled that I gasped and said, "You must have the wrong number!" slamming down the receiver. "Who was that man, Mama?" I heard Jaffe asking. "It was a wrong number, I'm sure it was, honey! I'm going to call Daddy quickly before we leave."

"No, Mrs. Duvall, he hasn't gotten here yet but I'll have him call the minute he comes in."

"Thanks, I'll wait here until he calls." Pacing the floors quietly, waiting for Carter's call I thought of everyone I knew in the entire world and wondered if any of them might really want to kill me. The sound of the ringing phone startled me. "Catherine, what's wrong? You scared my secretary to death."

"Sorry, but I needed you. Right after you left some man called and when Jaffe answered the phone he asked Jaffe for his mother. When I answered, he said that he had a gun and was going to kill me. I hung up on him after I told him that he had the wrong number." Carter started laughing so hard that I thought he was going to cry. "What's so funny?"

"It's not funny, honey, but I can't believe that you'd tell a would be murderer he has the wrong number."

"What do you think I should do, Carter?"

"What were you going to do?"

"Go shopping because it's storming."

"Well, go shopping, and I'll check on you later but don't stay out too late, please."

I locked all the doors as we left the house. Driving toward the interstate I spotted a police officer on the side of the road and I was still a little uneasy about the phone call so I pulled up behind him. He instantly got out of his car and came towards me. I rehashed my phone call before he immediately started interrogating me. "Who might want to kill you? Do you have enemies? Are there any workers near your house? Does your husband have enemies? After I'd answered a barrage of questions, he agreed to be at the house at 6:30 pm to check out the house before the boys and I entered. The storm was brewing with black clouds and lightning as the thunder roared. It was barely visible to see as the boys and I sped off to Charleston for the afternoon but there was not a cloud in the sky as we reached the city. Stepping out of the car the heat rose to our faces and the pavement was scorching. "Boys stay close to me, please."

"After we leave Dumas' and the Market, can we go to Cannon Park, Mama? "Okay Jaffe, if y'all behave."

I watched the boys play until they were soaked with sweat. Jaffe chased Peter, and Drayton toddled after them both with his little stubby legs as fast as he could. Sitting on the bench gazing at the harbor, I forgot about the phone call. The sun was beaming down on Fort Sumter as I visualized the soldiers their wool uniforms, enduring this summer heat. Pigeons fluttered and cooed as they wandered through the streets, unafraid of the multitude of tourists that were feeding them. I glimpsed a pigeon just as it pooped on an unsuspecting passerby while the rest of the travelers chuckled. I caught myself grinning at the sight of it all. Looking down at my watch I shouted, "Boys, hurry, we've got to hurry! It's time to go home!"

I wanted to be home at the same time as the police officer. The boys fell asleep on the ride back to Summerville with their little heads nodding back and forth before plopping on their chins. As I quietly parked in the driveway, each of the boys began yawning.

"We'll stay in the car until the officer arrives," I said but at seven o'clock, the boys and I decided that we were brave enough to go into the house alone. "Okay Jaffe, here's the plan I'll unlock the door and turn on all the lights, Drayton and Peter will stay with me, while you and I open all the closets and check under beds. If you see anything start screaming and run. I'll have the phone ready to call the police."

"Okay, Mama. Tell me when we're ready 'cause I can run fast."

"Go!"

We were yelling like fools, turning on lights, opening closets, and looking under beds. Jaffe was like a streak and I was like a whale carrying two baby boys with me. "I don't see anything, Mama."

"Okay, come out here with me and let's lock all the doors." The phone started ringing, and we all just stared at it before it stopped and we took a deep breath. Then, it started ringing again so this time I picked up the receiver and listened without saying a word. "Catherine, is that you? Say something!"

"Yes, Carter, it's me! We just got home and Jaffe and I've been casing the joint together but the doors are now locked, and we'll be fine until you get home. By the way, I told a local police officer about the call and he said that he'd be here when we came home. Can you believe that he never showed up."

"Yes, I'll try to get home early, be brave and keep the doors locked."

"Okay, boys, bath time!" After bath, dinner, stories and prayers, my three darlings were fast asleep. I tried to be brave but the night sounds really had me spooked. Carter kept a .22 rifle in his closet, and I reached into the back and pulled it out before searching through his chest for bullets. I wasn't sure what I'd do with them, but I found four shiny bullets tucked in a handkerchief underneath his underwear. I fumbled with the gun, dropping the bullets several times and chasing them across the floor. Finally, I had it loaded but I wasn't sure how to use it so I decided I needed backup. First I tiptoed into Jaffe's room to get his baseball bat and then I was off to the kitchen to get a butcher knife. By now it was 9:30pm and I was exhausted so I stashed my arsenal on the sofa beside me and started watching Peyton Place.

As I dosed off, I was suddenly awakened by a noise. Listening carefully before gathering my weapons, I headed for the kitchen door. My back was against the wall and I was shaking with terror as I watched the doorknob begin to turn. As quietly as I could, I put the bat and the knife on the floor and pointed the barrel of the gun toward the door as I heard fumbling keys just as the door sprung open. I almost fainted as I watched Daddy grab the gun from my trembling hands. "You need to be careful with that, Catherine." I ran into his arms mumbling, "What are you doing here? I thought you were at the hospital with Mama."

"Carter gave me a call and said he was worried about you, so I left the hospital early and came to check on you and the boys. Are they sleeping?"

"Uh huh, they've been asleep for a while."

"I'm going to check out the entire house. You go on in there and watch your TV show. "Daddy."

"Yes."

"You scared me near to death, why didn't you call me?"

"I was in a hurry to get over here!" Daddy stayed with me until Carter came home, and I never received another murdering wrong number again but my unusual experiences didn't stop with that night.

My whole life was consumed with love and affection for my family. Mama had been in the hospital most of the summer, and I tried to visit her every day. The summer was unbearably hot and long but the daily trips to the hospital gave me time to meditate on her health and my life.

I often felt a mystic power when I was with Mama in her antiseptic room but the stench of death seemed so near. The hint of her lavender fragrance kept her alive: Mama, lying in her bed with oxygen, her fancy mules waiting on the floor to carry her to the bathroom for a puff on a Lucky Strike. After my visits with her, I was always overwhelmed with sadness, constantly searching for answers but not sure of the questions. I found myself seeking healing techniques through every dimension available because medical science just couldn't give me the answers I needed. I focused on anything that was a positive connection in life with others since I had always been deeply spiritual, I kept thinking about the time that Mama bought me that suit and again when I saw her in my dream when I was pregnant with Jaffe. I knew there must be a deep connection that could defy conventional explanations and so I meditated more often. Daddy was busy taking care of Mama, and it wasn't long after he had taken her home from the hospital that I had another ESP episode.

It was about 11:30, and Carter and I were lying in bed watching the late show when a cold chill came over me, such that the hair on the back of my neck stood straight up. I sat up straight the bed and whispered out loud. "Carter, something's wrong with Daddy, he's had a heart attack."

"You probably fell asleep for a few minutes and had a dream, Catherine."

"No I didn't! I was thinking about Mama and then Daddy appeared. I couldn't see him very well but he said he needed help."

"It'll be okay, honey, now go to sleep." I lay in the bed for over an hour squirming. Finally, I said, "I can't go to sleep unless I check on Daddy!" Picking up the phone I dialed his number and then I heard his long slow "hello."

"Daddy, are you all right?"

"What's the matter with you, Catherine? Of course I'm all right, except that you woke me up."

"Sorry daddy, goodnight." As I dosed off to sleep, I found myself wondering how I could have been so wrong.

The next morning began as every other day until just after breakfast. That's when Carter's brother, William, called. "Hey, Catherine, is Carter home?"

"No William, he's at work."

"Father had a heart attack around midnight last night but he's alive. Can you get Carter? I need his help right away. Mother's home alone and someone needs to be with her immediately."

"Sure, William, I'm so sorry."

I called Carter immediately. "Well, Catherine, it seems you were right after all but you had the wrong dad."

"I guess I did! Are you going to stay with your mother?"

"Yes will you go see my father for me?"

"Are you crazy? He'll probably die for sure if I show up. I hurriedly called my Daddy and asked him to go with me to the hospital. "Sure, Catherine, you have to go. You have no choice; you must go! I'll be there with you, honey"

I waited for my time to go into the cardiac care unit. I pushed open those huge doors as if I was marching off to war. There he was, hooked to tubes and machines, and I was trying to be as brave as a warrior. As I got closer to his bed, he tried to smile and actually seemed pleased to see me. Eight years had passed since I last saw him. William was with him while his wife Lacey was with Mrs. Duvall. Carter was now with his mother, too. She'd taken a dose of her medications and was in bed. Lacey and Carter decided someone should be with her at all times, and they locked up her medications. All the brothers were called. "Lacey, you call Jackson and Mathew while I call Jules then let's set up a plan for watching her until we know how father will be."

Jules and his wife Elaine came to the hospital immediately to be with me. Mathew and his wife Margie lived in Georgetown so it took them longer to get into town. Mathew was Margaret's favorite son so he went straight to the house. Jackson was a commercial pilot and out of town; the company contacted him and he called to say that he was on his way home.

Carter's large family was reunited, and it seemed as if the family might mend. Carter's father survived his heart attack and Margaret got to see Carter for the first time in many years. I hoped this would be a new beginning and my in-laws would accept the boys and me. Carter, however, was very uncomfortable with the whole idea.

Several weeks passed, and Mr. Duvall came home and called me to thank me for visiting him. "I know how hard it was for you to come, Catherine. I hope that you can forgive me and we can start over."

"I think that is a good idea, Mr. Duvall. I hope you're getting along okay."

"I'm doing fine. It's the wife who's having a hard time with this. She still stays in bed all day. I want to try to bring her for a visit soon."

"Give us a call anytime, Mr. Duvall." After I hung up, I called Carter to tell him the news. "Well, Catherine, I don't want either of them coming for a visit ever. They have never seen Drayton and I don't care if they do. The only Duvalls I love are you and the boys. Don't let them try and con you now."

"Okay, Carter. We can talk about this later. I'm late for a tennis match. See you later, honey." As I rushed off to the country club, my thoughts were on the Duvall's and all that they had missed in life by not knowing their son and grandsons. "Well, that will never happen to me and my children," I heard myself say out loud.

About two months later, Mr. Duvall called for an early Sunday afternoon visit. The boys were as adorable as ever, anticipating the visit of their long-lost grandparents. Carter was unusually quiet while he worked on his papers, and I was so nervous I could hardly sit still. Finally, they arrived. "How are you, Mrs. Duvall?" I asked. "Not so well, Catherine. You've really lost weight."

"I play tennis a lot and keep up with three little boys."

"Yes, I know. I had five boys myself, that's why I stay in my bed now. Couldn't take it, and Bernie was gone in the military so much."

"Now Margaret, let's not get started on all of that today, please. Let's meet our grandsons. You are Jaffe; I remember you, handsome as ever.

This must be Peter. You look like your mother! And you…you must be Drayton. You are dark like your daddy but I see Catherine in you, too."

"Hello, Grandfather Duvall." The boys all chimed at once. Say hello to your grandmother Duvall." The boys each gave her a kiss on the cheek as they said their hellos. "May we be excused now?" Jaffe asked for the group. "We're going to play in the side yard with our friends." Carter immediately stood up and walked the boys to the door. "Y'all know the rules. Be careful now…no jumping from the roof today, no gangplank walking and no hangings or rope burns."

"I know Daddy. You mean we can only play ball and stuff."

"That's right, Jaffe. You take care of your brothers; don't let your friends take over the games. Keep it calm, please."

The visit went smoothly, but as the Duvall's started to leave I saw a strange look on Carter's face. I couldn't decide if it was hate, pride, or suffering but it gave me cold chills. After the boys were tucked in, I sat by Carter, "How do you think the visit went?"

"I can't talk about it, Catherine. It's very painful for me to see my mother and I'll never forgive her." I looked into his eyes and I saw it again, the horrible look of suffering.

I was exhausted so I went to bed early while Carter stayed in the family room watching TV. I was fast asleep. Or was I? I kept seeing Jack, the boy-man across the street and I felt him looking at me through the bedroom window. The dream became more and more real, until I sat straight up in bed and looked at the window. I could see a man looking back at me. I let out a blood-curdling scream for Carter. As he ran toward me, the peeper ran away. "I saw him! He was right there!"

"Well, there's no one out there now. You must have been dreaming."

"Carter, I saw him!"

"Who did you see, Mommy?" By now all three boys were climbing into my bed. "Sorry boys, I just had a bad dream, I didn't mean to wake you."

"Can we watch TV with you?" Peter asked as he pulled his blanket up onto my bed. "I'd love that!" I gathered all three boys as close to me as possible listening to Carter as he went outside to look around. When he came back, he moved each sleeping boy back to his bed before climbing in beside me. "Didn't see anybody out there, Catherine, but I found dead fish thrown on the front lawn."

"Dead fish? What does that mean?"

"I'm not sure…guess it means something's fishy!" I threw my pillow at Carter before cuddling up into his arms. "You know, Lydia was telling me that there's a rumor about an evil cult that has taken up in town. Do you think they had anything to do with this?"

"Why do you talk to that busy body, Catherine?"

Just as summer had been so hot, this winter was phenomenal. Snow in Charleston was extremely rare but this year we had a real blizzard. The entire area was snowed in. The boys loved it as much as we did. Bundled up in as many layers as possible, we headed outdoors to teach the boys the fine art of making snowballs and snow angels. We delighted in watching our appropriately dressed neighbors from the north shoveling the snow from their driveway. As we giggled and threw snowballs, we whispered to one another "Should we tell them that no one will clean the streets?"

"No, let's watch them for awhile." The interstate to Charleston was completely shut down, and people were being housed everywhere. In our small town, there were no snowplows at all. This blizzard had blown more than twenty inches of the most magical white fluff southerners had ever seen. We enjoyed several days of snow angels and snowball fights before returning to reality and the slushy mess left behind.

After the unexpected delights of the cold winter, spring came early and magnificently. The azaleas, magnolias, and camellias were breathtaking. Carter and I stood admiring our garden. We noticed cars driving slowly by the corner of our yard. People were staring at one of our trees. "What are they all looking at, Carter?"

"I think they're looking at the tulip tree, but it doesn't bloom for a few more weeks."

"I see some new white buds on it."

"Catherine, it blooms purple! Let's go see what's going on down there." Carter and I reached the tulip tree just about the time Peter turned the corner of the house. "Do you like it, Mama? I fixed this tree for you. It wasn't blooming yet so I helped it. Isn't it beautiful?" Carter and I had to cover our mouths and laugh to ourselves before answering. "Peter, it's lovely and so white and fluffy. "I found a big box of these things under the sink in your bathroom, Mama. The strings were perfect to tie onto the tree. I pulled the hard pieces into these flowers." Chuckling, we said together, "We love it, Peter, but maybe these blooms would look better on that little tree in the back yard. We'll take these off so you can fix it." The minute he left to join his brothers, Carter and I hurried to pick the tampons from the tree.

Since Mr. Duvall's heart attack, Carter and his uncle had become responsible for Mrs. Duvall's aging father. Poppy, as Carter called him, was eighty-nine and ridden with arthritis. He was as crotchety as any old man could be. His lovely wife had died only ten months earlier and nothing could make him happy. Poppy was angry and depressed and he needed help bathing and preparing dinner. Carter stopped by his grandfather's after work several days a week to bathe him while Carter's uncle and his wife, along with their daughters, went by everyday to feed this cantankerous old man.

One particular day, I was sautéing some shrimp for dinner, the phone rang. I hurried to answer it, wondering if it was Carter calling to tell me he's on his way to bathe Poppy. "Catherine, is Carter home yet?" I heard the panic in Diane's voice. She was Carter's oldest cousin on his mother's side. "No, Diane, he's gone to bathe Poppy."

"Catherine, Poppy has been shot!"

"Oh my God! Was Carter there? Did he do it? Where? What time? Why?"

"Just a few minutes ago! He did it himself because he found out that daddy was paying us girls to go over and feed him and he was furious. He went into the bedroom, got down on his knees and called my sister to the door, hollering about her being paid to care for him. When she reached the door, he put the gun to his head and fired."

Just as Diane finished talking, Carter walked through the door. I hugged him tightly as I relayed the news before getting the boys ready to go as quickly as I could and calling a friend to pick up Jaffe and keep him. On the way to the hospital, we dropped the younger boys by my parents. Just after we reached the emergency room Poppy's heart stopped beating. He had ended his suffering, but he'd left a living hell for the rest of us.

A few days after the funeral, Carter announced that he was going fishing to meditate. The more that I thought about Carter fishing alone, the more I worried and urged him to stay home. "Please don't go, Carter! I have one of my feelings that something terrible is going to happen."

"What's going to happen, Catherine?"

"I don't know, but I know that something terrible is going to happen."

"I'm going fishing, you can come, too!"

"No, I can't. I need to be with the boys." I waved goodbye with a lump in my throat and a fear of the unknown as he drove away. The day crept by slowly because I couldn't get my mind off Carter and his safety. I didn't take my eyes off the boys and I checked on my parents every couple of hours. I watched the news every time it came on and fed the boys early and got them ready for bed. It was time for Carter to be home.

As I walked outside looking for his car, I saw our beautiful fluffy mutt, Nameless, crossing the street. Just as she reached our side a huge Lincoln raced around the corner running over her. I couldn't believe what I was seeing. As I screamed, they stopped and backed up over her again before speeding off down the road. Hysterically, I rushed to her and tried to pick her up. She weighed at least fifty pounds, and I couldn't lift her limp body. Carter drove up and found me sitting in the road with her. He quickly moved Nameless to the grass and took me in his arms. "I'm so sorry that I went. You told me something terrible would happen. Please forgive me, Catherine." I only sobbed, "She was so sweet."

Months, even years went by, and strange events still happened that I couldn't explain. Clocks stopped at midnight with Carter always trying to find a logical explanation. One day we learned a story about the house. It seems that the wife of the owner had died in our very bedroom. She had a headache for several days, went to the doctor and then came home and died in her sleep, in our bedroom. Lydia said, "The reason your back fence is bowed in the corner is her husband had been jumping it so much. He was fooling around with the French woman next door. Maybe the two of them killed the wife." Lydia's off-hand comments sent my mind reeling. I checked every nook and cranny of the house trying to find signs of unhappy spirits. I never did find any and tried desperately to ignore Lydia's gossip and my own feelings.

Fortunately, on the other side of our house lived our dearest friends, the Everett's. Dr. Johnny Everett was an orthopedic surgeon and his wife, Megan, was a nurse. In fact, she'd been his nurse. They had two lovely children, Stacy and Dawson and Megan and I were exercise buddies walking at least two miles every morning before the sun was high. Megan was trying to get rid of her behind but it never went anywhere, and I always felt fat no matter what size. "Thinner will be better," was my motto.

During our walks, we chatted about everything, including the dead woman and the mistress. But we never talked about the Johnny gossip. Johnny worked long hours in his new practice but everyone in town whispered about his philandering. I figured it was gossip until the day of Drayton's birthday party and Megan was there helping me get ready for the party. Lydia called just after lunch. "Have you heard?"

"What, Lydia?" Lydia's husband was also in Johnny's practice. "Johnny totaled his Jaguar during lunch turned it upside down. He's fine, but the nurse he was with isn't. She broke her leg and from the sounds of it she had it in the wrong place."

"Lydia, Megan is here."

"Oh, my God don't say a word to her! I don't know how Johnny will get out of this one." I felt as though I was going to choke and began torturing myself with thoughts, "If Megan is my friend I should be honest with her, tell her. Maybe I should protect her and not tell her." Where was Carter when I needed him? He'd know what to do.

The party started at four o'clock, just after school and homework. By now, Carter was getting ready to cook the hot dogs and hamburgers and kids were everywhere. I hadn't had a chance to breathe a word to him. "Megan is Johnny going to get home and help me cook these burgers, or am I on my own?"

"I haven't heard from him all day, Carter. He must be busy. You know how his practice is growing."

"I sure do. He's a great doctor." Megan was getting ready to walk home after the party when our phone rang.

"Hello, Catherine, sorry I didn't make it to Drayton's party. Is Megan still there?"

"She's right here, Johnny." Handing the phone to Megan, my heart sank to the floor and I should have walked away but I couldn't. As I listened she said, "Are you all right? Why didn't you call sooner? Do you need me to come get you? I love you, too." I just stood there, waiting. "Catherine, you won't believe what happened to Johnny. He had been to a meeting at the hospital and was hurrying back here to Drayton's party when a deer ran out in front of him. He swerved and his Jag overturned on River Road. He's fine. He's meeting with the insurance people now and then he has to go check on a patient with a broken leg. He said he'd see all of us later. Poor thing…he works so hard."

"Oh, no, Megan, that's terrible. I'm glad he's okay."

A few weeks later Megan came over to join me for lunch. As we chatted, she asked me a few questions about taxes and our CPA. "I don't know much about financial things, Catherine. Johnny takes care of everything. He's been working so hard and I think he's getting a little depressed. He seems very guarded these days. In fact, he just told me that he's going to Miami to work on our taxes. He even said that I shouldn't call him while he's there. He's not going to tell me exactly where he's staying so I won't be tempted to call and interrupt him. He doesn't want to be disturbed until he finishes his business. Can you believe how dedicated he is to his work?"

"You know, Megan, I really can't believe what you just told me. Johnny is really something. When is he leaving?"

"Next Thursday."

"Well let's plan to have a wonderful weekend while he's gone. We'll cookout and take the kids to the movies. We won't think about taxes or Johnny."

"It's a date."

I couldn't believe Megan bought this story, but again I said nothing. I was beginning to hate myself, and I already hated Johnny. Sharing the conversation with Carter was difficult for me, too, because I knew how much he admired his friend. "Maybe he's telling the truth, Catherine. You know how he is about his money."

"Bull! I'm not buying that story for a minute. Just wait. One of these days you'll know that I'm right."

On the Thursday morning, Megan and I walked as usual. "Johnny was up before me. He's packed and is leaving as soon as I get home from walking. Can we cut it short this morning so he can leave early?"

"Sure Megan, we'll turn around at the church." When we got home I gave Carter a big kiss. "What was that for?"

"because you get our taxes done by a local CPA." Carter smiled and said, as he hurried off to his office, "I'm coming home for lunch today just to be with you."

"Thanks honey, I'll make something good for you," I said, blowing him a kiss.

He looked very sheepish when he came home at lunch. As he grabbed me and gave me a big kiss, I could sense something was up. "Guess who I saw on the way home?"

"Who?"

"Johnny. He was in a brand new rental car packed with luggage and…a beautiful blonde. He didn't see me, but I saw him and he didn't look like taxes were on his mind."

"What time did you see him?"

"Noon."

"He left the house at six o'clock this morning. Told us he had to get to Miami in a hurry."

"I'll bet he did. Catherine, I have to admit you were right."

"I'm so sorry that you have to say that, Carter."

During those years, we discovered that our town was a mini Peyton Place. Almost everybody in town was sleeping with someone else's wife or husband. It was unbelievable. Tennis players were swapping more than their serves. Our dear friend Richard, a vet was having quickies with a technician during lunch. Faith left her two girls and banker husband for a vending machine operator, who we all called, "The sandwich man." The neighborhood marriage councilor was listening to the problems and married his patient. Mildred, across the street came over nightly to cry and drink our liquor because her husband, a corporate executive, was leaving her for his secretary. They were "doing it" on the boardroom table while Mildred was having another baby. Even the gay guys from New York were having a tiff over the new priest who just moved to town. And there was Johnny. The town was filled with deceit.

I didn't trust anyone except Carter. He was so caring and naïve that I kept a close eye on his every move. I guess that I kept such a close eye on him during this sexual uprising that at thirty-four, I found myself with an unquestionable surprise. Jaffe was almost thirteen; Peter was ten, and Drayton nearly nine. "That's right, boys. Your Mama is going to have a baby in March."

"How do you know that the baby will be coming in March, Daddy?" Drayton asked. "Because that's how long it'll take the baby to grow."

"Is it a boy or a girl, Daddy?"

"We don't know yet, but we hope to find out soon." The boys were thrilled at the thought of another sibling. I wasn't so sure about Drayton, after all he had been "the baby" for a long time.

I was busy chauffeuring Jaffe from baseball, football, and his tennis practice that I stayed in the car all afternoon. Driving the boys to cotillion and art lessons was a treat because they didn't smell so dirty and sweaty.

My pregnancy was flying by and my stomach was as round as a balloon. The baby moved all over the place when I was scrunched behind the stirring wheel of my aging Mercedes. All of us were hoping to find out the sex of the baby before the March arrival. Carter and I were thrilled about this baby that we weren't sure that we wanted to risk an amniocentesis test. I didn't fall into any of the high-risk groups, but I'd be thirty-five when the baby was born. After reading extensively about the procedure, we decided the risk of miscarrying was too great. So there I was again, not knowing what to do about colors, clothes, or gender. Deep down I knew the baby was a girl, but Carter was sure the baby was another boy.

The months went by quickly. Christmas was perfect, and everyone gave me some tiny, lovely piece of sterling for the new baby. I had a collection of silver juice cups, Chantilly feeding spoons, and a new shiny porringer that was intricately designed. I found an antique high chair that was an exact duplicate of the one I had seen in the Charleston Museum. The cane bottom was in perfect condition and its handle folded down and converted the high chair into a stroller. The little cast iron wheels rolled perfectly along the heart pine floors of our house. "Catherine, I think this high chair is a bit dainty for our new son," Carter warned. "Oh, Carter, it's such a find. Look at the details! I have to have it for the baby. Besides, now that we're going to have four children, think about how many grandchildren we could have. We'll need a lot of high chairs." Carter paid the dealer a handsome sum and we loaded our new purchase into his car.

Several baby showers were scheduled for February and another after the baby's arrival, but I already had so many boxes of disposable diapers that I was wondering how we'd use them all. Pampers weren't around when the older boys were born so Carter and I used a diaper service and washed diapers out in the toilet, just like Mama had done. In fact, we called the plumber often when Drayton was young because Peter loved to flush the toilet, and we often left a dirty diaper soaking. Times had sure changed.

By Valentine's Day I looked like cupid. Every inch of my short body was covered with baby. I felt wonderful but extremely tired. Carter or one of the boys rubbed my swollen feet every night while we watched TV. Peter regularly lay with his head on my stomach talking to the baby and listening to heartbeats. Drayton would give my stomach a touch but if the baby moved he always moved his hand and Jaffe would just look at me in bewilderment. My C-section had been scheduled for Friday, March 30, but I had a feeling that that the baby wasn't going to be born then. My clothes were packed and I was ready for delivery.

On Friday night March 23, Carter and I went to a party at Society Hall. The band was good but not like Maurice Williams and the Zodiacs that we grew up dancing to at Folly Beach. Mrs. Hannett and her crew catered the whole affair. She was really taking over the town with her delicacies. Carter looked so dashing in his Brooks Brothers tuxedo and I looked so pregnant in my black sequined maternity gown. We shagged until very late into the evening. "I think you had better take me home before I fall over on the floor, honey."

"Are you all right?"

"I'm fine, just exhausted." On our long ride back to Summerville I kept wondering what the baby would be.

The next morning, Carter and I took the boys out for breakfast at Ella's, one of the few restaurants in Summerville that served breakfast. It looked just like the one from Mayberry where Andy and Barney often ate. Carter was so predictable—I knew he'd order two eggs (over medium), bacon (crisp), rye toast (buttered), tomato juice and coffee just like Daddy. The boys ordered everything else on the menu but I only wanted fresh strawberries. "Is that all you're going to eat, Catherine?"

"Yes, I'm too tired to eat, all that dancing has done me in. I think I'm going to take a nap as soon as we get home."

"The boys and I are going to Azalea Park after breakfast. Do you want to come, or do you want me to take you back to the house?"

"Please take me home, I'm really tired, and I don't think I can walk anywhere." Carter drove me home and as I trudged up the massive steps to our Victorian home, I blew kisses to all my boys. Stopping on the front porch to admire the flowerbeds and the ferns hanging in their gigantic baskets, I took a deep breath the ferns had doubled in size, they were gigantic. Yawning, I turned and climbed the rest of the stairs.

I must have dozed off immediately before waking to the laughter of Carter and the boys. Glancing at the clock, I realized that I'd been asleep for more than three hours. It was lunchtime, and Carter and the boys were chattering and giggling like girls as they made sandwiches and fries in the kitchen. "I came up and checked on you but you didn't move. Here, I brought you some lunch." Looking at the enormous amount of food on the plate made me even less hungry. "Thanks honey, I'll nibble on it, but I'm just not very hungry. Thanks for fixing it, though." As Carter galloped down the stairs, I rolled over and went back to sleep.

Late that evening I finally came down. "Well, hello, stranger! We thought you were going to sleep all day."

"Sorry, hope I didn't miss much."

"Only one whole day in your life!"

"Well, now that I'm awake let's do something, let's grill some steaks and watch a movie."

Together we cooked the steaks and then started watching *Steel Magnolias*. The boys went up to their rooms to play and watch their TV. Carter fell asleep, and I started crying softly because the movie was so funny and so sad. I cried and cried until I finally woke Carter up. "Why are you crying, honey?"

"Because the movie's sad, because the baby hasn't moved in days, because I slept all day, because I love you," I sobbed. "Okay, now why are you really crying?"

"I don't know!"

"Come on, Catherine, let's go to bed." As we climbed into bed, I knew that I could never sleep. Just a little before midnight my water broke. "Carter, wake up. We're going to the hospital. I called the doctor; my water broke an hour ago. I'm ready, so wake up and let's go. Daddy's on his way here to stay with the boys," I whispered. By the time Carter was fully awake and ready to go, I heard Daddy climbing the porch steps. I quietly opened the door and waited for my kiss. "How are you feeling, Sis?" Daddy was known for calling girls Sis. "Fine, Daddy, just ready to see this baby."

"Hello, Truman. The boys never woke up; I'll call you in awhile. The coffee pot is ready for you to turn on."

"You call me as soon as you know anything."

"I will." Off we headed to the hospital one more time on an early morning. As was the case the last three times, the full moon guided our path to the holy city for a birth.

8
Chamberlain

"Hello, Duvall residence."

"Truman, you have a beautiful granddaughter. She was born at 7:30 this morning and weighs 8-lb. 1 oz. She's so pink and precious and nineteen inches long. She looks just like Jaffe with really bright, blue eyes."

"How's Catherine? What are you going to name the baby? Are you sticking to the family names?"

"Catherine is sleeping now. She was so tickled that the baby's a girl. The C-section went fine, and she got to see Chamberlain before the doctor drugged her. We are going to call the baby Chamberlain but her full name is Elizabeth Calhoun Chamberlain Duvall. She's named after Rachel Elizabeth and my mother's maiden name, Chamberlain. My grandparents would be so proud."

"I know they would, Carter, and so am I. I'm calling Rachel as soon as we hang up. When the boys get up we're picking up Rachel and all heading down there to see Miss Chamberlain and her mother."

The ringing phone woke Catherine. It was Rachel and she was so excited so I handed the phone to Catherine. "Hey Mama, have you seen her yet?"

"I sure have, and the nurse let me hold her while you were sleeping. She looks just like your granddaddy, Drayton, I think. How are you feeling, baby?"

"I'm tired, but thrilled. No more babies for me now, I'm getting too old. I'm going to go to Church Street Children tomorrow and buy her every pink Feldman gown and dress in the shop. I'll put the big pink bow on the garden gate as soon as we take the boys home. Is there anything else you need me to do?"

"Thanks Mama, I love you so much. No, I think we're fine except for watching the boys." The doctors let Chamberlain and me go home on Friday and Carter took the boys out of school so they could help bring their sister home. "Let me hold her!"

"No, let me hold her."

"I want to hold her first! I'm the oldest."

"Boys, your mother's going to hold her until we get her home, then you can all hold her."

"Okay, Daddy," they chanted at once.

Mama had a huge pink bow neatly attached to the gate when we got home. Bottles of champagne, balloons, and gifts lined the buffet in the foyer. "Who brought all of this stuff?"

"We'll look at the cards later, Catherine but first let's try and get you up these stairs. I'll carry Chamberlain to her new room." After many breathless moments, holding a pillow over my stitches as I slowly climbed the stairs I reached the nursery. When Carter opened the door I couldn't believe my eyes. "When did this happen?"

"Last Tuesday, do you like it? I know how much you wanted it done."

"Carter, I love it. It's so girly. The powder pink walls are just perfect. Where did you get this adorable rug?"

"Beth helped me with everything. Your sister has a very good eye for decorating."

"She certainly does, and she knows just what I like. Thank you so much, it's wonderful."

"Anything for my girls!"

The boys couldn't get enough of their little sister. They hurried home from school each day and gathered her for a walk in her pram. If she cried at night, they were in her room before I could get my feet on the floor. Before I knew it, she was two months old and ready to be christened.

The white gown, worn by generations of Drayton's, as well as her brothers, hung to the floor as I held her tightly in my arms. Beaming with pride at the sight of our angel, I caught a glimpse of the church pews filled with friends and neighbors. They were all smiling at Chamberlain. When I looked back down at her, her face was as red as a beet and she was straining as hard as she could. Carter gave me a look of embarrassment as the priest anointed our daughter with water while she yawned, stretched, and smiled as if she was in control of the whole service. As soon as the Baptism was over, Carter raced to the back room in the church to change Chamberlain's diaper.

Bessie Lou spoiled Chamberlain even more than the rest of us. She kept her smocked dresses as crisp as toast, and the bows for her strawberry blonde hair were lined up neatly to match each outfit. She bathed and changed her in the mornings after breakfast and again just before leaving in the afternoon.

Chamberlain always loved it when Bessie brought her nephew by before taking him to his sitter's. He was a month younger than Chamberlain but taller and bigger. His skin was like dark chocolate, and Bessie kept him shinning brightly in his white shirts and diapers.

Bessie had custody of Tom because his mother was in jail on drug charges, and no one else in the family could take him. He adored Bessie Lou and was very distressed every time she had to leave him. "You can bring him here with you, Bessie Lou."

"Lord, no, Miss Catherine. I'd never get my work done with the two of them all day." Tom was the joy of her life but she had two older sons who lived with her mother. Bessie always said, "They can get a better education with my mother looking after them while Bailey and I work to provide for them." Bessie was a natural mother though, and as soon as she took Tom into her life, he meant everything to her. The children were now toddlers and growing like two little weeds together.

Temperatures reached record highs as Carter and I prepared for our annual July fourth birthday celebration for Peter. He was turning thirteen, and we wanted everything to be extra special for him. The caterers were busy putting trays on the tables. The tables were covered with blue and white checked gingham linens and topped with pots of geraniums with gigantic blooms of red. They seemed to smile with happiness as the flags flew proudly throughout our yard, and torches burned in the gardens to keep the mosquitoes at bay. The younger children were having a parade and marching right in front of them, leading with her tiny American flag, was Chamberlain. Her white dress was smocked with small red, white, and blue flags around the top while the ribbon on her Charleston bonnet was cocked to the side. Her tiny feet were marching in step to the music.

Promptly at one o'clock, Peter's guests began arriving as I noticed how much all of his friends had grown. The thin, lanky years were definitely upon them. As usual the girls swarmed around Peter. He smiled wrapping his long arms gently around them. He was definitely a ladies man just like my father.

The food was about to be served when I noticed a dark cloud approaching from the lake. "Carter, do you think we should move everything inside? Look at that cloud!"

"I think we'll make it, honey, don't worry yet. Would you like me to get you a drink?"

"Yes, I'd love a mint julep. I put a silver dish on the bar with Kentucky Colonel Mint in it for the drinks. Randy knows how I like it. I'll mingle in the garden." As I walked into my beautiful garden, something told me that that cloud was an omen even though Carter assured me the dark cloud would not foreshadow our party.

The party for Peter was a glorious event. Mama and Daddy left early so Mama could rest, but everyone else continued to eat and drink into the early evening. I was sitting in the wicker swing on the front porch sipping another julep when the phone rang. "Can someone get that for me, please?" I called to the staff in the kitchen. "It's for you, Mrs. Duvall."

"Hello, this is Catherine Duvall."

"Catherine, it's…Mama!"

My mother was gasping for air and crying so hard that I couldn't understand a word she was saying. "Mama, stop crying! Just sit there for a minute and get a breath. Where's Daddy? Is he hurt?"

"No," I heard her faintly whisper. "Okay…let's try again." I strained to listen to her words. She was sputtering incoherently while sobbing and gasping. "Oh my God! No, Mama! This really didn't happen. What should we do?" By now Carter was beside me.

"Catherine, what is it? You look as though you've seen a ghost."
Trembling, I tried to speak. "Bessie Lou's niece got out of prison. She was trying to get Tom back but Bessie wouldn't let him go with her. Then, she didn't like it because Bessie was getting some money assistance for Tom's food. Anyway, I'm not sure of all the details, but DSS got involved and told Bessie that she had to let the natural mother have visitation. Tom's mother picked him up today, and they were going fishing together with some people around two o'clock, Tom's naptime, and he started crying, saying that he wanted his Bessie Lou. His mother got furious and told him to stop crying for Bessie Lou. When he didn't stop asking for Bessie, his mother picked him up and threw him off the bridge and drowned him. He's dead, Carter!"

"Oh, God, what's this world coming to? Where's your Daddy?"

"He's with Bessie Lou. Can you finish up the party? I'm going to stay with Mama and make some phone calls. This is just crazy. I can't believe Tom's dead." Carter held me close as we looked out on our party and our four wonderful children.

Driving to Charleston alone, I cried for the small boy who had touched so many lives in such a brief time.

Bessie Lou was never the same. She always smiled, but I could see sadness in her eyes except when she was caring for Chamberlain. She watched Chamberlain grow just as I did, but both of our hearts still ached for Tom. As I watched Chamberlain play, I shuddered at the thought of the tragedy with Tom. I promised myself I would always watch over my baby girl. I knew she would grow too fast for my liking—just like her brothers had done. After Tom's death, I never left Chamberlain with anyone other than her daddy, her brothers, my parents or her special sitters, she called Pop-Pop and Lala, and of course Bessie.

Pop and Lala were well into their seventies but loved keeping Chamberlain. Pop would bundle her up and walk all the way to Azalea Park with her while Lala stayed home and baked cookies from her duck eggs. These two remarkable people had kept many children in their day, but they considered our child their own. "You know, Catherine, I believe Chamberlain is gifted. She's real smart, I can tell."

"I think she is pretty smart…Lala, but I'm not sure about her IQ yet. We'll just let her grow and enjoy her for now." By the time Chamberlain was two, she could sing her alphabet and say each letter and sound when I held them up. She knew all the TV ads and when I was getting ready to watch a movie with her she said, "Mommy, the movie is over."

"How do you know that the movie is over, honey?"

"'Cause the words are going up!"

"Oh, well, Mommy will get another movie." While I found another movie, Chamberlain started reading her storybook out loud…"A is for apple, B is for ball."

"Can you read the whole book, Chamberlain?"

"Yes, Mommy, Drayton taught me."

"Good, for you now run on out in the garden and play for a while."

Her perky blue eyes twinkled and her strawberry blonde locks glistened in the sun as she played in the garden with her best friend, Katie. They were playing school in the playhouse but weren't exactly sure of all the rules since Peter and Drayton had given their version of school rules. Chamberlain and Katie were so excited about starting first grade in the fall.

The girls took a break from role playing to come inside for drinks just as the phone rang. "Catherine, I can't wake up your Mama."

"Is she breathing, Daddy?"

"Uh huh, but I can't get her to open her eyes."

"How long has she been like this?"

"Oh, a couple of hours."

"I'm on my way." Hurriedly I walked the girls to Katie's house and asked Anne to keep Chamberlain for me.

Driving to my parents' house, I knew this wouldn't end happily. Rushing in their house I shouted, "Mama, wake up. It's Catherine. Can you hear me? Have you called the doctor, Daddy?"

"No, I was waiting to see what you thought."

"We need to call an ambulance and the doctor immediately!" I could see that Daddy just couldn't face the idea that Mama might not get better this time. I couldn't believe he'd waited so long. Just as I picked up the phone their neighbor walks in and called Mama's name several times with no success as I dialed 9 1 1. "What's your emergency?"

"It's my mother. I think she's in a coma, please hurry." As I gave the operator the address I saw Daddy gently rubbing Mama's arm and I could hear him saying, "You're going to be okay, Sis." Waiting in front of the house for the paramedics seemed an eternity as I watched goose bumps rise on my arms. I knew Daddy wasn't going to deal with this very well. He had cared for Mama for so long and she always got better, but I knew the end was near.

I climbed into the ambulance with Mama's still body while Daddy followed in the car. I told the paramedics about her condition, medications, and doctors while they feverishly worked on her all the way to the hospital. My Daddy and I sat motionless in the lobby waiting for news. I called Carter. "I'll be down there as soon as I can, Catherine. I love you. How's your Daddy?"

"I love you, too. He's fidgety, biting his nails, coughing, and now he's pacing. You know how he gets. See you soon, honey."

Suddenly Dr. Davis appeared. "Truman, Rachel definitely is in a coma. I'm doing everything possible to keep her going. I'll have more information for you by morning. Do you have any questions for me?"

"No, Doc. You always take such good care of her so I'll see you in the morning."

Daddy and I stayed beside Mama until near suppertime when Carter arrived and paced the floor with Daddy. They decided to get a bite to eat and asked what they could bring me. "I'm not hungry. Y'all go ahead. I'll stay here with Mama." I called Beth, who was now living in Daytona Beach. She was recovering from a hysterectomy, and Daddy didn't want her to know about Mama. "How are you feeling, Beth?"

"I'm still in pain and really having trouble walking."

"Well, try to rest and take care of yourself. Don't do too much like you always do."

"Yes, ma'am, little sister and who do you think you're bossing?"

"My big sister, that's who, and you'd better not mess with me…I'm not nearly as tall as you, but I can jump."

"Don't make me laugh, Catherine. It hurts so much to laugh."

"Okay, I'll call you later." I got off the phone before she could ask if I'd seen Mama and Daddy. The nurse walked into the room as I hung up the receiver. "How's Mama doing?"

"She's comfortable, but she's not going to last long with all this morphine she's getting."

The next morning Daddy and I had a long talk about telling Beth. "I know, Daddy, but she needs to know. If something happens and you haven't told her, she'll never forgive us. Plus, if Mama wakes up, Beth can talk to her on the phone."

"Okay, Catherine, whatever you think. I'm going for a walk." Daddy was gone for five hours.

"I was so worried about you, Daddy. Where have you been?"

"Oh, I had lunch with my buddies and walked the dog and picked up Bessie so she can get the house clean for your Mama's homecoming."

"Daddy, we're calling Beth right now!"

"Okay"

"No, honey, you don't need to come, your Mama's doing fine. Just a little sleepy, can't seem to stay awake. You stay there and take care of yourself. How are Gregory and the children?"

"Daddy, we're all fine. I want to talk to her when she's awake."

"I promise I'll call as soon as she's ready to talk."

Mama stayed in her coma for over a week before opening her eyes and surprising the daylights out of me. I hadn't left the hospital except to go home and get more clothes. The children were well taken care of and Daddy couldn't bring himself to stay at the hospital. "What are you doing, Catherine?" Mama's faint voice startled me from my reading. "Well, hello there!" I grabbed the call button and pushed for the nurse. "She's awake and talking." Three nurses came running. One bound for the monitors, one checked charts and one said "You are unbelievable, Mrs. Jaffe. I'm going to call Dr. Davis right now."

"What's going on?"

"Well, give me a kiss, beautiful...I knew you'd be just fine. You really scared me this time."

"Hold my hand, Truman." Daddy had just returned from one of his many disappearances. "Beth wants to talk to you. Do you feel like talking?"

"Okay."

"Catherine, will you get Beth on the phone while I freshen your Mama's pillows?"

"Sure Daddy." As I dialed Beth's number, I knew I should tell her a few things myself. "Hey, big Sis, how are you feeling?" I said normally but then I whispered, "Tell her you love her, tell her anything you've ever wanted to say, say it now Beth. " While they shared their words of love and adoration, I sat with the biggest lump in my throat unable to swallow. Daddy motioned me to take the phone. "Catherine, is she dying?"

"I think so, Beth, but nobody will say for sure."

"Should I come now?"

"No, I'll call you in time, I promise." Mama was in and out of consciousness for five more days but each time she was awake, she wanted me to tell her about the boys and Chamberlain. "How much has she grown? Is her hair still like spun gold? Can you bring her to see me? And then she'd lapsed back into a coma.

I convinced Daddy that it was time to have Beth come home after the night nurse came in with a hypodermic syringe filled with morphine. "Honey, do you want to help your Mama stop her suffering?"

"What do you mean?" I asked. "Just between you and me, she's getting so much morphine I can bottom her out if you say so. No one will ever know!"

"I ought to report you! Don't ever ask me that again," I sobbed as I ran out of the room. "Sorry, honey, but her days are few." I stayed with Mama for about another week but she didn't utter a sound or open her eyes. Then, one night her eyes popped wide open and she said, "Jesus, hold me…hold my hand…I see the light." Nurses ran in the room checking her completely but said that she wasn't awake and they couldn't believe she had the strength to talk. Mama's life on earth ended just after she reached for Jesus.

When I finally walked into my house, I found Chamberlain giggling with her brothers in my bedroom on my antique bed with the mattress collapsed on the floor. "Sorry, Mommy, I guess I jumped too hard," my smiling daughter was saying to me as I climbed past her onto the rumpled pile on the floor. "It's okay, honey, Daddy will fix it later." I covered my eyes with a pillow and fell into a deep sleep.

When I woke up, I was totally disoriented for a few minutes because things were such a mess. I felt as if I had just had a horrible nightmare. Carter came through the door as I said "I just had the worst nightmare. I dreamed that I'd been at the hospital for weeks and my mother died."

"Oh Catherine, it isn't a dream, Rachel is gone. I'm so sorry." Carter held me in his arms for a long time. "Have you told the children?"

"Yes, they're okay but they're worried about you and Truman. Let's go down stairs and see them."

Walking out of the room, I turned and looked at the collapsed bed as I shuddered at the sight. "What will collapse next?" I asked myself, knowing full well that this was another omen for me. The children were sitting on the sofa, their eyes filled with tears. They were trying to be so brave as they rushed to put their arms around me. "Let's all say a prayer for Granny," I heard Drayton whisper and we bowed our heads.

Chamberlain insisted on going to the funeral against my better judgment. I decided to let her go only to the church where she cried so loudly I thought I'd lose the last thread of my own control. The boys sat like soldiers, softly wiping away tears. Daddy was the most pitiful soul sitting next to Beth and me with his huge hands shaking as he sobbed like a baby. Carter and Gregory were two of the pallbearers carrying Mama to her rest and I held Chamberlain tightly as she bawled, "I want my, Granny. God can't have her, I need her, come back, Granny."

Months passed as we grieved for mama and helped Daddy clean out her things. Each time I went to his house, I realized that things were really missing. "Where's the loveseat that was over by the window, Daddy?"

"Oh, I gave it to the neighbors." When I got home I picked up the phone. "Beth, he's giving all the furniture to the neighbors."

"No, he's not Catherine."

"Yes, he is! You come up here and see for yourself." By the time Beth arrived, Daddy had given most of the furniture away to the neighbors and Bessie Lou. "I don't need all this stuff, girls. Y'all take it, just leave me a bed, TV, and lounge chair but get the rest out of here." Beth and I divided everything left in the house and Daddy lived like a hermit in two rooms of his once—gorgeous home.

"Let's go to Granddaddy's, Mama. I'll take my skates and skate in the house 'cause it's so empty."

"I don't think that will do, Chamberlain. We can go see him but you can't skate inside, and it's too cold and nasty outside for skating."

"How are you doing, Daddy? "Okay, just moseying along day by day. Come here, little Sis, how are you?"

"I'm fine, Granddaddy but I miss Granny."

"I know. We all miss her, but we'll have to keep on going. How about helping me fix some cheese toast? You get the bread and cheddar cheese out of the fridge, and I'll get the grater and knife." I watched as my daughter and her grandfather cooked in the kitchen. He hummed and she chatted as they made hot chocolate and sat down to eat their cheese toast. "Catherine, come in here and sit with us. You don't have to eat, but its real good."

"You know I can't resist your toast, Daddy, it's the best in the world," I said taking a bite. "Have you seen Carter's family lately?"

"Not really. They call once in a while. I have their Christmas presents wrapped. I guess we'll see them during the holidays."

"You are eating Christmas dinner with us, aren't you, Granddaddy?"

"Twist my arm, Chamberlain."

"Sir?"

"Of course, I'll be there, the way your Mama cooks, I wouldn't miss it."

Carter delivered the Christmas presents to the Duvall's on Christmas night. He later sat telling me about his trip to Charleston. "I'm glad that she was in bed so I didn't have to see her. The house was dark as usual and my father was sitting there drinking red wine. I don't know, Catherine, it just felt weird being there."

On a cold evening in January our phone rang. "Hello, William, sure he's right here. " I listened as Carter talked with his brother but I could only hear Carter's side, and could tell the conversation wasn't pleasant. "How long has she been sick? Why didn't you call before now? No, I'm not coming. Why should I? She's never been there for me and I really don't care." Watching Carter pour himself bourbon as he hung up the phone, I waited for him to say something but he didn't. Finally, I couldn't wait any longer. "What's going on?"

"My Mother's in ICU at Harris Regional. She has double pneumonia and is on a respirator. She had the flu but my father didn't take her to the doctor because she stays in bed anyway."

"Carter, you need to go to the hospital."

"I'm not going, Catherine. I will not do a thing for her."

"Then, I'll have to go because someone from our side of the family needs to be there."

"Go if you want to but I'm not going." Carter poured more bourbon into the Waterford glass clinched tightly in his hand. "You need to slow down on those so you'll be sober when I call you in a little while." Climbing behind the wheel of my car, I shuddered not only at the cold but because I'd seen a side of Carter that frightened me. As I reached the hospital ICU waiting area, I saw most but not all of my in-laws. "Where's Carter?" they all asked at once. "Home with the children…I'm going to call him if he needs to come."

At that moment, the nurse announced that two of us could visit Margaret Duvall. She looked like death with the respirator breathing her every breath. William and Lacey began rubbing her arms and then her blue feet that were in desperate need of a pedicure. As I looked at them, an insane thought crossed my mind. "Catherine, always get pedicures 'cause no one can ever see your feet in that shape." I wanted to run out screaming, but I took a deep breath and stood like a statue staring at a dying woman who had been so negligent of her son, grandchildren, and me. "You can get through this, you can do this," I kept repeating to myself.

I'd been there about an hour when she began to get worse. I knew that I needed to talk with Carter but I wasn't sure what I'd say to get him to come. "Your mother isn't going to make it and I think you need to come now. You really sound funny. Are you drunk?"

"Of course not, my head is just stopped up. I'll get the babysitter and see you in a while." Carter arrived at the hospital an hour later reeking of bourbon. I was furious, ashamed, and sad for him all at once. Within minutes of his getting there, his mother died. I left my car at the hospital and drove my drunken husband home in his car. He sat staring into space before I heard. "She was a terrible mother but I'm glad she's gone out her misery all though I won't miss her at all."

"Think about what you're saying. Would you want Chamberlain or the boys to say that? I'm so sad for you, Carter. No one should feel so alone and unloved. Even if she neglected you, loss of any life is sad and I love you, the children love you. Now, come here and let me hold you." We sat together grieving in our own ways.

Carter and I were so busy taking care of the children and helping Daddy that we'd forgotten about Carter's father. William called out of the blue and asked if he could come over to talk. "You do know about Hildegard, don't you?"

"Who's Hildegard?" Carter and I asked simultaneously. "Remember, she grew up across the street from our grandparents in the green house." William shared with us. "You mean Hildegard North? Yeah, I remember her, she certainly wasn't a beauty growing up…real plain and not bright. She's my age. Why do you bring her up?" Carter seemed to remember her well.

Then William and Lacey relayed their story. "It seems that our daddy had been visiting her at the store where she worked long before mother got sick. The day of mother's funeral Hildegard came over to offer her condolences and she's still there…moved right in with him."

"You're not serious. Are you?"

"We're dead serious! Lacey was able to spend a lot of time with mother when she was sick. Mother told her that our father was seeing someone. "William, Mother was a drug addict and mental case and you can't possibly believe anything she had to say."

"Well, Carter, I do believe this because I see Hildegard there now and she's doing a number on our father."

Now it was Lacey who spoke. "I think your father killed your mother."

"Y'all are really losing it! Mother died from pneumonia."

"Yeah, but your father didn't take her to the doctor until it was too late."

"Well, Lacey, you were there, you could have taken her."

"He wouldn't let me. I'm telling you, he killed her."

"You know what? I don't really care about either of them. I'm sorry it disturbs y'all so much, but I'm over it. They are both out of my life, and I'm glad," Carter said as he walked to the bar. "Can I fix anyone a drink?"

Within seven months after Margaret's death, Mr. Duvall married Hildegard North. He didn't invite any of his sons or friends to the ceremony. We finally met her a few months later when I invited the newlyweds for Thanksgiving dinner. I nearly collapsed when she walked through the door. She was a year older than my forty-one years, but she looked sixty-five with her gray hair fixed like the blue-haired ladies of my mothers' generation. Her outfit was gruesome polyester with cheap beads for an accessory. She also wore brogan shoes and carried a plastic box looking purse. She smelled of cheap cologne, and the minute she opened her mouth I knew that her education level wasn't comparable to my mother's boarding school years.

Dinner seemed to drag forever with Hildegard buttering up my daddy. I kept a close eye on her that day and knew I would every time she was around. She was obviously a gold digger and I couldn't imagine what Mr. Duvall saw in her. As my Daddy was leaving that evening, he leaned over to kiss me and said, "He's gotten himself into a real mess with this woman."

Messes seemed to pop up everywhere after that. Carter's company down sized and he was laid off. That day was a shocker when he walked through the door early one spring afternoon to tell me that he lost his job. Quickly, I sent Chamberlain over to play with Katie as my heart sank. "They didn't give you any warning?" I asked as he sat at the table hanging his head in gloom. "You didn't have a clue?"

"None, Catherine, we have some savings but with four children and this huge house and the beach house I don't know how long it will last."

"Let me think, Carter. We'll figure this out together."

"I need a drink, Catherine. Do you want one?"

"No, thanks, it's only three o'clock, Carter."

Carter drank while I contemplated before calling Daddy for his support. "You know I'm here for you, honey, you'll make the right decisions. It'll work out. Why don't I pick up Chamberlain and Drayton to go to supper with me tonight? Do you think Peter and Jaffe might want to go?"

"Daddy, supper would be great! I'd love for Chamberlain and the boys to be with you for a while. They need to have fun and happiness."

After much deliberation and a good severance package, Carter decided that he should start his own business. He loved building and had a great eye for detail. He developed his company slowly, and within two years it really took off. He was making a name for himself in the construction world, building several top-dollar homes . Some of these fantastic homes just sat on the market for many months. According to our bankers, the recession was lingering much longer than anticipated. "The market is drying up, no one is buying because of the interest rates. I'm sorry, Carter, but we can't loan you any more money at this time."

"Thanks, R.C. I appreciate you seeing me today. I'll try to figure something out."

Chamberlain was starting second grade and hated riding in the carpool because the other mothers were always late picking them up. "Please come get me every day, Daddy. I like it when you or Mama come to get me."

"Okay, baby, just keep an eye out for me." Carter picked her up almost everyday and took her straight to the park. "You should see how high Daddy lets me swing, Mama and you know that witches hat?"

"Yes, I know the witches hat."

"Daddy makes it go around so fast that I get dizzy and can't walk when I get off."

"You two need to be careful at the park. I'm not sure who's watching whom." I watched as Carter and Chamberlain bonded more each day but he became more silent and withdrawn from me.

It took only six months for our lives to fall completely apart—and I didn't even know it was happening. Carter never discussed finances with me, and I had no clue that I was about to face some of the biggest decisions of my life.

Decorating the Christmas tree that year, I noticed that Carter was extremely quiet. "This tree is enormous, Carter. Where did you find it?"

"I went over to Spell's and they had lots of trees. I took the children while you were shopping, Catherine. Sorry, we didn't wait on you as usual." Carter continued putting the lights on and when our masterpiece was completed; I turned off the lamps so we could admire our tree of peace. Standing straight in front of it I asked Carter if he thought it was standing straight. "It seems to be leaning a little to me. Do you think it could fall over? I don't want to break all Mamas' antique ornaments."

"It's fine, Catherine, you worry too much. The tree is standing the way it should be."

The children and I finished our eggnog before heading off to bed while Carter stayed up drinking a few more shots of bourbon. Just before the alarm went off the next morning, I heard a thunderous crash.

Dashing down the stairs, I arrived in time to see my befuddled husband trying to lift our fallen Christmas tree. "I'll fix it, Catherine, I promise!" I ran hysterically back up to my room where I stayed for hours, trying to control my emotions. "Christmas should be a joyous time. What had happened to us?" I continued to ask questions but had no answers. Christmas day was filled with mixed feelings. It was great time for the children, especially Chamberlain, but I felt a real distance between Carter and I and I couldn't figure out his behavior.

Carter must have been confiding in Jaffe because the day after Christmas, they started taking pictures off the walls and talking about the plan. "What are you doing? Leave our things alone. Have you lost your mind? Stop this absurdity now!" I couldn't believe what he was doing. "Catherine, I've tried to tell you but you just don't listen to me. I haven't paid our mortgage in six months, and the house is being repossessed. We have to move immediately."

"No, we can't move! What about the children and their schools? We can't put Chamberlain in just any school...she is so brilliant. Where are we going?"

"That's for you to decide. Find a place immediately."

"How much can we afford to buy, Carter?"

"Catherine, we can't buy so find a place to rent!" Carter was glaring at me by now. "RENT! Oh, my God! You are joking, aren't you?"

"No, Catherine, I'm not." I ran into the bathroom and threw up. As I sat with a wash cloth on my head unable to believe what was happening, I cried and cried before the numbness took over.

The next day I contacted Father O'Malley. "What should I do, Father?"

"Move near the water, Catherine, the ocean is always healing source."

"But the children will have to make so many changes."

"They'll survive, Catherine, and so will you." As Carter and the boys packed, Chamberlain and I searched for an acceptable place to live. We found a lovely rental overlooking the Atlantic Ocean "I like this house, Mommy. It's perfect for Olivia and me. Olivia was a Lhasa Apso that Chamberlain had named after Olivia Newton John. "Okay, honey, this is where we'll move."

My thoughts were only of my children and their sacrifices but I also knew Summerville was too small for us to remain. The gossip couldn't hurt them if they didn't hear it. Driving back from Seabrook Island to Summerville seemed an eternity while I kept hearing my own voice in my head, "If only Carter had shared with me sooner, I could have sorted this all out better! I feel so out of control! I want to do what's right for him but I have to protect the children. Damn him! I wonder how long he's been planning the move. How am I going to fix this? I just need some time."

As I walked into the house, my footsteps echoed on the empty floors and boxes were everywhere. Furniture had been moved near the doors. The boys were eating pizza and watching TV so I sent Chamberlain in to join them and tell them about our new house. Walking upstairs, I heard a funny sound before I found Carter doubled over in pain. "What's wrong with you?" I asked. "I don't feel well, my stomach hurts," he said. "Well, my heart hurts and I can't fix it, but I did find a house for us. It's available immediately. Here are the keys."

Carter and the boys continued to load the huge truck that was parked outside. Nosy neighbors started to arrive while I smiled and nodded as they asked where we were moving. "Oh, we're moving to Seabrook Island but we'll be seeing all of you. We're not going far. Carter and the boys will get to do a lot of fishing and I hope you will come for a visit. We'll give you a call." When they all finally left, I was so exhausted that I disappeared to my room to meditate.

Later that night, I heard Carter moaning, he was delirious with fever. I called our doctor friend next door who came right over. "I'm going to send Carter to the emergency room, immediately." Carter was admitted into Harris Regional that night. "Catherine, he's really sick. He has acute diverticulosis. It's going to take a while for him to get better." I listened as Carter's doctor gave me his diagnosis. I remember thinking, "He's lying in bed being waited on and I'm left to move four children to a rented house far from my safe and secure world." Then, I was ashamed of myself for thinking such a thought.

Drayton was so proud of himself when he hung our treasured portrait of Robert E. Lee on a nail left by the last renters. "How do you like it here, Mama?"

"It's perfect, Drayton, but is that nail strong enough?"

"Yes ma'am." I left to head back to Summerville to get more boxes and check on Carter at the hospital but I felt so hurt and angry with him for being sick. I couldn't understand him or myself and it was hard for us to look at one another. "Are you going with me to see Daddy, Chamberlain?"

"No ma'am. I'm staying with the boys but will you please sneak Olivia here?"

"Honey, I want to bring her, too, but Daddy says it's safer to leave her at the house until we are completely settled. I'll go by and feed her and give her a kiss for you."

"Okay, Mama, I love her so much. Tell her for me, please."

"I will."

Our friend, Bill, the doctor, was standing beside Carter when I arrived. I could tell that I had interrupted a manly conversation. I was flabbergasted when Bill looked at me and said, "Catherine, you should be ashamed of yourself! Carter almost died, and you've been angry with him. It's not his fault that there's a recession and you've not gotten a job or helped him in any way." Tears welled in my eyes as I shouted "You bastards, I didn't cause any of this. I've been rearing four children and trying to be the best wife and mother I can be. You can both go straight to hell!"

I ran to my car, sobbing so heavily that I couldn't breathe. When I finally managed to drive to my now deserted home, I sat on the steps and cried even more when Olivia came to comfort me. The phone hadn't been disconnected yet and was ringing off the hook. After it rang for the twentieth time, I finally went in and picked up the receiver. "Catherine, you misunderstood what I was saying."

"Bill, you and Carter can both drop dead. Take good care of him because I won't be back. I'll be with my children." With that said I slammed down the phone and cried for my entire family.

Carter came home from the hospital after two weeks while my confusion and anger still consumed me. "I've completely settled our children into this place while you've done nothing but lie in bed, Carter. I'm trying to work through my anger so please give me some time. This whole mess—losing our home, your being sick and adjusting to a new place—is overwhelming for all of us." As I continued unpacking, I found myself muttering to myself, "If I could only find time for myself, maybe I can stop feeling so angry." What's the matter with you, Catherine? This isn't like you. Get a grip. Maybe you're depressed."

Carter was going to Summerville the next day so I asked, "If you feel like it tomorrow would you please bring Olivia home? Chamberlain misses her so much."

"Okay, Catherine, all I can say to you is that I'm so sorry. I didn't plan things to turn out like this."

"Oh, Carter, I know you didn't. I'm sorry, too and I'm so glad you're well.

Carter had a job interview the next day at Palmetto College just north of Charleston. After the interview, he called to say, "Chamberlain, get all of Olivia's toys ready, Daddy's bringing her home."

"I'm so excited, Mama. I can't wait to let her sleep in my bed." Chamberlain heard his car before I did. She came rushing past me into the kitchen and we both dashed to the top of the stairs. "Where is she? Sniffing out the yard?" I asked Carter. "I couldn't find her. She's gone. Let's call the SPCA and put an ad in the paper.

Chamberlain and I jumped into my car and headed for Summerville. As I ran out the door, I hollered back to Carter, "Did you get the job?"

"Yes, I start on Monday."

"Great! We'll talk later." We traveled every inch of Summerville looking for Olivia asking everyone if they had seen her but no luck and the SPCA hadn't seen her. We were exhausted when we got home. "If we don't find her, Chamberlain I'll get you another pet."

"I don't want another pet, Mama. I want Olivia."

"I do, too, honey." I sat with Chamberlain in my arms as she cried. I drove to Summerville everyday for a month but couldn't find our precious dog.

It wasn't until a year later that I found out exactly what happened to Olivia. Our neighbor just to the rear of the house, Hazel Locke, visited me at the beach. I had been hospitalized for a large kidney stone so Hazel came to visit. "What's lithotripsy, Catherine?" They have a new machine in town that shatters the stone and I'm getting it done tomorrow." Hazel was known for being a strange and interfering in other people's business but as I lay in my bed stunned as I listened to her talk. "Catherine, you certainly have been through a plight all at once and I really miss seeing all of you everyday. I'm so glad Jaffe and Peter continued to drive back to Summerville to finish their high school years. Drayton seems happy with the Island School and I know Chamberlain is doing well at her new private school, Rutledge Academy. Carter seems to like his new job as Director of Operations at Palmetto College, and you'll get better soon my dear. Oh, by the way, don't search for Olivia anymore because I know where she is. I was so heartsick when I watched her playing in your yard without her family that I scooped her up and took her to the pound to have her put down. The pound didn't know she was yours because I said she was a stray. I knew you'd understand my concern for her." I looked at Hazel as if she was a witch and then I politely smiled and said, "Yes, Hazel, I do understand."

Hazel had once confided to me after drinking too much vodka that her ailing husband, Brad, would have survived longer if it hadn't been for her. "When you're there day and night taking care of them, you know."

"You know what, Hazel?"

"Oh, you know when it's time to slip them a little too much of this or that. Brad didn't need a strong dose. I can tell you this he departed quickly." Once Hazel left, I grieved quietly for my darling Olivia and the life that I used to know. I missed being near my friends daily but I promised myself to make new ones as soon as I got out of the hospital and vowed not to tell Chamberlain about Olivia for a long time. She'd been through so much and I wanted to protect my little girl from the cruel world awhile longer.

Jaffe was a junior now at Palmetto College and majoring in business and Kim Johnson. Every time we looked around Kim was sitting on his lap or attached to him somewhere. Chamberlain was beginning to feel really left out. "Perhaps you can get the girls to bond, honey," I advised my eldest son. "Come on Mom…Kim and I are in love and we want to be together forever."

"She's only seventeen and too young, Jaffe. She and your sister act about the same age. "Well, you and Daddy have messed up our lives and I don't need you to tell me what to do."

"You might think we messed up your life, but someday you'll understand. If you don't think you need anyone to tell you what to do, you're wrong. First of all, you're not going to talk to me this way and next, you need to listen because Kim is very young. I'm begging you to please slow down with this relationship because I don't want to see you hurt." The final straw with Jaffe and Kim came the night Carter and I found them completely naked in Chamberlain's bed. "What do you think you're doing in here? This is your sister's room. Where are your clothes?"

"We're going to have sex."

"Are you crazy? You can't just come in here and tell me you're going to have sex together, Jaffe."

"Our clothes are over there, and sex is the plan, Mrs. Duvall," Kim said matter-of-factly. "I want you out of my daughter's bed! Put your clothes on now! I'm not leaving this room until you do. What would your mother think?"

"Oh, she'd be all for it; you should hear her with her new husband."

"Jaffe, get her out of Chamberlain's bed, now!"

"Okay Mama, calm down."

The next morning Jaffe told us that he was going to marry Kim no matter what we thought and that he was twenty and could do whatever he wanted. "But Kim is only seventeen."

"Her Dad's going to sign for her. She's just finished talking to him."

"Is he crazy?"

"Stop it, Mama! I'm getting married and out of here."

Two weeks after Jaffe's graduation from Palmetto College, our entire family including Daddy, Beth and her family, and an assortment of friends drove to Easley to watch the most dubious wedding imaginable. Chamberlain was a junior bridesmaid and wore a dress that Kim had chosen. "It's ugly," Chamberlain cried every time she saw it."

"No, it's not, honey. It's just different from what you usually wear so stop crying and get dressed because your brother needs you to be pretty." The only bridesmaid was Kim's sister, who was pudgy but beautiful. I had arranged the rehearsal dinner to take place in the only hotel in town. The menu turned out to be quite delightful, especially, the dessert: a pastry swan filled with whipped cream and berries or chocolate custard. All went well that night, but the next morning turned into a fiasco. I started crying and begged Jaffe not to marry Kim. "You're marrying her for all of the wrong reasons, son. I know we've had some problems in our family lately, but getting married to someone so young isn't the answer." It continued right up to the time for the wedding when Jaffe had stopped by our hotel room. "Son, take a trip to Europe for a year. Mom and I will pay all of your expenses if you'll change your mind."

"No thanks, Dad I'm getting married today."

"Jaffe, you know your grandparents didn't want me to marry your dad, so I understand how you feel but I agee with your Dad."

"I'm getting married to Kim within the hour, Mama." I looked over at Chamberlain who was still threatening to run away if she had to wear the dress. "I hate this balloon dress it looks stupid on me. Jaffe, please don't marry her, so I won't have to wear the dress." Beth knocked on our door, "It's almost time to go to the church."

"Beth, will you get Chamberlain ready and please use the curling iron on her hair."

Minutes later, there was a horrendous shriek from Chamberlain as she came running through our door. "Mama, she burned me, it hurts; it really hurts and I want to go home." Beth was right behind her, "I'm so sorry! I've never used a curling iron before because I only use hot rollers. Let me see your face, Chamberlain." The left side of Chamberlain's cheek was a scarlet red. Carter grabbed the first-aid kit as tears ran down my face. "It'll be okay, honey, I know it hurts, let me put this on it. Now, let's put on your dress and get this wedding over."

Kim's father was standing in the vestibule, with his shoulders convulsing as he sobbed. His much younger third wife was consoling him as Kim's mother escorted by her fifth husband arrived on a motorcycle. The nuptials were being held in the local Baptist church. As customary the bride's family sat on the left side and grooms sat on the right. Glancing over my shoulder at the bride's family, the thought of my days as a Baptist returned as I mumbled, "Baptist's might not drink, but the group really does divorce."

After we finished taking wedding pictures I found the church hall only to find that the reception was as dry as a desert, not a drop of liquor could be found. The special event looked more like a family reunion—friends and family rushed in with plates, casseroles, and desserts. Our young son and his bride stood before God and their families with the beautiful Waterford goblets Carter and I had given them as grape juice was poured before they toasted to their wedding bliss. Carter nudged my arm, "I need a stiff drink, honey."

"Me too Carter, when can we leave?"

"Not yet." The knife wasn't through the cake before Carter started edging toward the door. "Not yet," I mouthed to him. As soon as the rice fell to the ground and I heard the newlyweds crunching the hulls under their feet I motioned to Carter. As he tucked my arm in his I whispered, "Say thanks and good-bye at the same time and then we can go."

Mulling over the day, I realized the photographer hadn't taken a single picture of me. "Are you sure, Catherine? You were pretty upset, maybe you're wrong."

"I'm not wrong, Carter, wait and you'll see."

After we accepted that Jaffe was definitely marrying Kim, Carter and I gave him the money for their honeymoon to the mountains. We still remembered how the Duvall's had treated me, and Jaffe was our first born so we tried hard to put his happiness first. I was already feeling guilty about my behavior at the wedding and I loved Jaffe so much and only wanted him happy. "They'll be okay. Love conquers all!" I kept saying to myself.

When the honeymooners returned Jaffe called, "We're back; Mama and we have the wedding pictures. They look great. Are y'all going to be home for a while? We want to bring them over."

"Sure, son we'd love to see you."

"These are really good. Chamberlain looks cute. Thank goodness the photographer didn't get a picture of her burn."

"I see some really good shots but I haven't seen one of your Mama," I heard my husband say. Kim chimed in at this point, "Oh, the photographer apologized about that and he said it was just a mistake." She gave me a long, low smile, that I knew she was going to haunt me forever.

A few months after Jaffe's wedding, Carter and I had a huge argument because he'd been drinking and was threatening me. "We aren't as intimate as we used to be, Catherine. If you don't get your act together, I'm going to find someone else."

"I'm sorry Carter, but I need help. I'm still trying to deal with losing the house and you not confiding in me. It's been really hard for me to adjust to moving so unexpectedly and I miss Summerville, my friends and my gardens. I miss Olivia and I don't like you when you're drinking. I know I need a counselor. Will you go with me to see someone, please?"

"Absolutely not I won't waste money on a shrink like my mother did and you need to get your act together!"

"And you need to join AA. You do nothing but get drunk every night and I don't know you any more. I'm beginning to hate you."

"That's just fine! I'm going out so don't wait up!"

My heart sank as he walked out of the door. I knew that I had pushed him to do it and when I tried to sleep I couldn't. I listened to every noise and checked on Chamberlain at least a dozen times. When I heard the clock strike four o'clock, I knew Carter wasn't coming home and this was definitely the longest night of my life.

I was sitting beside the phone at 7:30 the next morning when it rang. "Hey, it's me and I need you to do something for me."

"Where are you? You sound funny. Where have you been all night? Are you okay?"

"I had drinks at Jester's Lounge while I watched the strippers. I headed home around four this morning but got stopped on the street before our house. I'm in jail and need you to bail me out. How much money do you have?"

"Maybe $50, how much do I need?"

"$500."

"Where am I going to get $500 this early in the morning?"

"Go to my favorite liquor store right over the bridge and knock on the door. He gets in early. Tell him what you need. Take a check from my checkbook and he'll give you the cash. Bring the cash to the jail on Leeds Avenue." I didn't want to wake the children but I had no choice. When we left Summerville Carter had sold his car, so we were down to mine. Carter had taken it out last night so I went quietly into Peter's room. After gently waking him I said, "Daddy's got a little problem because he had too much to drink last night and tried to drive home. He's in jail."

"What do we need me to do, Mama?"

"Will you give me a ride in your car? I need to get some cash and bail him out."

"I'll be ready in a few minutes." Next, I went into talk with Drayton. "Please take care of your sister and don't breathe a word. I don't want her to know about this."

"I want to go with you, I've never seen a jail."

"I really need for you to stay with Chamberlain, son."

"I'll go and get the girl across the street to come over and sit with her, Mama. Please let me go."

"Okay, honey but hurry." Drayton dressed and marched straight across the street returning with the sitter. "She probably won't wake up, but if she does help her fix some breakfast and tell her that we had to run an errand. I'll call if we are going to be gone too long. Thanks for coming."

The boys and I climbed into Peter's black Trans Am, its dark tinted windows hiding our faces, as we headed out on our dirty deed. Knocking on the liquor store window, cars rushed by as I tried to hide my face until the proprietor opened the door. "What can I do for you, ma'am?"

"I need this check cashed immediately so I can bail my husband out of jail. He shops here frequently."

"I know he does, he's one of my best customers. They caught him, huh? Sure, I'll cash his check but please tell him I'll see him next week."

The boys and I headed north to the county jail. When we drove up, there were plenty of strange sights to see arriving to post bail. After taking a number we took a seat when an officer asked, "Who are you here for?"

"Carter Duvall."

"I was the officer that arrested him and he was pretty slick. His blood alcohol level was .23 and I think he's still drunk in his cell. Before he started running from my partner and me he told me that I was ruining his life. You look like a nice family so I suggest that you get him into a program before he destroys himself or someone else."

"Thanks, Officer Reynolds, I appreciate your concern."

Just then Peter and Drayton walked out escorting their father. "Let's get him into the car quickly, he's still drunk," I heard my sons saying. I was so angry with Carter that by the time we were heading home I couldn't say a word. He was in the back seat giggling and burping and the boys started to smile at the ridiculousness of their father. My face remained granite until he fell over and passed out and the boys and I burst out laughing and discussing how long he should be punished.

As the new school year approached, I knew car trips to the city from the beach were going to be long so I began searching for a new place to live closer to Chamberlain's school. She needed to be near her friends where she could ride her bicycle and play in a neighborhood. I found the perfect house on South Battery close enough to the water for all of us. We could walk one block and look out at the harbor and Fort Sumter and the boys were thrilled to be moving into the city because they had so many friends downtown. Chamberlain had really missed Katie but now she had a new best friend from Rutledge Academy, Leigh Anne McNamara, who lived only a block away.

This time things went smoother because Carter participated in the move. It was a mild September weekend with the fresh breeze blowing in off the water that made decorating this house a real joy. I was back in an old charmer and in my glory. Betsy and Jefferson McNamara, Leigh Anne's parents, were our first visitors. Carter and Jefferson were becoming great friends enjoying their evening libation together. Jefferson was a tax attorney with a local firm and a very dedicated Irishman and a glorified member of the Leprechaun League. The Leprechaun League was an elite group in Charleston where a member must be signed up at birth. Betsy worked as an administrator in the education system. In fact, according to her stories and gift of gab, she could have invented the entire system. A teacher, turned administrator, Betsy had an answer for everything. From the beginning of our friendship, I knew that the only way to please Betsy was to listen to her and then do whatever I wanted. She consistently tried to tell me how to rear Chamberlain…forgetting that Chamberlain was my fourth child and Leigh Anne was only her second. Both girls were in second grade at Rutledge Academy and adored being together. Chamberlain hadn't been this happy since we moved from Summerville.

Jaffe and Kim seemed to be getting along okay, although we only saw them for a quick visit once in a while. Chamberlain often asked Jaffe, "Can I come spend the night?" He would tell her that she needed to ask

Kim, and Kim would say that they were too busy. A silent wedge seemed to be growing between our families.

Peter and Drayton were thrilled in our new house, and life again was good. I was desperate to pull my family back together, and knew we must get back to church. Saint Ann's Church was my choice for this reconnection and since it was the oldest Catholic church in the southeast I knew it would help our chances of survival.

Since Carter worked at Palmetto College, I received a discount on my graduate courses so I began work on my masters degree so Chamberlain and I set up a study area and did our homework together.

One day as I drove toward the Furman Building at the college, I saw Kim nose to nose with a nice looking young man who was not my son. I watched as they put their arms around one another, oblivious to their surroundings. Quickly, I drove my car in the opposite direction. "I tell you, Carter, she's having an affair, and Jaffe doesn't have a clue. No, I'm not going to tell him. Do you think I should? He'll never believe me, and I'll be the bad guy in all of this."

"How do you intend to handle this, Catherine?"

"I'm not sure yet; I'll let you know."

Months passed and I continued to catch peeps of an affair that I couldn't believe. I did some investigating and learned that Kim's other man was much closer to her age and wasn't married. He was on the tennis team with her so I tried to get information from Jaffe but it was useless. He didn't have a clue about his deceitful wife.

In March we invited Kim and Jaffe to our house for hamburgers and Chamberlains birthday. Jaffe arrived without Kim. "Where's Kim, honey? Does she have to work again tonight?"

"Uh huh, she's working, Mom."

"Are you feeling okay, son? You look really pale."

"I'll be okay, Mama."

"Okay everybody let's eat!" As we ate and sang and did the whole birthday thing, I kept a watchful eye on my eldest son who looked terribly sad. "Hey, Jaffe, Drayton and I are going out for a while. You wanna come?"

"Where y'all going, Peter? Will we be out late?" We're going to the Blind Bats to listen to Bluegrass, Stephen's playing tonight."

"Sure, I'd love to come."

All three of my boys left with their arms tightly wrapped around one another. As they thundered down the stairs, I couldn't help but feel a burst of pride. "You three are certainly a handsome bunch!"

"Thanks, Mom!" Then they were off. It must have been two o'clock when I heard them all come home. The next night, all three boys went out together again and didn't come in until three o'clock. The next night was the same routine. I'd had enough.

Peter and Drayton dragged themselves out of bed just after lunch. "Where's Jaffe? Did he go home last night? "I'm right here, Mom. It was too late so I didn't want to drive over the bridge."

"You boys go ahead and get something to eat. I left food in the kitchen for you." I waited until they had finished eating. "You boys don't need to clean up. I'll do it in a few minutes but I do want to talk to Jaffe. I waited for the two younger boys to leave the room before looking at him. "Son, where's your wife? Why have you been going out with your brothers every night and why did you really spend the night here? It's time for you to tell the truth."

He looked at me in disbelief before saying, "I'm sorry, Mama but I just didn't know how to tell you. It was the night of Chamberlain's birthday and I hurried home from work to pick up Kim so we could come over here. She wasn't home, but she left me this." Jaffe dug a crumpled letter out of his pocket and passed it across the table. After I read it, I grabbed my son and smothered him in hugs and kisses. "Jaffe, I'm so sorry. I'm so sorry that you're hurting." Carter came home and into the room while we sat crying. "What's going on?"

"Here, read this."

Dear Jaffe,

I am writing this letter to tell you that I'm not going to your silly sister's party tonight or to any party at your parent's house. I know that you have been asking me to get pregnant, but there's no way that I want your mother's genes inside a child of mine. I detest her! I know she told you about my affair with Chris. I love him very much, and I'm moving in with him as soon as possible. I could never have children with you because I don't love you and never did. I thought your family had money. According to you, they are Charleston's finest. I know you'll find someone else, but I'm sure your mother will run her off, too. You will never get children because of her. Tell the bitch she won!

Kim

"Come here, son," Carter said, giving Jaffe a hug. "Thanks, Dad. What am I going to do? I had no idea that she was having an affair. What is she talking about that Mom told me?"

"Your mother saw her kissing and carrying on behind posts and other places on campus. I finally saw her, too, but we decided that it was best not to tell you. We were afraid you wouldn't believe us, and Kim would lie. I'm so sorry. What are you going to do now? How can we help you, son?"

"I don't know, Dad. I'm going to call Kim and try to talk with her…after all, she is still my wife. No one in our family has ever divorced. I can't tell granddaddy Truman about this, he won't understand."

"My father certainly will understand, in fact I'm sure he'll help you financially with your divorce, son. There's always a first in every family. You are his first grandson, and he adores you. Do you want me to call him?"

"No, I'll call him myself, Mom." Jaffe did call his grandfather who was very supportive and suggested that the two of them visit Bishop John the next day for guidance. Jaffe called Kim and she refused to talk to him or see him. After two months of her avoiding him, Jaffe started proceedings for an annulment. Once the Bishop read Kim's letter, he confirmed that Jaffe was entitled to an annulment. The two of them hadn't been married in the Catholic Church but the contributing factor was the statement that she never wanted children with Jaffe. That letter was backfiring on her. "I went over to tell Kim the news about the annulment and to explain the details to her but I couldn't believe what I saw, Mom."

"What is it, son?"

"She's huge…really big. She has gained so much weight."

"Maybe she's been stress eating, honey."

"No, Mom, she's pregnant!"

"Oh my God is it yours?"

"No, it can't be because I haven't been near her in quite sometime. Can you believe her?"

"Yes, honey. I can."

Chamberlain was delighted to have her big brother back in her life, as we all were, but his heartbreak and loneliness made us sad. "Will you come over more now, Jaffe? I've missed you so much. Let's go to the park and play tennis."

"Okay, little sister, but I want you to remember all of this and never let a guy do this to you. I'll be watching every boy who comes near you. Let's go."

"Jaffe, you're so silly, I'm only nine." Watching my children reconnecting warmed my heart.

Chamberlain seemed to blossom under the watchful eye of her big brother. He'd bought her a fluffy toy poodle that she named Ruffle. She loved Ruffle so much and was getting over her loss of Olivia. "Come on, Ruffle, I know you're a boy, but let me put this little bathrobe on you. You'll look so cute."

"Chamberlain, I think you should be a fashion designer."

"Thanks, Jaffe. Doesn't he look cute?" I looked through the doorway to see a very adorable hooded dog with his bathrobe tied beneath his tummy. At this very moment, Ruffle jumped down and ran out the screen door to the back yard. We all ran to the door and watched as he hiked his leg and totally soaked his new wardrobe. "I guess I need to work on my designs a bit more!" I heard my strawberry blonde giggle as she got out her scissors.

Chamberlain was getting ready to go back to school so we'd shopped in every store in town. She bought the cutest lunch box and monogrammed book bag from Sarah Anne's, her favorite shop on King Street. Chamberlain thought Sarah Anne's was her personal boutique. Sarah Anne's had really grown over the years beginning with toys and gifts and now into beautiful apparel, accessories and even shoes. Shoes were our passion, and we'd been in every shoe store. "Do you need anything else, honey? I'm getting pretty tired."

"I don't think so, Mommy. Where are we going for lunch? I love shopping with you, Mama "Let's go to the King Street Café. I know you love it there."

"Can we call Leigh Anne and her mom to meet us?"

"Sure, use my phone and tell them to meet us in thirty minutes."

"Hey! Glad y'all could join us; I see you have been shopping too, Betsy. "We went to Sarah Anne's."

"We did too but didn't see y'all, we must have just missed each other. Chamberlain got a lunchbox and book bag."

"I know, Sarah Anne told us that y'all had been in so Leigh Anne got the same ones." Chamberlain gave me a vexed look as I smiled trying to console her with my eyes. "Let's order, I'm starved!"

"Can I get a virgin strawberry daiquiri, Mommy? Sounds delicious, I'll have one, too.

9
Hugo

September was gliding by and Chamberlain was comfortable in school. Jaffe was working hard and staying with Daddy while Peter and Drayton were busy with their studies. Carter was absorbed in his new job, and I was busy finishing my masters' degree. I was completely immersed in studying, knowing that I wouldn't be satisfied unless I made all A's. I was so wrapped up in my school work that I hadn't read the newspaper, watched TV, or talked with any of my friends in ages.

The only person I called daily was Daddy and he'd been disappearing regularly for the last several months while Carter and I worried about his health and safety. Finally, I found out the reason for his disappearances, her name was Priscilla LeBlanc, twice widowed. Daddy was smitten from the very beginning and we were too. Ms. LeBlanc was very attractive, charismatic, and spontaneous particularly when sharing details about my father. I remember just after meeting her as we sat on sofa, "You know, Catherine," she gushed, "According to your father, your mother Rachel was always so sick that he never…"

"Never what, Priscilla?" Blushing she gushed, "I'm talking too much, oh, I'll tell you another time when we get to know one another better." My face turned beet red when I realized what she was talking about Daddy's sex life. Daddy and Priscilla became a real item, although he always declared, "There'll be only one wife for me, and that's my Rachel."

Late one September afternoon in 1989, I whizzed up to Betsy poking along in her Mercedes. We stopped on the side of the street and double-parked to chat. "I'm going to pick up Chamberlain. Do you want me to get Leigh Anne?"

"That would be great, I'm rushing to the store to stock up on groceries and supplies."

"Are y'all going to have another party?"

"No! I'm afraid that thing is going to sit out there and spin and then get us."

"Goodness, Betsy, what on earth are you talking about?"

"You mean you don't have a clue? Don't you watch the news or weather?"

"Haven't had time with all my studying, I'm just too busy."

"Well…I suggest that you tune in tonight, girl 'cause there's a storm brewing off the coast and I think it's after us."

I picked the girls up from school, dropped them off at piano lessons and headed home. Turning on the TV, I saw Charlie Hart describing the conditions developing off the eastern coast. "Folks, I'm telling you not to worry yet but stay tuned for updates. Hugo is its name and it's not budging at this point." I called Carter at work. "Did you know that we have a storm off the coast?"

"Yeah, I've been in meetings with the emergency preparedness people all day. It looks like we might get this one, Catherine. I guess we'd better get ready."

I picked Chamberlain and Leigh Anne up from piano lessons and took Leigh Anne to her house. By now Betsy was home and walked out to my car. "The stores are empty!"

"Where'd you go to shop?"

"The Teeter."

"Well, I'll head to Piggly Wiggly right now." Betsy asked, "Chamberlain, do you want to stay here with Leigh Anne and me?"

"Please, Mama, can I?"

"Sure, honey, I've got a lot of things to get; I'll pick you up on my way home."

They were putting out the last supply of water just as I got to the store. I grabbed a dozen gallons before heading off to the canned goods and bread. Carter was stopping for batteries and first aid supplies. Exhausted,

I finally checked out of Piggly Wiggly after filling three grocery baskets and drove straight to home, hoping that Carter and Drayton would be there. "Hey, Mom, have you heard about the big storm?"

"I have! As a matter of fact, I have the car loaded with groceries and supplies. Do you mind helping me get them inside?"

"You go on in, Mom. I'll get them."

Drayton surrounded me with bags faster than I could possibly unload them and Peter's' chocolate lab, Morgan, and Chamberlain's poodle Ruffle couldn't keep their noses out of the bags. "Do you think you bought enough stuff, Mom?"

"It won't go to waste if the storm passes us by, and if it blows in here we'll have plenty. You know we'll lose our power, so I got loads of canned goods."

"All I know about hurricanes comes from TV and the stories you've told us about Gracie. Do you think we'll really get this one?"

"I don't know, honey, but Charlie Hart and the mayor seem to be getting very anxious."

A few more days passed and finally on the morning of September 21, we sat glued to the TV while commentators predicted that Hugo was going to hit Charleston. "Folks, the storm surge could be between ten and twenty feet high."

"You know, Catherine, the wanes coating in the living room was added after Gracie and it marks the height of water during that storm."

"Oh my God, we'll have to move everything to the second and third stories." I said, "Let's wait a little longer before we start moving things" just before a flash came on the TV. "The Mayor will make a speech and we'll be right back as soon as he's through." Not one of us budged from our seats. "And now, the honorable Mayor of Charleston."

Surrounded by a throng of reporters sticking microphones in his face, the Mayor began his speech. "Thank you. Folks I want you to know that this hurricane is mighty and there's a very good chance that it will strike Charleston. It could be one of the worst disasters of this century. The wall of water could be eight, ten, maybe fifteen feet above sea level and severely flood low-lying areas. People in one-story houses could have a real problem! Many of your neighbors, friends, and family have voluntarily left the area, but now I am ordering everyone—all of you who are located in or near Charleston—to evacuate immediately. Let's keep it orderly and swift, check your emergency evacuation routes now. Stop boarding up your houses and go…get out of here!

Following the Mayor's speech, FEMA personnel added their evaluation of the situation before Charlie Hart came back on the screen. Charlie had been at the station since my family bought our first TV in the late 1950s. I'd watched him in black and white back when the station came on around 4:30 or five o'clock in the afternoon. As children we sat and watched the test pattern until Flash Gordon came on. Charlie Hart was a household word, and everyone trusted his opinion.

Charlie was giving the latest weather update…"Please, folks, listen to all the warnings. Take this storm seriously…it is not a joke! This storm is very dangerous! Please, listen to the Mayor, evacuate now!

"Boys, start grabbing furniture and get it upstairs. Catherine, pack the sterling and your jewelry in the car. Chamberlain, pack some games and enough food for Ruffle and Morgan to last for a few days and carry a big pan of water to the bathroom on the third story for your cats. Take the litter box up there for Sara and Magic, too. We won't be able to handle both the cats and the dogs so put enough dry food down for the cats because they'll stay here. "Do we have to leave them, Daddy?"

"Sorry, honey, but we're going to the College and there could be other dogs that'll go after them. They'll be safe here at home, I promise."

"Okay, Daddy." Everyone was scurrying and preparing for our departure. "Carter, I really don't want to leave the house. Can't we send the kids to Daddy's and stay here?"

"I have to get back to the college, honey, you know I'm responsible for keeping things moving there. They'll have students who can't go home, and who knows what this storm will destroy. I have to be there and so do you. I'm not leaving you here alone! Now, get busy getting our things together, please!"

Carter and the boys moved all of the furniture that they possible could, except the grand piano and Chippendale sideboard that were too heavy to get up the stairs. "They'll have to stay where they are. "They were my great grandmother's!"

"I know but they'll have to stay."

Carter left for the College around one o'clock while the children and I stayed to finish up the smaller things. "Did you put all the picture albums in the Jeep, Peter?"

"Yes ma'am."

"Okay, Chamberlain and I are leaving with the dogs so you boys hurry behind us, please. I'll be worried if I don't know where you are."

"We know, Mama but Dr. Pruitt just asked us to help him move some of their things upstairs. It won't take long."

Chamberlain and I headed up the interstate heading west away from Charleston at three o'clock. The dogs and everything else possible was crammed into our Jeep Cherokee. Morgan was panting and hopping all over the car. It was obvious that he was playful and sweet but in dire need of obedience school. Ruffle licked Chamberlain's face all over before settling down in a tiny spot beside her. As we approached Cosgrove Avenue, it appeared that we might be sitting on the interstate when the storm hit. Inwardly, I was panicking, but outwardly, I tried to stay calm for my young daughter. I kept questioning my every action: "Why didn't you leave sooner, Catherine? You should have anticipated this backup on the interstate. What if this traffic doesn't clear? What's your plan now?"

"Mommy, there are the Sullivan's waving at you. Let the windows down."

"Hey, this is a mess isn't it?"

"Hello, Catherine!" John and Susan were both chatting rapidly. Where are Carter and the boys? Where are y'all staying? I just heard that they are going to open more lanes to get us out of this."

"Carter's already at the college and the boys are coming behind me. We're staying at Palmetto. I hope we start moving a little faster soon."

They waved as the policeman shouted, "Cross the median; drive north using the southbound lane of the interstate." Chamberlain and I arrived at the dorm room reserved for us just after 5:30. Carter looked as though he'd been put through a ringer. "What took you so long?"

"Traffic!"

"What time did you leave?"

"Three o'clock."

"It took you two and a half hours to drive fifteen miles?"

"That's right and we both need to use the bathroom. I need to pee! Have you seen the boys yet?" I yelled over my shoulder as I ran past him.

"No. I'm getting worried about them too. What time did they leave?"

"I'm not sure. Bill Pruitt asked them to help him move some things. They should be here soon."

Peter and Drayton arrived not long after I got back from the bathroom. "You should see the line of people coming out of the city, Dad," Peter exclaimed. I heard Drayton chime in with, "They're saying that the water's going to rise even higher than they thought earlier."

"You boys did get all of the portraits moved to the upstairs, didn't you?"

"Most of them, Mama," Drayton sheepishly confided. "Which ones are still hanging downstairs?"

"Robert E. Lee, Great-grandmother Jaffe and George Washington."

"Boys, those are very valuable pieces and can't be replaced." Before I could say another word, they jumped into their Jeep and took off, the top puffing up with the wind that had begun blowing. "We'll be right back!" Peter yelled as Drayton waved and smiled his devilish grin.

As they headed back toward the interstate, my heart sank to my feet because clouds and rain had already begun. "Can they make it back here before the storm gets too bad, Carter?' He looked at the sky and at his watch. "It's 6:15 and the storm's not supposed to hit until around midnight. I think they'll be fine, but it depends on the traffic and whether anything goes wrong."

I paced in our tiny dorm room listening to the various scenarios on the radio stations. Chamberlain was on the bed playing Nintendo and talking to the dogs. It was getting really dark outside and the wind was blowing harder. Charlie Hart told us on the radio that waves were now washing over the piers at the beaches. Just as I was about to have a panic attack the boys burst through the door. "Boy, you should see it out there especially off the Battery. The water is whirling around like a washing machine and it's up to the railings. There's nobody around...Charleston's' like a big ghost town! Deserted! You know the sign over that hotel by the

Dorchester Road? It kept flashing over and over...'If you can read this, you're going the wrong way! Turn around, now!' It was awesome going back without anybody there, wasn't it Drayton?"

"It sure was and I can't wait to go back in the morning and see what the storm did. Oh by the way, we checked on the cats, too, Mama. They're doing fine."

As we all settled down to wait, Carter was busy checking the glass atrium and looking for objects that might get blown around. Before ten o'clock that evening, the wind had increased, and all power was out. Chamberlain was fast asleep in one of the single beds. Carter and the boys had carried in several extra mattresses earlier so we'd all be comfortable. The minutes past by excruciatingly slow while we sat silently; listening for every minute sound outside. The screeching winds turned into very low howling as their speed climbed to 135 mph and gusts reached 185 mph. The air conditioner in the wall of the concrete building was shaking so hard that we were sure it was going to fly through our room.

The boys grabbed the mattresses and pulled them over their heads. I lightly covered Chamberlain with a mattress to protect her in case the wall blew in. Carter sat with his arm around me and we were praying about the time we heard a tremendous crash. Carter carefully opened our door in time to see the rest of the atrium glass walls tumble down and through the air. Shaking, I thought, "This is it we're not going to survive this storm." I didn't realize I was holding my breath until I got light headed and almost fainted. "Catherine, take a deep breath, I need you to help me, please. Breathe."

"I'm sorry, honey, I'm just so scared. I wish Jaffe was with us, too."

"He'll be safe with your Daddy; you know they'll make it together."

"Do you think they stayed at Daddy's or went to Priscilla's?"

"I'll bet they're in Mount Pleasant at Priscilla's house. You know how much your Daddy cares about her."

We heard more crashing and the winds were so loud that we couldn't hear one another talking sitting side by side. I prayed for everybody I knew and worried about Sara and Magic. I figured by now our house was completely torn apart and without a roof. "Poor cats," I whimpered to myself. Suddenly, the wind stopped and I took a breath. "Hurry, y'all, get the dogs out to the bathroom while I check out the damages here." The boys and I quickly and quietly put leashes on the dogs and walked out the back door of our dorm.

All the visible pine trees were cut off half way down to the ground and debris was everywhere. Carter softly walked up behind us. "Things look pretty gruesome on the other side of the atrium, but no one's hurt. Where's Chamberlain?"

"Still sleeping, she doesn't have a clue that the storm's even hit."

"We'd better get back inside before the eye passes over and it won't be long now."

Chamberlain was still fast asleep, and we didn't want to wake her. The storm was bad enough without listening to her tears. It wasn't long before the low growling started again. I was hoping this quadrant of the storm wouldn't be so violent, but the gusts were even stronger and so furious that I covered myself with a mattress. The dogs were so freaked out that they joined me. Carter kept trying to open the door to the hall to check on things but the winds were so strong that he couldn't budge it.

I'm not sure how many agonizing hours we held onto our mattresses and each other, praying for our lives but I do remember the moment it ended. The silent calm was eerie. Exhausted and thankful, we carefully uncovered ourselves to peep out and see if anyone needed help. Disbelief quickly replaced our fear and panic.

Harris Regional Hospital was across the street from Palmetto College and the whole side of it was missing with stretchers hanging out the side of the building. The cars below were strewn with concrete, hospital equipment, and trees and there wasn't an entrance to the hospital any more. Cars were everywhere thrown about like Matchbox toys.

The situation at Palmetto was much the same according to Carter. He surveyed the needs of the facility while jumping over live electrical wires scattered throughout.

Just before the sun came up, the entire Duvall family jumped into our son's two Jeeps and headed for Charleston. We knew we had to get there before the National Guard had time to get into place. We'd decided that if we didn't hurry, they might not let us back into the city. Chamberlain was in total disbelief that she had missed the entire storm! We drove around downed power poles with wires sparking all around. Cars and trucks were thrown all about on the interstate and several eighteen wheelers were flung like trash. Closer to the Charleston port, huge containers had been tossed onto the interstate. We rode in the median to dodge rooftops, signs, and boats that had been swept wild by the winds of Hugo.

As we tried to get near our South Battery home, the water was too high for even the Jeeps. They stalled out at Colonial Lake so decided to walk the rest of the way. I climbed out of the Jeep, forgetting that I was only 5'2"tall. "How deep do you think this water is?"

"Probably four or five feet." As my feet hit the mucky water and felt for the ground, I took a deep breath finally touching the ground with the water a few inches below my shoulders. "This feels yucky! Wait for me, y'all. I'm coming."

Peter had Chamberlain, with Ruffle in her arms, on his shoulders because she didn't want to get wet. Carter and Drayton carried chainsaws and tools on theirs while Morgan swam as fast as he could go.

Houses floated from their foundations and closed off streets. Carter finally came back to help me through the turmoil as we reached our home. "Oh God" I cried "It's still here. Look at the Pruitt's tree through our front door." I tried to climb past the limbs to get inside but Carter insisted I wait until he and the boys cut them off. Before the loud buzz of the saw began, I thought I heard a cat meowing and strained my ears but all I could hear was the buzzing. Once the doorway was clear enough to enter, the boys scampered through the water and muck inside up to the third story to get the cats. Each boy came down with one severely traumatized cat in his arms. They wouldn't stop meowing and their eyes told the story of their fright. After we all petted and cooed over them, I said "With all this water down here, you'd better take them back up stairs where they'll be safe. Move them into Chamberlain's room with fresh litter, please."

Carter yelled, "Watch out!" I turned around to see my refrigerator floating upside down come through the dining room door. I quickly moved as my husband tackled it and pushed it back into the kitchen. The boys were busy chasing crabs and fish that were swimming throughout the living room. Drayton played Beethoven's Fifth Symphony on the floating piano as he and Chamberlain turned it round and round in the water. "I think we'll need to get it tuned, Mom."

"I think it's going to need more than that, son, but at least it's still here." Many weeks of cleanup began for us and all of those in Hugo's path.

We finally located Daddy and Jaffe at Priscilla's in Mount Pleasant. They had property damage when an oak tree fell through the roof at Daddy's house and tons of water damaged the floors. After finally getting through to us by phone, Beth loaded her car with water, paper towels, toilet paper, and other supplies—particularly bourbon for Carter—and drove up from Florida.

Charleston was sheer chaos and the National Guard was a welcomed sight. Called in to protect all of us, they were wonderful and great at doing their job. Our nightly curfew was strictly enforced—even the nights that I drove to a Broad Street corner to give them some special treats. "Now, Mrs. Duvall, you know that you're not supposed to be out after curfew."

"I know, young man, but I wanted to bring you this. I'm heading straight back home."

"Okay. You hurry now, and thanks for the supper." We hadn't had electricity in over a week so everything was pitch-black. I carefully headed home.

Before Hugo, I'd stocked the freezer with the fresh fish the fellows caught. It was also loaded with turkeys, steaks, roasts, chickens, pork chops and butts, venison, pounds of shrimp, crabmeat, and tons of frozen vegetables. We kept things frozen for as long as we could, but without electricity things were thawing. Carter had put our gas stove upright after it floated through the kitchen door into the back yard. After I don't know how many hours, he'd blown enough water out of the vents so that it actually worked. None of our neighbors had gas stoves but everyone had a thawing freezer. I became the South of Broad Street Cooker. There wasn't anything else to do but clean or play cards so I cooked for everyone, including the National Guardsmen.

Bill and Rebecca Pruitt lived across the street. He was a successful doctor and Rebecca was absolutely charming but pretty reclusive. I watched as Bill walked across the street to talk with Carter and they went back through the gates. They began scampering through the gardens of the Pruitt estate, connecting orange cords over to our house. A short while later, Carter came inside for a drink. "Bill's partner brought him four new generators so he could hook up pumps to his ponds. If he doesn't, he's going to lose all of his prize-winning fish. You've seen how many they've already lost, haven't you?"

"Dozens and I saw Morgan carrying one over here. He was barking and jumping at the poor thing while it was dying. They're really starting to smell bad."

"I'm helping him hook up the generators because he doesn't have much time and he's frantically trying to save the rest. He said that we could use one of the generators over here."

"That's wonderful!"

"Rebecca said they'd be over for dinner again tonight. I guess they like your cooking."

"It might be that there's no where else for them to go silly."

Our house had severe structural damage so we couldn't have air conditioning or heat until the house was completely renovated. The force of the water had moved our staircase, and the outside walls were bowing. We would definitely have to move out for a while. Four weeks after Hugo, we still had no electricity one night while Betsy and Leigh Anne were sitting on my bed with Chamberlain and me. By candlelight we were talking about our lives before Hugo when suddenly there was a spark right outside my bedroom window. "Look at that firefly!" the girls shouted. "That's not a firefly, girls. It's an electrical spark!" I told them as I looked out the window. Down on the corner of our street I saw men from the Georgia Power Company working on lines but before I could say another word, our power came on. There were cheers and tears as we all ran to thank them. People were everywhere hugging and dancing in the streets for such a truly joyous event.

By the end of October, Carter and I had finally cleaned the muck out of the house and were trying to find another place to live. "There's nothing available because everybody's in the same mess we are. Do you want to move in with your Daddy?"

"It's so far away from Chamberlain's school and her friends. Let's look a little longer." We finally found an upstairs apartment on Trapp Street. It had three bedrooms, a kitchen, living room and dining room and a huge closed-in sun porch so we squeezed furniture everywhere and stacked box after box on the sun porch. "This will just have to do," I said to Betsy as we finished our drinks. "Where are y'all going?"

"We're going to stay in our house but we've gotten a bunch of space heaters and we'll use the fireplaces. Our house didn't get the structural damage yours did. Hey, it's getting close to Thanksgiving. Ya'll want to have dinner together?"

"Sure, this place is pretty small. Can we come to your house? I'll help cook. What do you want me to bring?"

"Of course, we'll do it at my house; you know how Jefferson is about his house. Invite your Daddy and Priscilla, too, if you want. We'll get together on the menu later. Right now I have to go over to the Leprechaun League to go over the details for my parents' fiftieth wedding anniversary party. Y'all will get your invitation."

We received our invitation on December 19, the day before the party. Mail carriers were having trouble finding houses and people because so many had been destroyed or the people moved.

Everyone was trying to get back to normal routines but it wasn't easy. Chamberlain and the boys finally were back in school. Jaffe was working hard trying to forget Kim and his failed marriage. Stress was getting to Carter and me, and we were arguing all the time over stupid things. I never saw Daddy because he was always at Priscilla's and life was confusing and dreadful in our Trapp Street apartment. I tried to smile all of the time to cover my feelings although I wasn't sure why I was angry. My life, as I knew it, seemed to have come to a screeching halt and the only thing that kept me going was the fact that so many of my friends said they felt the same way after Hugo. I was so sad, but I had no one to talk to about it because everyone seemed to be smiling just like me. I was so thankful when Thanksgiving was over because I didn't feel thankful for anything these days except my four children. I certainly wasn't thankful for a husband who drank all the time. I was always so exhausted and tired; some nights I could hardly stay awake past 8:30.

Carter poured himself three shots of bourbon while we were dressing to go to Betsy's parents' anniversary party not once noticing my new outfit or me. By the time I finished my glass of wine, I was ready to stay home and go to bed. "Why don't you go on without me?"

"You know Betsy and Jefferson will be upset if you don't show up. Now hurry up, and let's go."

The music from the band filtered out on to King Street. As we entered the hall, the elaborate staircase was filled with guests eager to help Betsy's parents celebrate. The beautiful staircase spiraled up to four elaborately decorated ballrooms. The gigantic Ionic columns supporting the staircase were trimmed with ornate motifs. Looking up at the massive crystal chandeliers inside the ballrooms, I saw a tremendous gold four-leaf clover with a leprechaun peeping over the edge of its leaves and I wondered how they'd managed to suspend it from the ceiling. Tables were covered with food, and bartenders were stationed in all directions. Not long after we arrived, I found Betsy to ask if she needed any help. "Everything's under control, Catherine. Just enjoy yourself; I'll see you in a little while."

As Betsy started to walk away, I shouted, "You'd better hurry over there!" We both dashed across the room grabbing vases as the whole side of beef started sliding off the collapsing table almost crashing to the floor. A few men caught everything. "Seems the leg on this table didn't get caught, Mrs. McNamara. We're so sorry." Betsy looked frazzled as we put everything back together. "Great catch, Catherine."

"Thanks."

The great hall was filled with people dancing and laughing, but I couldn't see Carter anywhere. "Would you like to dance?"

"I'd love to, Charles." Charles was very good looking and had recently divorced his wife of twenty years because she'd fallen in love with an insurance executive. "Is Carter with you?" Charles asked as he whisked me around the floor. "He's here somewhere. I haven't seen him since we arrived."

"He doesn't know what he's missing, Catherine. I'd keep you close by my side."

"Oh, Charles, you're so sweet."

Carter finally showed up several hours later. "Where have you been?" I asked. Before he answered I knew, "You've had too much to drink. You've been going from bar to bar haven't you? Come on. Let's get you some food before you embarrass both of us." I couldn't wait for this party to be over because I was exhausted. I had promised Betsy that I'd stay until the very end of the party in case she needed help gathering the silver trays and crystal that we'd brought.

I was as tipsy as Carter after midnight when we went into the back kitchen to get silver. As we loaded the trays in our arms and started down the steep back steps, I stubbed my toe on the banister. "Ouch!" I yelped sitting down right on the steps I took off my heels. "I think I broke my toe."

"No, you didn't," Carter slurred. "Come on, Catherine." I stood up and proceeded to take off my other shoe and pull down my panty hose right there. "Yes, I did, damn it and it hurts like hell. Look at it!"

"Pick up your stockings and shoes and let's go home before everyone hears you!" I scooped up my stuff and hobbled toward the front of the hall where there was Charles. "Catherine, are you hurt? Let me help you to your car. How are you, Carter?"

"Drunk! Great party wasn't it, Charles? "It sure was!" he said as he rubbed his hands across my shoulders.

By the time I climbed up the stairs to our apartment, my big toe felt like it was the size of a balloon and it was throbbing so badly that all I could do was cry. "Be quiet. You're going to wake up the children."

"Go to hell, Carter," I cried as I took several aspirin and climbed into my bed. Carter gathered a blanket and headed for the sofa. As I tried to doze, I heard the crystal top on the decanter clank beside the bottle as I rolled over and passed out.

I slept about three hours before waking in the most excruciating pain. As soon as it was morning, I went next door to the Callahan's because Marshall Callahan was an orthopedic surgeon. I was standing on their porch trying to decide whether to knock or not when the door opened. "Marshall! Thank God you're awake."

"Well, hello, Catherine, I was just coming out to get the paper but I see that you're delivering today, thanks."

"Oh, yeah, here's your paper, Marshall. I am in a lot of pain! I think I have broken my toe. Can you look at it?"

"Sure, have a seat. Want some coffee? Sylvia's still sleeping. She sleeps late on Sundays. Now let me look at that toe. Yep. You broke your big toe and the one next to it. In fact, I'm sure they're broken in half but I'll take you down to the office and x-ray them later."

"Then what will you do?"

"Nothing!"

"Nothing? But they're broken, and they hurt so much."

"I know. Broken toes are painful, but all I can do is splint them and tape them together to keep them from moving. Sorry Catherine!" Marshall buzzed around me with his tape and splints before sending me on my way with a prescription for painkillers. As I gingerly walked back to my apartment, I cursed stairs in general and particularly the ones I had to climb.

Carter woke up unaware I had been in pain all night because he had no memory of the night before. Grumbling, he headed to Calhoun Street Pharmacy to get my much-needed pain pills. Chamberlain and the boys got up before he came back. "What's for breakfast, Mom?" Each of them asked as they came into the living room. I just looked at them and started to cry. "Nothing!" And I hobbled into my bedroom. They all burst through my door with an astonished look on their faces. "What happened to you, Mommy?" Chamberlain asked. "I broke two toes coming down the back steps of the Leprechaun League." Peter walked out of the room saying, "I'll fix breakfast. Drayton, come help me." I heard the boys whispering together, "It must have been a good party."

"Mommy, will you still be able to come to my Christmas play this afternoon?"

"I wouldn't miss it for the world."

When Carter finally came back, I took the painkillers and slept for hours. "Wake up, Catherine, it's time to get ready for the play."

"Have you already taken Chamberlain to the church?"

"Peter went with her awhile ago." I tried to hurry, but I was so groggy that I couldn't think straight. When we arrived at the church there were throngs of people. "You get out with Drayton, and I'll park the car, honey." Peter was inside with Jaffe, Daddy and Priscilla. "Do we have enough seats?"

"I took care of it, Mama."

"Thanks son. Daddy'll be here in a minute, he's parking the car." Sitting on the hard pew with my foot touching the floor was miserable and I was dying to prop it up. Carter slid in beside me just as the shepherd blew her horn. I whispered, "I'm miserable. Can you help me prop my foot up?" Carter started to quietly stack hymnals and then put his coat on top. "Try this." It was better, but my foot was still throbbing like the worst toothache imaginable. Chamberlain skipped and jingled down the aisle wearing her radiant purple suit and beautiful smile like a perfect jester for a king. As she jingled her bells and tumbled down the isle in front of her majesty, all eyes were on her because she was hysterically funny. Watching the angels climb one by one into the beautiful stained glass windows of the church, I glimpsed their soft faces as they spread their wings. I started to weep with Carter quickly giving me his handkerchief. I cried for my dead mother, Olivia, my lost house in Summerville, Hugo, and my throbbing toes.

Two days later as I baked a chocolate birthday cake for Drayton, I cried again because he was nineteen and I didn't know where my life had gone. When he walked into the kitchen and found me in tears he asked, "Why are you crying, Mom? "Because I love you so much, and you've grown up too fast, happy birthday, baby! I'm making your usual for your party. Do you want anything else or maybe something different?"

"Are you kidding? I can't wait for your French onion soup. It's the best in the whole town! My mouth has been watering waiting to taste it. I don't know how you always manage to make it for so many people and the week before Christmas."

"I don't either, son, but that's just what moms do. Now, you go enjoy your afternoon because everybody's going to be here at 6:30.

With the last few months being so horrendous, I hadn't found time for Christmas shopping. I had decided to wait until the week before to do my shopping but now I found myself unable to walk very fast or far. I thought I'd wait a little longer and hopefully my foot would feel better. Here we are on December 23, and the weather looked pretty ominous. "It looks like it's going to snow, Carter."

"It doesn't snow in Charleston, but those do look like snow clouds, honey."

"Mommy, come outside quick there are snow flakes on the walk but they're melting."

"I'll get down there in a few minutes, Chamberlain."

"I still need to go shopping, Carter."

"Well, you won't be doing it this evening because I just heard on the weather that they're closing down all the malls and stores due to icing tonight." Carter fixed us a plastic cup with bourbon and diet coke, a "go'ey", as he often called them, to keep us warm outside with Chamberlain and the snowflakes

Snowflakes were still falling the next morning as I listened to the TV while Chamberlain and I made Christmas cookies. I heard the commentator say, "Well, folks, Charleston's definitely going to have a white Christmas! The malls are opening for three hours today but then everything is shutting down."

"Chamberlain, go find Peter for me, please and ask him to come in here and see me."

"Ma'am? You wanted to see me? "All the shops downtown are closed because of the weather so will you drive me to the mall and help me shop really fast? See if Drayton will go, too."

At ten o'clock Christmas Eve morning, the boys and I climbed into Peter's Jeep and headed for the mall. "Here's a list for both of you. If you're not sure about something, come get me and we'll find it together. I'll be in Fines Department Store. Peter, please get some more wrapping paper and tags, too."

"Are you finished, Mama? It's almost 12:45, and the mall's closing at one o'clock. It's really snowing outside. We'd better hurry and get back over the bridge."

"I just need to buy some candy for Chamberlain and I'll be ready."

Climbing into the Jeep I exclaimed, "I can't believe all of this snow! It hasn't snowed like this since the early '70s." As Peter pulled out I yelled, "Watch out, son, look at that car sliding. It just missed that telephone pole." Cars were sliding, wrecking, and stalling all over the road. Between dodging them and the snowflakes, it took us more than an hour to get home. "I was worried about y'all. Did you get what you needed?"

"We did. I'll never wait to shop for Christmas again as long as I live."

"You always give too much anyway, Catherine."

"And you never give enough, Carter! Now do you want to start another fight? Maybe you need a drink. No, I see you're already drinking."

"Merry Christmas to you, too, bitch."

Carter stormed off while I went in and gave Chamberlain her candy and sat down to finish wrapping the gifts we'd just bought. It was hours before I finished wrapping. The whole time I was alone thinking about Carter, our family and why I was the only one buying and wrapping for everyone. Every year I was Santa, and Carter got all the thanks. I was sick and tired of this game we always played.

I'd worked myself into fury, so I went into the kitchen to take my frustrations out on a rutabaga. As I chopped and diced, I remembered every Christmas that I felt completely exhausted by Christmas Eve. When the rutabaga started boiling, I turned to attack the turkey. "I'll bet you felt the same way about Thanksgiving and Christmas before you gave up your life."

"Who are you talking to?"

"If it's any of your business, Carter, I was talking to the turkey."

"Okay. But I hope it doesn't talk back. Would you like me to help you dress the turkey?"

"I'll do it. Will you find the roasting pan for me? I can't find a thing in this apartment."

"It's in grandmother's trunk. I saw it last week. I'll get it for you. "Something sure smells good in here. I've come for free liquor; pour me a drink, Carter."

"Hello, Jefferson. What'll you have…bourbon or beer?"

"I'll have bourbon, Carter."

"How are things at your house, Jefferson?"

"Betsy's in a panic over dinner for tomorrow and she's afraid that no one will be able to get to the house after she's spent all her time cooking. You know how she always overdoes it, especially with all those sweets she insists on making. I'll bet she's already made one hundred dozen of her meringue pecan sandies. Leigh Anne's waiting on Chamberlain to come over so I thought I could walk her back. Can you believe this snow? I've built a huge fire in the upstairs fireplace. Why don't y'all come over after a while and we'll sing Christmas carols and the girls can play. I don't think that there will be services at the Cathedral because of the road conditions, but if there is we can walk together."

"I'll talk with the boss in the kitchen. She hasn't been very happy with me lately, not since your party at the League. It was a good time though and I certainly had plenty of good food and drinks." I could hear their conversation in the kitchen, and just as I stepped into the living room to tell them so, a sudden hush fell over the room.

As we stared at one another in disbelief, Carter said, "The power lines must be freezing and the tree limbs are falling. I wonder how long we'll be without power this time. I still have Bill's generator so we can have a little heat from the space heaters. Come on, everybody. Let's walk down to Jefferson's house for a while." The power didn't come back on that evening. Carter, Chamberlain and I stayed at the McNamara's house until late on Christmas Eve and around six o'clock, I started to feel really tipsy and knew that I'd better get myself home. Carter insisted that I stay while he and Jefferson had one more cup of cheer so by the time we staggered home at nine o'clock I put on my nightgown and said goodnight. "Catherine, it's Christmas Eve, you can't go to bed now. There's Santa to do when Chamberlain goes to bed and I don't know who gets what or where everything is."

"You know what, Carter, I really don't care. I don't care about Santa, Christmas, or you. Go have another drink, and leave me alone."

I closed my door and totally passed out, thinking that I should really quit drinking. Carter was the one with a problem, not me."

"Wake up, Mom. Wake up! Santa came. He brought me everything I asked for and some things I didn't."

"What do you mean, Chamberlain?" Well, he brought all the things I put on my list, but he put the candy you brought me yesterday in my stocking even though I'd already eaten most of it. Santa didn't take price tags off of my things either, and this year he didn't arrange things very pretty. He just dumped them in piles."

"Well, honey, maybe Santa was in more of a hurry because of the snow and the power outage. I'm sorry he gave you eaten candy."

"You know, Mommy, I think that you must help Santa each year because you know how to always make things perfect."

"Come here and give your Mama a big Christmas hug." As I hugged my young daughter, I smiled, knowing the turmoil Carter must have experienced the night before. My sadness immediately returned as innocence had been left behind. There'd be no need for Santa pretending in the Duvall house ever again.

Several months passed in the Trapp Street apartment while we made decisions about our future. We didn't have enough money or insurance to totally fix the house. Jefferson and Betsy suggested that we move into their good friend's house. It was occupied now but he wanted to replace the renters. "I don't want to rent again, Carter."

"Catherine, you know our situation, and if you want to be near Rutledge Academy this could be our answer. Call Betsy and let's go see it anything would be better than staying in this tiny apartment."

"Hey Betsy, yes, Carter and I would love to look at Clyde's house."

"I'll set up the appointment for you and Jefferson and I will go with you, okay?"

"Sure, we'd love to have your company."

As we were driving over to Clyde's, the very Irish McNamara's were hoots as they described the house. "Now there's a lot of Gothic crap still in the house that belongs to Clyde but it's a really nice house. Just try not to look at the purple and lavender bathroom, the '70s light fixtures that look like runway lights and you won't be able to avoid the rosettes—they're everywhere. You'll love the game room on the first floor, Carter and on the second floor there's a living room, dining room, library, bedroom, kitchen and two baths. Right outside the sliding glass door is most beautiful view over looking the water. If you look the other way, you'll see the city. Clyde has jasmine growing all over the back of the house, and the scent of it really takes your breath away."

As we approached the house, I saw no beauty in it whatsoever. As we climbed the tall flight of stairs I held tightly to the railing but I was still not interested. Meandering from room to room with Carter right behind me, I could hear him talking with Jefferson. I knew that he was very interested in moving into this house. It definitely was a man's house. As I looked, I thought, "Did he have a decorator? He must have had help from a female." I couldn't figure out the purple bathroom and rosettes until Betsy said, "Clyde had his mother help him decorate when he built this in 1971 before he got married."

As I stood on the top porch looking at the water, my thoughts wandered back to the priest in Summerville. "Go to the water, Catherine. It will heal you and your family."

"So what do you think, honey?" Carter asked wrapping his arms around me. "We could certainly enjoy some evenings up here."

"I think we can make this place something. We'll have to remove the Gothic fixtures in the bathrooms, and the ceiling lights need changing. The paneling is so dark, we'll definitely need more lamps. A little fresh paint in the bedrooms and a ton of yard work will help it come together. We won't stay long, Catherine; the lease is for only a year."

We moved into Clyde's house the first of February, thinking it would make our lives and our children's lives much more normal. The boys were doing well in college, and Chamberlain was receiving awards at Rutledge Academy. I had finished my masters' degree in administration. I wasn't looking for a job, but one of my professors insisted that I look into a position at Holy Divine School. "You already have degrees in elementary education and early childhood education, Catherine. This will be perfect for you and they need a director who loves children as much as you do. Please go for an interview."

"Okay, Dr. Bean, I'll look into it."

Holy Divine School had a tough board of directors conducting the interviews. There were so many degrees sitting around the table that I wasn't sure whether I wanted the job. The only person in the room who didn't petrify me was Father Paul. He was handsome, and his warm smile filtered kindness throughout the room. The board interviewed me for quite a long time, even Father Paul interrupted every now and then for a question of his own. They left the room for a short while then came back into the room with Father Paul at the lead. "Welcome to Holy Divine, Catherine. We're glad to have you if you want us," Father Paul announced as he gave me a welcoming hug.

Holy Divine was located just beyond the Ashley River Bridge in the Regency neighborhood. Father Paul was an absolute delight to work for. His kindness radiated into every facet of the organization. A financial officer oversaw bills and payroll, and I focused on my teaching staff and the wonderful children attending the school. As I continued to focus on my work, things began to return to some sort of normalcy in my home life again.

It was definitely a problem that I was working until five o'clock and getting home late. Chamberlain was missing her mother so much and really needed me at home. Peter, Drayton, and sometimes Jaffe would pick up her carpool from school and stay with her. When I got home one Friday afternoon in April, she was telling the boys about her ride home from school with Leigh Anne and Betsy. I listened carefully to her every word. "She told me that I wasn't allowed to say such things in her car. She said I was being rude. I tried to tell her that it would be okay with my family but she yelled at me and told me to stop talking."

I stepped into the room to ask questions. "Who yelled at you, Chamberlain? What is this all about?"

"Oh Mommy, you're home. It was Betsy. I was telling Leigh Anne that Shirley invited me over to spend the night because she's having a party. Betsy told me that I couldn't talk like that in her car. She said it might hurt Leigh Anne's feeling because she wasn't invited. I tried to explain that I meant nothing by it, but she started yelling at me."

"Did you say anything else to her, honey?"

"No ma'am."

I waited until later that evening after supper to call Betsy. "Betsy. It's Catherine. Chamberlain mentioned there was a problem in the carpool today. Can you tell me what happened?"

"Chamberlain was very rude talking about what she's going to do this weekend and I reprimanded her and told her she was out of line."

"Well, you know, Betsy, it doesn't sound like Chamberlain was the one out of line, I believe you were. If my daughter does something wrong, Carter and I will be the first to reprimand her...not you. I won't have you yelling at her and embarrassing her in front of her friends." From there, our conversation grew more heated, and we were each talking at the same time. Then I heard, "Well, I'm calling everyone in the carpool, and I'm having you and Chamberlain put out of it."

"You're doing what?" There was a click on the other end.

I walked into Chamberlain's room. "From now on you'll only be riding to and from school with a member of your family. Oh, and I don't think you'll be seeing as much of Leigh Anne. You and I are no longer in the carpool, but it'll be fine."

"Okay, Mom, did you and Betsy fight?"

"Not exactly, I just didn't put up with her stuff this time. It'll be okay, honey. You have plenty of other friends, and you'll always have these two," I said as I rubbed Morgan and Ruffle's ears.

During the next few weeks, Jaffe volunteered to drive and sister sit. As classes were letting out one Wednesday, Carter called me at work. "Catherine, are you in the middle of something?"

"Why? What's wrong? I can tell by your voice that something's wrong."

"I can't leave work right now, but you need to leave and get home as fast as you can. Jaffe was at the house painting the bathroom. He was outside washing his brushes and left the door open. Morgan and Ruffle ran outside. Before Jaffe could catch up with them, a car ran over Ruffle. He's dead. Jaffe carried his body back to the house, but he needs one of us there before he tells Chamberlain. He's on his way to pick her up from school."

"I'm on my way, Carter!" Chamberlain took the news as well as could be expected and I only hoped every tragedy made her stronger.

Holy Divine School had been financially strapped for years before I took the job as director but after Hugo, the financial burdens mounted even higher. Father Paul, the board of directors and the Episcopal

Diocese decided that the school would be closed at the end May. Several board members were teachers or administrators in Creek County school district and we'd become close friends since my horrendous interview. "What are you going to do when the school closes, Catherine? "I don't know. The boys are grown, probably stay home with Chamberlain. I haven't decided."

"You're too good at what you do, Catherine. We need you in Creek County. You don't need to stay home...your teaching skills are really needed, we have the perfect school for you, Tracy Elementary. Think about it!"

"I live in downtown Charleston. Creek County is forty-five minutes away if I drive fast."

"Creek County pays more and is much better to work for than all those disgruntled people in Rice County."

"I'll talk with Carter and think about it." Carter and I did talk about supporting two boys in college and Chamberlain at Rutledge Academy. "I haven't been able to catch up since those spec houses, Catherine. I'm still trying to pay everyone and you know Chamberlain wants to go to Europe with the Velvet Choir next year. I'm not sure we can afford it. Your Daddy's already given us so much—I don't want him to pay for the trip."

"If I take this job at Tracy, I'll be driving the opposite direction from rush hour traffic. It'll only take about an hour each way. I'll miss being home with Chamberlain, but I'm willing to do it if it means giving her more money. I'll give the Holy Divine board chairman a call in the morning. "Hey Ellen, this is Catherine. I've thought about what you said and I would like to interview at Tracy Elementary."

"Great, Catherine, I'll call the principal right away."

10 Daffodil

Carlos Rourk stood in his office brushing his snow white hair out of his face while I sat just outside the secretarial area waiting patiently. As I watched teachers parade in and out of his office, I caught a glimpse of a familiar face. "Well, hello there! I haven't seen you in awhile. How's that adorable, Peter?"

"Hello, Natalie Flynn! It's so good to see you. Peter's doing fine. He's in college and all grown up. How's Drew? Still playing tennis? Do you teach here?"

"Drew's fine. He still plays tennis sometime, but he hasn't played nearly as much since Peter moved from Summerville. I do a little bit of everything around here, but most of all I keep Carlos straight. I'm his assistant principal. Are you here to see him?"

"Yes. I had an interview almost an hour ago but I guess he forgot about it."

"You come with me right now. Carlos, this is a dear friend of mine, Catherine Duvall, our sons grew up together, and she has the most adorable little girl named Chamberlain. I believe Catherine has an interview with you."

"I'm so sorry I've kept you waiting." Carlos gave me an enormous smile and waved toward the only other seat in his office. "Please be seated."

During my interview, Mr. Rourk seemed more interested in my friendship with Natalie than in my credentials. After chatting for an hour, he said, "Thank you for coming, Mrs. Duvall. I have two more people to interview, and then I'll give you a call." A week passed, and Carlos Rourk did call. In fact, he kept calling. He called two times for more interviewing, each time questioning me about Natalie. "How long did you say y'all have known each other? Are y'all good friends? What do you think of her husband, Elton?" Mr. Rourk couldn't seem to get enough information about Natalie but on the final interview he hired me as a first grade teacher. "Come back the first week in January ready to go to work."

I heard from one of the other teachers, Harriet, that the teacher who'd been with my new class had resigned. As Harriet put it, "the children are out-of-control hellions, and they all need to be tied up and gagged!" After hearing this story, I wasn't so sure I'd made the right decision.

Right after Christmas, I headed for Tracy to get my room ready. As I laminated my materials as fast as I could, Carlos Rourk watched my every move. My students arrived on the fourth of January and they were the largest first graders I'd ever seen. "Nobody told you, Catherine?" Harriet stood there with her mouth wide open and her hands on her hips. "Every one of them is a repeater and some of them several times." The students themselves confessed that they had thrown desks and chairs around the room with their other teacher. "She cried all the time, and begged us to behave, Mrs. Duvall," Bart said. "Thank you for sharing that," I said. "Now, you and I are going to tell all the other boys and girls that I'm not going anywhere and that they're not going to behave like that for me. Here's why: We are going to start all over this year, and you are going to have fun with all of the wonderful things planned. If you don't behave, you will go home. Not me."

My normal teaching practice was to offer rewards, and I loaded this class with rewards…stickers, candy, toys, and gift certificates to their favorite burger joints. After several weeks, they were walking in a line, using their manners, and acting like real people. As we walked to the cafeteria, a colleague stopped me in the hall. "How'd you do it?"

"Excuse me?"

"How'd you get them to shape up so quickly?"

"Love and a little bribery!" By the time we finished in June, my heart was broken over losing my misfit class. They were all moving on to second grade and as I hugged each and every one, I hoped that maybe I'd made a difference in their lives.

I couldn't wait to be with Chamberlain for the summer. At twelve years old she loved to shop as much as I did. We frolicked all over Charleston, shopping and eating lunch in every restaurant possible.

It had been over a year since I had spoken to the McNamara's but the girls still spent time together at school. Chamberlain hadn't mentioned the carpool incident at all and I had totally forgotten about it until early one evening the doorbell rang. I opened the door and there stood Betsy, Jefferson, and Leigh Anne. "Well, hello."

"Hello, Catherine. Leigh Anne wants to play Barbies with Chamberlain. May we come in?"

"Why…yes…sure…come on in."

So, that's how the McNamara's came back into our lives and nothing more was ever said about carpool. For the rest of the summer, the girls played together as often as possible while Betsy and I shuffled around each other gingerly. "Chamberlain, I have to go to Tracy to get my room ready and I don't want to leave you home. Will you come with me? I can use some help. You can put the toys out in the centers and cut out some shapes for me."

"Okay, Mama, but promise you won't stay all day like you usually do."

"I promise."

"Hey, Josephine, I see your room's as messy as ever."

"Thanks a bunch, Catherine. I wish I could get as neat as you; so why don't you organize my room?"

"I will after I finish mine." Josephine and I had become great pals at Tracy and Chamberlain adored her young children who were in diapers, kindergarten, and second grade. "Hey Josy, do you want any of these magazines?" I hollered as I threw a stack of them off the shelves above the counter I'd climbed. "I'm getting rid of all of this mess," I squealed, jumping right off the counter onto the slab floor catching the heel of my tennis shoe on several magazines that started sliding. I landed with a terrible thud right on my tail bone. As I lay on the cold floor groaning, I heard Josephine start running. I rolled in pain and saw Chamberlain's face. "I'm okay, honey, sit down…please don't faint, I'll be okay."

"Catherine, where do you hurt?"

"All over, I'm not sure, Carlos."

"Catherine, it is Natalie and I'm calling an ambulance and Carter. Josephine has Chamberlain and she'll be all right." I lay on the slab floor with Carlos trying to cheer me up until the local rescue squad arrived.

When they arrived, they were a motley looking crew, but I was thankful for any help I could get. Once they strapped me on to the stretcher, off we flew to Harris Regional. Carter had called our doctor, Bill, who was standing in the ER waiting for me. "Guess you took a real fall, Catherine, let's get some x-rays." I moaned and tried to move, but hurt too much. After two hours of lying on my back as straight as a board, I was about to scream. Tears trickled silently down my cheeks. I could hear the doctors in the other room discussing my x-rays. "Can we let her go?"

"Yeah, I think so." And then I heard, "Hold on there, boys and get her a room. See right there in lumbar four? She has a fracture." Two minutes after I heard Bill's statement, a nurse came in with a hypodermic syringe filled with a painkiller. "Thanks," was all I could muster."

After I was admitted to the hospital, Natalie and Carlos came up to my room. "Now, don't you worry about that classroom because I'll get in there and fix it myself! It may not be as good as you'd do, but I'll do my best."

"Thanks, Natalie. You're such a dear."

"I'll get you a long-term sub. We'll need to find out how long you'll be recuperating."

"Oh, Carlos I'm so sorry! It's entirely my fault. Please forgive me."

"Don't you worry about it, Catherine, just worry about healing."

Carter tried to call Daddy, but he had disappeared and we knew Priscilla was occupying all of his time. I spoke with Beth in Florida. "Will you be paralyzed? Can you walk?"

"No, I'm not paralyzed, and yes, I'll be able to walk. I just have to be real careful until the bones heal. A couple of weeks or months will do it.

Have you heard from Daddy? Carter tried to call him, but we can't get him."

"I talked to him a few days ago. Keep trying. Take care of yourself and I'll check on you tomorrow."

My third day in the hospital, Carter caught Daddy at home. "Tell her I'm sorry. I've just been busy but I'll get by to see her soon. I stayed in the hospital over a week before finally going home but Daddy never made it by to see me.

Carlos had hired a fantastic sub for my class. She came to the hospital and then to my house to discuss lesson plans and students. "You have a very young class this year, Catherine. Carlos gave you a readiness first grade class."

"You mean they aren't ready for first grade, but they're too good to stay in kindergarten?"

"You've got it! That's what you've got, we've got…in your class. There are some adorable children in the class and I can't wait until you see them, especially Daffodil Simmons. She's so tiny, petite and very precocious. I'm not sure what her story is, but Carols spends a lot of time with her. Maybe he'll share some of her story with you."

"I'm anxious to see all of them and Miss Daffodil. You've been wonderful, Missy. Thank you for everything you've done, I really appreciate it."

By the middle of October, I met my class, Miss Daffodil included. My teacher's assistant, Mabel Brown, had helped Missy with the class, so she was very familiar with the kids. "You're going to have your hands full with that one," she said as she nodded toward Daffodil. "I'm going to change her seating arrangement in just a few minutes. I'll keep her near me, Mabel. Do you know why Mr. Rourk has been keeping her with him?"

"No, he said something about she had a sore on her foot and he didn't want it to get worse."

"That's odd. I'll talk with him during lunch if you don't mind watching the class."

"We'll be fine. I'm so glad you're back, Catherine."

"Thanks."

"Hey Carlos, may I come in?"

"Hello, Catherine. Glad to see you. How's the class?"

"They're adorable. That's why I'm here. Missy told me that you keep Daffodil with you most of the time, and Mabel just told me the same thing except she said something about a sore on Daffodil's foot. Does she have diabetes? Her medical records are not in her permanent folder. The nurse doesn't have them. Do you know where they are?"

"Yes, I do. Please shut the door and sit down. I've been waiting until you got back to talk with you about Daffodil. What I'm about to share with you cannot go out of this room. Natalie assures me that I can trust you completely."

"If you tell me not to say a word then I won't."

"Daffodil lives with her grandmother. Her brothers live in New York with their aunt. Daffodil's mother is in jail on drug charges, and she has AIDS. Daffodil was born HIV positive. If it gets out that she's HIV positive, parents will remove every child in this school. I don't even want the nurse to know because she's scared to death about contracting the disease. No one knows except the superintendent, Natalie, me, and now you. Due to the confidentiality laws, we can't say a word about Daffodil's condition but you need to watch her carefully. If she bleeds, get her into my office."

"That poor baby girl. Is she on medication?"

"Yes. That's another thing I need from you. I can't have her come into the office for her medication like all the other students because the office staff watches the students and they'll know right away. Can you hide her meds in your room and administer them? I'll give you the proper forms to sign."

"I'll be happy to. I'll lock the AZT up in my cabinet and I can give it to her when the other children are at recess. Does that time work?"

"It's perfect."

"What about telling Mabel? Are you going to tell her?"

"Absolutely not! No one else will be told, just you. I know I've given you a big responsibility, but I know you can handle it. I have faith in you, Catherine." This is how my life with Daffodil Simmons began.

As I walked back to my classroom, I could hear Mabel's voice. "Stop that. Don't you do that, Daffodil, that's nasty." I walked into the room quickly. "What's she doing?"

"Trying to spit on Randy because he called her a baby."

"Randy, we are not going to call people names, and you, Miss Simmons, will step outside into the hall with me."

"I'm not going!" She cried as she sat down on the floor. "Oh, yes, you are!" I said as I dragged her as she kicked and screamed. Once she stopped crying, I sat down beside her. "Now, little lady, you and I are going to have to work some things out. If you are going to be in my room, you are going to behave. I have a lot of fun things planned for my class, and I'm going to need a helper. It could be you but only if you behave. We're going to cook every Friday and you can be in charge of the kitchen. I have made hundreds of new games to play while in the learning centers. Now, you need to decide whether or not you are going to stay in my room because I'm not going to put up with the outburst I just heard from you. Sit here and think about it for a few minutes. When you've made your decision, come back into the room and let me know your answer. Ms. Brown, will you come out here with her for a few minutes?" I went back inside and began reading a story to the class. Mabel and Daffodil came back about five minutes later with Daffodil marching over to my chair and putting her hands on her hips until I finished the story. She glared right at me before saying, "I'm staying, Mrs. Duvall."

"Well I'm glad, Daffodil," I said as I gave her a huge hug.

I spent the next weeks in medical books, gathering all the information I could on AIDS and children born HIV positive. I scrubbed all of the desks with bleach every afternoon after Mabel and the kids had gone home. Carlos decided that Daffodil couldn't go to the special area classes like PE, music, and art because those teachers didn't know about her condition. "She'll have to stay with you, Catherine, every minute of the day."

"What about me…will I ever get a break? "Only if Ms. Brown has her."

"That's not fair to her. She doesn't know Daffodil's condition either!"

"She's an assistant not a teacher and I can't tell her. I'm sorry. This is the way it has to be."

So, my little ball and chain stayed with me day after day. When I sat in the rocking chair reading to the class, she was always right beside me sucking her thumb and gently rubbing my arm. She became so attached to me that on several occasions she called me Mama.

I talked with Bill Pruitt hypothetically about AIDS and his medical advice was to be careful because all the answers weren't in yet on the disease. I cried for Daffodil in Carter's arms many nights. I couldn't keep this secret from him, and I knew he wasn't going to tell anyone. "I don't just worry about her, Carter; I worry about the other children too. Her lips bleed all the time because they're so chapped and she lost a tooth last week and was sucking her bloody thumb. This afternoon, she was eating a lollipop and had just about finished it when she decided to trade it with Antoinette for a cookie. Before I could grab it from Antoinette, she'd put the lollipop in her mouth and was eating it. I feel so responsible. What am I going to do?"

"I think that you need to talk to Carlos. He'll help you make some decisions."

The next day I went straight to Carlos about all my concerns. "And I'm also worried about all of the other kids in the room. Their parents have no clue what's going on."

"Do you want to talk to the superintendent? I'll go with you."

"I don't know if it'll help, but I guess it would make me feel better."

The next week, Carlos and I went to the Creek County District Office. "Mr. Clemmons will see you now."

"Hello, Mr. Clemmons, this is Catherine Duvall. She's Daffodil Simmons' teacher."

"Hello, Mrs. Duvall. Hello, Carlos." Mr. Clemmons listened carefully as I relayed the activities that had taken place with Daffodil. "She is precocious, isn't she?" He said smiling at his thoughts of her. After I ended with my concerns about all of the students, he said. "Mrs. Duvall, I understand your concerns, we all have them. However, there is nothing I can do to change the situation. None of us can break the confidentiality law, and no one knows except us. Just go back and do your best. Don't worry because there's nothing anyone can do!"

As Carlos and I climbed back into his car, he saw that I was shaking. "Are you okay?"

"No, I'm furious! I am so angry with Mr. Clemmons!"

"It'll be okay, Catherine. I'm so sorry that I put this burden on you."

"It's fine, Carlos, I'm just so mad that no one cares about the other nineteen children in my room."

That Christmas, I made sure all of the children got plenty of gifts, but I made doubly sure that Daffodil got everything on her list. Her grandmother brought me her Santa list and my daddy bought her a doll, shoes, and a new coat. Carter and I bought the tea set, Barbies, and books. Carlos and Natalie bought her a bicycle and she had the greatest Christmas without knowing we bought anything.

When we returned to Tracy Elementary in January, Daffodil didn't come back and I was petrified. I couldn't help myself. "Carlos, is she okay? What's going on?"

"I don't know because I can't get anyone on the phone. I'll keep trying and let you know." That afternoon Carlos came into my room. "Boys and girls, I just visited a friend of yours. She's in the hospital because she has pneumonia. Do you know who I'm talking about?"

"Daffodil!" They all shouted at once.

Daffodil came back to school just before Valentine's Day but she was much weaker than I had ever seen her. She was skin and bones. Carlos was holding her hand when they came into the room. "Mrs. Duvall, I've brought you a special young lady."

"You certainly have!" I said bending down to scoop her up. "Hello, Princess. It's so good to have you back. Ms. Brown is waiting for her hug too."

"Come outside with me a minute, Catherine."

"What's going on, Carlos?"

"Her meds have been increased, here's the new dosage. She's no longer HIV positive. She's crossed over. She has full-blown AIDS."

"Oh, Carlos, I'm so sad." We stood there hugging and grieving together.

Right after Easter and spring break, we all regrouped to finish out the school year. Many of the children were coming down with viruses, spring colds and allergies. The building was filled with mold and mildew left from Hugo, so I wasn't surprised when Daffodil said, "Mrs. Duvall, I don't feel good." I touched her forehead. She was burning up with fever. "Ms. Brown, will you read the boys and girls a story? I'm going to take her to the nurse to check her temperature."

"It's 104°. Walking to Carlos' office, I opened his door and said, "She's sick. Can she stay in here until I get her grandmother?"

"Sure. She's about to fall asleep, I'll lay her down." The next day Daffodil came back to school with a fever. "Daffodil, what did your grandmother say yesterday after she took you home?"

"She spanked me for being such a baby and told me to get better because she had to work and didn't have time to stay home with me."

"Ms. Brown, will you read the boys and girls another story today? I'll be back in a few minutes."

"Carlos, can you believe she spanked her with a temp of 104°? What can we do?"

"Call social services, Catherine. See what they can do." Carlos had heard about Tom's story and wasn't surprised when I said, "You know my feelings on DSS, but I'll give it a try." Carlos walked in just as I hung up the phone. "How'd it go?"

"They said that they couldn't do a thing but they were sorry that she had AIDS. Her problem was out of their hands."

"What do you want me to do with her?"

"I'll take her in my office for a while, but Natalie and I have a principal's meeting."

"Bring her back to me before you leave."

It was after lunch when Carlos brought Daffodil back to me. She was lethargic and hot. "Give her to me, I'll just hold her while I teach. That's exactly how the next three days went. Ms. Brown took care of nineteen children and I tried to keep one away from all of the rest. When Daffodil came back to school the next Monday, she was as perky as ever. There were no outward signs of sickness at all. I was sure that stubborn, adorable Daffodil Simmons was going to defy all odds.

11
Abby

Jaffe had been working very hard and had moved into his own apartment after his stay with Daddy. Kim hadn't been mentioned in a long time. Our son came by our house to visit regularly but mostly to see Chamberlain. As he walked through the door one Friday afternoon in early May, I noticed a glow about him that I hadn't seen in years. "Hey, Mom, what's going on? Why are you not at school today? Give me a big hug."

"I'm fine, honey, and teacher's work day so I got home early for a change. How are you doing?"

"I'm doing great! Where's Chamberlain?"

"I'm right here!" she said galloping down the stairs before jumping into his arms. "Let's go hit some tennis balls, little Sis!"

"Okay. Did you bring me a racket, or do I need to get mine?"

"I've got you one."

"See you later, Mom. Love you," they chimed as they shuffled down the stairs to the car.

I continued watching Oprah and sat wondering how many hours a day she had to work to make her show look so easy and good. I stood leaning next to the doorframe, trying to scratch my back. It had been itching for weeks. Earlier in the week I'd gone by Bill's office to get it checked out. "Looks like your body is making too many histamines, Catherine and I really don't want to give you prednisone. I'll give you some samples of a topical cream."

"I don't want to take prednisone either, Bill. I fight my weight as it is. Any suggestions about the weight?"

"Eat less and exercise more, or have your jaws wired."

"Thanks, pal."

Carter came in just as I was reaching for a wooden spoon. "What are you cooking?"

"Nothing, I was scratching my back. Look at it for me. Is it red?"

"You look like a lobster back here. I'll put some more of your cream on it."

"Thanks, honey, that does feel better. Jaffe and Chamberlain have gone to hit a few tennis balls."

"Great, do you want a drink?"

"No, thanks. I'm going to take a Benadryl."

As Chamberlain and Jaffe came through the door I heard, "Mom, Jaffe's got a girlfriend."

"He does, does he? Jaffe, you want to tell us something?"

"It's true! I met her out at the Kiawah Tennis Center where she works. She's absolutely beautiful and has the best personality. Her name is Abby Harrison York and she's never been married, and she's Catholic."

"How long have you known her, son?"

"About a month, Dad, you'll love her. She's funny, and she's older than I am. She's not a baby like Kim."

"How much older is she, son?"

"Only a year and a half and I can't wait for you both to meet her. You too, squirt!"

"Why don't you invite her to dinner tomorrow night? We'd love to meet her. I'll fix a real Duvall dinner. Let's say seven o'clock?"

"I'll ask her and let you know, Mom. Gotta scoot…I've got a date. Bye. Love y'all."

I did make a Duvall dinner the next night, right down to my famous homemade pound cake with a dozen eggs in it. I topped it with fresh coconut icing and put it in the refrigerator to chill. About an hour before dinner, I put it on Mama's Gorham cake plate and set it on the buffet in the dining room. As I was adding the finishing touches to the she crab soup and asparagus wraps, I saw Morgan coming from the dining room.

Something was wrong. His whiskers were white, as though he was foaming at the mouth and he started licking his lips. Suddenly, realizing what it was, I rushed into the dining room to find that our Chocolate Lab had moved the entire coconut pound cake onto the floor. The only evidence was a few crumbs that were being eaten by Chamberlain's new Yorkshire terrier puppy, Witherspoon. "Morgan!" I shrieked. "Where are you going dog?"

"What's the matter, Mom? What did he do this time?"

"Peter, your dog is a pain and I wish that you could take him back to school with you. He just ate my whole coconut pound cake."

"Not the family favorite?"

"That would be the one. Jaffe's going to be here with Abby soon and I don't have a dessert."

"I'll run to the Teeter and buy something. I'll be right back!" Peter came back with a frozen Pepperidge Farm coconut cake. He beat Jaffe and Abby to the house by ten minutes. "Put it on the silver cake plate, but make sure it's pushed to the back of the sideboard, please, son."

"Mom, Dad, this is Abby."

"Hello, dear, please come in. It's so nice to meet you."

"Hello, Mrs. Duvall. Jaffe has told me so much about both of you and you must be Chamberlain. You are just as I imagined with that beautiful strawberry blonde hair. Why, your eyes are as blue as Jaffe's. Your brother never stops talking about you. I know he adores you. You really are a lucky girl having so many big brothers."

"Hey, Abby, I'm Peter."

"Well now…you look just like Jaffe but you have big brown eyes. Then, you must be Drayton. Gosh, I wish I was as tan as you are. I guess you get that beautiful dark complexion from your Dad. "Come on into the living room, Abby, there's no need to hang out in the foyer. I guess you've met everybody important in my life other than my granddaddy, Truman."

"Now, let me see if I remember correctly, that's your mother's father. Right, Jaffe?"

"That's right. You'll meet him soon because I'll take you by his house. He's been in a real slump lately or he'd be eating with us."

"Has he been sick?"

"No, Abby, just heart sick, he's been seeing lady friend, Priscilla, for several years and they've had a real thing going. She suddenly got sick and Granddaddy's been staying at the hospital with her and her children. They just did brain surgery because the doctors were sure that she had Mad Cow Disease."

"You're joking, right? Nobody around here has had Mad Cow Disease."

"She did, and she died several days later. Now Granddaddy's grieving and refusing to eat meat. He never ate chicken because he had to wring their necks when he was a child but now he says he'll never eat beef again. In fact, the last two times I've eaten with him he's had the same thing…two eggs scrambled, bacon crisp, toast dry with jelly on the side and one cup of coffee. You'll fall in love with him. We'll go for a visit tomorrow, Abby."

Abby was a genuine delight. There was no comparison between her and Kim. We all enjoyed her company that evening and hoped to see her again with or without Jaffe. As dinner ended and Carter poured more wine for all of us, I looked around. "Peter, where did you put the coconut cake?"

"Yum!" exclaimed Abby, my favorite. "Right over there!" Peter said pointing to the sideboard. We all turned to stare at an empty silver tray. Peter jumped up and ran into the kitchen yelling, "Morgan!" He came back with a sheepish grin on his face. "I'm sorry y'all. What can I say? He just loves coconut cake!"

When I woke Sunday morning I wasn't feeling well. I couldn't eat the breakfast Carter had made for me but I mustered up enough energy to put on a pot roast with carrots, onions, and potatoes because I knew all of the children would be around for Sunday dinner. I made macaroni and cheese while Carter snapped beans and filled the rice steamer to turn on later. "I think I'm going upstairs and get back into bed for a little while. Do you mind, honey? I think I drank too much wine last night."

"Go ahead, Catherine. I'm going for a walk around Colonial Lake.

I must have fallen asleep as soon as my head hit the pillow, because before I knew it, I heard, "Catherine, are you all right? It's getting late. Dinner's ready. Do you want to eat?"

"I'm not hungry, Carter. I'll be down shortly."

"I listened to my family laughing, sharing the Sunday meal but couldn't bring myself down the stairs. I drifted back to sleep and slept several more hours before I could make it down the stairs. Jaffe had gone out to see Abby, and Peter had gone to see his girlfriend, Lucy Gallagher. Drayton, Chamberlain, and Carter were stretched out on the sofa and chairs watching a movie. I snuggled in beside Carter. "How are you feeling?"

"Weird!"

"Weird, how?"

"I don't know, just weird." Around four o'clock I started feeling really cold. "Would you get me a blanket, honey?"

"I'll get it for you, Mom."

"Thanks, Drayton, you're so sweet." As I sat on the sofa covered in a blanket, I started rubbing my neck and my hand moved up to the top of my head and I slowly moved my fingers around on the top of my head. "Feel this. The top of my head is mushy feeling."

Drayton zoomed over to inspect my scalp. "Hey Dad, look at this. The top of her head is filled with water or something. It's all swollen under the skin."

"It's your imagination, son!"

"No, it's not, Dad! Feel it!"

Chamberlain moved closer to the TV because we were making too much noise. By six o'clock, Carter had rounded up three quilts and piled them on me but I was still freezing. "Will you call the doctor for me?"

"I don't want to bother Bill on a Sunday, Catherine."

"Will you at least call the answering service and see who's on call?"

"Okay, I guess." Dr. Holden, Bill's partner is on call."

"Will you please call Bill at home and ask him what he thinks? I'm getting worse."

"I really don't want to call Bill."

"Please, Carter."

"Hey, Bill. This is Carter. Catherine's got something going on. She's all red and freezing and the top of her head is swollen. It feels like a water balloon."

"He wants me to take you to Harris Regional ER. He's going to call Dr. Holden and have him meet us there. Drayton, will you stay her with your sister until we get back?"

"Sure, Dad, I'll keep her entertained."

By the time we reached the hospital, I was gasping for breath. A nurse came outside with a wheel chair and whisked me inside. I was shivering and gasping while the receptionist asked those inane insurance questions. The triage nurse came over to Carter and said, "Sir, take her on back where there's a bed, go right in there. You can give the information later." Dr. Holden arrived shortly behind us. He kept saying, "Catherine, try to breathe normally, slowly now…don't panic. You're going to be okay." The nurse started an IV and gave me several drugs. Hours passed and I vaguely remember hearing Dr. Holden say, "I'm getting her a room. She's staying!"

When I woke several days later, Carter's face told me things weren't looking good. "Hey, there, honey, you've been gone for awhile. It's good to see you."

"Where am I?"

"Harris Regional."

"What's wrong with me?"

"Nobody seems to know that yet and you have some new doctors. I'm sure they'll all be here in awhile."

"Where's Chamberlain? We're supposed to be getting her ready for her trip to Europe."

"She's shopping with your Daddy. Now, you rest. "What do they think I have?"

"Well, they are checking you for Lupus and other infectious diseases."

"My hands are so swollen that I can barely bend my fingers, look at my left arm. The skin looks like an alligator's. What's happening to me, Carter?" I started crying and one of the nurses came into my room. "Are you in pain, honey? Why are you crying? We don't want you upset now, so try to stay calm."

"What's wrong with me?"

"That's what everyone wants to know, honey. I'll be right back. "I'm going to give you a shot. This will make you feel better."

Days later I heard, "Hello, Catherine, can you wake up for me?"

"Hey, what's wrong with me, Bill?" He put my hand in his as he said, "I don't know. I have called in the best team of doctors I can find. We are sending your blood all over the place: California, Iowa, and Texas. We just have to wait until we get some answers. I need you to rest as much as possible and stay calm because when you get upset strange things start happening to your blood tests. You got to the hospital just in time because we almost lost you that night. You certainly have a lot of people baffled."

"Could I have AIDS?"

"Why do you ask that?"

"Remember that little girl I discussed with you who is in my class?"

"I sure do."

"Well, she used to sit and rub my left arm after she sucked her thumb and look at my arm now."

"I've ordered a biopsy to be done on that arm tomorrow, it won't be painful. Your face seems to be not as red."

"I wouldn't know. I haven't seen a mirror."

"Here, I'll get you one."

"Oh, my God! I look like a freak, my eyes are swollen shut! My whole face looks like a moon—I look like a clown painted huge cheeks on me! Please help me, Bill. This is terrible."

"I know, but the moon face is coming from the prednisone that I had to give you to boost your immune system. I'll find out what's causing the rest. I promise. Now you rest, and I'll see you tomorrow morning."

"Tell Brittany hello for me."

"I'm sure that wife of mine will be over to see you soon."

The next day was Saturday and Bill still had no news. Natalie and Carlos had just come in to visit me when I heard Natalie's sweet voice softly said, "Hello, girl. How's it going? How are you feeling?"

"Scared. They took blood to check for HIV, but I have to wait almost two weeks for the results."

"Give me a hug, Catherine."

"You might want to stay away from me, Carlos. There's no telling what I have."

"You don't scare me, now give me a hug."

"I'm so glad y'all are here. What's happening in my classroom?"

"Missy has taken over again and you are not coming back for the rest of the year. You're only going to worry about yourself."

"If I make it out of here, can I come tell them all good-bye? "Of course you can."

"Here comes your supper, Catherine."

"I don't want it, Natalie. Just move it out of the way or let Carlos eat it."

"Looks pretty good to me," Carlos was saying as he ate a spoon full of mashed potatoes. "Is there anything that I can fix you that you'll eat, Catherine?"

"I'm just not hungry, Natalie, but you're such a good cook that I'm sure I'd try."

"I'll bring you some good homemade chicken and noodles tomorrow."

"Please don't go to any trouble."

"Catherine, your roast beef was great and that layer cake was better than my ex-wife's."

"How is Elaine, Carlos?"

"Psychotic as usual."

"Hey, Mom."

"Hello, honey. Hey, there, Abby. Jaffe, introduce Abby to everyone, please." Abby walked right over and gave me a big kiss and hug. "Gosh, Mrs. Duvall, I'm afraid that I'm the one that made you sick. You've been sick ever since the night I came to your house. Are you feeling better?"

"I feel pretty lousy, and I thought we agreed that you'd call me Catherine. You didn't make me sick. In fact, your visit was wonderful."

"Catherine, I met your father. He's a hoot and really knows how to flirt with the ladies."

"He does do that, Abby."

"How is Truman?"

"He's fine, Carlos. "How's Priscilla?"

"I haven't had a chance to tell you, Priscilla passed away from Mad Cow Disease."

"Oh, no! How's your Daddy dealing with it?"

"He's grieving."

"Well, I'm sorry to hear about Priscilla, but back to you, Catherine. It's time for you to get well and there's no need to join Priscilla yet."

"Very funny, Carlos, I don't plan on it, and besides Priscilla and I never ate beef together."

Carter and Chamberlain came into the room just as they were all leaving. "Oh, Chamberlain, It's so good to see you! "Hello, Miss Natalie. It's good to see you, too."

"What adventure are you undertaking this week? Your Mama usually keeps me informed."

"I'm trying to get ready to go to Europe with the Rutledge Academy Velvet Choir. We leave in four days, but I'm having a little trouble packing without my Mama." She walked over and gave me a big kiss and smiled. "Carter, how are you holding up?"

"I'm doing fine but I need to get Chamberlain packed and on the plane. She's driving me crazy because I don't know the latest trends like Catherine."

"You know, Chamberlain I'm making your Mama some chicken and noodles tomorrow. Why don't I pick you up early in the afternoon and we'll go shopping and then get your suitcases packed. Is it a deal?"

"Miss Natalie that would be wonderful, I'll be dressed and ready."

"Carter, why don't you take a few hours to yourself? I'll come and stay with Catherine while the girls shop."

"You don't have to do that, Carlos."

"I know I don't, but I want to. I need to."

"Do you mind, Catherine?"

"I think it will be fine. Y'all don't worry about me. Just get my daughter ready for her trip, please."

Just as she said she would, Natalie brought chicken and noodles before going to pick up Chamberlain. "I don't think I've ever tasted anything so good in my life. Thanks, Nat."

"I'm glad to see you finally eat something now I'm off to pick up our girl. Is there anything in particular that she needs?"

"I'm not sure at this point. She has a list. Please make sure that she has plenty of underwear."

"I'll do it. Get some rest before Carlos gets here because I think he's bringing poetry to read to you."

"Thanks for the warning."

I was still in the hospital four days later when Chamberlain was scheduled to fly out. "Will you let me leave the hospital to go to the airport with her, Bill?"

"You're really not strong enough, Catherine."

"I really need to do this Bill. I know you're the doctor but I'm the mother, and I need to be there."

"Will Carter be with you?"

"Of course."

"Okay but you come right back and get back into bed, promise?"

"I promise."

Chamberlain was beaming all the way to the airport. She and Natalie had bought everything on her list and more. "Natalie thinks I should be a hat model and she put hats from every store on me. She particularly likes the Laura Ashley ones on me. How do you like this one, Mama?"

"You look as adorable as ever."

Carter grabbed a wheelchair, and we headed inside to join the group just in time for boarding. "Chamberlain, give me a big kiss. Now you be safe, and make sure you come home to me."

"Don't try to get up, Mama. I'll get down to you."

All of the other parents were kissing and hugging their daughters, too. As the girls buzzed around Harvey, the Velvet Choir director, getting instructions and tickets, the chaperones started walking slowly toward the loading gate. I noticed they kept staring at me. Waving good-bye to Chamberlain for the last time, Carter wheeled me back to the car. While he was putting the wheelchair back inside the terminal, I pulled down the visor to look into the small mirror and when I saw how horrible my face looked, I knew why they were all staring. Poor Chamberlain! I know I embarrassed her coming here. I shouldn't have come. "Why are you crying Catherine? She'll be back in two weeks."

"That's not why I'm crying, Carter. I'm crying because I feel and look so bad. I'm crying because I feel like I'm dying, and I want be here in two weeks to see my daughter. Please get me back to the hospital as fast as you can."

Bill released me from the hospital the day before Chamberlain returned home. None of the doctors came close to finding a clue about my illness. My AIDS test came back negative, but I was told I'd need another one in a few weeks. Jaffe and Abby were at the house when I got there. "It's good to see you, Mrs. Duvall, I mean Catherine, I'm so glad you're home."

"Hi, Mom."

"Hi, honey, what are you two up to?"

"Just came by to see you before going to dinner down on Market Street. There's a good street band playing tonight."

"I know you'll have a good time."

"Abby, be careful driving back to James Island after drinking tonight."

"She's not driving back to James Island, Mom, she's moved in with me. I took her by my apartment the other day, and she saw how organized I am. Now, I can't get her to leave. She brought her clothes and hasn't left since," Jaffe said winking at me. "Oh, Jaffe, you are so full of it. He begged me to move in with him. Now, who do you believe?"

"Both of you because you both know how to tell some tales. Who's going to help me up these stairs to my bed?"

"Come on, Catherine. I'll help you," Abby said as she put her arm around my waist.

Chamberlain slept for two days after returning from her trip. "Hey, sleepy head, here are your pictures from your trip. Abby just picked them up for you and brought them by."

"Where is she?"

"She had to go to work."

"I just love her, Mama, she's just like a big sister. I think she likes me, too."

"I'm sure she does. We'll have to keep our fingers crossed that it works out for Jaffe and Abby. Are you ready to tell me all about your trip?"

"In a little while, after I wake up more."

A few days later, Carlos came to pick me up, so I could see my school children before they left for the summer. "Do you feel up to this, Catherine?"

"I think so, Carlos. It's so nice of you to come and get me." Missy was having a great party for all of the children. She and Ms. Brown worked very hard to keep them from climbing all over me. "We've missed you so much, Mrs. Duvall."

"I've missed you boys, too. I think you've grown a foot, Victor. Maurice you are getting more handsome with each day. Well, hello, little one. Did you miss me?"

"Why did you leave me? I'm mad at you."

"I don't think you're really mad at me because you know I've been thinking about you every day. I put the pictures you made me all over my room at the hospital. Now, don't you think it's about time for you to give me a hug?" As she climbed into my arms, she whispered, "I love you so much."

"I love you too, Daffodil. You'll never know how much."

During June, the specialists continued to check me for Lupus, AIDS and any autoimmune diseases they could think of. When my knees started hurting so badly that I was screaming, Carter and Jaffe quickly carried me to the car. On the way to Bill's office, Carter listened as I prayed, "Dear God, please end this for me because I can't take another episode of whatever this is. Please help me."

"Try not to think about your pain, honey. We'll be there in a few minutes."

When we arrived Bill stood over me holding my hand. "You have really been through it, little lady and I can tell you're really hurting. I'm going to give you a shot for pain and I'm calling in a rheumatoid specialist, Dr. Franks."

"Carter, his office is a few buildings down from mine and he's expecting you both. Take her over there as soon as the Demerol kicks in and I'll call you later."

"Thanks, Bill."

"Hang in there, Carter." Dr. Franks put cortisone in both of my knees with needles as long as knitting needles. "It should feel better real soon mean while I'm going to take some blood for more tests, Catherine. Are you up to it?"

"Sure," I slurred.

Dr. Franks called me several weeks later, "Catherine, I just got some results from the blood that I sent to Iowa. You have Fifth's Disease."

"You're kidding?"

"Nope it's positive."

"I know a good bit about it from teaching school because they're always warning pregnant teachers. I know it will kill a fetus and little children get it all the time. I do have the slapped cheek look, don't I?"

"You do. Did any of the children have it in your class?"

"Not that I know of."

"Did any of them have a high fever and a rash?"

"One, she's the little girl who has AIDS."

"You sat and held her, didn't you?"

"Yes, for many days."

"I'll bet she put out more of the disease because her body is so messed up, and you sat right there and inhaled her virus. I'm making some phone calls and I'll call you back." I put the receiver down before picking it right back up. "Hello."

"Hi, honey. Dr. Franks just called. I have Fifth's Disease."

"What's that?"

"You know a children's disease like chicken pox, measles, mumps, and whooping cough. Well, this is the fifth disease that children get, but it was never named. According to Dr. Franks, if an adult gets it they usually die and he said only a handful of adults in the world have contracted it. He said I'd probably be in medical books."

"How do you treat it? What's the plan? Can you cure it?"

"I don't know. He's making phone calls and then he's going to call me back."

Several days later when Dr. Franks called back, he wasn't very helpful. "It just has to run its course and there's nothing I can do except treat the symptoms as they come up. It should have been gone, but obviously it isn't. Let's just see what happens next."

"I don't have much choice, do I?"

The night sweats got worse. I never knew when the chills would come, but when they did they were so severe that I thought my teeth were going to crack. I couldn't go out of the house because the sun made things worse. I felt like a prisoner with no one to talk to except my doctors. I began having pain in my groin every day and I asked Bill about it, but he blew it off as a pulled muscle. I asked Dr. Franks about it, and he said that it was probably a pinched nerve. Over the next months, my excruciating groin pain increased so much I could hardly tolerate it. I called doctors at least once a week describing my pain. "Catherine, I'm going to send you to the Medical University to an infectious disease guy named Eric Lawrence. He's an old friend of mine so let's see what he can find out."

"Does he have a wife that teaches at Rutledge Academy?"

"He sure does. Do you know her?"

"Not very well but she teaches Chamberlain at Rutledge Academy. I've met her husband a few times."

The next week my groin burned like fire as I hobbled from the car into Eric Lawrence's office. After waiting for more an hour to see Dr. Lawrence, I was really in pain from sitting. Some how I managed to make it to the exam room. "Well, hello, Mrs. Duvall. How are you? Bill tells me that you've really been through a lot. I'm going to run some more tests and see what I can come up with."

"Imagine that," I thought to myself. "I need you to come back in two weeks for your results." Hobbling back to the car, I cursed doctors the whole way.

Jaffe had moved back into our house to save money, and Abby came right along with him. They were inseparable but she was such a joy to have around, and Chamberlain was thrilled to have her company.

In the evenings, I stayed in my room trying to control my tears. As I raised my leg to put it on the bed, I shrieked like I had Tourette's syndrome and the pain was more than I could bear. Tears burst from my eyes and I couldn't control them. I knew my family had had enough of my illness the morning I heard Jaffe in the hall and I called out, "Jaffe, will you bring me a glass of water?" My eldest son replied, "No, get up and get your own water and get out of that bed and get yourself together."

"Jaffe, shame on you! I'll get you some water, Catherine. Here you go."

"Thank you so much, Abby. I can't believe he's treating me like this."

"I'll talk to him."

"It's okay, Abby, just let it go."

I could barely make it back to Dr. Lawrence's office two weeks later because walking was becoming more and more difficult. "All of your results are in and I can't find a thing wrong with you."

"But, I'm so sick."

"Maybe you should start looking into other avenues, Mrs. Duvall."

"What do you mean, Dr. Lawrence?"

"Perhaps you should see a mental heath person...maybe a psychiatrist?" Slowly, I started to rise from my seat as I felt the blood rushing to my face. "You know, Dr. Lawrence, I've been waiting for one of you quacks to say that my condition is mental and I just wasn't sure which one of you it would be. What I really need is a doctor who's not so worried about his fee and one who doesn't keep his patients waiting, one who is worried about helping me get well."

"Well! I guess that won't be me since it seems all I did was make you angry."

"Good day, Dr. Lawrence!"

"Good day, Mrs. Duvall." I was so angry that I sobbed all the way back to my car.

I tried to stay downstairs more often so I didn't have to ask anyone to get things for me. I knew I wasn't crazy, but everybody was starting to treat me as though I was. Just as I finished the book I was reading, Abby burst through the front door. "Chamberlain! Catherine! Come see it. I did it. I really did it." Chamberlain squealed, "You did what, Abby?" Jaffe was right behind her beaming. "I finally got somebody to ask me to marry him. Look!" She stuck out her hand with a sparkling new sapphire and diamond ring sparkling in the light. "Oh, my God, it's beautiful!"

"Well, Jaffe...you're just full of surprises, aren't you?"

"Yes, ma'am, I am." Carter joined us all in the kitchen as his eyes filled with tears and I was afraid that he wasn't happy. "Are you okay, honey?"

"I'm so happy for them and I'm so happy that we'll have Abby in our family."

"Me too, give me a hug, daughter."

"Me, too!" Chamberlain shouted as she grabbed Abby and they danced across the floor. "Congratulations, son, this calls for a celebration. I'll get the champagne. "Please get the flutes from the china cabinet, too, Carter."

After Carter poured champagne for everyone, including Chamberlain, we toasted the happy couple. I asked, "So have you decided on a date?"

"Not yet, we've got a lot of details to work out...like how much my parents can afford."

"Let us know how we can help, Abby."

"Thanks, Mom." And she's called me Mom ever since.

My condition was getting worse every day but I tried not to talk to any one to hide my pain. I'd called Dr. Frank's office so many times that I was sure the staff hated me. On my last visit, I cried and cried, begging him to do something. "I'll schedule an MRI for next week and that's about all I can do."

It was the end of August and time for school to start. Carlos promised he'd hold my job for a while until I felt better. One of my dear teacher friends, Heather, offered to drive me to Harris Regional for my MRI. "You are so sweet, Heather, I really appreciate your help. Carter can't afford to take more time off from work."

"I'm glad I can help, Catherine."

"I saw Daffodil at registration the other day, she's really missing you. Carlos is putting her in Nell's class this year and I hope she'll behave for her."

"Nell will have her hands full, that's for sure." Heather helped me inside the room where the technician was waiting. "We're ready for you, Mrs. Duvall, come right in here. The doctor has ordered a little something to help you relax so I'm going to start the drip now." I slept through the entire procedure and woke up just as the machine was sliding me out.

Heather was sitting patiently in the waiting room. "Are you okay, Catherine?"

"I'm fine, just anxious to get home to my bed."

Heather helped me climb the twenty stairs to my front door trying to comfort me each time I shouted out in pain. As I stopped on the porch, Chamberlain flung open the door. "Your doctor just called, Mom. I told him that you weren't home yet."

"Does he want me to call him?"

"No, Mama he said to tell you as soon as you got home to come right back to his office."

"It's going on five o'clock. Won't his office be closed?"

"He's waiting for you and said for you to hurry."

"I'll take you, Catherine."

"I'm so sorry to bother you, Heather. Are you sure you don't mind?"

"Positive! I think you need to call Carter, here, use my cell phone. Don't lean over to get yours."

"Hey. Yeah, I'm finished with the MRI. Heather and I just got home, but Dr. Franks called the house and wants to see me in his office immediately. Heather's taking me there now."

"I'll meet you in his parking lot."

"Thanks, honey, I love you."

"I love you, too, Catherine."

Heather took her phone back and called Carlos and Natalie with the news. When we got back to the hospital, there sat Carter, Natalie, and Carlos, looking very concerned.

"Hello, Dr. Franks, what's going on?"

"Sit down, Catherine. Do you want all of them to listen?"

"I sure do they've been my support through all of this."

"I have some bad news, Catherine. Your MRI showed that your right hip is in stage four of avascular-necrosis and your left hip is in stage two."

"What does that mean?"

"It means that the blood supply to your bones has been cut off, and your hipbones are breaking apart into little pieces and dying and the chips have been sticking into you when you moved and causing you pain."

"How can it be fixed?"

"Well, I'd recommend that you can sit in a wheel chair for a year and hope the bones heal. You can have hip replacements."

"Have you talked to Bill?"

"I talked with him just before you got here and he's going to call you tonight." I sat in Dr. Franks' office, surrounded by my well wishers and bawling my eyes out. "Come on, honey, I'm taking you home. You're exhausted. We'll make decisions later." I kissed my friends and left with my husband.

Bill and I talked that night and again the next day. "I want a second opinion."

"Okay, I'll get you in to see Dr. Jones, he's one of the best orthopedic doctors in Charleston, but he doesn't have much of a bedside manner."

"Thanks, Bill."

"Keep in touch, Catherine."

Dr. Jones was about as friendly as a rock. "You definitely need a hip replacement, young lady. I can't believe Franks told you to sit in a wheelchair for a year. Your hip's never going to heal. Now, your left hip may be salvageable. The head of orthopedics at Duke University is doing fibular grafts on young folks. Let's see, you're forty-seven, that's young enough. I can refer you there if you'd like."

"Yes, I definitely want another opinion."

Two weeks later, Carter and I were on the road to Durham. Looking at Duke University, I thought we'd traveled back in time. The Gothic buildings were a far cry from any thing in Charleston. The hospital was amazingly organized. Dr. Fisher's PA whisked us right into a room at ten o'clock and put me right into a gown. "Someone will take you to x-ray, and then you'll come back in here to wait. Dr. Fisher will be with you shortly. He's a very busy man but we're definitely going to work you in today, Mrs. Duvall. At noon Carter went to the cafeteria and brought back lunch. By three o'clock, we'd read every magazine in the room and waiting area. At five o'clock Carter said, "Maybe we should just leave."

"No! I'm not going anywhere after waiting this long. Besides, I want to know what he has to say." At six o'clock that evening, Duke's head of the orthopedic department walked into my room. "I understand that you've had an extremely long wait. I'm very sorry…every time I thought

I'd get in here, something else happened. Hello, I'm Richard Fisher." Dr. Fisher looked at my x-rays. "Who did this to you, Catherine? Your hips are a mess. Did you take steroids?" I told him about my long ordeal before answering, "Prednisone. Can I be fixed?"

"You need a hip replacement immediately on the right hip. I can do a fibular graft on the left one, although you're older than most of my graft patients. "How soon can you do it?"

"I'm booked for months, but given the severity of the damage I'll do it in two weeks. I'll send you upstairs to the labs and to meet the anesthesiologist now. I'll make you better soon."

"Will you do the surgery yourself?"

"I promise that I'll do the surgery and your husband can watch from behind the glassed seating area."

"I'm not sure I want to do that, Dr. Fisher."

"Well, you can decide, Mr. Duvall."

Beth's daughter Ann was getting married in Macon, Georgia, on September 16, our anniversary was on the 17th and Abby and Jaffe were getting married December 29. I desperately wanted to be at both weddings so I scheduled my surgery for Monday, September 18, I had it all planned: Carter and I would drive to Macon for the wedding and enjoy our anniversary the next day. Then I'd undergo surgery.

The wedding was glorious, and the guests looked like Who's Who from Charleston. Beth and Gregory had gone all out, nothing was forgotten. Ann and Donald both worked for the CIA. Donald's groomsmen, also agents, looked the typical part when they stood outside chatting with their sunglasses and black suits, I wondered if we were all under surveillance. My Daddy looked handsome dancing with all of his girls. I watched smiling from my wheel chair as he whirled the new bride, then Chamberlain, and moved on to Abby. "How are you feeling, Sis?" He said as he came over to give me a kiss. "I'm okay, Daddy. You certainly can cut a rug. The girls are having so much fun with you."

"I'm enjoying myself, too."

Right after breakfast we headed for Durham. "Now, make sure you call when y'all get back to Charleston. Chamberlain, you listen to Abby and the boys. Granddaddy will be checking on all of you. I love y'all."

"We love you, too," they were all saying as Carter pulled out of the hotel parking lot.

After checking into our room in Durham, Carter and I showered and dressed for an anniversary dinner. We found a cozy, cute restaurant not far from our hotel. "Can you believe that we've been married twenty-eight years?"

"No. It really is flying by. We certainly have beautiful children, don't we? At least we did that right. Are you nervous about tomorrow?"

"I'm petrified! If I die, please keep the family close. You know how important that is to me. I don't want our family to be separated like yours, Carter. Promise me. I updated my will last week."

"I promise, but you're not going to die, Catherine."

"I just feel so weak. I'm really scared. Let's not talk about it any more, okay?"

"Okay. How's your lobster and steak?"

"Perfect, just like you. Happy anniversary."

We arrived at the hospital promptly at four o'clock in the morning. My surgery was scheduled for six o'clock. I put on the gown, cap, and paper shoes and climbed onto the bed just as I was told. Carter sat silently holding my hand until time to leave. Around 5:30, people started moving all over the place and the anesthesiologists started an IV, I started shaking. "Are you cold, Mrs. Duvall?"

"No, I'm terrified."

"I'll give you a little something to help with that." By the time they wheeled me off to the operating room, I was feeling no pain. I didn't have a care in the world. "I'll be upstairs watching you. I love you, Catherine."

"Me, too," I waved at Carter as the door closed.

Being cut in half as I call it is absolutely no fun but I survived the surgery even though it took months to recuperate. Patients around me, who had the same surgery, were walking and doing fine. I was in so much pain that I refused to let the physical therapists touch me. "Come back later or I'll need to take some pain medication before you come, then I'll try harder." I ended up staying at Duke until the second week in October.

The drive home was the longest ride of my life. I'd had pain medication, and pillows were tucked all around the Mercedes to make me comfortable but still the trip was exhausting.

Carter had an ambulance company waiting at the house when we got to Charleston to lift me up the stairs. They almost dropped me over the banister rail so by the time the two people carrying me turned into the door, I was hysterical. Carter had moved my bed down to the first floor and put it in the library. As I climbed onto my bed the phone began ringing. "Catherine, it's Beth. Can you talk?" I shook my head yes, but as soon as I heard my sister's voice I started to bawl. Carter took the phone away from me and helped me get comfortable and covered me up before going into the kitchen. He fixed me a glass of water and brought me a pain pill. "Try to rest, honey. You've had a very long day."

Carlos had been to see me several times while I was at Duke and on the last visit, I watched him fidget. Finally, he started talking. "You know, Catherine, since you caught the virus from Daffodil and had to take all that Prednisone to keep from dying, I do believe you're entitled to a Workman's Compensation settlement."

"I don't know anything about Workman's Comp, Carlos. I just know that I'm running up major hospital bills, and I'm not helping Carter pay them. I haven't gotten a check in months."

"Well, I'll call you tomorrow with some numbers to call at the district office." Weeks passed as I lay in my bed wondering what I should do. One morning I woke up with my decision to pursue the Workman's Comp route.

"Yes, Mrs. Duvall, there is a possibility that you're eligible, but it's a long process, and you'll have to prove that you caught the virus from the child. I don't think that we've ever had a case where it was proven that a person caught a virus from a certain person."

"So, I'm just supposed to lie here and do nothing?"

"I didn't say that, but without an attorney you are going to be fighting a losing battle."

Since we were living in Clyde's house knowing that he was a prominent attorney and a genuinely kind person, I gave him a call. "I'm so sorry to hear you're having trouble, Catherine. Of course I'll be happy to talk with you. Come on over to my office tomorrow." Carter and Peter had built an extremely long handicap ramp down the back stairs of the house but if Carter made one mistake rolling me down, I could have been a runaway wheelchair headed straight for the Ashley River. "Now, I've put the breaks on. Put your hand on the wall of the house. I'll hold on tight. Drayton, you get in front of your Mom just in case."

"Oh, so you want me to be trampled thanks a lot, Dad! Just kidding, I've got her covered. Let's go."

"Can you come back later and help me get her back into the house, son?"

"Sure Dad, just give me a call."

Clyde's office had four flights of stairs. "What are we going to do, Carter?"

"You sit right here. I'll be right back." Carter returned with Clyde. "Let's meet right in here in the conference room, folks," Clyde said opening the door to a colossal table with ornate chairs. It took two hours to document all of the events that had taken place in the past.

Clyde agreed to take the case but warned me not to expect a large settlement because of how Workman's Comp calculations worked. "I just want my salary, Clyde. I appreciate your help." Back at home, Carter called Drayton, and the two of them slowly wheeled me back up the steep ramp into the house that I had grown to appreciate. "Are you sure you have her, Dad?"

"Yeah, this damn ramp is like climbing a mountain. You got the back?" Just at that moment there was a thud. "I slipped down, Dad, but I'm still holding on. Just stand still until I get up. There, now, I'm ready."

"Is there anything I can do?"

"Just sit still! We'll get you inside, honey." Once they got me over the threshold, Carter and Drayton burst out in laughter. "Good job, Dad."

"Couldn't have done it without you, son! Now that's a ramp!" I knew I wouldn't be traveling very often from that moment on. I called Clyde for updates often but his secretary was always very polite when she told me that he wasn't in or that he was out of the country on a month-long vacation. "I'm sure he's working on your case, Mrs. Duvall. These things just take a lot of time. Be patient, it'll work out."

By November, I was getting around better, and had a huge list of things to do for Abby and Jaffe's wedding. Abby's family had been wealthy at one time but their business had gone under about the same time as Carter's. Abby and Jaffe had decided to have the wedding on Wednesday, December twenty-ninth. "The church will still be decorated from Christmas and that'll save money on flowers, Mom," Abby said with pride. Saint Ann's is gorgeous no matter what time of year, but Christmas is especially pretty."

"I think you're right, Abby."

Since we'd had a large rehearsal party at a restaurant for Jaffe the last time around, I wanted this one to be different. "Do you mind if we have the rehearsal dinner here at home, son? I promise you it'll be lovely. I think it'll be so much more personable than at a restaurant."

"I agree with you, Mom. I'll talk it over with Abby."

Abby was busy looking for the perfect dress. "Do you feel like joining my mother, Chamberlain, my sister and me, Mom?"

"I'd love to, honey, but I can't stay out long because I get too tired. Why don't you narrow it down and call me, then, I'll join all of you. Did Jaffe talk to you about the rehearsal dinner?"

"Yes, ma'am, he did and I love the idea, but want it be too much trouble for you?"

"No, honey child, I love decorating, and I'll have it catered. We'll talk about it later. You'd better get going before your mother gets too anxious. Watch out for Chamberlain and don't let anything happen to her."

"I'll take good care of her; after all she's my little sister now."

Christmas was barely over; in fact Chamberlain hadn't even put her gifts in her room when Carter and Jaffe started rushing around taking down decorations. They looked wild as they accomplished their mission. "The hall needs painting over here, Dad. You get the paint, and I'll paint it tomorrow."

"Let's get out back and remove the dead limbs, too. I've picked up most of the front lawn, son."

"Catherine, are you sure you have the catering arranged?"

"How long have we been married Carter? Of course, I've done my part. All you have to do is pick up the liquor and I've called in that order but I'll confirm again on Monday. "December twenty-eighth arrived and the entire Duvall family was scurrying to make things perfect for Jaffe and Abby.

When they arrived for the party, I knew that we had succeeded. "Mom, everything is gorgeous: the candle lanterns leading to the house, the bows, the roses tucked everywhere with those long white ribbons flowing…it's absolutely beautiful. Look! You even have my favorites, candytuft and baby's breath. Oh, their white, lacy clusters are so beautiful."

"Don't cry, Abby, you'll mess up your make-up! I'm so glad that you approve."

"Approve? I love it!"

"Me too, Mom! Who designed my grooms' cake?" Jaffe said, kissing me on the cheek. "Charmer's Bakery, they're wonderful, aren't they? Best chocolate in town."

"I see Bessie's been here polishing silver. It must have taken her hours."

"It did, son, but she loves doing it."

As the guests arrived, I watched the happy couple great their friends and ours and felt a sheer joy in their love. "I guess sometimes a person just needs a starter marriage before getting it right," Carter said smiling as he put his arm around me. "Have you had a good time, honey?"

"It's been a perfect rehearsal dinner, Carter. I'm so glad Jaffe's happy." The night ended with love and happiness as the guests waved and kissed cheeks as they staggered happily down the street.

Going back into the house, I noticed there was chocolate all over the dining room rug. "I wonder who spilled all of this." Peter came up behind me quietly. "I'm sorry, Mom. I let Morgan in a few minutes ago and he made this mess. I don't know what to do about him eating cakes but I'll clean it up."

"Thanks, son, your dog definitely has a sweet tooth, doesn't he? You need to really watch him tonight; chocolate can make him sick.

The next day arrived much too quickly but when we got Chamberlain to the church, Abby was already in the church hall waiting with her parents. "You look beautiful in your wedding dress."

"Chamberlain, looks adorable in hers, Mom."

"Thanks, baby. She's quite put out that you've paired her with Alex and says he's the only groomsman that she doesn't know."

"Just do it for me, sis, please?"

"Okay, Abby, but I won't dance with him." Carter, Peter, and Drayton looked dashing in their tuxedos. I felt like a stuffed toad in my velvet green suit with its long skirt and rhinestone buttons. I refused to use a cane to walk down the aisle so Peter and his long legs walked me down the aisle. Smiling, I whispered, "Slow down."

As Daddy slid in beside me, he mouthed. "Are you okay? Peter was traveling a little fast for you."

"I'm fine, Daddy," I whispered back, wishing I'd taken a pain pill.

The Monsignor was getting so old that he didn't like evening services any more. He had recently changed the Christmas Eve midnight mass to a seven o'clock vigil. As he sat slumped over on his altar seat praying, I saw him look cautiously over at the deacon who was assisting him. Deacon Sam was fast asleep. Monsignor motioned to our friend, Thomas, who was in charge of the readings and Thomas walked over and gently touched the Deacon's shoulder before walking to the podium. I smiled at the scene and understood how tired they were and I hoped God would keep them alive and awake long enough to finish the ceremony. Both of my younger sons stood there beaming as they offered their arms to escort me back up the aisle. "Thank you, gentlemen," and we slowly descended the church.

When the photographer finished the wedding party photo session the group headed out into the night. The horse drawn carriage had to be cancelled due to near-freezing temperatures. In fact, it had started freezing as the limos drove toward the Fort Sumter Hotel. The reception gala was well under way, and music filled the air as the Southern Party Band played. Guests were parading everywhere, kissing and hugging one another. The band stopped suddenly. "Ladies and Gentlemen, please welcome Mr. and Mrs. Jaffe Rutledge Duvall," I heard the bandleader announce. Turning, I saw my radiant son and his beautiful new bride enter the ballroom and whirl around the floor as I was filled with pride and joy. "They're a perfect match and this will be forever," I thought to myself.

Each time Carter and I tried to dance together, another friend cut in, this time it was Carlos. As I danced with him he said, "How are you feeling, Catherine? I'm worried about you but you certainly have help put on quite a party here. The kids look splendid."

"I'm exhausted, Carlos. Please dance slowly, and don't let me go because I might fall over. My hip is really hurting. Thanks, Abbey's parents have done a great job, everything does look wonderful, doesn't it?" Carlos whirled me around a few more lyrics before taking me over to Natalie's table. "Hey there, girl, you're really cutting the rug out there."

"Hey, Natalie, give me a big hug. You too, Elton Flynn, it's so good to see you."

"You too, Catherine, when's the next surgery?"

"February first." As I hugged my dear friends, the caterer came to get me. "It's time for the cake cutting, Mrs. Duvall."

Jaffe and Abby downed their glasses of champagne and headed for the cake table. After the cake ritual, the newlyweds started saying their good-byes so the honeymoon could begin. Abby's mother came rushing over, "Now, don't let anybody throw rice. If we throw rice, I'll lose my deposit."

"Oh please, Mother! No one's going to throw rice. See? There's birdseed in the bundles Catherine fixed. Will you please calm down? "I just don't want to lose my deposit."

"I know, and you won't. Don't ruin this for me."

"Well, who's going to clean up this mess?"

"Look, Mother. Jaffe and I will leave, when the guests are all gone, we'll sneak back and help clean up. Now, stop making a scene." Abby gave her mother a beautiful smile and put her arm through Jaffe's as he whisked her away. Everyone tossed birdseed and shouted happy cheers as Carter put his arm around me, "Maybe he's done it right this time."

"I hope so because I do love Abby."

"Me, too, let's hurry and help her Mom and Dad for a few minutes and get out of here before the serious cleaning starts."

"I know. I do feel sorry for them, but I'm too exhausted to really care tonight. We did our clean up last night and they went home. Come on, let's hurry."

January sped by, and before I knew it Carter and I were off to Durham again. Dr. Fisher looked as confident as the last time I had seen him. "Hello, Catherine, are you ready for your graft?"

"I guess I'm as ready as ever but let me make sure I understand what's going to happen. You're going to cut my fibular bone out and graft it into my hip?"

"That's it!"

"What will go where my fibular is now?"

"Nothing."

"Oh."

"Will this surgery be just like a hip replacement with long scars and all? "Exactly."

"Can I have a plastic surgeon finish the lower part of my leg?"

"You sure can."

"Okay, let's do it."

Surgery went well, but again I stayed at Duke Hospital longer than anticipated. I was still weak from my surgery the previous September. "I'm so sorry that I missed Valentine's, Carter. I completely forgot about it and I didn't do anything for the children either. These roses are beautiful and they're as pink as a strawberry milkshake. Thank you so much."

"You're welcome, honey, I just want you to get stronger so I can take you home. Don't worry about the kids, the boys don't care about Valentine's, and I had a bouquet sent to Chamberlain at school from you and me."

"You are so thoughtful. Hopefully, I'll get out of here and home before my birthday."

"I certainly hope so."

This time I went back to Charleston by ambulance while Carter drove ahead of us on the interstate. Carter and Drayton were becoming an acrobatic team as they wheeled my stretcher up the ramp from hell. "Thank you for coming, son."

"It's so good to see you, Mom. I'm glad this is the last surgery for you and that it's over and you can get well. I love you."

"I love you too, Drayton."

Two days later Carter invited the children, Daddy, the McNamara's, the Pruitt's, the Flynn's, and Carlos to the house for my birthday. As they sang, I started to cry, "I never thought I'd make it to forty-nine, y'all." I really thought I was going to die. It's been a long haul, and I wouldn't have made it without all of you."

"Don't cry, Mama, you'll make me cry."

"I'm okay, Chamberlain. Don't you worry, I'm going to be fine."

Blowing my nose in the soft hanky that Abby handed me, I looked at Carlos and Natalie. How's Daffodil?"

"Now Catherine, don't you worry about her, she's just fine. Nell has her under control."

"Does Nell know, Natalie?" Carlos looked straight at me and said, "I've made sure that she knows everything. How's the Workman's Comp coming along?"

"I haven't heard from Clyde in awhile. He keeps saying that I'll never be able to prove where I got the virus. I really don't think I'll win the case because he doesn't seem positive. I'm beginning to wonder if I should find another lawyer but I don't want to ruin our friendship with Clyde."

"I think you should get a second opinion, Catherine, give me a call tomorrow and we'll talk."

"Okay, Carlos."

That night, I lay in bed thinking about my conversation with Carlos. I was taking enough pain medication that I wasn't sure I was making a wise decision when I browsed through the phone book for attorneys' names. I didn't know anything about Workman's Comp attorneys. I only new one name, and he had been Daddy's attorney after the car accident so I dialed his number. "Good afternoon. Grayson Howard's office, may I help you?"

"Yes. Is he in?"

"May I ask whose calling?"

"This is Catherine Duvall, he doesn't know me but he handled a case for my father, Truman Jaffe."

"Mrs. Duvall, I'm sorry Mr. Howard's not in but I'll be happy to give him your name and number and have him get back to you."

"That will be fine."

Knowing how prominent Grayson Howard was in town, I figured that it would be weeks before he bothered to call me back. Witherspoon was digging himself down under the covers on my bed. "It is chilly in here, isn't it boy? Here, get closer to me." I snuggled up with Witherspoon and fell fast asleep. I was dreaming that the phone was ringing and as it got louder I knocked over a glass of water reaching for the phone. My tongue was so thick that I could barely speak. "Hello."

"May I speak to Catherine Duvall?"

"This is she."

"Catherine, this is Grayson Howard. How can I help you?"

"I'm sorry that I sound so out of it, but I was sleeping, Mr. Howard," I said and proceeded to tell him my story and ask for his help. "I'd love to take your case, Catherine. It sounds very interesting however, I don't do Workman's Comp cases."

"Oh, no! Is there anyone who you could recommend?"

"There are several good ones out there, but I believe Hershel Cohen might be your best bet."

"Is he in the phone book?"

"Yes, he's located on Broad Street. Is there anything else I can do for you?"

"No. Thank you very much for your help."

" Good luck, and say hello to your dad, Truman is a fine man."

"He sure is and I'll give him your regards." I hung up the phone, then picked it back up, and placed it on the table, listening as it started to beep, I turned over and pulled Witherspoon closer. We snuggled down in the covers and dozed off. Drayton opened my door late in the afternoon, "Are you still sleeping, Mom? I'm sorry, I woke you up. You've really been a sleepy head today. This is the third time I've come by." What time is it?"

"After four o'clock."

"Where's Chamberlain?"

"At chorus, I'm going to get her in a few minutes. You haven't eaten all day. Do you want something to eat? "No, but I'd love something to drink, maybe a Diet Coke?" Drayton came back upstairs with my Diet Coke and a Mountain Dew for himself. "I let Morgan out like Dad asked me to do, but I can't find Witherspoon. I figured Chamberlain has him decked out in doll clothes and hidden somewhere."

"He's right here." I tossed back the covers so Drayton could see him. He'd been under the covers so long that his hair was sticking up like a porcupine. "He looks like a little dirty dust mop. Come on, boy, you need to go out."

Drayton left carrying Witherspoon in one hand as I slowly dragged myself up to drink my Diet Coke. Before I could drink a few sips, Witherspoon was at the side of my bed barking for me to pick him up. "I can't bend down little guy so you'll have to wait." He barked even louder, reaching a shrill octave. "I'll get him, Mom. He barely went outside. By the time I carried him down the stairs, he hiked his leg and took off running back to you." Drayton plopped the tiny dog back onto my bed. "I'm going to get Chamberlain and tell her that she needs a nursing outfit for Wither. I'll be right back, Mom." I smiled at the thought of Witherspoon in a nurse's outfit.

"Well hello, honey. It's good to see you smiling."

"You're home early."

"I thought I'd come home early and surprise you," Carter said as he held up a beautiful bouquet of balloons. "They're great! You are so thoughtful, come here and give me a kiss." Carter sat on the bed while we talked about his day at work and my day in bed. As he headed toward the bar to get a drink, I shouted, "I talked to Grayson Howard today, he doesn't do Workman's Comp." I heard Carter filling his glass with ice, then his footsteps on the stairs. "I'm back, honey. What do you want for dinner?"

"Aren't you going to say anything about Grayson Howard?"

"Who's Grayson Howard?"

"Didn't you hear a word that I said?"

"I didn't hear you say anything."

"I told you last week about my Daddy's attorney, Grayson Howard. I called him today but he doesn't do Workman's Comp and suggested that I call Hershel Cohen. What do you think I should do?"

"I think that you should give him a call. It couldn't hurt to get another opinion."

Hershel Cohen wasn't available when I called, but his secretary assured me that he would call soon. By late afternoon, I began to think that I had another Clyde situation when the phone finally rang. "Hello."

"Catherine Duvall, please. This is Hershel Cohen calling."

"Hello Mr. Cohen, this is Catherine speaking." I proceeded to tell him my saga while he jotted down notes. "Catherine, I believe you have a very good case and I want you to come in so we can go over the entire order of events again. I'm going to work you in tomorrow afternoon at four o'clock. I'll see you then."

Carter came home early to take me to the attorney's office. "You look pretty all dressed up, honey. I haven't seen you without a nightgown in a long time."

"I feel like a swollen pig."

"Well, you look nice. Now, come on, and let's get you to your appointment."

Hershel Cohen had an office on Broad Street. As Carter wheeled me into his office, I knew that he was accustomed to luxury. The leather sofa was a rich, velvety chocolate and in front of it was a plush, copper and ivory Couristan covering dark heart pine floors. Hershel's lanky body stood up straight as I entered the room rushing over and pulling out a chair for me. "I'm sorry it takes me a few minutes to navigate around, Mr. Cohen. Hi, I'm Catherine."

"I'm Hershel. It's nice to meet you and you must be Carter."

"I am. It's nice to meet you, too." Carter and I began to tell my story to this charming, eager young attorney.

As we finished recounting every detail, he said, "I feel that you have a solid case and I'm going to take it but the first thing that you need to do Catherine is release Clyde as your attorney."

"How do I do that? He's a friend."

"Write him a letter. He'll understand. It happens all of the time."

"But, how am I going to pay him?"

"I'll take care of that for you. Once we get a settlement, I'll get a third of your money and I'll pay Clyde, if he'll agree. It won't be a problem. Trust me. Now, I know you're tired from all of my questioning so go home and write that letter. Call me as soon as you know it's in the mail." Hershel stood, extending his hand. "It's a pleasure doing business with you both."

"Thanks for giving us hope," Carter said as he took Hershel's hand. "Do you mind giving me a hug? I asked. "I'm so grateful to you for taking my case."

"By all means, you can have a hug," he said leaning as low as he could. "I'll be waiting for that call!" Writing the letter to Clyde was much more difficult than I had anticipated. After Chamberlain put it in the mailbox, I sat in my room and watched until the mail carrier arrived and put it in the truck. Quickly, I picked up the phone. "May I tell him who is calling?"

"Catherine Duvall." Immediately I heard, "Hello, Catherine. You've finished the letter, and it's in the mail? He should get it tomorrow but I'll wait until the day after to give him a call. I'll get back with you as soon as I talk with Clyde."

It was late in the afternoon exactly two days later when the phone rang. "Hello, Catherine. Clyde's fine with everything so now you're mine. I'm sending a new attorney with the firm over to see you. He's going to document a time line for me. His name is Sam and he'll be calling you."

"That's fine because I never get out of the house anyway."

Sam Bennett wrote feverishly on his legal pad. "Would you like something to drink?"

"No, ma'am, I just want to finish up this statement. Thank you for letting me tape record your answers."

"You're welcome. If it's for winning the case, I'm all for it. When will I hear something?"

"I'm not sure, but Mr. Cohen will be back in touch with you in a few days. Have a good evening." I did hear from Hershel in a few days. "I just want you to know that all of the appropriate papers have been filed. Now, it's a waiting game. Sometimes these cases take years to get court dates, Catherine. You're going to have to be patient but I'll keep you informed." The waiting and hoping would prove to be much longer than I ever expected.

My fibular graft seemed to be healing normally. I was improving daily and had finally mastered walking up and down the stairs alone. It was quite a trip and still extremely difficult, but I was doing it myself. The only outing I went on alone was to physical therapy and the therapist would send her assistant out to my car to help me hobble inside.

It was October and signs of autumn were everywhere as I looked out at the deep waters of the Cooper River. Crossing the massive bridge on my way to Mount Pleasant, I looked at the steel girders; I could see fog rolling into the harbor and just below was an enormous cargo ship. I stepped on the accelerator as I remembered a story mother had told me when I was younger. "It was a stormy day, Catherine and a tugboat was guiding a cargo ship into the port when some lines broke on the cargo ship. The captain lost control and the ship hit the bridge knocking out one of the spans causing cars to fall deep into the water and killing people. All of the people died." I shuddered as I looked at the cargo ship and imagined my car falling deep into the water with me inside.

By the time I arrived at the therapist's, I had put the bridge image away but I knew it would reappear. Gloria came walking out wearing a jet-black cardigan covered with tiny pumpkins over her uniform as soon as I arrived.

"Hello, Gloria, you look very festive today."

"Hello, Mrs. Duvall. Yes, my grandchildren love this sweater and I'm picking them up after school today. We're going to the germ factory."

"You must mean Cheesy Pizza."

"You've got it. Let's get you inside. I've got a new machine for you today other than the recumbent bike." As I climbed up on the machine and was about to tell Gloria that I wasn't sure that it was good for me when Christy came in.

"Hello, Catherine. How are you doing today?"

"Fine, Christy and you? How's the business going?"

"I'm getting new patients every day and things are booming. I see Gloria's put you on our new leg-a-seizer. She loves it."

"Do you think that it's okay to use with my graft, Christy?"

"It's been nine months so I don't see why not. Go ahead and give it a try." I lifted the weight bar with my right leg and it was just fine. "Do at least ten repetitions, Catherine, on each leg. "I finished my ten lifts with my right leg and started on my left but just as I got the bar half way up I felt a tear in my hip. "Christy, I think I just damaged my graft."

"How many repetitions did you do?"

"Ten on my right and a half of one on my left."

"I think you'll be fine. You're just favoring that side because you're scared so we'll work on the left side another day, Catherine." After I refused to do any more lifts on my left side, Gloria helped me out to the car. "You seem to be moving slower today, Mrs. Duvall. Are you tired?"

"I'm not sure what's going on but my hip feels different."

"Well, you take it easy, and I'll see you next week."

"Thank you, Gloria and you have fun with those grandchildren. I really can't wait until I have some."

"They are wonderful, but exhausting. I'll see you next week, Mrs. Duvall." Climbing back into my car, I noticed a tinge of pain in my hip. "Oh, Catherine, you're over reacting." I told myself.

Driving back over the bridge, I tried to keep the cargo ship scene out of my mind but as soon as I hit the highest span of the bridge it was right back. I put my foot down and dashed back into the city.

That night I told Carter about my leg-a-seizer machine incident. "Christy's a good therapist, Catherine. She's probably right, you're just afraid of damaging your graft." Days went by without my saying another word about the graft but in my heart I knew that something had changed. I didn't go to physical therapy the next week because I was experiencing pain.

Carter, Chamberlain, Jefferson, and Leigh Anne were sashaying door to door for their yearly Halloween jaunt. "Don't you think that Chamberlain's getting a little old to go trick or treating, Carter?" I asked without her hearing me. "She's fine and besides, Jefferson and I only go to the houses where we can get toddies." The trick or treaters were in abundance because they were being transported by carloads from the east side. I traipsed back and forth to the door and every time I thought they were finished there was another crowd. Finally, I went upstairs a little after ten o'clock when I heard Chamberlain giggle as she and her drunken father came weaving through the door. "He's really lit, Mom."

"Did you have a good time, Sweetie?"

"It was okay, but Leigh Anne and I've decided not to go next year so we'll have a party instead because we felt out of place."

"Are you mad at me, Catherine?" Carter slurred as I turned and started toward my bed. "You're really a role model, aren't you?

All Saint's Day was filled with apologies from my remorseful spouse. "I promise I'll do better, Catherine and I won't go "toddy trotting" next year. I'm really sorry! I'll make it up to you and Chamberlain."

"You need to stop drinking altogether, Carter because you've got a real problem."

"I'm going to work on it, Catherine. Now, say you'll forgive me because I can't stand it when you're mad at me."

"Okay, but I'm not kidding about your needing help, and if you don't work on it I'm going to intervene."

"I'll start right away. I promise. I have a plan."

My hip was causing me so much pain right before Thanksgiving that I picked up the phone and called Dr. Fisher at Duke Hospital. "Yes, sir and that's exactly what happened. I've had pain ever since."

"Here's what I want you to do, Catherine. I'll call your family physician and request x-rays. When they're done, I want you to send them directly to me but get this done as soon as possible."

"I will, Dr. Fisher and I really appreciate your help." Bill called me to say that he had talked with Dr. Fisher and had ordered x-rays on me. "You'll need to call the x-ray department at Harris Regional. They're expecting your call, Catherine. I'll call you as soon as I look at them."

"Thanks, Bill."

I went to Harris Regional the very next day just two days before Thanksgiving. I didn't feel very thankful as I drove home from the hospital, so I decided to stop by the grocery store to get fresh cranberries and sweet potatoes. Slowly pushing the basket down aisles as I thought about the fabulous meal that I was about to prepare, I piled food higher and higher in the cart. More than an hour later, I trudged to the register. "That will be $328.62, ma'am. Do you need help with this?"

"Thanks!" I reached into my change purse. "Here you go, son. Happy Thanksgiving, dear."

"Wow, five bucks thank you, ma'am!"

Driving home, I phoned Drayton, "Where are you, honey?"

"A few miles from the house."

"Do you mind helping me unload groceries into the house? I over-did it again at the Teeter."

"Just leave them in the car and I'll get them in a few minutes, Mom."

I struggled slowly up the stairs and into the house but just as I reached the door, Drayton pulled into the driveway. "Hey, Mom, where do you want all of this stuff? Good Lord! Did you buy enough for the neighbors?"

"Thanks, honey, I don't know what I'd do without you. I did buy a lot, didn't I? You'd better get real hungry because I'm going to cook all of your favorites."

"Are you going to make that chocolate stuff that Aunt Daly calls 'Better than Robert Redford'?"

"Uh huh, and macaroni and cheese, sweet potato soufflé, rice and gravy, turkey and cornbread dressing, ham, squash casserole, butter beans, waldorf salad, turnip greens, green beans, pound cake, pumpkin and pecan pies, and homemade ice cream."

"Are we eating at the usual two o'clock?"

"Of course we are, two o'clock on the dot."

"I'm starving now, Mom. Got any Mountain Dew?"

"Look in the fridge…you'll find some and get a piece of that cheese, too. It's awesome." I smiled as Drayton ate his snacks looking like a little boy sitting in his Mama's kitchen. He quickly devoured every morsel, hopped up and was off to see his girlfriend.

"Good morning, Bill. Have you seen my x-rays?"

"Yes Catherine, I'm looking at them now. I just talked with Dr. Fisher so I'm sending them to him by express mail. It looks like there is a problem but he's the expert. Try and have a happy Thanksgiving and give the family my love."

"I will, Bill and the same to you and yours." I was too busy cooking to worry about x-rays. "Hi, honey!"

"Glad you were able to come home early. Can you put this turkey in the roaster for me?"

"Sure, have you heard from Bill?"

"Just got off the phone with him and he thinks there's a problem, but he's sending the x-rays to Dr. Fisher. I guess I'll know something Monday."

"Do you want a Bloody Mary, Catherine? I'm going to have one."

"Sure. Why not? It's almost a holiday but I've still got a lot of cooking to do."

"I'll help if you tell me what to do."

Being with all of the children, Abby, Daddy, and all of the McNamara family made Thanksgiving wonderful, and Betsy included her parents. We ate and drank until well into the evening so by the time everyone said their good-byes I was exhausted and in pain. Chamberlain went to spend the night with Leigh Anne and Carter poured himself bourbon. "Don't you think that you've had enough?"

"Mind your own business, I'll drink if I want."

"You really know how to ruin a perfectly beautiful day, don't you?" Carter didn't answer me and as he walked past and picked up the crystal decanter to pour himself another. I trudged up the steps to my room quickly stripping off my clothes before putting on a soft nightgown. Covering myself with my mother's quilts, I buried my face in a pillow sobbing uncontrollably until I fell asleep in exhaustion.

The Friday after Thanksgiving traditionally is "get the tree day" in the Duvall Family. By noon, all of the children had arrived for the journey. "Are we cutting at Tailgate Farms this year or going to a tree lot?" Carter asked everyone. "The farm doesn't have tall trees this year and I want a really tall tree, Daddy."

"Chamberlain votes for buying."

"It doesn't matter to us," Jaffe chimed in. "Us either!" Drayton said pointing to Peter. "I guess we're buying so let's go. "We'll follow right behind you in our truck, Dad." We scampered from lot to lot in search of our magnificent tree before a purchase at Home Center. "Anybody ready for lunch?"

"Yeah, Drayton, are you buying?"

"You must be kidding, Peter, I just meant that I'm hungry."

"Why don't we all go to the Mimi's? You kids want to join us? I'm buying?"

"Thanks, Dad. We'll meet y'all there."

After lunch, Drayton, Peter and Carter secured the tree in the stand. "What do you think, Catherine? Do you like it?"

"It's perfect and it makes Chamberlain happy, so I'm happy."

"I'm going to get all of the decorations out of the attic," Carter shouted before returning with boxes stacked precariously high. "There's a ton more up there. Why do we have so much stuff, Catherine?"

"I love Christmas and Daddy gave us some of Mama's decorations, too." After Carter finished stringing the lights on the tree, I carefully started searching for the perfect spot for each ornament. Carter turned on the Christmas music and fixed himself a drink before opening the French doors and lighting a mammoth fire. It didn't matter that the evening temperature was in the mid sixties because he just wanted the cozy atmosphere.

Together, we worked on decorating the tree as we reminiscenced over holidays past. Yawning after several glasses of sherry, I mumbled, "I'm off to bed but leave the door unlocked for Chamberlain. Betsy is bringing her home around ten o'clock."

"Okay, I'm going to finish up here and clean up the mess. I'll be up in a while and the door is unlocked." As I climbed the stairs, I heard ice clanking into his glass.

It was bright and crisp the next morning as I peeked into Chamberlain's room. She was in her favorite position with Taddy, her favorite bear, tucked under her arm looking so long and grownup. She was just a baby when she got her Taddy bear but every night she still dressed Taddy in pj's. I'd found a pair of pj's for Chamberlain to match and they looked so adorable this morning in their sleepwear. She looked so peaceful, her strawberry blonde hair covering her pillow so I softly closed the door and tiptoed down the stairs groaning in pain. The coffee maker was ready so I quietly flipped it and the TV on.

The aroma of the coffee was heavenly this morning as I sat in front of the TV peering into my cup, as if it held the answers to my future. I looked up at the enormous Christmas tree sparkling in all its glory with my thoughts cascading over the last few years. I didn't hear Carter as he quietly came up behind me putting his hands on my shoulders as he whispered, "I love you," into my ear. "I didn't hear you come down."

"I know, I've been watching you. I know you've been thinking about my drinking, haven't you?"

"Along with many other things, yes and you've got to stop because It's going to kill you."

"I know and I promise to do better."

The holiday weekend zoomed by with Dr. Fisher calling early on Monday. "You're right, Catherine, the graft is torn and there's nothing I can to do but a replacement and it needs to be done immediately."

"Dr. Fisher, it's almost Christmas, and coming to Duke is so hard on my family. If I find a orthopedic surgeon in Charleston will you work with him?"

"I'll do whatever you want me to do, Catherine."

"Can you suggest someone?"

"I'm sorry but I don't know who to recommend in Charleston but give me a call when you decide." I called several physical therapists looking for recommendations, "Who does the most surgeries on your patients? Who do you hear is the best?" After hours of phone calling, I thought I had my new doctor.

I placed a call to the office of Dr. Ronald Carlyle. Fortunately, they scheduled me for the very next day. "So why are you here, Mrs. Duvall? You said that you've had your surgeries done at Duke and I can see by your x-rays that you need a hip replacement. How can I help you?"

"I'm here to see if I like you enough to let you perform my surgery, Dr. Carlyle. Durham is a long way and it is Christmas time. If I select you, can you do the surgery and get me back home for Christmas?"

"I'll have to check my schedule but first I need to know if you're going to let me."

"I think you seem qualified so yes you are the man for the surgery if you'll get me home before Christmas."

Carter escorted me Christmas shopping in my wheelchair before surgery was scheduled for December 14. Having three hip surgeries in one year was almost more than I could imagine so I just wanted it over. Dr. Carlyle did as he promised and I was home by December 24 when we opened presents together and settled in to wait for the rest of the family.

Carter plopped the turkey in the oven that Christmas morning with me giving instructions from the sofa. After visiting their girlfriends, the boys came back for dinner with the four of us and Daddy. Abby was still working at the tennis center and had to work. I listened as Chamberlain, Jaffe, and Carter called out to me for help on a recipe while they clamored around the kitchen.

Christmas dinner was served promptly at 2:00 so Daddy came in to see if I was going to join them in the dining room. Putting my walker in front of the sofa he waited as I slowly tried to get up and managed to shuffle into the dining room. I was so drugged; I didn't care who was there or how I looked as I smiled at everyone and sat down for the blessing. Abby phoned just as we began dinner to tell us how much she missed us. "We miss you too, dear. Hurry home and we'll save your dinner." I heard Carter telling her after Jaffe handed him the phone. "Catherine, I can't believe you're sitting here at the dining table."

"I can't believe it either, Daddy, now let's eat."

Slowly I improved. I still had a long way to go and by the spring I was climbing the steps and venturing out on my own. Carlos came to visit often with his conversations centering around me. "So, when do you think you'll be able to return to the classroom, Catherine?" And my answers were always the same, "I don't know, Carlos, I'm taking it one day at a time but I hope it will be soon."

Abby helped me ready my classroom when I went back in the fall of the next year and I heard, "I moved your room closer to my office so I can check on you, and you'll be near me if you need anything."

"Carlos, you are so good to me, thank you!"

"It's the least I can do, Catherine. I put that child in your room!"

"That's ridiculous and you know it and don't think like that."

Carlos moved me to second grade because he thought he was helping. I had a room full of children: one had irritable bowel syndrome, another was on too much Ritalin and always fell asleep, three others were definitely ADHD, one was a kleptomaniac, and then there was Gary. No one told me about Gary's condition only "Watch this one." After several weeks of Gary darting out of my room and Carlos and other school employees chasing and retrieving him, I found out that he was extremely bright, working with the mental health department, and diagnosed with multiple disorders. On top of that, he was a runner and I couldn't keep this child in my room much less get him to read or write. I started locking my door during the day and had someone escort him when we went to the cafeteria for lunch.

During lunch I always picked a helper to wipe tables and sweep the floor where we sat. Each day Gary begged to do the cleaning so on this particular day when we returned to our room, I took Gary aside. "Gary, I've been watching you and I know that you really like cleaning with the broom so I could use some help keeping our room clean. Are you interested?" He nodded but he wasn't much on talking. "Well, Gary, here's the plan I have. I'll get you a broom to keep in our room and it'll be yours and only yours. You'll sweep our carpet when the boys and girls are at their desks, and when they're on the carpet you'll sweep under their desks." Gary was so excited about his duties that he actually smiled. "There's just a little more, Gary, you need to promise that you'll read for me when it's your turn. Do you promise?" Again, he nodded his head, so my experiment began.

Abby laughed hysterically as I described the scene of Gary sweeping while the other children read. "I swear, honey, when I called his name he'd come running to read but he never let go of the broom and it wasn't long before he was walking down the hall in a straight line and I was able to unlock my door. The staff noticed the changes and asked what I had done and my answer was simple: I gave him a broom. I tell you, Abby, shortly after I had him under some kind of control; the system moved him to a special program through mental health. They wouldn't let him take his broom and he was heart broken." Abby immediately stopped laughing and started to cry. "You're such a good teacher, Mom but I don't know how you stand all the heartache you see."

"You just do what you have to, honey, and you need to stop that crying right now. Let's have a glass of wine together so go get the goblets."

Abby and I were as close as two females could be and her love for Chamberlain was as strong as mine. When I saw her radiant smile or heard her hearty laughter I was thrilled for my eldest son and all of us. I continually tried to get her to resign from the tennis club requesting, "Honey, you can get a job doing anything you put your mind to and you'd have more hours with us and for yourself. That club is so far away and I worry about you driving that long road. I'm sure most of your money goes on your gas traveling back and forth." Abby always agreed with everything I said, but I knew she'd never leave on her own.

Abby and Jaffe finally moved into their own apartment shortly after I returned to school. They were very happy decorating their place and Chamberlain was with them as much as she was at home.

Fortunately, Chamberlain was with Abby the day that Carter came running in the door gasping, "Catherine, you've got to help me. Hurry! I've got a hysterical woman in my car and I need help."

"What's going on, Carter? What are you talking about?" He was white as a ghost. "I was stopped at a light near the bottom of the cross town and this woman ran into the back of my Jeep but I'm not hurt and I don't think she is either although she won't stop crying! She says that she was on her way to her psychiatrist and she's acting crazy. She doesn't have insurance and neither do I. It seems that her father just gave her the car, and she's afraid to tell him."

"How old is she?"

"I don't know, forties maybe? Please help me, Catherine!" I wiped my hands on a kitchen towel and walked toward the door.

By now Carter had the frantic woman in our foyer. "Hello, I'm Catherine. What's your name?" She was crying so hard that I could barely understand her so I asked, "Did you say, Jean?" She nodded her head. "Please sit down. Can I get you something to drink, how about a glass of wine?"

"Yes, please," she sobbed. After I calmed them both down, I called Jean's physiatrist so the two of them could talk. Later I helped Jean as she called her father to tell him about her damaged car and finally put Jean in her car and sent her on her way.

Climbing the stairs up to the house, my face started turning red when I realized how furious I was with Carter. "What did you mean when you said you don't have car insurance? Why would you drive without it?"

"It's too expensive since my DUI, so I've been driving illegally and that's why I was so worried about Jean acting so crazy. Thanks for your help!"

"Carter Duvall, I don't know you any more. What are you thinking? I think you're losing your mind. Tomorrow you're going to get insurance and I mean it."

When Abby brought Chamberlain home later in the evening, Carter told her his Jean story. I heard her first sympathize with him but two bourbons later, I could hear them rehashing the story while Abby giggled and said, "Way to go, Dad! Let them hit you and bring 'em home to Mom. You might be starting a new trend or TV series."

"Abby, shame on you, don't encourage him!"

"I'm sorry, Mom, but he's so funny. Fix me another drink, Dad and make it a 'Daddy Carter!' Fix Mom one too, she looks like she needs it." As usual, Abby had everyone laughing and giggling with her as she rattled on with her stories and ours.

12
Flame

I finally heard from my Workman's Comp case on a morning in February. "Catherine, will you settle for $175,000?"

"Absolutely not Hershel! I have been through so much and you're going to get a third and my bills are much more than that."

"Okay. I'll see what I can do!" We talked throughout the afternoon and each time I rejected the offer but as the day ended, I knew it was time to accept the offer. Hershel couldn't believe that I held out as long as I did. "Catherine, he says this is his final offer and that he's never gone this high before so what do you think?"

"Okay, I accept."

"Well, I'm thrilled because you've just put two of my children through college!"

"I'm glad I could help! Thank you, too because I couldn't have done it without you."

I put the money in savings temporarily trying to decide my next move. "Carter, I think it's time we built another house, don't you? "

"I guess so, but I don't know where."

"Summerville is out of the question and I don't care for Mount Pleasant. Since you don't want to live in the city, Carter, how about Johns Island? Do you think you would like it there? Peter told me about an island that's starting new development."

"Go ahead and start looking, Catherine, but remember we have plenty of time."

"No Carter, you have plenty of time but I don't...I need a new home for my family! It's called nesting and I need a new home now!"

Driving around looking at land for days was exhausting and I couldn't decide the best place to relocate my family. I couldn't traipse through the woods with the grinning, yapping realtor as he tried to sell every snapping twig in the forest so weeks passed before I chose a lot. It was nestled on the inside of the island that Peter had divulged to me. It seemed perfect because the land was higher in elevation than some others, but most of all it was the right price.

Once the location was decided, I moved on to the details for the house. Peter, of course, was going to be in charge of the construction. "How does this all work, sir? I have deposited a good deal of money into your bank, but I need you to explain the details of my construction loan, Mr. Harold."

"I'll be happy to do that, Mrs. Duvall. But first let me say welcome and thank you for choosing us, on behalf of our President here at the Southern Palmetto Bank." Mr. Harold and I sat together for two hours as I seemed to sign my life away. Peter arrived to be introduced just as we were initialing the last documents. "Mr. Harold, this is my contractor and adorable son, Peter Duvall."

I watched as the two men shook hands and slowly sized up one another. "Your mother is a very lucky woman to have a contractor in the family."

"Thanks but I learned everything from my father, he's also a general contractor. He taught me well. Is everything taken care of here so I can begin my operation?"

"I'll have your first check ready for you on Monday, son."

"Thank you, Mr. Harold I look forward to doing business with you. Come on, Mama Let me escort you to lunch."

"I'll see you soon, Mr. Harold but please keep my money safe."

"I'll do exactly that, Mrs. Duvall. Now, you have a nice lunch, and call me if you need anything."

Waiting for the maitre d' at the restaurant, I beamed as all of the young women turned to look at my handsome son. "Your favorite table, Mrs. Duvall?"

"That's perfect, Claude, what's your favorite on the menu for today?"

"I'd recommend the crab cakes, but I know how you love our chicken livers and grits, Ma'am."

"Disgusting, Mother! How do you eat those things?"

"Hush, Peter, and don't forget your manners."

"Hello, Claude, it's good to see you again."

"Hello, Mr. Duvall. Your mother's always so full of her mischief."

"That she is, Claude. That she is!" Peter and I finished our delicious lunch and drove straight to the island discussing the marvelous plans for my new home.

I sat in the car as Peter walked the land. "Did you know that you have a pond in the back of your lot, Mama?"

"I did not!"

"Yep…there's a big one with a nice alligator about four feet long. I'll bet it'll love Witherspoon."

"Stop that, Peter. That's not funny. Can we have it removed?"

"We'll worry about that 'gator later, Mama. Now, let's go over these plans." Watching over every detail progress, I drove to the property every day. I watched as they cleared the land and poured the foundation. Finally construction began. Each day I drove across the bridge to John Island, I noticed an intriguing building: Stackhouse' Fruits and Vegetables. From the road, this fruit stand appeared to be loaded with fruits, plants and some yard statues but a charmingly mysterious house just beyond the stand always caught my eye.

Moving day finally arrived on my birthday in March. What a gift moving my family back into a home of our own. "I'm going back to pick up a few more things from the old house. Will you be okay by yourself, Catherine?"

"I guess so, Carter. Sure, I will. But it's really dark out here on this island!"

"I'll set the security system before I go. Turn on a few more lights if that'll make you feel better." I watched as Carter went down the long staircase to the ground. Then, I walked to the French doors. Looking out, I remembered the alligator over in the pond. "Witherspoon, where are you?" The pitter-patter of his tiny feet brought a smile to my face. "Come on, boy let's go turn on a few more lights."

I heard every frog croaking within a mile. One bullfrog was so boisterous that I thought he was just outside on the back deck. The hoot of the owls echoed louder and louder. I heard leaves rustling beneath my bedroom window. I quietly tiptoed to turn on the side floodlights. As my hand reached the switch, Witherspoon started yapping and running back and forth. He scared me so badly that I jumped back quickly and I almost fell. Hoping no one was spying on me, I peeked through the windowpanes and stared straight into the eyes of a doe and her fawn grazing on trees right in our side yard.

It seemed like an eternity before Carter pulled into the large, scary garage under the house. I listened breathlessly and counted as he climbed the stairs. "Catherine, where are you? What's going on? It looks like a landing field for airplanes outside. You must have every light in this house on and all of the ones on the outside! Where are you?" Climbing out from behind the boxes in the guestroom, I tried to look totally in control. "Here I am! I was just looking for a few more boxes to empty. Glad you're home. Did you bring more stuff?"

"You were scared, weren't you? I can tell by that look on your face. Come on, now. Tell me the truth. What happened? "Okay, you're right. Wither and I just aren't use to all the critters, yet. "Oh, so Witherspoon was scared, too, was he?"

The days and nights passed as we adjusted to our new life on the island. The critters were everyday occurrences, and I began to look forward to their appearances. The house was very stately and absolutely beautiful. The boys and Carter had built an elaborate, ornamental kitchen garden for me for Mother's Day. "It will be a great for your herbs, Mama. I saw a sign down the road where they sell them."

"I saw it too, Chamberlain. Do you want to stop by there with me?"

"Sure, but I'm off to Caroline's now. I'll be back early."

As I got out of the car at the Stackhouse Fruit Stand a delightful young lady with porcelain skin and fiery red hair greeted me. "Welcome to our place! I'm Flame."

"Hello. I'm Catherine Duvall. Is this your place?"

"It sure is…my husband, Ash's and mine! We have a partner, too. His name is Toby. These are our sons, Smoky, and Cole. We have another baby. She's asleep over there in the house. Her name is Amber."

Flame and I hit it off right away. We spent over an hour discussing plants for my garden, as well as, her marriage to Ash. "Please tell me, Flame, are your names for real? How did they all come about?"

"Well, they are all real except for mine. Flame is a nickname because of my hair. My real name is Lavenia. We named the oldest Smoky because of his gray eyes and the youngest Cole because of his jet-black hair. Amber has my hair. All the names go great with Stackhouse. You do know the Stackhouse family that lives on front Battery, don't you? They're the people with miniature stackhouses on either side of their driveway."

"I do. Everyone in Charleston's heard about them. You mean that's Ashley's family?"

"Yeah, that's his family. But they don't get along very well."

Ash loaded my car as we discussed a proposal for landscaping. It seemed odd to me that this 5' 6", broad shouldered, balding, tanned to a crisp man was born and bred in one of the finest Charleston families. Here he was running a fruit stand. Ash's partner Toby returned just as I was leaving. I recognized him as an old friend of mine from college. "Hello, Catherine. How are you? How is Carter?"

"We're both doing fine, Toby. How are you doing? How long have you had this place? I had no idea that you were so close to us. We live right over there on the island. I knew you were into horticulture in college. You'll have to come over and visit Carter. I was just talking to Ash about landscaping. Please go over the details and give me a call."

"I'll do that, Catherine. See you soon."

A few days later, Toby called with the landscaping quote. "It sounds great, Toby. Why don't you come by about six and have a drink? We'll go over the details with Carter."

"It's really good to see you, Toby. How long have you been a partner with this Stackhouse guy?"

"Over a year, Carter and I'm thinking of going on my own. He's really a strange guy. My sons are old enough to help me now. You know how it is when you have a partner you can't trust."

"Well, are you staying long enough to finish our work? Should I sign this contract?"

"I'm planning to finish your place before I move on to greater adventures, Carter."

The landscaping project was to take about three weeks. Toby and his sons came every day for two weeks. The third week no one showed up. I called Ash Stackhouse several times a day, but never got any return phone calls.

I got into the car and drove to the Fruit Stand. Ash was giving a tour of the plant garden to an elderly group. I watched in amazement as he kept Flame very close by his side, leaning down to listen as she named the plants and their various culinary uses. Toby had said that Ash was cunning and a real "know it all "but I had not been around him long enough to watch him in action. Once the geriatric tour was completed, I walked right up to him.

"Why haven't you returned my phone calls?"

"Well, hello, Mrs. Duvall. I'm so sorry about that. I have been doubly busy with the landscaping. I'll get back to you next week, I promise."

"Where's Toby? Why hasn't he finished the job?"

"Oh, there's been a little problem. I had to get rid of Toby because I found out that he was stealing from me. It has taken its toll on the business, and I just couldn't let it go on any longer."

"Really? That's hard for me to believe. Toby is such a nice, religious man. I can't believe that he would do something like that."

"Well, believe it! I'll be at your place next week and I'll give you a discount for your inconvenience."

Flame didn't take her eyes off of me as I slowly climbed back into my car. The grave look in her eyes told a story but I wasn't sure I wanted to hear the words. Ash arrived alone early the next week. I grabbed my cane and began walking outside as he unloaded his truck. "The boys and Carter laid out this garden as a replica of a Renaissance design into these geometric shapes. Isn't it fabulous? Please make sure you keep the box hedges clipped low, so I can reach the sorrel and other herbs."

"Yes, it is fabulous, Mrs. Duvall. I see that Toby finished the ornamental garden and the water garden. Did you order that fountain special?"

"No. Toby brought that in from Georgetown for me. It's a lovely piece, isn't it?"

"Yes, it really is," I heard Ash mumble, "I wonder where Toby bought that fountain."

It only took a few days before the job was done, and Ash came into the kitchen to deliver my final invoice. I sat looking over the final bill before saying anything. "This is a good bit more than we agreed on, Ash. I'm trying to find why there's an increase."

"Oh, I can explain that. It's the cost of the fountain that Toby put in. I couldn't get him on the phone, but I found out where he bought it so I added the price right there on your invoice."

"I see! Well, you're going to have to take it right off. I was in Georgetown and bought it myself. Toby just brought it back here for me and I personally paid him for his services." Ash was as red as a beet as he sat re-figuring the invoice. I signed a check for the work completed before saying another word. "Ash Stackhouse, I hope that you don't try to bamboozle anyone else the way you tried with me. Your family may be well-to-do in this town, but I promise I'll ruin your business if I hear of it again. "I'm terribly sorry, Mrs. Duvall. I can assure you it was an honest mistake."

Months passed and Carlos was calling to see if I was coming back to school. "You know your job is still here waiting for you. I'll put you in a room right beside my office. It'll be much easier on you, I promise."

"Let me talk to Carter and I'll get back to you soon, Carlos. " I did return to school, and it was a true struggle each day trying to limp down the halls and stay out of harm's way.

Just before Christmas my leg gave out right in the hall. The pain was excruciating. I sat in Carlos' office with tears running down my face, "Please call Carter to come and get me."

"I'll drive you home, Catherine."

"No, Carlos. You have your meeting at the district, and I need Carter right now." I watched as Carter wheeled in my wheelchair from the car.

His usual smile was gone. "Here's your chariot, my dear. Careful now. Where are you hurting?" I started sobbing again. "I don't know! Everywhere!" It was a long, quiet drive home.

As we passed by Stackhouse Fruit Stand, I saw a small sign that read "Space for Rent." Looking over at Carter, I said, "I want to retire from teaching and open an antique shop right there at the fruit stand."

"Take your time and think it over, Catherine. The Christmas holidays are almost here, and that gives you some time to think. Then, if that's what you want to do, you should do it."

Chamberlain, Carter and the boys helped with all the Christmas festivities. I sat and wrapped a few gifts, watching as my family buzzed around me. I knew my answer would come shortly in the New Year. School reopened on January 7 that year, and I was as happy as ever to see my students again.

Our daily routine came right back as we started preparing for an upcoming test. As I went about my tasks, something kept telling me to revisit the fruit stand. On the way home that day, I stopped to visit Flame. "Is that space still for rent?"

"It sure is. Do you want to see it?" As Flame walked me through the small space, I had visions of a lovely little antique shop. "Do you get pretty good traffic in here, Flame?"

"Oh yeah, we have tons of customers all year. I have another woman who is interested in taking that room over there. She's going to sell her jewelry."

"I'm just on my way home. I need to talk with my husband and decide on a few other things. I'll call you back by tomorrow."

Climbing the staircase to the house was almost impossible these days, but I never said a word to anyone. As I reached the landing, Carter came out smiling. "You're home a little later than usual...I was getting worried."

"Sorry, I ran an errand." I waited until after dinner when Carter had had his usual shots of bourbon. "I stopped by the fruit stand today. That space is still available. Do you think you could help me if I opened an antique shop?"

"I'll be glad to move things for you, but I don't want to work in there."

"Will we be okay financially if I stopped teaching? I'll get some disability but it won't be much and it'll take a long time to start coming in."

"Don't you worry about the money, Catherine; I'll take care of everything. Have you made your decision?"

"I have. I'm going to open the shop on my birthday this year. I'll have the grand opening on March 16."

"Have you chosen a name for your antique shop?"

"I have. It's going to be *The Wobbly Wares.* I decided that some antiques come in wobbly, and I surely wobble, so I think the name is appropriate." Carter was still laughing as he went to fix another drink.

"Carlos, I really need to talk with you. May I come in?"

"Sure, Catherine let me get this chair for you."

"Carlos, teaching is overwhelming for me now, and trying to do all the things that I used to do is tough. I need time to heal."

"I understand, Catherine. I'll find someone to replace you next year." My eyes started to water, as I said, "No you don't understand, Carlos. I want to resign now. I'm giving you two weeks notice."

"Don't cry, Catherine. We'll work this out. Will you help me hire your replacement?" Nodding my head yes was all the strength I could come up with. This is how my teaching career came to a pause.

Flame was thrilled with the news of *The Wobbly Wares* and quickly took me under her wing at the fruit stand. We spent many hours together decorating my space in the shop. Ash was usually outside barking orders to Flame or on his computer adjusting bills. Smoky was always around chattering and demanding attention or in the back room with a TV as his babysitter. Cole was still a toddler who spent his days eating and napping and Amber cried all the time. From what I could see, these children were in desperate need of two parents. I was sure that both of theirs lacked good parenting skills.

Several weeks passed, and I was ready for *The Wobbly Wares* grand opening. I was as nervous as the first time I gave a speech in front of a large group. People were perusing through the shop, enjoying some refreshments and buying pieces here and there. My family had turned out to assist in every way. Flame was in her office with two manly looking women I'd never seen before. "Come here, Catherine. I want to introduce you to someone."

"Hello, I'm Catherine Duvall."

"This is my sister Betty Lou and her partner, Wynell."

"I would never have known that you're Flame's sister. You look nothing alike. Nice to meet you both."

I saw my Daddy walking in the door. I knew that he would have a problem with this scene, so I excused myself and walked toward him. "Hey there, I was just about to grab a bite to eat! Come with me in the kitchen."

Just as I was ready to slip into the kitchen for lunch with Daddy I heard a voice say, "Hello, Catherine. You've done a beautiful job." Trying to hurry without falling, I wrapped my arms around his neck saying, "You are so dear. Thank you for coming, Carlos."

"I miss you, Catherine, and so do all of the children."

"I miss all of you, too, but this feels so right. Come on in the kitchen with Daddy and me. I want you to meet Flame and her family. Drayton, will you help the customers while I'm gone? "Sure Mom. Hello, Carlos. Good to see you again."

"You, too Drayton, how's the FBI?"

"Great! I came home from Virginia for the grand opening. I'll be leaving tomorrow."

Carlos seemed really thrilled that I was following another dream. He sat with me at *The Wobbly Wares* for quite a while. I was helping a customer when I noticed Carlos watching Flame, who was talking to Drayton. Carlos had a foreboding smile on his face. For a long time I wondered what his smile was about.

Things at the shop were going okay but not as exciting as I thought it was going to be. Customer traffic was steady, but not great, and Ash seemed to take more and more advantage of me. He needed my help with his customers and often asked if I minded watching the kids while he ran errands.

Flame had started leaving the shop, going to antique shows by herself. First she went to Greenville, then to Atlanta, and now she was scheduling one for Myrtle Beach. I wondered why, at thirty-eight, she always went alone to the antique shows. Then one day Ash came in and said that he was leaving the shop for several hours. Shortly after he was gone, she climbed on a stool to look out the kitchen window. Then she yelled, "Cool beans! He's gone."

She picked up the phone and dialed. I couldn't help but listen as she made her plans. "Okay, I'll meet you for lunch at the country club. I'll be there at noon. I can't wait to see you either." Then she turned and looked at me. "Okay, Catherine. You can't say a word. I'm meeting this gorgeous attorney for lunch in Myrtle Beach. He's been meeting me at the shows. I can't wait for you to see him. He's so handsome. Says he's divorced, but I found out that he's still married. That doesn't matter because I'm just having fun. Ash is driving me crazy. He's always putting demands on me, but that's another story I'll have to tell you. Now that we are truly friends, I just wanted you to know why I've been leaving so much."

"My goodness, Flame, I thought you and Ash were the perfect couple with a little family. I knew his mother didn't like you, and you've told me that she thought he married beneath his family's means. Gosh. I had no idea that all of this was going on!"

"You've got to keep good secrets if you're going to be my friend, Catherine."

"Mum's the word for me, Flame."

This was my introduction to a life that was totally against everything I believed in. Carter and I had no secrets that I knew of and we had always been faithful in our marriage. I was consumed with sadness for this little family that I had come to know way too much about.

Things at home had begun to take on a different tone. Carter was becoming more and more withdrawn. He was drinking more than ever during the evenings and on weekends. I wasn't sure if it was because I knew Flame's secrets that Carter now seemed to have a dark side. I felt as if I didn't know who he was anymore.

By now, Chamberlain was seventeen and a junior at Rutledge Academy, happy as ever, though she had become reluctant to bring her friends home in the evening. When I asked her about her friends, she responded, "If I bring them here, Mama, I'll be embarrassed. Daddy's always drinking, and y'all bicker all the time." She had visited France several times over the past years and was fluent in French and Italian. She was only thinking of colleges these days and searching for her dreams.

Peter at twenty-seven had recently broken up with his girlfriend. His construction business was prospering, and he worked all of the time. Drayton, now twenty-six, was back in Virginia but kept returning home for short weekends. Carter and I weren't sure if the FBI was sending him home or what was on his agenda.

Abby and Jaffe had moved to Atlanta where Jaffe was working for a large advertising firm. They seemed as happy as a couple could be except for the two miscarriages they had suffered. Abby was certain that they were not going to be able to have children. We were all devastated over her news.

Our lives coasted along for a while, but just as things seemed to resemble normalcy, something always happened. I picked up the ringing phone. "Yes, this is Catherine."

"Catherine, this is Corporal Davis with the North Charleston Police Department. Your father has been in an accident. It's just a fender bender but I noticed that he was slurring his words so I called for an ambulance and had him transported to Harris Regional Hospital. I believe he may have had a stroke. I came to his house to see if I could locate some phone numbers. The neighbors gave me yours."

"Thank you, Corporal Davis. I'm on my way to the hospital."

Carter met me at the hospital. The doctors confirmed Daddy's diagnosis. The stroke had paralyzed his left side, and he now slurred his words. They assured me that the aphasia would probably improve. I called Beth as soon as I could. "I'm still teaching, Catherine. I'll come up next weekend and see how he's doing." Carter and I stayed at the hospital until late that night. We finished eating dinner around 10:30 and were just heading for bed when the phone rang.

"Yes, this is Catherine Duvall. I'll be right there." I told Carter to stay home with Chamberlain and I'd call him. Then I called Flame. "Can you go back to the hospital with me? There's a problem with Daddy."

"Sure, pick me up." I grabbed my car keys and quickly started across the porch toward the steps when I saw a man coming up the stairs. I was so startled that I almost fell on the step. "Where did you come from? You scared me to death. Why are you home?"

"Hey, Mom sorry I scared you. I grabbed a plane as soon as I heard about Granddaddy. How is he?" I'm on my way to the hospital now. Throw your things inside and come with me." Drayton had a heavier foot on the gas pedal than I did. "Don't forget to stop by and pick up Flame. I just called her, and I don't dare call back. You know how weird Ash is." The three of us raced to the hospital.

Rushing into Daddy's room, I couldn't believe my eyes. It looked like something had exploded. There were pieces of white strewn all over. Two orderlies were standing by the nurse, who looked as if she'd been fighting a war. "What's going on?"

"It's him! He won't let us do a thing for him," the nurse said pointing to my Dad. I walked over to Daddy and whispered. "What happened?"

"I gave him a piece of paper and a pencil. He started scribbling out letters, something about a damn straight jacket. Finally, one of the orderlies gave me the story. It started when they tried to bathe Daddy. He didn't want help and started hitting and throwing things so the nurse restrained him. He became angrier and somehow ripped it off and into smithereens. I turned to the nurse. "I thought I told you before I left that he was not to be put in a restraint."

"You did. But these old folks get really confused at night, and we have to do this a lot. If you don't want him in a restraint then someone will have to remain with him at all times."

"Someone will stay with him, I assure you and I don't want you near him again. I'll see what I can do about you tomorrow."

Drayton was beside his Granddaddy calming him down. "How about you letting me wash you off and then you and I can take a little nap." I thought I was going to start weeping but I didn't want to upset Daddy. "Flame, why don't you get Mama home? I'll call in a while and let y'all know how he's doing." I gave my son and my Dad a kiss before leaving. I dropped Flame off at her house around two o'clock and headed for home. Carter never heard me enter the house or climb into bed.

Weeks passed with Carter, the boys, and me taking turns at the hospital. Every time a decision had to be made I had to call Beth in Florida. Being the oldest child, Daddy had given her power of attorney and appointed her as executor of his estate. The only problem with this was that she lived out of town.

After weeks in the hospital, Daddy came to stay at our house. "Is your room comfortable? Do you need anything else?" His speech was still slurred and so I was utterly amazed when he said, "I'm fine, honey. Do you think that if I'm up to it tomorrow we can ride over to my bank? After the visit to the doctor, let's go to the cafeteria for lunch, so I can see my friends?" This became our daily routine.

I barely had time to speak to Carter and Chamberlain. Daddy wanted me to stop by and pick up Flame and take her to lunch with us. "Sorry, I can't go today. Ash just got in a new shipment of plants that I need to pot." Daddy thought she was so adorable but he wasn't very fond of Ash. He was constantly giving Flame money for her children and telling her to put it to good use. "Thank you, Truman. I'll do just that. I'll give it to the boys and Amber. They'll really appreciate it."

"Flame, do you mind watching my shop for me again today? I'll be back soon." It took about two months before Daddy was strong enough to return to his house. Everyone in the family thought it was better for him to stay with us, but he insisted on going home.

Once Daddy was situated and on the mend, I talked Flame into going on a trip with Chamberlain and me. Carter didn't want to take time off from work and said I should take Chamberlain. Chamberlain was going to have a fit if we didn't visit colleges soon. "Do you think Ash will let you go away for about four days, Flame?"

"I don't know. "I really need you to do the walking with Chamberlain. It will be too hard for me, and she'll be embarrassed if she has to push me in my wheelchair."

"I can probably get my sister to help some with the children, Catherine. You know Ash will make me do something for him if he lets me go."

We were as excited as three little girls going off to school. As we traveled to Dickenson College, Northern Virginia University, and

Wilson and Grant, we giggled and chatted about everything imaginable. The music was loud, and we sang every song. Just as we rounded the off ramp to Dickenson a big sign read Chamberlain's Stop and Go. I thought Chamberlain was going to have a cow. "That's my name. Let's go take my picture beside the sign." We stopped and went inside, where she bought drink holders with her name on them. Then we took her picture under the sign.

Dickenson College was absolutely beautiful. Flame and Chamberlain went on all the walking tours without me. Since my hip replacements, I moved very slowly, and I didn't want to embarrass Chamberlain. Everyone in the Dean's office was so helpful and tried to make me comfortable while the girls were gone.

From Dickenson, we were off to see NVU. The campus sprawled all over town, and Chamberlain immediately decided that this school was far too big for her. The next day we drove to Wilson and Grant. The backdrop of the beautiful mountains was a perfect setting. After visiting the grave of General Grant Wilson, the girls toured the campus. The atmosphere was pleasant but not quite as warm as the reception at Dickenson. Chamberlain didn't seem to care that there was also a wonderful military school right next to Wilson and Grant. She was very impressed with everyone with whom she spoke. After dining in a local restaurant in the small town, we climbed back into the Mercedes and headed for our hotel room. "Chamberlain, have you made your decision? "Either one, Mom, it depends on whether I get accepted." As I looked around the town the next morning, I hoped her choice would be closer to Charleston.

I don't know what happened while we were on that trip, but things were never the same after we got home. Carter was drinking more and more. The more I tried to stop him, the angrier and more belligerent he became. He started kicking at me to get away or acting like he was going to hit me. Finally, it happened.

It was late October, and I was fighting another bout of bronchitis and could barely move because I was so sore from all the coughing. The medication was making me sleepy. Carter was so drunk while he was watching a football game that I thought I was going to fall out of his chair.

As I went by the TV toward the kitchen, I reached over and turned off the set. He flew into a rage. "How dare you turn off the set while I'm watching a game?"

"You weren't watching it. You were slumped over in a drunken stupor." He pushed me and I pushed him back. He was so drunk that he stumbled. Then he came after me, hitting me in the face several times. I tried hitting him back, but I was too short to do any good. He was trying to hit me again as I moved into the kitchen and pulled out a butcher knife.

"Don't come near me, or I'll use this. I swear! I will use this!" I yelled. He started wobbling toward me as I backed up he grabbed the knife. Just as he got nearer to me he stumbled again. "Now you've done it. You stabbed me."

"I did not! I don't even have the knife. Let me see." He showed me a tiny hole in his shirt but there was no blood and no puncture wound that I could see. "Please just leave me alone and go to bed, Carter and give me that knife before you really hurt yourself. You've had way too much to drink, and I really don't feel well." Sick, exhausted, and hurt I climbed into my bed around ten o'clock. I kept asking myself, "How could the love of my life treat me and himself like this?"

About two o'clock I heard a crashing sound. I jumped straight up in my bed. Carter was not in the bed beside me. I screamed, "Carter where are you?" He started climbing up from the floor on his side of the bed. "Are you still drunk?"

"I fainted, Catherine. I'm hurt. I'm really hurt. I've been stabbed!" Just as he said this, he started toward the bathroom and fell on the floor again. I picked up the phone and dialed 9 1 1. "It's my husband. He says that he's been stabbed. He's falling all over the place. Please hurry!"

"Ma'am, an officer and paramedics are on the way. Stay on the line until they get there." About this time I heard footsteps coming up outside. I ran to unlock the door just as the officer reached it. I couldn't believe my eyes. There stood Joe Cromwell, an old friend who I hadn't seen in years. I didn't know that he had been transferred to the island. "Oh, my God, Joe, it's so good to see you!" We hugged as we rushed into the bedroom. "It's Carter. He's drunk but he keeps saying that he's stabbed himself." As I told Joe about the kitchen incident, Carter tried getting up again. "Hey, buddy. Stay still. The paramedics are on the way. What happened?"

"Hey Joe, haven't seen you in a long time. This is a mess, isn't it? Cut myself with a knife." The paramedics arrived and began working on Carter.

I was really confused when Peter came running up the front steps with Drayton right behind him. Chamberlain was scared to death and had called them. They ran inside to check on their little sister. She had also called Flame, who called me and said, "I'll meet you at the hospital."

"Where do you want him transported, ma'am?"

"Take him to Harris Regional, please." Joe stayed with me until I got dressed and then followed me to the hospital where Flame was waiting. "He's going to be okay, Catherine. Try to stop worrying. "It was awful, Flame. I hope he'll be fine. He needs help and so do I." The doctor came out glaring at me. "Your husband needs surgery immediately. I need to fix the hole in his stomach. The puncture missed all major organs. You're a lucky woman. Do you know how much he has had to drink? His blood alcohol is extremely high."

"I'd guess he's had at least a quart of bourbon. Is he going to be okay? Can I see him?"

"I'll come out after the surgery and let you know how he is. You can see him briefly, but hurry."

Following the doctor into the room I was shaking so hard that I was sure everyone could tell how scared I was. "Hey, there, how are you feeling?"

"Better since they gave me something for the pain in my side. I'm sorry about tonight. I love you. I'll be all right. I promise to stop drinking after this." I kissed him on his forehead before they wheeled him out of the room.

As soon as I saw Flame again, I started crying like a baby. I cried so hard that I threw up in the bathroom. About five o'clock that morning the glaring doctor came back out to tell me that Carter was going to be fine. "The surgery went well. He's doing great but if I might make a suggestion: You need to get yourself into an anger management group. You're lucky he's not pressing charges." I tried to explain the evening, but he excused himself and walked away. "Come on, Catherine, let me take you home. Leave your car here, and I'll bring Drayton back to pick it up later."

Chamberlain and the boys were fast asleep when I got home. I was climbing into the bathtub to ease the pain in my body when the phone rang. I quickly grabbed the portable that was lying on the side of the tub. "Hello, Catherine. It's Joe. How's Carter? I've been really concerned."

"He made it through the surgery just fine. The doctor says he's going to be okay. Thank you, Joe, for all of your help."

"You're very welcome, Catherine. I'll be over to see you soon." I tried to keep this incident as quite as possible because I knew how embarrassed Carter would be but it seemed that all of Charleston knew about it. There were a dozen calls each day and flowers were everywhere.

Following his stay in the hospital, Carter worked with a counselor and promised to join AA. This was very short lived. The counselor said that he needed quite a few more sessions but Carter started adding up the dollar signs, and that was the end of that. He was getting back to his old self, and that included drinking. Only now when he was drinking he really frightened me.

"You're so unhappy with me, I'll kill myself. I'll go down to Benny's Creek and drown myself, or you'll find me hanging by a rope in the garage. Just wait, Catherine. You'll get your wish. Then, my dear Catherine, I won't be drinking." He made these comments to me so often that I finally said, "Go ahead and kill yourself if that's what you want. I don't know you any more, and I don't care."

Flame was still having problems with Ash. Chamberlain had called her and asked her to come over and watch a movie after the children went to bed. When she arrived, she was as white as a ghost. "What's wrong with you?" I asked. She kept saying that nothing was wrong. Drayton had moved back home permanently and was living with Peter. Right after Flame arrived he came through the door. "I hear that there's a good movie to watch here tonight. Can I watch it, too?"

"Oh, Drayton, I'm so glad you're here. I love you so much."

"I love you, too Chamberlain. Let's go pop some popcorn."

While they were in the kitchen, Flame burst into tears. "He made me give him a blow job before he'd let me come over here," she blubbered. "He did what?" I found myself shouting. "He does it all the time. When I'm home, all he does is sit and watch porn and make me act out the parts. I've even found his porn tapes in the boy's room and one in Amber's room. He's got hundreds of them." Drayton came flying back into the room when he heard Flame crying. "What's wrong, Flame? Don't cry. What did that creep do this time?" It was obvious that Drayton had been privilege to other information about Flame.

Despite the twelve-year age difference, they seemed to have a close friendship. As the details of Flame's story came out, I heard my son swearing "I'll kill that S.O.B."

"That's not going to help anything, son. Let's put our heads together and figure out how we can help Flame and the children." Having been a teacher for so many years, my first concern was for the little children. Finding porn videos in the kids' room definitely sent up red flags. Flame sat there blowing her nose and sobbing. "I haven't loved Ash in a long time. In fact, I despise him. I can't do this any more. I want out. Please help me, Catherine. I'm so afraid of him. He'll kill me if I take the children. I don't know what to do!

We all sat that evening and put together a plan. Flame would get into counseling, find a good attorney, talk to her family and find an apartment. "If you need money, we'll help you with your expenses. Be positive, Flame. Everything will work out."

"You're so good to me, Catherine. Let me give you a hug."

"I want a hug, too!" I watched as her hug with Drayton lasted a little too long for my comfort.

Christmas was just around the corner again. Flame had moved out of her house. She had gotten a restraining order to keep Ash away from her because she was terrified all of the time. Drayton had become her bodyguard almost twenty-four hours a day.

I had noticed strange cars passing our house. Someone was keeping us under surveillance. On Christmas Eve, Flame was served papers stating that Ash wanted custody of the children because she was immoral. The papers also sighted her as having an affair with ME! I couldn't believe my eyes. I had been accused of many things in my life, but being a lesbian was a far cry from who I was.

On Christmas day, Carter gave all of us tickets to the Peach Bowl in Atlanta. He thought it would be great for all of us to visit Jaffe and Abby. He even bought a ticket for Flame, who was constantly by my side or at our home. She and the children had become permanent fixtures. Flame often said, "I want to be a part of a family as close and loving as this family. I only wish that there was an older Duvall son left, Catherine."

13
Catherine

On an early January morning, I woke to the most hideous scream I have ever heard in my life. It was one o'clock in the morning. I had gone to bed around nine because I was ill again. This time I had walking pneumonia and my medication was very strong. The scream was very frightening but I was dazed and trying to orient myself because it was Chamberlain!

I watched as she frantically ran screaming down three flights of stairs. I tried to see who was after her. She was still screaming as she reached the garage, and I stood unable to move as she screamed, "NO, DADDY! NO! I watched her drag Carter out from behind the wheel of the Jeep. The car was running with hoses attached to it. She laid her unconscious father on the ground and tried to resuscitate him. I dialed 911, again. Carter regained consciousness just as the operator answered. He staggered up the stairs into the house with Chamberlain right behind him screaming "NO, please don't!"

Carter went absolutely crazy when he saw me. He started ripping the banisters apart and throwing the pieces all over the place. He was screaming, "I hate this house! I hate every bit of it! I hate this world! I hate my mother! I hate you, Catherine! I want you to die! I want to die! "The operator could hear what was going on. She yelled for me to get out of the house or lock myself in somewhere until the officers arrived. As I frantically tried to find Chamberlain and get us both onto the porch, Peter ran past me, and then I saw Drayton". "Daddy, stop it! Stop it now!" I heard Peter shouting at his father. The boys grabbed Carter just as the officers arrived. Out front we had at least ten police cars, a fire truck, and an ambulance. As the paramedics strapped Carter to the stretcher, I tried to comfort Chamberlain. "He'll be all right, honey. You saved his life. "She was sobbing uncontrollably. In her hands was the note he had left in the car, a picture of the family and a book we had given him about fatherly love. "Ma'am, I'm going to need those as evidence. Where do you want the paramedics to take him? "I don't know, officer. I guess to the nearest psychiatric ward. Harris Regional, if they have one. Do I need to come with him?"

"No, ma'am, they're not going to let you near him for a while. He has so much alcohol and carbon monoxide in him that they'll be working on him for a while. You can call this number after a few hours, and they'll give you some information."

After the police finished going over the crime scene and the investigators left, I fell apart in my room. The boys were with Chamberlain upstairs so I knew they would take care of her. I sobbed into my pillow for hours until I finally dozed off.

Around seven o'clock the next morning the phone rang. I grabbed the receiver quickly, not wanting to wake the children. I must have sounded pretty rough on the other end of the line when I whispered, "Hello."

"Catherine, Catherine is that you? This is Betsy. Catherine, I'm sitting here in my Daddy's hospital room reading the paper. Did you know that your house is being repossessed?"

"No! I'm really sick and Carter tried to commit suicide last night. I'll talk to you later." I hung up the phone, closed my eyes and cried again. I finally dragged myself out from under the covers a few hours later saying, "Get your act together, Catherine. You can do it. Do it for the children."

Who could I turn to? I didn't need to worry about Carter's job. Many people were still on vacation for the holidays. I was thankful that I didn't have to deal with that, yet. Daddy was too old and sick himself to worry about this mess. I felt so sad and alone. "What on earth am I going to do this time?" I kept asking myself.

Chamberlain was my biggest concern right now. Witnessing such a horror could really damage her. Carter was being taken care of. I called the number the officer had given me and spoke with the psychiatrist who was treating my husband. He wanted to talk with me later in the afternoon.

Flame came over as soon as she was able to leave the children with her parents. "What are you going to do, Catherine?"

"I have no idea. Right now I have to take care of my family. I have to get well, and then I'll have to find us another place to live. Will you help me, Flame?"

"I'll be right here beside you. Just let me know what you need."

"You know Flame, I have never been so mortified in my life and I don't feel a thing but numb. I can barely think or move because I'm so depressed. How could he do this? Do you think it is genetic? You know his mother tried to commit suicide several times. He used to be so loving, kind, and generous. He was always so devoted to God and us. What happened? Where did he go? Why?"

"I don't know the answers, Catherine, but I'm sure you'll get your answers someday."

Slowly putting one foot in front of the other, I was able to get dressed and meet with Carter's doctors. They assured me that he was doing fine, but the family was not allowed to see him for a week. I made several appointments for Chamberlain and myself to see doctors during that week. They were confident that Chamberlain was handling the tragedy well and they said that they had determined that I was strong willed and a survivor.

Flame and I started searching for a new home for my family, another rental. I was beginning to see a pattern here. Was God telling me that I didn't need a fine home and maybe He had another plan for us? The rental was lovely, small and near the hospital so Carter wouldn't have a reason for missing his appointments.

The day finally came for me to visit my husband. The lump in my throat must have shown. I could barely swallow as I looked into his face and asked, "How are you?"

"I'm fine. They're treating me very well. I have classes, visits from doctors, recreation time, and the meals are great. I've made some good friends but a few of the patients are really crazy." I didn't know how to respond because all of a sudden I was furious.

He had friends, good meals, and recreation! I was busy every minute worrying about him and the children, trying to find a place to live and finances and in my spare time packing boxes. I decided to cut my visit short and gave him a quick kiss and departed. Outside the locked doors guilt started eating at me for leaving. I found an empty room, stepped inside, and wept.

The next week when I met with Carter's psychiatrist he said, "Mrs. Duvall, Carter is not crazy at all. He's probably one of the noblest men I have ever met. He only tried to end his life to give you and your family the millions from his insurance money. He had checked everything out and had his affairs lined up perfectly. He is terribly sorry that he hurt you, but that wasn't his intent. He didn't want you to know that you were in debt because you're not well and he didn't want you to have to go back to work. He's doing so well that I'm releasing him from here tomorrow."

"You can't do that! It's way too soon. He needs to stay longer, please."

"He has assured me that he will follow up on his visits. It's settled. I'm releasing him tomorrow."

Carter's homecoming was very strained to say the least while Flame and I continued to pack boxes. I had contacted the CEO of the mortgage company and he worked with me on the foreclosure. Within a month of that dreadful January night, I had my family on its way to recovery once again.

Carter quit his job and joined Peter in his business. The two of them were as happy as could be with their new partnership. Carter continued to go to counseling, but was back to his old bourbon routine after six months. This time he was more in control of himself, but I worried all the time.

Watching Chamberlain graduate from Rutledge Academy with high honors was the highlight for our entire family. Everyone showed up for this grand event except my sister, Beth, who was too busy with her own family in Florida. All of Carter's brothers and their families attended. We all were so proud of her. Now she was off to Dickenson. She had been accepted to W&G but chose to be nearer to Charleston because of my recent failed hip replacement.

Shortly after Chamberlain's graduation, I drove back to Duke for a revision of the hip replacement done by the surgeon in Charleston. Things didn't go as planned but as usual, Carter was right beside me. The bone on top of my prosthesis fractured, and I had to stay in bed about six months. Carter came home every day to fix my lunch, bathe me, and be as devoted as any husband could be.

Flame didn't come around as often anymore. When I talked to Abby and Jaffe about her, they told me an abominable story. "I promise you, Mom, we're telling the truth. She's feeling guilty. That night she went out to Folly beach with Drayton and us, remember she was still married to Ash, well, I swear she screwed Drayton right there in the sand."

"I don't believe you, Jaffe. She told me that she had rug burn from Ash dragging her across the floor."

"Well, just remember what I've told you. It'll all come out someday!"

Drayton had found a job back in Charleston and was faithful about checking in on me. On one of the visits I tried to get answers to the accusation. "Who are you dating now, son? "Since I broke up with Karen, I haven't been dating anyone."

"Are you seeing Flame?"

"Yeah, I see Flame often, we're just good friends. I have fun when I'm with her and I enjoy being with her children, too. Is that a problem?"

"No, but you're so handsome and young and I think you need to find someone your age to date. Flame's a good bit older than you."

"She is, but don't worry, Mom, we're only friends." Carter and Peter were extremely busy in their business and had grown into only accepting commercial contracts. I rarely saw Peter because he was dating Delilah Turner, and she made sure that she kept him all to herself.

During my time of seclusion and loneliness, I often reflected on my life and its twist and turns. I lay there wondering, "Do others have as many wonderful and horrifying adventures to tell as I do?"

Now that Chamberlain was gone and the boys grown, I longed for grandchildren. Carter wasn't as sure about longing to be a grandparent as I was. I had been through so many surgeries that I was uncertain about surviving another so I felt I needed someone to carry on my life for me. The hopes of grandchildren seemed lost for now and maybe forever.

"If only Jaffe and Abby could have a baby. Carter, I'd be so happy. Beth already has six grandchildren and we can't even get one."

"Maybe we'll get good news this Christmas."

Christmas was not the same because Jaffe and Abby stayed in Georgia, Peter went to Hilton Head with Delilah, and Drayton had dinner with us but hurried off to have dessert with Flame. Melancholy was my new name and I really hadn't been myself since Daddy died in April. I just couldn't get it together. "You'll be okay, Catherine," I promised myself, "Cheer up, things could be worse."

I was still down in the dumps when Peter called me early in January. "Hey, Mama, I've been thinking about you a lot lately. Sorry I haven't been over much, but I know Daddy has told you how busy I am...we are. How are you feeling?"

"I'm fine, son, now that I'm talking with you."

"What are you doing today? Are you busy? I have something I want to show you. Can you go for a ride?"

"Sure. Just give me time to get dressed." Peter arrived about an hour later.

"Here, let me help you up into the Jeep. Step on this stool I brought along because I don't want you to mess up that hip."

"You're so thoughtful. Where are we going?"

"We're going to Wadmalaw Island."

"Gosh, I haven't been out there in years."

As we bounced together over the bumpy road, not noticing the musky stench of the Jeep Cherokee, I gazed through the windows of grime, sensitive to my son's excitement on this crisp January day. At twenty-six, he still gnawed at his nails, biting to the quick always a sure sign of his nervousness. Predictably dressed in his khakis, freshly ironed Polo shirt, and highly polished Timberlands, Peter was strikingly handsome. Taller than his three siblings, his strong Celtic features were unmistakably a product of the ancestral Feagin Clan. His honey blond hair was closely cropped, and his deep caramel brown eyes and flaxen skin were truly an image of his grandmother, Rachel. A closer scrutiny often revealed a remarkable resemblance to the kindly face of his grandfather, Truman.

I grasped the seat belt, clumsily pushing the clasp downward into the lock. Peter's size ten shoe pushed down onto the gas pedal. The Jeep thrust past the modest clapboards needing a fresh coat of whitewash. I hadn't visited this curvy, kudzu-draped island in years. The long afternoon shadows extended their arms through the windshield, lulling me into a trance. My eyes were open, but I didn't notice that my journey had suddenly come to a silent halt. I sat motionless until I heard my darling chauffeur say, "Mama, are you all right?" Peter searched my eyes as they welled with tears. Speechless is an uncommon trait for me because I'm known as a perpetual chatterbox. I was unable to utter a sound as I leaned forward overwhelmed. I was truly silenced by what lay before me. "I told you it would be tough, but I promised I'd do it some day, and I did! I've built another plantation house, and this one's yours, Mama!"

These were the words my adorable offspring announced as he hastened around to open my door. As I stepped out into the afternoon breeze, Peter gently placed a parcel wrapped in tattered brown butcher paper in my arms. "I have more excitement in store for you. This will be the first treasure that enters your new home because you are going to need it."

My eyes burned with salty tears as they overflowed down my round cheeks. I cherished the contents in this carefully done-up bundle. I trembled as I held my life's memories. Peter's smile widened as he watched for my expression. I looked into his eyes and smiled as happiness danced over the lines of my face. The anticipation of another generation vividly dashed through my mind.

Before I could say a word, he whisked me to the front door. "Slow down, son. I can't walk that fast." Reaching the door he handed me a shiny brass key. I turned it in the lock and heard the click. As the door opened wide, I almost crumpled to my feet. They were all there, screaming, "Surprise!" Drayton left Flame's side and scurried over with a chair for me to sit down. Carter came over to put his loving arms around me. Chamberlain rushed over with her usual peck on the cheek. Jaffe leaned and kissed me, "Hi, Mom. Sorry I didn't make it for Christmas."

"Where's Abby? Don't tell me that…"

"No, Mom. She's in the bathroom."

"Here I am, Mom. You know me. I'm never on time!" As she came closer, her smile was as wide as her stomach was big. "Oh, my God! You are very pregnant."

"Yes I am, and that's why we didn't come home for Christmas. We didn't want to ruin your surprise. Now, I think that you need to open that bundle, and let us see it."

I could barely unravel the layers of tissue beneath the butcher paper because I was trembling with excitement. As I reached in, I gently touched the tiny garment. I was trembling as I unfolded each layer, protecting it like a fragile cocoon. It was as exquisite as ever. Delicately sewn by hand centuries ago, it was made of soft batiste, trimmed with French lace and silk ribbons. My life delicately unraveled right before my eyes. Through tears, I read the sacred names that were beautifully stitched beneath the tiny tucks of this gorgeous family Christening gown. As I turned the gown around and around, slowly undoing it, I read the names of my family. First there was great, great grandfather Rutledge, my great grandmother Calhoun and then Rachel Elizabeth Drayton, Elizabeth Ann Jaffe, Catherine Drayton Jaffe, Jaffe Rutledge Duvall, Christopher Peter Duvall, Drayton Carter Duvall, and Elizabeth Calhoun Chamberlain Duvall. I hesitated, looking at Abby. "Do we know the next name to be placed on this treasure?"

"We sure do, Grandma."

"It's Isabelle Catherine Calhoun Duvall. You're having a granddaughter in a few months."

"How wonderful, I'm thrilled!" I said sobbing again but this time with tears of joy.

"One more thing, Mom, while we have everyone assembled here," Abby said. "What do you want your granddaughter to call you? Grandmother, Grandma, Granny, or do you have a preference?"

I stopped weeping long enough to think for a minute. Then, smiling with my whole heart, I looked at each of my children with a gleam in my eyes and uttered softly, "I started out as Khaki, and I think I'd like to end my time here on earth the same way. I want them to call me 'Khaki'."